PRAISE FOR
LAST NIGHT AT THE HOLLYW

"Part historical fiction and part murder mystery, *Last Night at the Hollywood Canteen* lures its readers into the World War II, celebrity-populated venue exclusively for servicemen called the Hollywood Canteen. Glamorous and suspenseful in equal measure, Sarah James has delivered a story that is both a delight and a puzzle readers will clamor to solve."

—Marie Benedict, *New York Times* bestselling author of *The Only Woman in the Room* and *The Mitford Affair*

"This vibrant, utterly delightful mystery expertly captures the drama, glamour, and absurdity of wartime Hollywood. Sarah James's swift dialogue, dry wit, and clever characters transport you into a 1940s movie, where the jokes are quick, the love affairs scandalous, and the cast as charming as they are flawed. Underneath it all, James's deep knowledge of the era's movies and music lends an authenticity that makes the rest shine even brighter. I laughed, I gasped, and I never wanted it to end. This should head straight to the top of every must-read list."

—Brianna Labuskes, author of *The Librarian of Burned Books*

"Delivers the humor, wit, and dazzle of WWII-era Hollywoodland while asking darker questions about the seductive price of fame and trade-offs artists make to earn a living."

—Lori Rader-Day, award-winning author of *Death at Greenway*

LAST NIGHT

AT THE HOLLYWOOD CANTEEN

A NOVEL

Sarah James

Published by Sourcebooks Landmark, an imprint of Sourcebooks
P.O. Box 4410, Naperville, Illinois 60567-4410
(630) 961-3900
sourcebooks.com

Cataloging-in-Publication Data is on file with the Library of Congress.

Printed and bound in Canada.
MBP 10 9 8 7 6 5 4 3 2 1

For my upstairs neighbors

ONE

‒‹‹‹◆›››‒

When I tell you this story, I'm going to sound like a stalker. You have to trust me that that's not the case.

I was only sneaking around the side of the building that night because the back door of the Hollywood Canteen—the one volunteers entered through when we arrived—was locked, and I was heading around to the front of the building. There was a concert going on. In between all the jitterbugging with movie stars and the endless supply of free sodas and sandwiches, the Hollywood entertainers put on all kinds of wonderful shows for the servicemen at the Canteen. Nearly every evening in that converted old nightclub, you could see someone there you'd have to pay big money to see anywhere else. Sure, you had to stand packed like sardines with six hundred buck privates, but who cared when Frank Sinatra, Duke Ellington, or Dinah Shore was your entertainment?

July 25, 1943, was no exception. Victor Durand was there, playing the solo in Henry Hilbert's piano concerto. I had heard him play on the radio before and never thought too much of it, but something about that live performance had enraptured me. The full-body effort it seemed to take, the pain of it. The only problem was that I had neglected to fill out some of my volunteer paperwork, so I'd been ban-ished to an unfinished room upstairs, experiencing the work of our greatest living composer played by our greatest living pianist through a thin sheet of glass. It simply wouldn't do. So once I finished filling out the forms, I headed downstairs.

I came out the stage door into the alley and tried to go back in through the volunteer entrance just a few yards up, but like I said, it had been locked. I could have gone around the block, but the concert was almost over. I decided cutting between the buildings would be faster. It was nighttime and it was dark—the streetlights having been turned off completely due to the war—but enough light was coming out of the window from the Canteen kitchen that I thought it would be okay.

So it wasn't that I wanted to "see the fruits of my handiwork" or whatever else the papers printed about me. In fact, I'd do anything to unsee the image I saw through the window that night. When I close my eyes, I can still see the three of them, posed like some sick mockery of a Renaissance painting—Jack doubled over, wailing; Terry's wide eyes, her arm outstretched, calling for help that was already too late; and Fiona Farris, a cup of coffee tumbling from her hand, her eyes seeing nothing—bathed in the warm, patriotic light of the building that stood for how good and selfless we in Hollywood could be.

TWO

-<<<<>>>-

March 1943
New York City

Not to be dramatic, but being a playwright half an hour before curtain is the worst situation a human being can possibly experience. Everyone else has business to be doing: actors have makeup to put on, stage managers have props to set, wardrobe has hems to finish up and shirts to iron. The director is probably the only other person in the building without a task to distract him, but he can't relate; directors don't get the blame for a bad show, just the credit for a good one. No, being a playwright half an hour before curtain is like being tied to the tracks of an oncoming train. Everyone's about to discover you're a hack, and it's too late to do anything about it now.

And that's before I found out what I had just found out.

I barged into Bev and Adam's shared dressing room without knocking. Adam was already in costume, his silver glasses and a book of Auden's poems in his hand the only things keeping him Adam Cook of the Upper West Side rather than Fitzwilliam Abbott of the Newport set. Bev was still in her underwear, her sandy-blond hair in rollers, lining her lower lid in white with a preposterously steady hand.

"You won't believe what one of the producers just gave me," I said, holding up the telegram with my shaking gloved hand.

"What?" said Bev, swiveling around on her stool, eye pencil midair.

Adam, more sensibly, held up a hand. "How about a drink first, darling?"

"I simply couldn't," I said.

"Not even a martini?"

"Fine." I took a deep breath as Adam pushed himself up from the chair, then slunk over to the gold bar cart that had been stocked in the dressing room in anticipation of opening-night celebrations. "I probably shouldn't even tell you two," I said. "I don't want to upset you before you have to go on."

"Now you *have* to tell us," said Bev.

"Come on, we're unflappable," Adam added, using tongs to drop a few ice cubes from the bucket into a cocktail shaker.

"Fiona Farris is in town," I began.

Both of them seemed unimpressed by that, at least. Adam poured a few glugs of gin into the shaker. "So the reign of terror has begun."

Fiona Farris had been the notoriously brutal theater critic for the *New Yorker* in the early thirties. She had personally ended the careers of five composers, three playwrights, and too many chorus girls to count. One particularly devastating review of *Titus Andronicus* in '33 had resulted in not a single production of Shakespeare himself being mounted in the greater New York area for eighteen months. When she'd moved to California around '35, she switched to covering movies for the *Hollywood Dispatch*, and anyone who had ever dreamed of a career in the theater on the East Coast breathed a sigh of relief. Then the *Dispatch* editors decided it would be amusing to send her back to us for one week a year to cover dozens of shows playing on Broadway all at once. Fiona's annual visits were like a tornado, leaving a trail of shuttered shows in its wake.

"Is she seeing our show?" asked Bev.

I waved the telegram in my hand. "She already has."

That got their attention. Adam slammed the cocktail shaker down on the bar, and Bev leapt to her feet. "We haven't even opened yet!" she cried.

"She came last night to the preview," I explained.

"Critics aren't allowed to come to the previews. It's an ethical violation," said Adam.

"She doesn't bat an eye over ruining people's lives—why would she care about an ethical violation?" I said.

"Is that it?" asked Bev, nodding toward the telegram.

"Not all of it. Just a few choice quotes. One of the producers has a pal in the *Dispatch* offices. He sent it over."

"You haven't read it?" she said.

I shook my head no.

The three of us shared a look, all thinking the same thing but none of us wanting to be the dummy who gave the thought a voice. Finally, Bev piped up. "Maybe it's a good review."

"It's not," Adam and I replied, practically in unison.

"Fiona Farris doesn't write good reviews," Adam continued. "If she filed one at all, it's mixed at best."

My heart was pounding so hard in my chest I could see the black crepe of my new dress rising and falling. "Let's not read it now," I said. "We'll read it at the party, with the others, when there's more booze to go around."

"If we wait until after the show, we'll all spend the whole performance distracted," countered Beth.

"Let's get it over with," agreed Adam.

I pushed the cursed telegram into his hands. "You read it, then."

Adam turned the telegram over as I headed for the bar cart, straining my gin into a gold-rimmed glass and then taking a sip. He had forgotten to add vermouth, but straight gin seemed more appropriate anyway. After a moment, Adam folded. He handed the telegram to Bev. "You read it," he said. "I can't."

Bev wasted no time in unfolding the thing and holding it up. She was always the brave one, Bev. Adam was too concerned with being liked, and I was too concerned with being asleep, for either of us to engage in much courage, but Bev approached everything like a Girl Scout: rosy-cheeked and ready to fix things. "'*Altogether Too Many Murders* is a perfectly serviceable murder story—'"

"'Serviceable'!" said Adam happily. Bev held up a finger to quiet him.

"'—even if discerning audience members will find the twist obvious from the first scene.'"

"Most audience members can't even discern where their seats are. I'm not too worried," I said.

"'The show features two lovely performances from real-life married couple Adam and Beverly Cook,'" Bev went on.

"This is a fine review," said Adam. "What were we all worked up for?"

"'Playwright Annie Laurence writes so lovingly for her two leads one wonders if the three don't spend their off-hours running lines among an extra-large bedroom set.'"

I felt all the blood drain from my face. Bev lowered the telegram, looking at me. I glanced at Adam, who was worryingly biting his lower lip.

All of us were silent, each privately scanning our history for the moment that had done us in. Had someone been round to ours for a party and snooped in the bedroom? Had we all shown up at rehearsal together one too many times, left a party—all three of us—while the wrong person was watching? Adam and I had gone to the Cloisters a month ago and held hands the whole time; had someone spotted us? Bev and I had gone dancing at a nightclub uptown two weeks ago; had someone figured out my hands were a little too tight around her waist for the two of us to be just friends?

"How did she…? How did she know?" I finally asked.

"She doesn't," Bev assured me right away. "It's a joke."

"Some joke!" cried Adam. "My parents read the *Dispatch*. We can't have this out there. Can John call his friend and make her change it?"

"I'll ask him," I said.

"No, don't. That'll only make it worse," said Bev. "Fiona Farris thinks she wrote a meaningless quip, and then she gets a call from her editor saying we've gone over her head to make her change it? She'll know for sure it's true after that."

"She's nuts. Didn't she try to slit her own throat once? Who lets people still write for the trades after they try to slit their own throat?" muttered Adam.

"No one who doesn't already know about us would think this is anything but a cheeky one-liner from a woman who is known for writing cheeky one-liners," said Bev. "Really, put it straight out of your heads. It's a decent review from Fiona Farris! That means the *Post*, the *New Yorker*, they'll all be raves—we'll run for a year!"

A stage manager called fifteen minutes from outside the door, and Bev was suddenly off in a flurry to put on her costume. I leaned into Adam, resting my cheek on his tweed-clad shoulder. "I do write lovingly for you two, you know. I hear your voices with every word I type."

He wrapped an arm around me, twisting one of my red curls around his finger. "The future's at our feet. You, the wildly successful mystery playwright. Us, your doting muses. We've worked so hard for this, and now it all begins tonight."

I leaned up to kiss his cheek before pulling away to take a sip of my not-quite martini. "Did the telegram say anything else, Bev?" I called out.

Even though she'd been standing around practically nude for fifteen minutes, Bev had ducked behind the lacquered privacy screen to put on her costume. "Just that Mrs. Farris thinks the murder weapon?

The cherry laurel leaves? She thinks it wouldn't actually kill anyone in real life."

I snorted, a bit of gin burning my nostrils. Adam and I shared a look. "Oh, it would," I muttered. "She's welcome to try it on herself if she doesn't believe me."

Two hours and twenty minutes later, the drama of whatever Fiona Farris had written about our love life was entirely forgotten. I could tell by the way the audience leapt to their feet the show was a hit; by the way they screamed for Bev, tossing flowers at her feet, she was a star. We drank champagne until the sun rose and then slept all day. When I woke at 6 p.m., with Mr. Cook on one side of me and Mrs. Cook on the other, stage makeup still staining the corners of their faces, I thought of the future Adam had promised me that was now here. I thought I must be the luckiest person in the world.

That future lasted six weeks.

It was after they got back from the show one night. We were all in the living room, listening to the radio and talking, but something seemed off. They were both acting distant, which didn't itself bother me—humans are entitled to their moods—only they were both pretending that they weren't being distant, getting lost running their fingers through the carpet pile and then immediately acting as if everything were normal. Then there were the looks. They kept sharing meaningful glances between them. That happened sometimes with an arrangement like ours. Some nights, two of the three were on the same page, and the third felt left out. I was trying my best not to be too bothered by it.

There was a lull in whatever stilted conversation we were having, and Adam cleared his throat and announced there was something we needed to discuss. I was actually relieved. At least now, whatever it was would be out in the open. At least now, we could all three deal with it together.

Judy Garland was on the radio, crooning out some sad old Hilbert tune about being foolish for falling in love so hard. How aptly trite. Adam was on the couch, the new green velvet one we had all recently picked out together. Bev and I were lying on the carpet—pale green and dotted with geometric pink roses, bought at the same time. What had brought us to lie on the floor, I no longer remember. All I recall is glancing over at her, blond curls framing her head like a halo, and the smile she gave me. It was the last time I knew, without a doubt, she loved me.

My first assumption to Adam's declaration was that Bev must be pregnant, which would put a dent in our cozy little situation but wouldn't be the worst thing in the world. It could be nice to have a baby in my life, especially one I didn't have to grow and push out myself. We could take her to the zoo, watch her run around and imitate tigers. We'd share a knowing look whenever Adam or Bev referred to me as "Aunt" Annie. It could be fun.

The news was not a baby.

"We've been offered contracts at MGM," said Adam.

How naive, that my first reaction was pride. "Oh my!" I cried, propping myself up on my elbows, a grin spreading across my face. MGM was the tops; everyone knew it. Paramount, Pacific, Columbia—sure, they made a good movie now and then, but an offer from MGM was real validation of their talent. Not that they would ever take it, of course. The money was better out there, but theater had always been what we wanted to do. "That's incredible!"

I could see from their faces that my reaction had not been what they were expecting. A sour taste crept up the back of my throat as I began to sense the storm coming for me. "You want to take them?" I asked.

Adam didn't seem to have the guts to say it, only exhaling loudly and casting his gaze to the floor. Bev sat up and placed a soft hand on top of mine. "They want to turn us into stars. Whole movies made for us, makeovers, money… It's not the kind of offer you pass on."

"So we'd move to California?" I asked. The very thought was making the room spin. I sat up and pulled my hand away from Bev's, then pressed it to my temple. Maybe this was all a trick of the martinis I'd been drinking. "I don't know about that. I like it here. I like New York. It's closer to my family, and all our friends are here—and I don't know the first thing about writing for pictures."

They were looking at me with both pity and guilt, as if I were an injured animal they had tried to put out of its misery but was refusing to die. "Annie," said Bev gently. So very gently. "Adam and I would move to California. Just the two of us."

A few years ago, my brother Joe and I had been in a car crash. He'd been telling me about the girl he was seeing, laughing at her ingenious technique of scheduling a second date later in the night so she would have an excuse to leave early if Joe was boring her. Out of nowhere, a driver had run a red light and made direct contact with the tail of Joe's brand-new Ford, sending us spinning out of control. Other than a few bruises and bumps, we'd both been fine but badly shaken up. You think events like that—that are so momentous, so frightening—you think you will see them coming. Their gravity is so massive, their impact so pronounced, how could you not? How could you be laughing about a sneaky girlfriend one moment and screaming for your life in the next? How could you not feel at least the air shift around you beforehand, sense that the universe was coming for you?

"What about the future?" I managed to stammer out.

"What future?" asked Bev.

What future…! The future where I would continue to write plays, and Bev and Adam would continue to star in them, and all three of us would become enormous stars and go home every night to collapse on our couch, laughing and embracing. The future where I'd keep getting too anxious on opening nights, and Adam would calm me down with a hand in my hair. The future where we'd continue to humor Bev's attempts to cook Christmas dinner before giving up and going out. The future where we'd one day have enough money to buy a vacation house upstate or sail to Rio or open up a theater of our own. The *future!* I didn't know how else to put it.

"We would of course finish out our contracts in your show," said Adam, looking at me with an expression so earnest it made my eyebrows raise in anger. Is that what they thought I meant by *the future?* Our *business* future? And since when was it *my* show and not *our* show?

Miss Garland had switched to "Don't Get around Much Anymore," and Adam leaned over to switch off the radio, the tune distorting before it gasped away. In the awkward silence, Beverly began smoothing down her hair, which had gone askew from lying on the floor. I hated her for doing that, suddenly. *Who are you preening for? Just leave it a mess.*

I looked at Adam, who looked away like the coward he was. His eyes met Beverly's mid–hair pat, and I was stabbed with the thought of a conversation that had revolved around me but did not include me. Had it been whispered under bedsheets while I was in the shower? Backstage in the wings on a night I didn't attend the play? When had they carved out their little moments to plot how they would ruin my life?

"So this is it," I said finally, looking again at Adam. He was running an unlit cigarette between his fingers. I willed the same jolt of hatred I'd just felt for Beverly to appear for him, but I couldn't do it. He was a horrible coward, a meek little worm of a man, and I loved him so much. I loved both of them so much. "You're ending everything we have to run off to Hollywood together."

"It doesn't have to be the end..." began Beverly, but I knew it was a hollow offer even before Adam cleared his throat and shot her another look. A tear slid down her cheek, which didn't impress me all that much because she cried on command eight times a week in Act Three of *Altogether Too Many Murders*. That is the hazard of falling in love with actors. "It's only because MGM wants complete control of our lives. Movie stars are products the whole world buys. We have to keep a wholesome public image."

"No one has to know," I said. "We've kept it secret all these years—"

"Not very well, if Fiona Farris is writing about it openly in her column," said Adam.

"You said that was a joke—that no one would know—"

"Well, it was a joke L. B. Mayer got," said Adam. "We had to assure them there was no merit to it. If they find out we lied? All it would take would be Fiona seeing us out to eat once, and that's it—our careers are over!"

"We have to sign a morality clause as part of the contract," added Beverly. "If they even catch a whiff that we're involved in a scandal..."

I knew that some people—most people, perhaps—would call our lives scandalous, but to me it was only our lives. That Adam and Beverly had apparently already denied our lives felt like a stab in the heart. "Then don't take the jobs," I said.

"We told you," said Adam, "it's not the kind of offer you turn down."

"Of course it is," I tried to say, but it came out in a babble. I was on my feet, although I don't remember standing. "Of course it is, if you love me."

"Of course we love you," Adam said.

"But not enough," I said.

Neither of them spoke.

In the silence, something began grasping at my chest, my throat. I gasped for air, turning away so neither of them would see me losing it.

"It doesn't mean that all the time we've had together wasn't—" said Adam, stopping abruptly as Beverly no doubt signaled to him to can it.

"I'm not waiting for you," I said, whipping back around to face them. "If you go out there and—and—and you hate it, and you want to come home, and you want to come back to this life, it won't be here. I won't be here. If you do this, I am done with you. Done forever."

"Oh, Annie, maybe you're right—" began Beverly, but this time it was Adam who cut her off, with a gentle "Bev" in a tone of *We talked about this*. My threat didn't matter, I realized. The shift had already happened. They were done with me. We had been "the three of us" for years, but the second they had gotten off the phone with MGM, we became "the two of us and Annie" in their minds.

Their contracts in the play lasted six more weeks. They were on the train to California before the curtain touched the stage floor, and I was alone.

With the two stars leaving, the producers decided to close the show at the end of April. Beverly and Adam didn't even bother to come to the closing-night party. Technically, I shouldn't be sour about this, as they'd asked and I'd given them my blessing to skip it. "*MGM is insistent we're there to start shooting a picture first thing on Monday, and it's a three-day train ride now that civilians can't take airplanes…*" What could I have said? Sure. Fine. Go.

I'd been living out of a hastily packed suitcase at the Algonquin for the last six weeks, keeping up appearances only out of sheer determination not to let the two of them know they had won. Once they left, they offered me the Upper West Side place since the lease wouldn't be up for a few more months. I didn't want to take anything from them, but writers whose shows close after three months don't have "live at the Algonquin indefinitely" money, so I did. I braced myself as I slipped the key into the lock, certain the emotions I'd been suppressing would come rushing back to me upon seeing the rooms where I'd once been so happy.

Only Beverly and Adam had stripped the place bare.

The rose-patterned rug, the green velvet couch, the grand piano we never had room for but Beverly insisted we keep anyway, even the mahogany end tables that had belonged to my grandmother— they'd all disappeared. They were kind enough to leave me the portable Electrola record player in a sleek black leather case I'd blown all my savings on four years ago, which was hardly a sacrifice for them since Adam had a much nicer model in its own oak cabinet. They did not, however, leave me any records. In the kitchen, the telephone remained—probably because it had been bolted into the wall. I found some uninspiring-looking apples in the refrigerator and a half-eaten box of Adam's favorite molasses cookies in the otherwise bare cupboards. The bedroom had nothing but the curtains, white and rippling gently from the cracked window. I had a bare, yellowing wooden floor, the clothes I'd managed to shove into a suitcase while fighting off tears the night they had dumped me, my typewriter, and nothing else.

I made an attempt that afternoon to buy furniture. I'd spent the last six weeks gritting my teeth and pretending I was all right—what was one more day? I packed myself into the crowd of sailors on leave on the IRT and went to the Macy's on 34th, where I ordered myself a mattress to be delivered right away. It was when the salesgirl in the horrible cotton day dress trimmed with an inscrutable amount of lace took me up the wooden escalator to the bedroom sets that I began to unravel. There were so many choices. Metal or wood, classic or modern, painted or stained, four-poster or plain. All I wanted, I realized as a flush came to my cheeks and something began to well up in my chest, was the bed we had been sleeping in. Yet when I found one that was similar—dark walnut, ornamented appropriately with walnut carvings—I hated it, thought it tacky and outdated. What I missed, of course, was not the bed frame but sharing the bed with them. Every wall I'd put up began to come crashing down. I choked out a thank-you to the salesgirl in the hideous dress and fled back uptown.

It was me. That was the part I'd been pushing down. Something about me was the problem. If I were different—more attractive, maybe, or more successful—when MGM had called, the answer would have been "Thanks, but no thanks."

The realization sent me into a stupor. I spent the next several weeks lying on my mattress, watching the light coming in through the window grow long and fade out, trying to figure out exactly what was wrong about me. Had I been too anxious, too needy? Had I not been born rich enough? Was I too boring? Not boring enough? What person besides Annie Laurence could I have been that would make me lovable for longer than just until a movie studio came along?

Friends came round to see me; I mostly blew them off. My mother came up on the train from Philadelphia to cheer me up; I told her to leave me alone. The producers of my plays wanted to know what I was working on next; I laughed in their faces. Eventually, everyone stopped trying to reach me, which I had thought was what I wanted but turned out to be far worse. I heard from the Cooks exactly one time, when they sent a letter with their new address and telephone number, so I could "update my Christmas card list." It was a generic greeting they had clearly sent to everyone they knew, and I was furious at myself when I didn't have it in me to burn it. I barely went outside anymore, barely ate, barely slept. I subsisted off cigarettes and self-pity. And just around the time I was beginning to suspect that I could melt into the floor and not a soul would miss me, that perhaps such a thing would be the best for all parties—as if they could sense that I was broken, weak, desperate—Pacific Pictures called.

"This is Irma Feinstein, secretary to Mr. Devlin Murray, president of Pacific Pictures," said the woman on the phone. "I saw your play in New York a few months ago. How would you like to move to Hollywood and write for us?"

THREE

-⟪⟨◆⟩⟫-

July 1943
Los Angeles

With civilian flights grounded, it took three days to travel across the country by train, first to Chicago on the 20th Century Limited and then on to the West Coast aboard the Los Angeles Challenger. Even with wartime flights closed to us, I was still one of the few civilians on board. Everyone who traveled, traveled with a purpose. Amid all the enlisted men going to bases in Los Angeles or San Diego and all the civilians traveling for war effort work or family emergencies, me, my record player, my suitcase, and my typewriter stuck out like sore thumbs.

Three days was a lot of time to think about what I was doing. I didn't want to think it, but the idea kept creeping into my brain: The future Adam had promised me—what if I could get it all back?

New York Annie hadn't been able to compete with an MGM contract and the promise of a shiny new career. But Hollywood Annie, with a shiny new career of her own—maybe she could. Obviously, it would be a much different future than I had previously imagined. Our cozy two-bedroom apartment would be a Beverly Hills mansion, and I would write murder motion pictures for them instead of murder plays, but it was better than nothing—and better than the last four months I'd spent on my own. Anything had to be better than that.

I didn't want to spend too long indulging the possibility. I couldn't get my hopes up. I was moving to Los Angeles to start over, and if Adam and Beverly Cook someday saw how well starting over had worked out for me, that would be fine. If not, their loss.

A driver for the studio met me at Union Station and took me a few miles west to my new home. I had been promised furnished lodgings and was expecting a nice hotel, but the squat apartment building to which I was driven was furnished in only the barest sense of the word. The entrance to the building led to a small courtyard, with my front door off to the right. It opened into a living room that was completely bare, lacking even a curtain to cover up the window looking onto the street. To the left was a kitchen with a counter and two stools; around the corner, a bedroom with a bed and an end table. The driver, who had helped me carry in my suitcases, tried to put a positive spin on the place. "Lots of room to make it your own," he said.

"I don't know what my own is anymore," I replied. "I was hoping Pacific Pictures would tell me."

The Pacific Pictures lot itself was tucked behind a privacy hedge on a block of Melrose Avenue in Hollywood, only a mile or so northwest of my new place. It wasn't much to see from the outside; it hardly looked like the property was any bigger than maybe a large hotel. Once you were through the front gate and past the wrought-iron sign bearing the studio's name, however, it unfurled itself at your feet, a maze of sound-stages and coffee carts, office buildings and cafeterias, music studios and costume storage. There was even a small schoolhouse building, where child actors were required to spend a few hours of their day. And plastered on the side of every building were posters. Outside, the billboards were all about buying war bonds or starting a liberty garden. Not on the Pacific lot. Some advertised upcoming Pacific movies, some advertised past successes, and some were only pictures of Pacific's latest stars. Just outside the rectangular L-shaped building that housed the writers' offices was one of June Lee wearing a red dress so skintight I was shocked it had gotten past the so-called morality clauses Adam and Beverly had warned me about. June Lee had been a serious actress back in her New York theater days—I'd seen her do Ibsen—but now she was barely more than a pinup girl, from the looks of things. "Pacific Stars Are Heating Up Hollywood!" the poster declared in bold orange text.

My first task as an official salaried writer for Pacific Studios was to meet with Mr. Devlin Murray for my assigned screenplay, which I was certain would be an adaptation of *Altogether Too Many Murders*. Why else would I have been brought here?

The morning of my meeting, I allowed myself to feel—for the first time in four months—something approaching optimism. It would be nice, I thought, to have a task. Something to do and someone counting on me to do it. I bought a new dress for the occasion, a gray one covered in tiny violet flowers. New York Annie had never been one for florals, but Hollywood Annie was going to be brand new.

Mr. Murray's office was all the way at the back of the lot, an elegant sandstone building surrounded by manicured lawns so green they looked artificial. I was met by Mrs. Irma Feinstein, an imposing woman of about fifty whose hair, pinned up in two severe victory curls, was such a stark shade of brown that it had to be from a salon. She greeted me with a handshake that knocked the feeling from my fingers. "Miss Laurence," she began. Her smile seemed forced, as if she had never attempted one on her own but was merely copying an expression she'd seen others use in similar situations. "I loved your play."

"Thank you," I said, feeling a little flutter in my chest. There was nothing like a compliment from someone in the position to give you money to take the edge off a four-month depression.

"The murder weapon was very interesting," she went on. "Cherry laurel leaves. How on earth did you come up with it?"

"A friend of mine from primary school had the hedges near her house," I answered. "We had no idea they were poisonous until one day, her dog ate a bunch of the leaves. He'd never shown any interest in them before, but he got a taste for them, I suppose. And then he died."

"The dog?" asked Irma. "The dog died?"

"Yes. Bud, his name was. He became terribly ill first, throwing up absolutely everywhere. Our shoes were ruined. But it wasn't enough to purge the leaves from his system, and he died a few hours later. Of course, for humans it would take a lot more than a few leaves, so I made it into a concentrate. That's when you boil the leaves in water and catch the condensation. Would kill someone in under half an hour, or so I'd imagine. I wouldn't know firsthand."

Mrs. Irma Feinstein frowned at me. "When you tell that story to Mr. Murray, say the dog lived."

"What? Why?"

"Better story."

Before I could argue that point, a male voice came booming out from the oak door behind Irma's desk. "I'll have your head and the heads of all your little friends on a platter!"

"You don't tell me what to write. I don't work for you!" a woman shouted back, seeming unfazed by the threat.

"Work for *me*? You'll never work for anyone in this town!" the man continued. "I will personally see to that! Get out of my office! Get out of my sight!"

The office door banged open, and a woman came storming out, moving so fast she was nothing but a blur in a checked skirt suit. The man shouted after her, "I'll ruin you, you hear me? You write one word of this, and I'll make your life a living hell!"

I met Irma's gaze, expecting her expression to match the one of disbelief that was currently on my face. Instead, she was perfectly calm. "Mr. Murray will see you now," she said.

"I'm not going in there," I whispered.

"Who's next?" shouted Devlin from inside.

Seeing as I was practically frozen in my spot, Irma went ahead of me, announcing my presence as she handed Mr. Murray a bound pile of papers. "This is Miss Annie Laurence, one of your new writers. She's a playwright from New York."

Devlin Murray did not appear large enough to have made the enormous ruckus I'd just overheard. He was a small balding man with a red-and-gray mustache, wearing an ostentatiously large gold wristwatch that was two sizes too big for his tiny wrist. "Pleasure to meet you, Mr. Murray," I said.

"I hate New York," he replied. "That's all, Irma."

Although I did my best to beg her to stay with my eyes, Irma shut the door behind her as she left, and Mr. Murray settled in behind his desk without offering me a seat. I stood awkwardly near the door as he kicked his feet up, hummed to himself, and flipped through the document. On one hand, I was relieved he didn't seem angry anymore; on the other, it was unsettling he'd been able to drop the rage so quickly.

"This your play?" he asked, snapping it shut and squinting at the front page. "*Altogether Too Many Murders*?"

"Yes," I said.

He yawned, tossing it aside. "Tell me about it."

I'd pitched the play probably hundreds of times over the last five years, but my nerves caused everything about it to evaporate from my mind. "Well, when I was a girl—um—my friend had this dog, and it ate leaves from a cherry laurel bush and...lived?"

"Is it funny?" he interrupted.

"Well, no," I said. "It's about a murder. Several murders, really. There's a lot of murdering in it."

"Where's it set?" he asked.

I perked up. At least I knew the answer to that one. "At an old society family's mansion in Newport."

"Pass," he said.

I blinked. "Pass? I—are you sure? It got rave reviews on Broadway."

"It's not personal," he explained. "It's just not what we do. Paramount does the highbrow stuff: drawing rooms and Newport. Warners does the lowbrow stuff: pratfalls and farmers. We do middlebrow—but not preachy like MGM. A thriller, but it's also sexy. A fun musical, but it kinda makes you think. That's our niche."

I'd been rejected before but not simply off the word *Newport*. "Why did you hire me if my play's not what you produce?" I asked, trying to sound calm enough to not get screamed out of his office like the last woman.

Mr. Murray laughed. "We're desperate. Why else? Half my writers have gone to war; the other half will get called up soon enough. You seen a picture lately? Duct tape and shoe polish since December 7, 1941. I tried to convince FDR that 'movie star' is a job essential to morale—why are you laughing? I'm serious. But he said no deferment for singing and dancing, so here we are. I'm desperate, you're desperate. You're not a fit—well, I'll make you a fit. You know how many stars I've made? I've turned cigarette girls into *Screenland* cover stars. And vice versa. You want a sexy thriller or a smart musical?"

This diatribe had been delivered a mile a minute, and I blinked, not sure I'd taken it all in. "Sorry—what?"

"I'm gonna give you a smart musical; the girl writers are better at those anyway. Say, can you write a part for Henry Hilbert in it? I'm trying to make him a star."

"Henry Hilbert the songwriter?"

"Yeah—who doesn't love Henry Hilbert? He was writing tunes for MGM, but he jumped ship fast when we offered to make him a star. He's almost forty-five and free from the draft. Pretty smart of me, huh? Now let me give you a title. I keep a list of phrases that are bang-up titles—where is it?"

As he shuffled through the papers on his desk, I took the

opportunity to speak up. "I don't want to write a musical for Henry Hilbert," I said. "I'm a serious writer. I'm interested in the darkness of the human soul. Pain and murder and mystery—"

Devlin sat upright, slamming his feet onto the floor. "Miss Laurence, I'm not sure you understand. You're under contract with Pacific Pictures, and you'll write what Pacific Pictures wants you to write. This isn't a negotiation about your career as an artist. This is your boss, giving you instructions for your job. Is that clear?"

I forced myself to nod.

"Wonderful," he said, picking up a yellow legal pad. "Now, none of these titles have stories attached to them yet, but that's your job. How about *Don't Count Your Coconuts*?"

"Sure," I said. "Sounds like a treat."

"That's the ticket," he replied. "And put that hilarious story about the dog eating leaves when you were a kid in there. I liked that."

I must have looked positively shell-shocked when I exited the office, because Irma smiled at me sympathetically. "Not how you expected it to go?" she said.

"No," I admitted. "I have no idea how I'm going to write this script."

"I can help with that," said Irma. She reached into the inside pocket of her blazer and produced a small notepad. "I always keep this on my person exactly for situations such as these." She scrawled something on it, tore off the paper, and handed it to me.

This was no ordinary note, I realized. She had written me a prescription. At the top, where a doctor's name and address would ordinarily be, it read simply *Pacific Pictures Medical Offices*, and underneath that, in smaller type, *Office of Mrs. Irma Feinstein, Assistant to Mr. Devlin Murray*.

"Take that to the pharmacy on the lot. It's just across from the cafeteria. You can't miss it—there's always a line out the door."

"What is it?" I asked.

"A little something to help you focus," she demurred.

I didn't press further. "Thanks," I said, shoving the paper into my purse and wondering how a movie studio's secretary got a hold of a personalized prescription pad in the first place.

"There's just one more thing," Irma went on. "It was sensitive enough that I didn't want to bring it up over the phone, but now that I've got you here in person—I'm certain there's nothing to this, but we need to know. Have you read this?"

She was handing me a newspaper column, carefully cut out from its original page. *Stars Shine, Ending Disappoints in Altogether Too Many Murders by Fiona Farris.*

"I don't read reviews," I lied, trying to hand it back to her. She wouldn't take it.

"There's an insinuation in there that you were having… Well, it's hardly appropriate to say out loud."

"I know what it was insinuating," I replied.

"So you *do* read reviews," Irma said, a slight smile coming to her lips. "Is there any truth to it?"

Just a few months ago, I had been certain that if I were ever to be asked this question, I wouldn't do what Adam and Beverly had done. I would tell the truth, no matter what it cost me, because I loved them more than I loved anything else in the world. But now, with Irma expectantly blinking at me, waiting for an answer—with my entire career on the line—what was I to say?

"No truth to it at all," I said. "They're friends, nothing more."

I went right home after that, stopping only at a liquor store to buy a bottle of vodka. By the time I was climbing the steps to the building, my new violet-patterned dress was soaked in sweat, and the silly pumps with little bows I had chosen to go with them had rubbed my heels raw. I was barely inside the front door before I was throwing them both off, nearly ripping the seams on the dress as I struggled to pull it over my head. Why had I even bought that dress? The sign in the window had said it would "lighten up any day like the gayest melody played on a cheery piano." I had fallen for that terrible writing? I ought to be ashamed of myself.

Dress puddled on the floor by my front door, I lit a cigarette and poured vodka into one of the two glasses my furnished apartment had generously provided me. Somewhere around the fourth drink, as the sun began to set and cast an orange glow around my blank white living room, I realized I was lonely. For four months I had felt next to nothing, in a depressive haze of smoke and apathy. Now I had finally progressed to feeling again, and the first thing my body could produce was loneliness? What a rotten deal.

The next morning, in my tiny windowless office on the Pacific lot, I fed a piece of paper into the Remington typewriter and began to type.

```
DON'T COUNT YOUR COCONUTS
       By Annie Laurence
           Act One
          Scene One
```

My fingers were still poised above the keys as I looked up from the paper and stared into a corner. I wasn't sure what to do next. It wasn't a blocked-artist kind of feeling but simply perplexing, like picking up a Sunday crossword only to find the clues are all in hieroglyphics. How exactly did a person…write? Where did you start? I couldn't remember.

How had I done it in the past? I thought back to all those years ago, scribbling out the first draft for *Altogether Too Many Murders* in our old apartment, the dark and dismal one in Chelsea. We'd all been so excited to live there, despite the oven never working right and water leaking through the ceiling whenever our upstairs neighbors took a bath. That play had started from a desire to see Adam play a Newport-set mama's boy and Beverly as the femme fatale who had ensnared his wealthy father. I thought their chemistry would make them compelling onstage rivals, a sensual tension underpinning their struggle. I also thought it would be amusing to see Adam in a sweater vest, and I'd been correct. The play before that, I'd wanted to see quiet, skinny Adam play a gangster and Bev, with her angelic crown of blond curls, a murderous madame. Even the first thing I'd ever written, a one-act play back at Sarah Lawrence for our little theater society, had been for them.

My breaths were growing shallower as I looked back down at the paper in the typewriter. Could I do this on my own?

I remembered clear as day being stuck on the ending of *Altogether Too Many Murders*, how I complained about it incessantly until one evening Adam shut his book, holding his page with a finger, crossed his legs, and took a drag on his cigarette. "The thing about endings," he said slowly, exhaling the smoke, "is they are intrinsically linked to beginnings. Whatever your beginning is, Annie, is also your ending."

I looked to Beverly, who was tickling out some Liszt on the piano, and our eyes met and danced with utter charm at Adam's ridiculousness. *Listen to our man. Isn't he impossibly silly? Don't you love him more than life itself?*

"I'd like to end it with me saying something cosmopolitan," said Beverly. "Perhaps 'I'll drink to that!' And then I swallow poison. Hamlet's mom but with a gimlet and a cocaine habit."

I'd used both of their suggestions—Adam solving the murder from a clue in the first scene and Beverly drinking poison to save his life. The more I ruminated on it, the more it seemed like I'd never written a single scene without their input. Four months ago I had thought of myself as two things: a writer, and Bev and Adam's lover. Was I neither?

The phone ringing interrupted this spiral, which scared me half to death. I hadn't expected anyone to contact me. I tried to answer professionally, but ended up sounding like a fool. "Annie Laurence, Pacific Pictures."

"Miss Laurence? It's Irma Feinstein. Are you all right? You sound tired."

I winced. "Just struggling with the writing, is all."

"Did you fill that prescription I wrote you?"

"Unless it's a cyanide pill, I doubt it'll help me much," I said. There was no response. I remembered her reaction to my story about the dog and cleared my throat. "Um, no. Not yet."

"You should," answered Irma. "It'll perk you right up. But listen—I'm calling because I thought of an idea for you. You still want to make your play into a movie, don't you?"

"Yes," I admitted.

"I want that too," she said. "Now, look. You're still going to have to write that other movie Mr. Murray assigned you. I can't get you out of that. But if you want a chance at your play getting produced as well, you need to go to the Hollywood Canteen tonight."

"What's that?" I asked.

"You don't know what the Hollywood Canteen is?"

"I only moved here a week ago," I pointed out.

"Yes, but the whole country is talking about the Hollywood Canteen," Irma replied. "You of course know that Los Angeles is the main port for boys shipping off to the Pacific."

I hadn't known that. "Of course," I said.

"That means servicemen come from all over the country and spend a few days here before they leave to go off to god-knows-where and see god-knows-what," she said. "So Bette Davis and John Garfield—you know who they are, right?" she asked sarcastically.

"Yes," I answered, at least being truthful about that.

"Well, they started the Hollywood Canteen. It's run entirely by volunteers from the industry. Stars perform, dance with the boys, serve them food. It's extremely popular, gets thousands of visitors a night. All the studios rotate days, and Wednesday is our night. All the Pacific stars are required to be there. Go make some friends who have more pull around this lot than you do. Henry Hilbert, Don Farris, June Lee—she couldn't play the lead, of course, but maybe there's a side character who's Chinese?"

"Did you say Don Farris will be there?" I said. "Fiona Farris's husband?"

"If he's under a Pacific contract, he'll be there."

"Will Fiona be with him?"

"I think she comes with him sometimes, yes. Are you worried about her printing more lies about you?"

"Yes," I lied quickly.

"Don't worry about her. You have the power of a studio PR department on your side now. She's nobody. Focus on your future. If you turn in an acceptable draft of *Don't Count Your Coconuts*, prove to Mr. Murray that it's worth it to him to keep you around, *and* you come into this office with a star wanting to make your other movie? It'll get made. The studio system is a lot like the solar system: it all revolves around the stars."

It was likely decent professional advice, but I could hardly focus on that. All I could think about was Fiona, the one sentence she had penned that had ruined my life. How much more did she know, and was there any way I could find out before she struck again?

"I'll be there," I told Irma.

"Excellent. It's on Cahuenga, just south of Sunset, but the entrance for volunteers is in the back around the block. Doors open at seven," Irma said. "And fill that prescription! You'll need some energy if you'll be jitterbugging all night."

The Hollywood Canteen was about a half an hour's walk from the studio, a faux Western–fronted place with a sign made to look like lasso rope. The light was only just starting to grow long, casting a cinematic purple haze over everything as I walked past the long line of waiting servicemen and headed for the back.

While the main entrance was on a busy thoroughfare, the back entrance was on a street that was little more than an alley. There were two doors, one labeled "Stage Door" and the other labeled "Volunteer Entrance." I was surprised to see autograph hounds and photographers waiting at each of them. Irma must not have been kidding about all the stars being here tonight.

I made my way through the volunteer entrance and into the small vestibule behind it, where I was met by a woman with a clipboard. She had curly brown hair that was streaked with gray and a presence so tall and commanding that I immediately felt like I was in trouble for something. "I'm here to volunteer," I told her.

"You work for Pacific?" she asked.

I nodded. "Just started. Irma Feinstein told me I should come."

She rolled her eyes at the name. "Sorry you had to meet Irma. You won't have to deal with her here, at least. I'm Terry Levine."

The name sounded familiar to me, but I couldn't place it, and something about the straightness of this woman's spine told me she wouldn't have taken too kindly to me getting it wrong. I attempted no guess. "Annie Laurence," I said.

"Welcome, Miss Laurence. You'll have to fill out some forms, get fingerprinted—standard stuff all the volunteers have to do. Head for the office; they'll help you out. Across the dance floor to the front lobby, and then it's the door next to the phone booth."

The door out of the vestibule led me to a short hallway with two bathrooms. Even though one was marked "Men" and one "Women," servicemen were queued up for both, loudly swapping stories and craning their necks to check me out as I passed. I guessed that I would just have to hold it.

This short hallway opened up to a large wooden dance floor. I had only begun to take in the giant Western-themed chandeliers, the colorful murals on the wall, and the stage immediately to my right, where a man was absolutely wailing on a trumpet with a full orchestra behind him, when I was pushed out onto the dance floor full of jitterbugging men. One of them grabbed me near instantaneously, launching me into a dance so frantic I felt like I perhaps should have stretched first.

"I can't dance," I shouted to him.

"You're doing great!" he shouted back.

"No, I—"

Before I could explain that wasn't what I meant and actually I needed to find the office, he interrupted. "What's your name?"

"Annie," I shouted. "What's yours?"

He ignored the question. "You famous? What pictures have you been in?"

"I haven't been in any pictures," I said. "I'm a writer."

He dropped his hands from my waist and walked away.

I barely had time to comprehend what had just happened when another man, this one a sailor, scooped me into his arms. "Hi, I'm Bob," he said.

"Hi, Bob. I'm Annie."

"Sorry about that other fellow. He seemed rude."

"That's all right," I replied. "Writers aren't known for their dance moves."

"You're doing just fine in my book."

As we danced, I studied the room in an attempt to get my bearings. The first thing I noticed was that it made sense why I'd been grabbed right away: the men outnumbered the women six to one, if not more.

The floor was absolutely packed with people, many of whom were dancing with such a flailing intensity that I had to assume there were multiple fatalities a night.

After Bob, I stopped trying to make conversation. I also stopped trying to make my way to the front of the room, letting men scoop me up and going along for the ride. It didn't take long before I became too overwhelmed to even get a good look at the men's faces. The uniforms had the effect of making each fellow blend into one another, which I supposed was the point, but it also made it incredibly easy to shut my brain off. Only a few details made it through: Crooked tie. Sweat stain on shirt. Freckles.

This went on for what felt like several hours but what was probably half an hour, if that. I was disgustingly sober. I could have killed someone for a cigarette, and I was starting to get dizzy, both from the whirlwind of faces and the actual whirlwind my body had been on.

"Sailor," I said to the next man who grabbed me midtune, "Would you mind dancing me over to that corner?" I tipped my head toward the front of the Canteen, where a curtain led to an area that had to be the front lobby. "I'm supposed to be filling out some paperwork in the office."

"Sure thing, doll," said the sailor, spinning me around and starting to work his way toward the other side of the dance floor.

That's when I saw her.

The crowd was so dense it was only a glimpse at first: the stark line of her blunt-cut bangs darting about as she tittered at some joke, no doubt one that had come from her own mouth. I had to crane my neck to confirm it was her sharp, small nose; her dark-brown eyes; her pale skin just starting to crease around the mouth from too many cigarettes. "Oh my god," I said to my companion. "It's her."

"Who's her? A star?" asked the sailor.

"To some," I said. "It's Fiona Farris."

She was sitting with a small group of other volunteers, whom I came to recognize one by one as I continued to stare through the mass of moving bodies. There was June Lee, whose face had been greeting me outside my office every morning, just as scandalously clad here as she had been in her Pacific promotional shot. The plum sequined number that matched her lipstick perfectly looked as if it had been painted on, yet she either didn't notice or didn't care that she was currently being eyed by every fellow in the place. Next to June was Jack Kott, the radio comedian, pulling a series of absurd faces as he recounted for the rest of the group some dramatic story. Leaning back in his seat between Jack and Fiona was a dark-haired man I didn't recognize, wearing an immaculately cut gray pinstripe suit and a wry smile. And there, at the end of the table, was Fiona Farris herself, in a crisply starched black-and-white-striped button-up and a black skirt. She looked smart, sophisticated, intimidating without even trying to be. I thought of the violet-printed dress on the floor of my apartment and vowed to burn it and never wear florals ever again.

The sailor, not being completely blind, noticed the way I kept spinning my head around to keep her in my field of view. "Want me to dance you over that way?" he offered. I nodded.

We managed to get a little closer before the song ended. The bandleader stopped to take a bow, holding aloft the clarinet he had both played and conducted with. I took the opportunity to bid farewell to the sailor and push my way a little closer to Fiona's table. The group was near the snack bar, where Rita Hayworth herself was handing out sandwiches and sodas. I maneuvered my way to the counter and asked Miss Hayworth for a water.

Filled water glass in hand, I inched back over toward the tables, closer to Fiona and her friends, hoping I'd overhear even a snippet of their conversation. For a moment of wild vanity, I even thought they might be talking about me, that Fiona might be telling the group about this wonderful play she'd seen in New York, with two actors who were so clearly involved with the playwright…

Obviously, they weren't talking about me. When I finally managed to get close enough to hear them—which was right over Fiona's shoulder, given how loud and crowded it was in that room—Jack Kott was still animatedly telling a story. "I didn't say anything all that terrible. Just that he was boring, thoughtless, slow-witted, dull, and ignorant."

"So nothing his wife didn't say on their wedding night," replied Fiona.

I half snorted, half guffawed, which made all four turn to look at me. All four expressions were identical: *Who the hell are you?*

Needless to say, this would have been the most mortifying thing I could have experienced, if not for what happened next. Desperate to pretend I was not standing there eavesdropping, only passing by, I took a large step to my right and was immediately slammed into by a jitterbugging couple. My water, which Miss Hayworth had so kindly filled to the very tip-top, went all over myself and Fiona Farris's white-striped shirt.

"Lovely," she said, slowly rising from the table. "Now I need to go towel off. Which is another thing Hal said on their wedding night."

FOUR

⫷⫸

If I had ever been so mortified in my life, I couldn't remember it now. I ran to follow Fiona past the snack bar, through a set of double doors marked "Volunteers Only!" and into the back kitchen, practically falling over myself to apologize profusely. By the time she grabbed a few dish towels from a cabinet above an industrial-size silver coffee carafe, she was rolling her eyes at me. "Stop apologizing; it's getting boring," she said.

"Sorry," I said.

"You must be new here," she went on as she handed me one of the towels.

"Was it my clumsiness or the fact that I have no idea where to stand that gave it away?" I asked.

"Just the look in your eye," she replied, pressing a towel to her soaked shirt. "You look like a deer post-headlights."

"It's my first shift, and I was thrown right into the deep end," I said. "It's only been an hour, and every bone in my body hurts. I think I might be too old for jitterbugging."

"Everyone over seventeen is too old for jitterbugging," she muttered. "Well, I can give you some pointers: Don't dance with the same person twice. Bette will get mad if she sees you doing it, 'cause there's way more of them than there are of us. But more importantly, dancing around prevents any of the boys from getting any ideas about you liking them. Last thing you need coming out of here is a puppy following you home—trust me on that. Now, if there's an emergency, like a fight breaks out on the floor, don't try to break it up. Go to the bandleader and tell him to start playing 'The Star-Spangled Banner.' That makes everyone stand at attention and go quiet, and it's long enough that by the time the song's over, everyone's forgotten what they were fighting about. And third—you're at Pacific, right?"

I nodded.

"I'm a free agent, but all my friends are at Pacific, so I've seen it firsthand that if you miss your shift, Murray's squirrely little secretary, Irma? She'll make your life hell. Because what good is patriotism if it's not performed loudly and incessantly?"

Even though Irma had seemed kind, if a bit old-fashioned, to me, I laughed, and Fiona seemed pleased with herself. She smiled, tossing the dishrag onto the counter. "You look familiar," she said. "Have we met?"

"You reviewed my play once," I blurted out. "I'm Annie Laurence."

If she had any reaction to the name, any feelings about me, she kept them under the surface. "Of course," she said. "*Altogether Too Many Murders*, I remember. But you're at Pacific? Not at MGM with your pals, the Cooks?"

I could only hope that my poker face was half as good as hers. I acted as if the question surprised me a bit. "Oh, Louis B. Mayer wouldn't have the likes of me running around his lot," I said lightly.

"Maybe MGM will loan them to Pacific for your first picture," she replied. "That happens occasionally. You write so well for them, after all."

Was it a genuine compliment, or was she needling me? I couldn't tell at all. To my surprise, this thrilled rather than terrified me. Here was one of the smartest critics of our generation, and I had the chance to outsmart her. "Maybe," I said. "As long as they pay me, I don't really care who stars in it."

"Hmm," Fiona said thoughtfully. "Well, regardless. It's always exciting to have another New Yorker out here. Say, you wouldn't be interested in a drink, would you?"

I peered around the kitchen. "I thought they didn't serve booze here."

"They don't," Fiona replied. "But after our shift, my friends and I are going drinking at the Cocoanut Grove. It's inside the Ambassador Hotel, down on Wilshire. Wanna meet us there?"

The Cocoanut Grove was a vast nightclub, with artificial palm trees stretching toward the ceiling and Moroccan chandeliers splaying geometric patterns on their wide green leaves. White-covered tables were packed together, both on the main level, where I currently stood, and on a slightly raised seating area toward the back of the room. Figuring stars like June Lee and Jack Kott would certainly be in the center of the action, I made my way around the edges of the dance floor first, occasionally losing my footing on the uneven line where wooden panels replaced green carpeting. Not seeing anyone I recognized, I headed for the back and up a few carpeted stairs, where I finally spotted Fiona and her friends.

As I approached the table, seeing the group talking and laughing, a wave of embarrassment washed over me. This crowd wouldn't want me there; why would they? Fiona had probably only invited me to be nice.

It was there that I stopped myself. Fiona Farris didn't do anything to be nice.

Terry Levine, the one who had checked me in at the Canteen that night, had joined the group and was currently holding forth. "Dev absolutely threw a fit over it. He was storming through the hall, shouting, 'If anyone's going to operate on my stars, it's going to be my guy.' Talking about all the money he's put into Irv over the years like he's a used car."

"Unbelievable," said June Lee. "Give me a penknife and a lighter, and I could remove someone's appendix."

"You can't sterilize a penknife with a lighter," said Jack Kott.

"The lighter's for cigarettes. I'm going to need something to calm my nerves if I'm operating on a guy."

Jack spotted me first. "Ah, you must be Fiona's friend Annie," he said.

"We're not friends," Fiona clarified. "We're barely acquaintances."

"You sure know how to make a guest feel welcome," I replied. June was standing up to greet me. I held out my hand to shake hers, and instead she pulled me into a hug. She smelled heavily of rum, which may have explained the familiarity.

"Oh god, June's gone full California," said Jack. "Don't expect any of the rest of us to hug you. We're clinging to some shred of New York dignity."

"Come on, being uninterested in hugging a beautiful woman is Victor's thing," June shot back, returning to her chair and encouraging me to sit down next to her.

Fiona gave Jack an icy look. "Perhaps if your mother had hugged you more, it wouldn't feel so foreign."

The banter prior to this remark had been fast, but now the table went quiet. Everyone looked to Jack to gauge his reaction and then looked away as we each realized we were all staring at him. Jack took a long gulp from his cocktail, draining it, and then placed the empty glass on the table.

"Nonsense. Jack's mother did a fine job raising him," said Terry. "That's why we all drink as much as we do: because our mothers did an excellent job."

The group laughed at that, and I did, too, a warm and comfortable feeling spreading through my chest. How long had it been since I shared a laugh with a group of people? Months, at least. It felt good. A waitress came by with another round for the table, and I ordered a martini, which was deposited in front of me with alarming swiftness. It was crisp and bitter and, on a stomach emptied by hours of dancing, went straight to my head.

"All right, let's do the introducing bit," Fiona said. "Annie, this is the club. That's Jack Kott. Even if you recognize him, pretend you don't, or he'll be insufferable all night. That's Victor Durand. Even if you don't recognize him, pretend you do, or same thing."

Durand had been the man in the gray suit I'd seen at the Canteen, which I should have guessed. He had become famous for playing Henry Hilbert's music, and he appeared regularly on Jack Kott's show to play the piano and insult people. "I've heard you both on the radio, of course. You're wonderful." To Victor, I added, "You're Henry Hilbert's friend, right?"

"That's one way to put it," he replied grimly.

"Well, I love his music."

"Everyone does."

Fiona didn't give me a chance to converse on that topic further. "You've already been acquainted with Miss June Lee, who apparently hugs strangers now. And this is Terry Levine."

"We met earlier," I said. "Hello again."

"I don't remember you," replied Terry.

"Terry's a producer at Pacific, so a good person to know if you want your little play turned into a movie," Fiona continued. "I should charge you a finder's fee for introducing you. Club, this is Annie Laurence. She's a writer from New York."

"Another writer!" cried Jack earnestly, and the rest of the table broke out into giggles.

June turned to me to explain. "Jack is one of the most important novelists of our time."

The laughs turned louder at that, and Jack rolled his eyes. "I wrote a novel that no one wants to publish, and that's the most hilarious thing in the world to this lot," he explained.

"I'll say this about Jack's novel," said Victor. "The pages were all in order."

"Oh, I wasn't nearly so sure," countered Fiona.

"It was all about his childhood in war-torn Europe," said June. "And he made the bold choice to make the experience of reading it as harrowing as growing up there."

"I'm a screenwriter at Pacific now," I said. "So maybe I'll adapt it into a picture, and then no one will enjoy it but in a different medium."

I hadn't been sure I was close enough to the friends to make fun of them the way they all appeared to make fun of each other, but my attempt was met with an approving round of laughter, even from Jack.

"That's me," said Jack. "Jack Kott: Terrible writer. Mediocre comedian. Excellent alcoholic."

This time, everyone laughed except for Fiona, who looked upward in thoughtful consideration. I felt Jack take a tiny, near-imperceptible breath in anticipation (or fear?) of what she was wording in her head.

"The thing is, you're not actually a terrible writer," she said. "It's only that no one wants that from you. Including anyone at this table. Jack Kott being serious is like learning that a dog is going to be performing your surgery: You don't exactly care whether or not he's good at it. You'd rather he just roll over and beg for bones."

Victor and June laughed, but Jack puckered his lips and polished off his second drink. Terry looked back and forth between him and Fiona. "I don't think that's true," she said.

Fiona looked a bit sour that her quip wasn't being treated with the proper deference, but Terry deftly changed the subject before she could respond. "We're all from New York, too, Annie. Met there near-ly…oh goodness, almost two decades ago."

"Christ," said Jack. "Almost time for us to start dying off."

"I reviewed her play the last time I was out there," said Fiona, nod-ding toward me.

"Oh, how unfortunate," June said to me immediately.

"If you want to kill her, we can ask the girl to bring out a steak knife," offered Victor.

"Did I say anything truly terrible about it?" asked Fiona, lean-ing forward and resting her chin in one delicate hand. "I don't remember."

Her dark-brown eyes met mine, holding there steadily. The same sensation I'd had in the kitchen came over me again, that feeling she was testing me. It dawned on me that possibly the only reason I'd been invited here was so she could fish for new column material, and the danger of it all sent a little thrill down my spine. "No, it was a rather positive review, actually," I said. "Only you didn't think the murder weapon would work in real life. Which I would beg to differ."

"Well, you're lucky," interjected June before Fiona could respond.

"Don't start," Jack warned her.

June ignored him, turning to me again and grabbing my wrist. "My first film that I did out here, I played this talented but troubled violin-ist—I thought it was a great film, that it really showed what I can do as an actress. Fiona reviewed it and absolutely tore it apart."

"Didn't I just say, 'Don't start'?" asked Jack.

"I'm not starting; I'm explaining. I'm telling the story to Annie," June snapped at him before turning back to me. "'Miss Lee acts about as well as you'd expect someone as attractive as her to act.' That's what she wrote about me."

"What's wrong with that? I called you attractive," said Fiona.

"Jack's right. Let's not get into it," Terry interrupted. "Well-trod territory. Besides, not being in good movies has really freed you up to be in the terrible movies that I make."

"I already told you, I don't care anymore," said June, although she suddenly pushed her chair away from the table and stood up. "Excuse me, I have to go powder something. Maybe my nose. I'm still weighing options."

"Did the studio put you up somewhere nice?" Terry asked me, but I only half heard the question, watching June squeeze her way off to a corner of the dining room.

"Actually I'm going to go powder things as well," I said. "Excuse me."

June was reapplying her lipstick when I entered the bathroom, looking far more calm and collected than I expected someone who had slunk away from the table possibly on the verge of tears to be. "Thought I'd touch up too," I said, pulling my own lipstick from my bag. "What shade is that? It's fabulous."

She smacked her freshly coated lips. "You seem like a doll, but I can't tell. Women must have their secrets, you know?"

"Sure." I looked down at my shade. It was called Big Apple Red, and I'd bought it at Bullocks, the department store near my apartment. A twinge of homesickness had made me reach for it, not the color itself, and as a result it looked a bit off on my face, clashing with my red hair.

"Are you having fun?" she asked.

"I'm having a swell time," I answered. "I haven't been on the town in ages. Feels wonderful to have a drink and hear some music again. I'm starting to feel like a person."

"I'm thrilled to hear it," she deadpanned. "It's not always the case when one of us brings a guest. Our little club isn't everyone's cup of tea."

"You're the best people I've met in Hollywood so far," I answered truthfully, leaving out the technicality that I hadn't met any other people. "Although I do feel as if I ought to ask..."

June seemed to read my mind. "Fiona," she said.

"She brings the mood down a little, no?" I remarked. "It seemed like she upset you a bit there."

"Oh no," said June. "Well, yes. But that's my problem, not hers. That's what friends are for, isn't it? To keep you humble? That's the difference between Hollywood and New York, you know. New York, everyone kicks you in the shins. Cabbies, grocers, critics. Out here, everyone just sucks up to each other all the time. No one wants to take the piss out of the person who could cast them in a picture. Problem with that is, you've got a town where everyone's full of piss."

"I hate people like that," I said. "To your face, it's all 'I love you, I love you,' but then they'll throw you away when they no longer need you. Just throw me away from the start so I know who I can trust."

June had moved on to fluffing her hair, twirling a few of the flatter strands through her fingers. "Exactly," she said. "And you can trust Fiona—in that you can trust that you can never trust her."

June's explanation, and the flow of quickly appearing martinis, allowed me to relax. Fiona wasn't needling me to trick me into revealing secrets of my scandalous past; she was needling me because it was fun, and if I needled her right back, not only would she take it, but she'd also laugh as loudly as anyone else at the table. The more I relaxed, the clearer the dynamics of this group became. June, Victor, and Jack would tease each other. Fiona would take it too far. Terry would calm everyone down, change the subject, soothe over any hurt feelings. As long as I stayed solidly in the first group—poking fun but not too much—I fit right in. By the end of the night, June was grabbing my arm and insisting that I knew enough of everyone's secrets to be named an honorary member of the Ambassador's Club.

Terry quickly jumped in to explain. "We named ourselves that because that's what the hotel is called."

"And we needed a name that's as insufferable as all our personalities," added Victor.

"I love it," I said. "The name and the hotel." There was a roar from down toward the dance floor. I craned my neck and saw that girls in hula outfits were currently streaming out from backstage, their hips swaying to the music. "I mean, what a spot."

"We know. It's awful," said Jack.

"I love the bold choice to exercise neither restraint nor taste," said Victor.

"The decor is almost as terrible as the drinks, music, service, and food," added June.

"Don't forget that it's also overpriced," said Terry.

"*Free* would be overpriced," countered Fiona.

I remembered when I walked in, how enchanted I'd been by the lights on the trees. That illusion was completely shattered now. The trees were plastic, covered in dust. The Moroccan chandeliers were tacky, a cheap knockoff meant to imitate some foreign land for boring Hollywood types who had no interest in experiencing the real thing for themselves. I wasn't disappointed by the magic evaporating. Quite the contrary—I was thrilled by it. It was like I'd peeled back a layer, like this group had given me the intelligence to see through to the truth of things.

"So you must drink here often, then," I said.

"Almost every night," answered Fiona. "Sometimes Jack or Vic has a show, or Terry makes those three work late on that awful Henry Hilbert movie she's producing, but except for that. Want to join us again tomorrow?"

She was perhaps the only person in the entire state of California I should stay away from or risk tanking not only my own career but Adam's and Beverly's as well, yet I found myself agreeing right away.

When we finally spilled out onto Wilshire Boulevard, it was almost 2 a.m. My apartment was nearby, so I decided to walk home, even though the lack of streetlights made the streets pitch-black. The darkness would have unnerved me—in New York, we'd only dimmed the lights for the war, not shut them off completely—if I hadn't felt on top of the world. For the first time in months, it felt as if I could do this. I could live in Los Angeles, I could make friends, I could get my picture made. I could become fabulous Hollywood Annie, and when Adam and Beverly finally saw me? Their jaws would drop.

That opportunity would come sooner than I thought.

I spent the next two days in my office, failing at writing *Don't Count Your Coconuts,* and the next two evenings at the Ambassador Hotel, succeeding at getting very intoxicated. Friday night, Victor showed up with a handful of pamphlets, tossing them at us. "Irma roped me into playing the Canteen on Sunday," he said. "Come or don't come—but if you don't come, I will burn your houses down."

"What are you playing?" asked Jack.

"Piano," deadpanned Victor. "The Hilbert concerto. What else?"

This caused some distress among the group, none of whom liked Henry Hilbert very much, I'd surmised. But I wasn't paying attention. The pamphlets Victor had tossed at us listed the week's schedule for the Hollywood Canteen. The upcoming "Symphonic Sunday" indeed listed Henry Hilbert's 1939 *Concerto in C Minor,* featuring the Hollywood Canteen Orchestra and soloist Victor Durand, conducted by Mr. Hilbert himself. It was the words underneath that caught my eye.

Sunday night is MGM night at the Hollywood Canteen!

FIVE

-‹‹‹◆›››-

The news that Sunday night was MGM night should have turned me off completely from going. If Fiona was the one person in California I probably ought to stay away from, Beverly and Adam would round out the top three. It could spell disaster to put all four of us in a room together, where Fiona would no doubt be watching our every interaction like a hawk. The smart thing to do would have been not to chance it, to make an excuse: a script deadline, a last-minute cold.

The thought never crossed my mind.

Instead, I was thrilled at the prospect. I'd spent three nights now with the Ambassador's Club, which was nothing on the years and years they had spent with each other but was enough to make me confident I could sit down at any table they were at and be welcomed. I could see it all, how it would play out. I'd join June, Jack, Terry, and Fiona in a prime spot to watch the concert. As Victor played, Beverly's eyes would scan the room, her heart skipping a beat as they landed on Fiona. Just as she would be tapping Adam's arm to whisper that Fiona Farris was here, she'd spy me, right next to Fiona. The tap on Adam's arm would become a frantic pat, which would annoy him. Adam loved classical music and would hate an interruption. *What?* he'd whisper finally. Beverly would point to me.

What had I told her, they would wonder. Did they need to worry about their precious little careers because the woman they had so dreadfully mistreated now had the ear of the most important columnist in town? They had been ignoring me for four months, but there was no way they could ignore me after seeing that.

I chose my outfit so carefully that night, eventually deciding on a black dress that showed off my legs and a simple gold chain to ornament it. I wanted to look like a knockout but not like I had tried too hard to look like a knockout. The wolf whistles I received from the servicemen in line waiting for the Canteen to open told me I had nailed it.

Even Terry, once again working the volunteer entrance, did a double take when she saw me. "You look like a million bucks," she said, passing me the sign-in sheet. "Fiona and June are inside. I don't think Vic and Jack are here yet. Probably off drinking somewhere. God forbid either one of them ever performs sober."

I was nodding to Terry and peering inside to get my bearings when all of a sudden, there they were.

They were coming into the vestibule from the back entrance to the kitchen, murmuring to one another. Beverly was wearing a white suit and a matching pillbox hat; Adam was in a pair of gray trousers and a white button-up. In the few heartbeats before they saw me, I looked at them. They were both different—Beverly's hair was a few shades lighter; Adam had ditched the glasses—and exactly the same. Something jumped into my throat, and I had the sudden, shocking urge to run away or cry or both. I hadn't expected it to happen like this, so fast. I wanted them to see me far away and indifferent to them, not up close, with all my emotions offered up on a platter.

They saw me at the same time, both stopping mid-whisper to stare at me. I watched them take me in, watched them notice how they wanted to react and then send that impulse away, watched them calculate exactly how a normal actor would respond to seeing a normal colleague in an unexpected place. The process took milliseconds, and before long, Beverly was hugging me—the way an old friend would, of course. "Annie Laurence! How lovely to see you!"

I hadn't steeled myself for the smell of her, for the weight of her hand on the small of my back. It took all my concentration to remain upright. She pulled away, and Adam extended his hand out to me. I looked at him like he was nuts. I didn't want to shake his hand like he was some friend of my father's and not a person I'd lived with for five years. But Terry was watching not ten feet away, so I reluctantly took it. "Hi," I said. "Fancy running into you here."

"Understatement of the century," said Adam. "Why aren't you in New York?"

"I moved out here," I said. "A couple weeks ago."

Even knowing how a normal actor would react to this news from a normal colleague, they couldn't bring themselves to do it. Their eyes both widened, and they were stuck bobbing their heads like owls. "Uh-huh," said Beverly finally. "You know, we were just going to take a smoke break, but I left my cigarettes in the car. Why don't you walk with us? It's just around the corner. Give us a chance to catch up."

I made my apologies to Terry, promising to return to my shift in a moment, and followed them north on the side street to Sunset Boulevard. We look a left and walked for a few more blocks in silence until I finally said, "I thought the car was just around the corner."

"We took a taxi," said Adam.

"Here," said Beverly, pointing to an alley. A few rats scattered as the two led me down past the dumpsters.

"Are you going to kill me?" I tried to joke.

"I don't know, maybe," replied Adam. "What the hell are you doing here, Annie?"

It certainly wasn't the fearful but impressed reaction I'd fantasized about. "I got a job at Pacific," I said.

"Why?"

"What do you mean, why?" I asked. "They offered me money, and I've found that's a useful thing to exchange for goods and services."

"Don't be sarcastic," said Beverly. "You know what we mean. You never had any interest in moving out here, and suddenly we're not here three months, and you've got a job out here too?"

"I didn't follow you, if that's what you're implying," I said. "My last play closed a lot earlier than expected. I needed the money. You two aren't the first people in the world to think of moving to Hollywood to work in pictures."

"Come on, Annie," said Adam. "We thought you understood. This would be easier on all of us with a continent in between us."

The comment took me aback. "Easier for all of us? What part of this hasn't been easy on you?"

"All of it, Annie—this has been so, so hard," said Beverly, absent-mindedly adjusting the angle of her hat. "We miss you every day. Just last night, Adam came home from work and accidentally made three martinis out of habit."

"Sorry, I…" I pressed my eyes closed, not believing what I was hearing. "This has been hard for you because you had to dump an extra martini?" I pictured every night I'd spent on my bare mattress on the Upper West Side, going weeks between baths, ignoring my own mother. I started to laugh. "Yes, how terrible, that the happily married couple had to forlornly pour one shot of gin down the drain and only talk to each other!"

"Let's not derail ourselves into a contest, who is more miserable than whom," said Adam. "Annie, you can't be here tonight. Fiona Farris is in there. If she sees us all together—"

"I know she's there," I said. "She invited me."

There it was: the wide eyes, the fear. I couldn't help but smile a little. It was satisfying. "You spoke to her?" said Adam, running his hands through his hair and exhaling. "You could ruin us doing that."

"Yes, I imagine that's the point," muttered Beverly.

"Will you relax? I'm not going to do anything to hurt you. I would never..." I trailed off. How had this gone so wrong, so fast? "Look. I'm sorry, I hadn't expected us to run into each other like this. I'm not handling it well."

They looked at each other, decided silently to accept my apology. "It's all right," said Beverly. "We're sorry too."

"But if you're so miserable, and I'm so miserable, why don't we forget this stupid mess? Go back to the way things were?"

"Because we're MGM contract stars now," said Adam. He said it plainly, as if this were a logical response and not a load of rubbish. "The studio is marketing us as a wholesome married couple. L. B. Mayer is considering hiring some child actors to play our kids—"

"He's *what*?"

"At press events and stuff, so we look more all-American. It's what the troops need right now—a solid American family to remind them what they're fighting for."

"You know what? Never mind," I said. "I don't want to be with someone who hires fake children—"

"We're not hiring them; the studio would be hiring them. It's common practice, to control a star's image—"

"I don't want anything from you two," I said.

"Then why did you just ask five seconds ago—" Beverly could hardly get the words out. "You asked us to take you back!"

"Because I want everything from you!" I said. "I want everything from you, and I want nothing. I want to see you every day, and I never want to see you again. I want you to hate yourself for what you did to me—hate yourself so much you beg me to come back—and also for you to never speak to me ever again. I want you to know you made a mistake."

"We didn't make a mistake," Adam said. "Let me be clear. Don't call us, don't come to our house, don't show up to places you think we'll be. Whatever we had, it's over now. Let it die."

They left me there in the alley. I watched them hail a cab on Sunset and waited for the car to pull away before I slunk back to the Hollywood Canteen, feeling so small I could vanish into the air.

Somehow the Canteen was even more packed than it had been on Wednesday. When I entered the main room, I was immediately grabbed by a sailor and launched into a jitterbug, except we had to mostly dance in place, as there wasn't anywhere to move. I kept my head on a swivel, looking around for Fiona. Obviously, I wouldn't be able to tell her anything about the conversation I'd just had, but I wanted to see a face that would be... *Friendly* wasn't the right word to describe any member of the Ambassador's Club—recognizable, perhaps?

But the room was so crowded—and I was short enough, even in heels—that I couldn't see more than a foot in front of me. I went on like that for about an hour, my feet getting calloused and sore and my throat becoming parched. I was starting to feel a little light-headed from it all when June finally swept into my peripheral vision. I was about to excuse myself from my dance partner and beg June to join me outside for a cigarette when I noticed tears were forming at the corner of her eyes and her cheeks were shaking from holding her smile. She pushed away the soldier she was dancing with and turned around. He put his hands on her shoulders, his fingers gripping too hard. He only let go when another couple lost their footing and tumbled in between them. June made a beeline for the kitchen.

I tried to follow her, but it was like digging a hole in wet sand. Every time I thought I saw a path, it filled with men, each one trying to grab me for a dance. I gave each one a polite couple of beats of swaying and a twirl before moving on.

It wasn't until I walked into the kitchen that I saw the reason it had been June's destination. Fiona was one of the half a dozen or so volunteers tasked with making sandwiches for distribution at the snack bar, and June was in the middle of screaming at her.

"...like I'm just a piece of meat to them. Not even that. Just a picture, just a—"

"How about you have some coffee and calm down," suggested Fiona, cool as a cucumber.

"—an idea or... I don't want your nasty coffee. I want to have never met you!" screamed June.

"Doll, having never met me wouldn't have stopped me from writing that review," countered Fiona. June let out a guttural screech, grabbed a box of raisins from a nearby tray, and threw it against the wall.

"What's going on?" I whispered to the volunteer closest to me, who was not even pretending to be uninterested in this drama.

"One of the servicemen groped June Lee on the dance floor," she whispered back. "And she's pissed at that lady for it, for some reason."

Fiona was starting to lose her temper now as well. "I'm not sure why you're yelling at me," she was saying, angrily slathering a slice of white bread with too much mayonnaise. "I didn't grab your tits. First of all, they're too small for my liking."

"It's your fault I'm even here!" June replied, but a little more meekly. Her anger was dissipating as she seemed to realize Fiona had a point. "I never wanted to be this: Recognized. A pretty face only, a thing men want to possess. I wanted to be serious. I wanted to be a real actress—"

I could see the thought hit Fiona, and in the milliseconds between when I saw her think it and heard her say it, I wanted to dive in between them, do something before words were said that couldn't be taken back.

"It's not my fault you're a bad actress," Fiona snapped. "It's not my fault you've done nothing interesting, said nothing interesting, thought nothing interesting. Maybe men only see you as a pretty face because there's nothing else there to see."

I almost felt for Fiona in that moment, almost sympathized with the shock of a rather uninteresting night of making sandwiches before a concert interrupted by an angry friend unfairly rehashing old grievances. But to see your friend's deepest weakness, her most tender bruise, and press down hard seemed cruel even for Fiona Farris.

June fled through the back door of the kitchen, the one leading back to the volunteer entrance. I tried to follow her but was cut off by Bette Davis, who appeared out of nowhere to grab me by the shoulders.

"We need you making sandwiches," she said. "After the concert, there's going to be a run on sandwiches. We need more people making sandwiches."

Let me tell you something: when Bette Davis tells you forcefully in that deep voice that you need to do something, you don't ask a lot of questions. "All right," I mumbled, stepping back into the kitchen and walking numbly to an empty spot by the island in the center of the room. Fiona was just to my right. I tried desperately not to look at her as I reached for two slices from a loaf of white bread.

"June is such a child," Fiona muttered to me. I could still feel anger radiating off her. "Can you imagine being the sexiest woman in Hollywood and complaining that no one wants to see you play Lady Macbeth?"

The last thing I wanted was to insert myself into the middle of an argument between two of the five people in this town that I thought could someday be my friends. "It's bad luck to say that word in a theater," I said.

Fiona rolled her eyes. "That's the least of my problems tonight," she said. Then her head snapped up to look at me, and any sourness disappeared, replaced with what could almost be described as a twinkle in her eye.

Only one thing could cheer her up that quickly, so I knew what was coming. "Your friends the Cooks are here," she remarked with a singsongy lilt to her voice.

"Yes, I saw them on my way in," I replied coolly. "I think they were leaving."

And that was the end of our conversation.

We were only making sandwiches for a few minutes before trouble started up again. "Oh, Christ, here comes Henry Hilbert's right- *and* left-hand man," she said.

I looked up to see Victor, dressed for the concert in a full tuxedo, with his hair pomaded back. "We need to talk," he said to Fiona.

"Did you hear what I said?" she replied. "Right- and left-hand man."

"I'm doubled over laughing," snapped Victor. "Come here."

Victor took Fiona to the corner by the coffee machine, where he started in on her with a low and intense voice. I felt myself wanting to eavesdrop, not because I was nosy—well, not *only* because I was nosy—but also because maybe this time I could stop Fiona before she said whatever sentence would hurt Victor as much as she had hurt June. Fortunately, Terry got there before I needed to. She came into the kitchen from the back entrance and must have sensed the tension because she swept over right away, breaking the two apart.

I glanced at my watch—eight forty-five. The concert was supposed to start at nine, so if I was going to get a smoke in beforehand, I'd better go now. I left the kitchen through the back door and went out to the side street, where things were significantly calmer than when

I'd arrived. The onlookers and photographers trying to catch glimpses of stars arriving for their shifts had dissipated, and the servicemen who wanted to smoke went out to the patio by the front, so I had the street all to myself. For a few seconds, at least. I'd barely lit my cigarette before Victor was in front of me, helping himself to another one from the open pack still in my hand.

"Jack took mine," he said, already lighting it as he asked, "You don't mind, do you?"

"What was that all about in there?" I asked.

He ignored the question. "'Right- and left-hand man.' Do you think she lies awake at night thinking of little comments like that?"

"I'm sure she keeps a notebook on her nightstand," I replied.

Our conversation was interrupted by the volunteer-entrance door slamming open and Bette Davis appearing again, this time holding a manila folder. "Hi, Bette," said Victor. "I saw *Now, Voyager*. You should have told them to call it *Two Hours, Voyager*."

She ignored him, looking at me. "Are you Annie Laurence?" I nodded. "You never filled out your paperwork," she said.

Realizing he wasn't going to be the center of this conversation, Victor abandoned us without a farewell and headed for the stage door down the street. "What paperwork?" I asked.

"Canteen volunteers have to fill out paperwork, get fingerprinted and background checked by the FBI. Anyone who works with servicemen does." She held the folder out for me to take. "Take this to the office and fill it out."

"Can it wait until after the concert?" I asked. "I was hoping to watch."

Mrs. Davis shook her head. "Unfortunately not. But there's a room above the sound booth; you could fill it out there. There's windows that look out to the stage. Go in the stage door right there and straight up the stairs on the left. You can't miss 'em."

I thanked her as she headed back inside. I thought I'd take a minute to finish my cigarette and enjoy the warm night air, but the second I was alone, I thought of Beverly and Adam. It had been easier to think of them as happy, living their blissful MGM existence and forgetting I had ever been alive. But knowing they missed me—that they did care about me but not enough—felt worse. I dropped my cigarette on the ground and headed for the stage door.

The stage door vestibule was smaller than the volunteer entrance and completely empty, although a lot of noise and activity was coming from a door in front of me that must have led out to the stage. I imagined that Victor and Henry Hilbert were probably in there right now, taking a few deep breaths or having one last drink or whatever unique thing constituted their version of the preshow routine all artists are required to have.

To my right was a staircase of unfinished wood. Whether this was a stylistic choice in keeping with the rustic "cowboy" feel of the rest of the Canteen or simply an unfinished bit of construction, I couldn't tell. The stairs led me to a small unassuming room with nothing more than a couple of tables and chairs. The walls were the same exposed wood with a few windows cut in, looking down on the stage and the Canteen's main room. The dancing had stopped, and soldiers, sailors, hostesses, and kitchen volunteers were all seated in a tight pack on the floor, while a few lucky folks got chairs along the side walls.

I always liked the feeling of a theater before a show—the room buzzing with excited small talk, the way even the particles in the air seem to know something is about to happen. Sometimes during the run of *Altogether Too Many Murders*, if I happened to be in the neighborhood, I'd sneak into the back of the theater before the show just to soak up some of that concentrated anticipation, the unique electricity of nearly a thousand individuals about to experience something together, in the same room. I wouldn't even stay for the performance sometimes.

Up in my unfinished wooden tree house, a sheet of glass between me and any emotion, I suddenly felt so isolated. That loneliness again cascaded through me, picking up steam and becoming a wash of incredible sadness that shocked me at how fast it hit. I had been only slightly annoyed a moment ago, but now I could put my head in my arms and sob. I wasn't a crier, but it seemed like the only appropriate response. What the hell was I doing here in this room? What the hell was I doing at the Hollywood Canteen? What the hell was I doing in Los Angeles altogether?

As Henry Hilbert took the conductor's stand to applause, I stepped away from the window and lay down on the unfinished floor. The applause died away and then started up again, presumably from Victor entering and sitting at the piano. I no longer cared about the concert. What I wanted was to disappear—melt into this unsanded wood, stop existing, maybe have my bones and muscles reform themselves into some other shape. Was there a way to die without actually killing oneself?

Then I heard the opening notes of the concerto.

The piano began alone, a few haunting chords surrounded by silence, like the tolling of a bell. The resonance of the low notes shook the wooden floor I lay on. I sat up and crawled my way to a window, kneeling up to look out. Victor, at the piano, was nearly right underneath me, his shoulders hunched. I'd heard him play on the radio before, but there was something about seeing him perform. His movements started slow, subtle—a nod of the head, a flick of the wrist—only to grow in intensity and emotion until it wasn't just his fingers striking the keys but seemingly a full-body effort. It was impossible not to watch him with awe, not to think that everything I could ever and would ever do would pale in comparison to this.

After a minute or so, the strings joined in, sweeping and low and melodic, joined a few moments later by a warbly clarinet. I knelt at the window, transfixed, as the music hit a crescendo and then took a turn for the upbeat. Victor's fingers moved the entire length of the piano, hitting more keys than it seemed humanly possible to do, before sliding back into a languid melody. The first movement came to a conclusion, and the audience, who had apparently been as enraptured as I was, burst into loud applause, punctuated with whoops and hollers from the boys. Victor didn't even flinch, just flipped away the tails of his jacket, readjusted himself on the bench, and took a deep breath.

I checked my watch and was shocked to see fourteen entire minutes had passed. It had been the fastest quarter of an hour of my life.

The second movement began, faster and more foreboding than the first. When the clarinets came in, they sounded less tender and melancholy but more ominous. A drum started to beat, its pace like a heartbeat, pounding faster and faster, shaking the window.

I was so caught up in the tension I didn't hear the footsteps behind me.

When I saw a shadow pass on the wooden wall, I whipped around in fright, then exhaled in relief when I saw it was only Jack. "You scared me," I said. "Here to watch?"

He didn't answer, just ran his fingers over the edge of one of the black wooden chairs as if it were the most fascinating thing in the world. His eyes were glazed over, his pupils wide, seeming to take in nothing and everything all at once. "Hey," I said, waving my arm this time. "You okay?"

He looked up, and the action sent him stumbling a bit. He was drunk, I realized. He opened his mouth to say something and then looked to the ground like he'd forgotten what it was. So not just drunk—very drunk. "You're not okay," he said finally.

"No, I'm not," I said. It wasn't the sort of thing I would normally admit to a near-stranger, but there was something freeing in the knowledge he would never remember this.

"None of us are okay," he said. "None of us are…"

He pulled out the chair to try to sit down but missed completely, landing on his butt with a thud. It didn't seem to hurt; in fact, he found it quite hilarious and slapped his knee a few times.

"Maybe you should get something to eat," I said. "There's sandwiches and coffee in the kitchen."

"Sandwiches and coffee," he repeated. "Sandwiches and coffee." It must have been an agreement because he started to stand and head for the staircase.

"You know where it is?" I asked.

"Sandwiches and coffee," he replied.

"You want me to go with you?"

"Kid, you can't come with me. At the end of it all is a journey we must take alone," he said.

"I'm not talking about death. I meant to the kitchen," I said.

"Death, the kitchen." He had already started down the stairs. "What's the difference?"

I followed him downstairs and outside to the back of the Canteen, catching the stage door and closing it gently so it wouldn't slam shut and disturb the show. Terry had just come out of the volunteer entrance down the street, and she looked over to us.

"I think Jack needs to eat something," I said to her.

She understood my meaning. "Ah," she said, taking Jack's arm. "I'll take him."

I was going to wait for them to go inside the volunteer entrance before going back upstairs, but Jack was walking pretty slowly, so I headed back to the unfinished room. I thought perhaps the interruption might have ruined whatever magical effect the concert was having on me, but I snapped right back into that emotional place, feeling my heart tug with every new variation on a melody. The end of the second movement a few moments later was so downtrodden—a petering out rather than a punctuation—that this time the room remained silent.

I thought how silence could be part of a song, just as important as the sounds. I wasn't sure if that thought was deep or just cloudy enough that I couldn't see its shallowness. I thought about Jack.

As the third movement started, robust and energetic, I grabbed the manila folder of forms and dashed to fill out my name, address, marital status. If I hurried up and finished them, I could go downstairs and watch the rest of the third movement from the dance floor. I wanted to be among the crowd for the bows and applause, wanted to shout, "Bravo," and have something besides glass and wooden beams absorb it.

But when I ran out to the back street with the completed forms under my arm, I realized the volunteer entrance had been locked. Terry must have closed it after taking Jack to the kitchen.

I should have gone back upstairs. Even better, I should have turned and left the Canteen forever, walked west on Sunset until I hit the ocean and then kept going, on and on until I became a speck in the horizon. But I was manic then. I *would* be watching the rest of the concert from the crowd on the dance floor. Not only would this act cure all my problems—it was the only thing that could.

I would go around to the front entrance, I decided, and I would cut through the alley between the Canteen and the building next door rather than going all the way around the block. The ground between the two buildings was uneven dirt, and it was dark outside, so I had to go a little slower than I wanted to so as not to lose my footing. I was grateful that just up ahead was the window into the kitchen, with at least some light streaming out of it.

As I passed by, I glanced in the window and saw it—saw her. Saw Jack on his knees, hysterical, saw Terry shouting for help. I saw it was already useless. I saw the empty coffee cup lying next to her. I saw Fiona Farris, her eyes already glazed over, on the floor of the Hollywood Canteen.

SIX

-«««◆»»»-

Bette Davis rushed to the stage to tell the packed house that no one was allowed to leave until a police officer and a Canteen manager gave us the okay. Each and every one of us would be interviewed, so grab a snack or a coffee if you need one and find a seat; it's going to be a long night. Immediately after she said that, a police officer shouted that none of us were to eat or drink anything from the kitchen—news that was met with more emotion than the fact that someone had passed away.

In some fairness, most of the one hundred and fifty or so volunteers and several hundred visitors to the Canteen only knew for certain that a medical emergency had happened, not that anything had been fatal. In the rush of ambulances and medics, there was some chatter that perhaps Fiona would be okay. I knew that wasn't going to be the case. I would have known that even if I hadn't seen her, just from the shock and pain and hollowness in Jack's eyes. He had seen something he would never forget.

Jack and Terry were already in a corner, talking with the police, so I scanned the rest of the room, telling myself I was looking for Victor and June but really looking for Beverly and Adam. They were nowhere in sight, so they must have left for good after our fight after all. Victor and June were both on the stage, huddled together, surrounded by several dozen friends and other musicians giving them supportive hugs and rubs on the back. June was dabbing at her eyes with someone's handkerchief; Victor kept looking back at the piano, as if he were wondering if he ought to sit down and finish the show. I recognized Henry Hilbert from New York—I'd never met him, of course, him being the most famous composer of the twentieth century and me being a nearly unknown playwright—but we'd been at a handful of the same opening-night parties over the years. At those affairs, he'd been surrounded by dozens of people hanging on his every word, but now he was lingering off to the side of the crowd, completely alone.

I thought about joining June and Victor but suddenly felt uncomfortable about doing so. For all the fantasizing I had done about Beverly and Adam seeing me with my new friends, I felt now that I didn't know them at all, that my presence would be an annoyance rather than a comfort. Not sure what else to do, I took a seat on the floor. It still didn't feel real. Fiona Farris couldn't die. I'd been hearing her name for so long, hearing her worst barbs repeated backstage and her nastiest reviews read aloud at cocktail parties for what felt like my entire life. She had seemed bigger than a human being. How could a person who loomed so large disappear?

My thoughts were interrupted by the chatter of the group of MGM chorus dancers next to me. "She was married to Don Farris? You know who she is," a blond woman was explaining to her friend as she did a few neck rolls. The fact that they were so casually discussing Fiona disgusted me—but on the other hand, I'd have been disgusted if they were discussing anything but Fiona. "She's completely neurotic. Tried to slit her throat once on the Pacific lot. Come on, you remember."

The blond woman's friend thought about it for a moment, then shook her head. "I don't remember that," she said.

"She's the columnist for the *Dispatch* who never has a nice word to say about anyone," the blond went on.

From in front of them, a third woman turned around to join in. "Ain't that the truth. She absolutely destroyed my last movie. Said it was worse than Nazi propaganda because 'at least Nazis have a consistent story.'"

"Be grateful she reviewed your movie," the blond grumbled. "She wouldn't even come to mine. Absolutely ruined our release." She went silent, then glanced around as she realized anyone could be listening. "Not that I would kill her for that, obviously."

"Oh, of course not," said the third woman quickly. "I would never do something like that."

"I know who you're talking about now!" the second woman chimed in. "She's the writer who accused me of sleeping with George Kaufman! She published it right in the magazine, for anyone to read!"

"You *were* sleeping with George Kaufman," said the blond.

"But she didn't know that," her friend shot back.

I looked around the room as stealthily as I could manage. I was surrounded by Hollywood folks: actresses, writers, singers, directors, dancers, producers. Any one of us could have had a grudge against Fiona. It was likely that *all* of us did. How many others had she published an indiscreet rumor about? How many dreams of stardom had been killed by her pen? No wonder we were being held in this room until we could all be questioned—what had happened in that kitchen was no unfortunate accident. Someone in this room, right now, had decided to make sure the critic never wrote again.

Bette Davis was on the stage, her hands anxiously running through her hair as she talked to two police officers. Joan Crawford was lingering by the snack bar, nervously shuffling around a stack of napkins. Marlene Dietrich was holding court at a table full of servicemen, doing her best to keep them calm with a story. Could it have been one of them? What about the gossipy chorus dancers next to me? What about them?

I probably would have sat there and looked at each volunteer one by one to try to suss out if they were a murderer, but I was interrupted by someone calling my name. A police officer on the stage was shouting into the crowd. I stood up and raised my arm. "I'm here. That's me."

He waved me toward the stage. "Come with me, please."

The gossiping trio next to me went silent as I stood, only to immediately start tittering again as soon as they thought I was out of earshot. I felt several hundred people all assuming I was a murderer as the police officer led me off the stage and into the sound booth.

The officer took me up the unfinished wooden staircase to the room where I'd watched the first two movements of the concerto. Inside was another officer, taller and more commanding than the first. He stood to greet me. "Miss Annie Laurence?"

"Yes," I said, shaking his outstretched hand.

"I'm Detective Kiblowski. That's my partner, Detective Cooper. We just have a few questions for you, if you don't mind. Have a seat."

The seat he offered me was next to his, which I thought was strange. Wasn't I supposed to sit across from the two of them? I sat, and Detective Cooper took the opposite seat. I studied his round face and receding hairline, which even a police hat was failing to hide.

"We heard you were one of the people who found the body," said Kiblowski. "That correct?"

"Not quite," I said. "Jack Kott and Terry Levine, they found her. But I saw the three of them through a window."

"And what exactly did you see?" asked Kiblowski.

I took a shaky breath. The image was still crisp in my mind. It was beginning to occur to me that it might be crisp in my mind for the rest of my life. "Fiona was on the floor, in front of the coffee carafe on the counter. It looked like she had only fainted, except for how pale she was. She was pale before but even more pale now."

"You knew her before?" interjected Cooper.

"I met her on Wednesday, here at the Canteen. We went to the Cocoanut Grove after our shift and then a few times later in the week," I said. "But I knew *of* her before then. Everybody did."

"What else did you see through the window?" Kiblowski asked. "No detail is too small."

"There was a cup next to her," I said. "And some coffee spilled on the floor."

"And Mr. Kott and Mrs. Levine...?"

"Terry was shouting for help," I said. "Jack was... He was a bit further away, um, just sort of...kneeling there. His head was in his hands. Someone had thrown up; I think it was him. He looked awful, just a wreck."

"Understandably so," said Kiblowski. "Mr. Kott and Mrs. Levine were Mrs. Farris's good friends, weren't they? They told us they spent most nights together at the Cocoanut Grove. Did you meet them too?"

I nodded. "And June Lee and Victor Durand."

Kiblowski smiled, shook his head. "What a crew. You never know who you'll meet in Tinsel Town. Right, Cooper? I'd love to run with friends like those."

"Didn't seem to help Mrs. Farris much," said Cooper.

Kiblowski nodded solemnly. "That's true." He turned back to me. "Mrs. Farris had some mental troubles, is that right?"

There was of course the story those actresses had been gossiping about: that Fiona had once smashed a bottle over Don Farris's head in his trailer and then gone for herself with the shards of glass. I had no idea if there was any truth to the story. "I've heard rumors," I said. "But I wouldn't know. Like I said, I only met her for the first time this week."

"How did she seem to you, earlier this week?" asked Kiblowski.

There was something going sour about this exchange, but I couldn't put my finger on it. I shrugged. "She seemed fine."

"What did you all talk about at the Cocoanut Grove?"

I shrugged again. Our conversations had mostly revolved around people we disliked, but I couldn't think of a diplomatic way to put that. "The normal things people talk about: Our careers. The war."

"Do you get the sense Fiona was happy?" asked Kiblowski.

"Oh yes," I answered immediately.

That got an eyebrow raise. "Really?"

"Why wouldn't she be?" I asked. "She wrote a must-read column. In a town where everyone wants influence, she had the most of it. Everyone was afraid of what she would write about them." I remembered the panicked way Adam and Beverly and I had stood in that dressing room opening night, scared to read the telegram with her words on it but equally scared not to read it. How could a person who can send three strangers into a tizzy with a few clacks of a typewriter not be happy?

"That sounds like a lonely existence to me," said Kiblowski. "Never anyone who likes you for you. Never anyone you can turn to in a crisis. Do you think Fiona had someone she could have turned to in a crisis?"

"Sure," I said. "She had friends. June Lee—"

Cooper cut me off. "But Mrs. Farris and Miss Lee had an argument this evening, isn't that right?"

"And Mrs. Farris and Mr. Durand did as well," Kiblowski pointed out. "And from what we've gathered, none of that is unusual."

"That's the kind of relationship they have," I explained. "And some would say that's a more honest sort of relationship than one where you fake a smile and pretend everything is fine when it's not."

Kiblowski wrinkled his brow, his bushy blond eyebrows nearly touching. "You know a lot about what kind of friendship they have, for only knowing them since Wednesday."

"That's the sense I got," I said.

Cooper put up his hand. "We're not interested in your senses, Miss Laurence, just what you saw and heard."

I leaned back and crossed my arms, annoyed at the remark. Why was my analysis worth nothing? They ought to be grateful they had someone like me to provide them with these insights. "What I saw and heard," I began evenly, "was every two-bit actress in Hollywood sitting out there, mouthing off about how Fiona panned them in this, wrote gossip about them doing that, ruined their career doing this. June Lee may have bickered with her friend a few hours ago, but there's an entire room full of suspects out there, any one of whom could have used the concert as a cover to sneak into the kitchen."

"So you don't believe Mrs. Farris could have committed suicide," said Kiblowski.

"There was coffee spilled on the floor," I said.

Both of them looked at me, confused. If the circumstances had been less dire, I would have smiled rather smugly. "I don't understand," said Kiblowski finally.

"If you're drinking lethal poison because you want to die, why bother to mix it with coffee?" I asked. "Someone wanted to trick Fiona into drinking it."

Instead of being impressed by my reasoning, the two only looked at me with thinly veiled annoyance. "We never said she was poisoned," said Cooper.

"She wasn't bleeding; there were no marks around her neck; she appeared to have collapsed while drinking a beverage—not a difficult deduction to make," I replied.

"You've given us a lot to keep in mind," said Kiblowski, although it was clearly a blow-off and not a serious thanks. "Before we let you go, mind sharing with us where you were during the concert?"

"I was in this room," I said. "Filling out my volunteer paperwork."

"Can anyone confirm that's where you were? Did anyone see you up here?" Kiblowski asked.

"Jack Kott," I said. "He wandered up here during the second movement."

Kiblowski and Cooper looked at each other before Kiblowski turned back to me with a smile. "Thanks, Miss Laurence. That's all for now. You're free to go."

The studio was closed on Monday, to give all the Pacific employees who had been at the Canteen a generous twenty-four hours to recover from their shock. But I wasn't surprised Tuesday morning when the front page of *Variety* that had been slipped under my office door by the studio paperboy proclaimed HOLLYWOOD DISPATCH CRITIC FIONA FARRIS FOUND DEAD IN APPARENT SUICIDE.

The article was full of one ridiculous detail after another, the least of which was that the Hollywood Canteen had been completely scrubbed from the situation. The way *Variety* reported it, Fiona may as well have died in the back room of some seedy nightclub, surrounded by gangsters and criminals. God forbid Hollywood's bastion of patriotism be tainted with the truth. There was also the suicide note, allegedly found in Fiona's pocket: *Please forgive me. I can't go on like this. The pain is too much.* Fiona Farris would never have written anything so hackneyed, so vague and unspecific.

I had a typewriter in front of me and a note card reading *Don't Count Your Coconuts* that I somehow needed to turn into 120 pages of dialogue, but every time I put down the newspaper to write, I picked it back up moments later. None of it made sense. Fiona had it all. She was happily married—Don Farris might have been twenty-five years her senior, but he was a handsome and wealthy movie star. What could possibly be the problem there? She had the career—a twice-weekly column in the *Hollywood Dispatch*, where she could cover whatever she wanted. She could personally make or break the careers of anyone in this town on a Tuesday's whim. Hell, she had so much power and influence that news of her death had thrown

MUSSOLINI ARRESTED below the fold. And not least of all, she had the friends. The sort of friendship the Ambassador's Club had was rare; it was intoxicating; it wasn't something you threw away and left behind.

The police had gotten it wrong; I was sure of it. But what could I do about it? I put down *Variety* and swiveled back around in my desk to face the typewriter.

What could I do about it? That had been the theme of my life lately, it seemed. Beverly and Adam wanted to abandon me for California—what could I do about it? Pacific Pictures wanted me to write *Don't Count Your Coconuts*—what could I do about it? I couldn't type a word without inspiration from my exes—what could I do about it? A woman who I thought could be my friend is murdered and the police do nothing—no. This time I wasn't going to lie on the floor helpless. This time was too important. What could I do about it? I could solve it myself. I'd constructed a murder for the stage. How much harder could working backward to solve one in real life be?

With the first burst of energy I'd felt in months, I left the writers' offices, flagged down the first page boy I saw, and asked him what stage was home to the Henry Hilbert movie.

The light above the door to Soundstage 13 was off, meaning no filming was going on, so I let myself in. I wasn't sure what to expect. I'd seen movie sets in movies about movies—large warehouses where cameras soared above colorful spaces while directors shouted into megaphones—but I'd never been on an active one before.

I would still have to wait for that day, it turned out. Stage 13 was completely empty. I tiptoed inside, gazing up at the high ceilings and the rows of darkened stage lights hanging from the scaffolding above me. There were three sets all crammed into this one room: a cabaret in

1920s decor, a living room of a similar vintage, and a simple office with a desk and a few chairs. They might have looked swell lit up properly and captured on film, but in the cold white work lights, they looked cheap and fake, no more impressive than the sets we'd built for our one-act plays back at Sarah Lawrence.

I stood there for a moment, feeling silly. Of course they would shut down production after a dear friend of half the cast passed away. Why had I expected that the rest of the Ambassador's Club would be hanging around here? They were probably home in their beds.

I was about to slink back to my office when I heard a slow romantic melody that I didn't recognize. It was beautiful, though, whatever it was. Stepping a little farther into the soundstage, I realized that I was not alone, that in the fake bar set was a real piano—and at the piano sat Henry Hilbert.

He stopped playing as I stepped into his sight, looking almost embarrassed. "I didn't mean to interrupt," I said. "Is that a new song of yours? It's lovely."

"It's not," he replied.

"Not yours or not lovely?" I asked.

He squinted at me. "Sorry—who are you?"

"Oh, I'm—I was looking for Fiona's friends," I stammered. I took a few steps into the bar set, noting how the backs of the tables—not visible to the camera—hadn't been painted. "But I've just realized they're probably all at home."

"You're a friend of theirs?" he said. "So they're replacing me already."

"Annie Laurence," I said, not sure how else to respond to that other than to offer my hand.

He took it, squeezing it in his own but not moving his arm. "The murder playwright?"

"Yes, the same."

"Pleasure to meet you, Miss Laurence," he said. "Henry."

"I know," I said. "I love your songs."

"Everyone does," he replied. "They're not at home, Fiona's friends. They're all here, their whole little club. Your whole little club. Spent hours holed up in Terry's office, discussing the fate of the production schedule of the picture that's launching my film career—which you'd think I'd have a say on, especially when she was my friend too." He stopped, seeming to realize he was becoming emotional, and busied himself with fiddling with his wedding ring.

"I'm sorry about Fiona," I said.

"Thanks," he mumbled, sliding back to the piano and returning to the melody. "They're shooting on 11 today. I'm behind on writing songs, so they banished me in here to work."

I thanked him and turned around, heading back for the door. "I'm no expert, but whatever you were playing earlier sounded pretty good to me," I told him. "So that's at least one song you've got."

Stage 11 was buzzing with activity. I should never have doubted how little tact Hollywood could have. This stage was home to the set of what was certain to be an elaborate dance number. Two white staircases dotted with footlights arced toward each other and met in the middle, and a white stage underneath had enough room for two dozen or more chorus girls. Now, though, the stage was empty except for a few stagehands—did they call them *moviehands* out here?—running around to orders barked by the director.

I spotted June off to the side, near a table set up with snacks and coffee, watching the crew run about with an expressionless face. I walked over to her and put a hand on her shoulder. She jumped, as if she had been in such a daze, she hadn't even seen me approach, but once she realized who I was, she smiled. "Hi, Annie," she said. "Are you working on this train wreck now too?"

"No," I answered. "Just wanted to stop by and see how you all were holding up."

She smiled again and nodded, then looked aside as if those two gestures weren't exactly the entire story. "Terry tried to get us shut down for a few days, but Devlin refused. This picture's cost him too much money already, he said. So I don't really have a choice but to be fine. I used to want nothing more than to be a movie star, but careful what you wish for, I suppose. Now I'm only a movie star, and I don't get to be a person at all."

"That's horrible," I said.

She shrugged. "At least it pays terribly."

The director gave another shout, and the crew jumped into action. The staircase set split down the middle in front of us to reveal the backdrop of a gorgeous cloudy sky painted in the colors of a rich sunset. June nodded toward them. "They've been working on this transition for hours. They built this set for Ginger Rogers to dance on. Terry convinced their producer to let us use it for my song before Ginger starts filming. Only problem is, Henry hasn't finished my song yet, so that's posing some production challenges."

From her chair behind the director, Terry shouted for them to stop. "It's not on the beat!" she cried. "You have to move the set on the beat!"

"It doesn't have a beat!" the director shouted back. "The fucker hasn't written the song yet!"

As the crew reset and Terry yelled to the director that since they weren't shooting a film about Strauss, he could assume the beat would be one-two-three-four, I leaned in closer to June. "Look, there's no easy way to bring this up, but there's something I'm wondering, and I want to know if you and your friends were thinking it too. I don't think Fiona's death was a suicide."

June's head snapped toward me. "Annie," she began seriously, "I know that it wasn't."

SEVEN

❄❄❄◆❄❄❄

June glanced around the set to make sure no one would miss us if we snuck away. Once it was clear that both the director and Terry were preoccupied with the doomed task of staging a musical number to no music, she led me off the soundstage and around a corner to a row of trailers. The doors literally had stars bearing the actors' names tacked to their center—I had previously assumed that was a cliché only in films. Backstage at the theater, we trusted the actors to simply remember which dressing room belonged to them.

June took me over to the door labeled "Victor Durand." I could hear Jack's voice as she opened the door without knocking.

"She once said I was so dedicated to drinking that soon I'd be brain-dead enough to finally be successful as a film actor," Jack was saying as he waved around a flask. The trailer was small, the four of us only barely fitting inside. Jack was seated in a curved wooden chair in front of a small vanity, and Victor was on a small gray two-seater couch on the other end of the room. June immediately went to the bar cart opposite the door and poured two whiskey neats in a glass for each of us. Neither of them seemed to mind that we'd barged in without knocking, although Jack did a small double take at the sight of me. "Annie! Hi."

"How's it going out there?" Victor asked June.

"Awful," she replied. "Can't you make Henry pick up the pace before we all lose our contracts?"

"If I could make Henry do anything, I wouldn't waste it on that," replied Victor.

"We were just discussing the worst things Fiona ever published about us," Jack chimed in.

Involuntarily, some kind of scoffing noise came from my throat, and all three looked at me. "What?" asked June. "Did she hit you, too?"

Of course the awful thing Fiona had written about me wasn't all *that* awful, unless you happened to know she had been one hundred percent right about me and the Cooks sharing a bedroom. But I wasn't prepared to get into any of that at the moment. "She said the murder weapon in my play wouldn't have worked," I lied, claiming one of the empty chairs that had clearly been dragged in from another trailer and stuffed in whatever nook they would fit.

"That's nothing," said Jack. "She once said listening to a song written by Vic was like hearing a drunk on a bus try to hum a song written by Henry."

Victor rolled his eyes. "Please, I've heard worse remarks than that from my own mother. That wasn't even close to Fiona's nastiest work. No, the worst was when she said I collected antiques."

"You *do* collect antiques," said Jack.

"No, darling, she said I *collected antiques*," Victor repeated. "She was upset at me because I'd yelled at her for telling me, 'Good luck,' before a show."

"Which you were right to do. That was monstrous of her," said June sarcastically.

"So that week, in her column, she wrote a whole paragraph about how I'd dropped several thousand dollars on a chaise longue and a Ming vase. Devlin chewed me out in his office for three hours about what the public would think, which I'm certain was her aim. I almost had to marry Joan Crawford to get out of that one."

This anecdote confirmed it for me: Fiona had known absolutely everything going on between me and Adam and Beverly Cook, and she had been trying to see how close to the line she could get. How much could she insinuate while maintaining the plausible deniability it was all harmless? After all, I did write well for Bev and Adam. Victor Durand did collect antiques. The woman was smart.

Had been smart.

"To collecting antiques," I said, raising my whiskey.

"Jack, tell Annie what you were saying this morning," said June.

Victor immediately groaned. "Oh, come on."

Jack straightened up in his chair, put the flask down. "I saw the murderer."

"No, you didn't," said Victor.

"Yes, I did," Jack insisted.

I leaned toward him. "What did you see? What did he look like?"

"Yes, Jack, tell her," interjected Victor. June smacked his leg to shut him up.

"That's the thing," began Jack, chuckling awkwardly and picking up the flask again. "I don't exactly remember?"

"He was drunk all night," said Victor. "You saw a streetlight and you thought it was a man. I've been there. Once, after too much cocaine, I tried to fight a picture of Eugene Ormandy."

"No, no," said Jack, looking at me with wide eyes, as if his entire sense of self in that moment depended on convincing me to believe him. "Before the show, I was in the sound booth with Vic. Then I realized I had a drinking problem: my flask was empty."

"Awful," muttered Victor.

"Hey, Vic, what do you call a bottle of vodka at a symphony?"

"Get out of my trailer."

"*Beethoven's Fifth!*"

"Could you stop amusing yourself and get back to the murderer, please?" snapped June.

"I left to go get more booze. Now I don't really remember doing that, to be honest. But I do remember coming back, walking down Cole Place to the back entrance, when I saw someone coming out of the volunteer door."

"How?" asked Victor. "The streetlights have been off for a year."

"It wasn't pitch-dark yet, and there was some light coming out of the door when it opened," answered Jack. "But after, that's where it gets hazy. Or hazier. I recognized whoever it was, but I don't remember *what* it was I recognized. Only that I shouted out to them to say hello because I knew them, and they ignored me. Just walked quickly down the street and around the corner, as if they didn't want me to see their face. I didn't think much of it at the time. People always try to get out of talking to me; I don't take it personal. But later, I thought, well, whoever that was, they must have come from the kitchen. That's why they were shielding their face. That must have been the person that poisoned her."

"You don't remember anything about them?" I asked. "Height, build, the way they walked?"

"There's one thing I think I remember," Jack began.

"Here we go," said Victor.

"I think the figure might have had...horns?"

"Case closed!" said Victor. "It was Satan himself!"

"Shut up!" said June, this time hitting him with one of the pillows on the two-seater. "That could have been anything... A hat—"

"Or a shadow—I don't know," said Jack. "But I remember calling out to whoever it was, 'Hey!' and them not answering. That, I know for sure. Why not answer me?"

The trailer door banged open, and we all jumped until we saw Terry making her way for the bar cart. "What a nightmare of a day. We're going to need you down there in a few, June," she said, doing a little jump of her own when she saw me sitting there. "I thought you were Fiona for a second. That was her chair."

I wondered if I ought to apologize and move, but there was nowhere else to sit once Terry settled in the other wooden chair. The conversation moved on. "I brought Annie to hear what Jack saw," said June.

"What, you mean his own shadow?" muttered Terry.

"I think she was murdered," I said. "And if you all help me, I think I can find who did it."

"Look, I understand why you might think that," said Victor. "She didn't have a nice word to say about a single person in the building—present company not excluded. But—"

June cut him off. "Exactly. Two hundred suspects, and the police solve it in a day? They couldn't have possibly checked everyone."

"They found a suicide note," Terry pointed out.

"Did you see the text of it, though?" I asked. "It didn't sound like Fiona to me."

Jack pointed at me. "Annie's right," he said. "That note's been bugging me all day. Fiona was a writer. She would have told us all why. Or told us to go to hell. Or something. It had to have been planted on her."

Terry shrugged. "The police said it was her handwriting."

"Oh, come on," Jack scoffed. "You believe a word the police say? Half of LAPD is corrupt, and the other half is lazy. They could have planted the note on her because they'd been paid to or simply because they couldn't be bothered to do any real investigating. The police are only out for themselves—"

"No one's in the mood for one of your Commie rants," said Victor.

"I don't know what those detectives were like when you all talked to them," I began. "But when they spoke to me, it sure sounded like they cared a lot more about calling Fiona crazy and closing the case than doing any real investigating."

"So the Los Angeles police are bad at their jobs. What do you want me to do about it?" snapped Victor.

"Torture them with one of your songs," replied Jack immediately.

"Ah, good one. Original. Too bad you're 4F. You could inflict a lot of damage overseas with the sharpness of that tongue."

Any goodwill was evaporating from the room. June must have sensed it too. "Knock it off," she scolded Victor. "Not everyone's as proud as you of being certifiable."

"None of you were there," Victor shot back. "The first time she tried it, with the bottle? I was there."

So that rumor was true—interesting. It didn't change my mind, and it didn't change June's. "That was *different*," she shouted over Victor.

"So apologies for thinking it's possible when I saw it was possible—"

"She was sick then. She'd gotten better—"

Jack chimed in. "And the police are here to protect capital, not to protect us—"

"Remind me, Jack, how many oceanfront houses in Santa Monica did Karl Marx have?"

It was all escalating like this, I realized, because Fiona wasn't here. Fiona would say something so perfect, so devastating, so *mean* it would shut everyone up. Then Terry could change the subject, and we'd all move on. But Fiona wasn't here, so the only way I could see to get this group to function again was to be her myself.

"Look, folks, I've only spent a few evenings with the Ambassador's Club, and that's been enough to make me want to kill myself," I said. "The point isn't if Fiona *could* have done it; it's if she did. Don't you want to know for sure? Because I do."

Everyone went quiet. I could feel my heart pounding in my chest but not in an uncomfortable way. The air had a crack to it, that electric feeling of being exactly where you are supposed to be.

All four of them looked at me. Finally, Terry broke the silence. "What do you want us to do?" she asked.

"Whoever did it had to have motive, means, and opportunity," I said, shocking myself at how confidently the words came out of my mouth. For someone who had been sitting at her desk a few days ago, certain she'd forgotten everything there was to know about writing, the elements of a murder came right back to me. "We don't know what specific poison the murderer used, so means will be tricky. Motive's the best place to start. You all knew her so well; you're the best ones to have a sense of who might have had it out for her. I'm sure it's a decently long list, so we can cross-reference it with whoever was at the Canteen that night—"

"I can get the volunteer sign-in sheet from Sunday night from the Canteen office," volunteered Terry.

"That's perfect," I said. "We can come up with a list of suspects, then meet tomorrow night at the Canteen to see who was there on Sunday."

Jack scoffed. "Come on," he said. "We don't need to do all that."

"Why not?" June asked.

"We all know who was there who hated Fiona the most," said Jack. "What, do we have to sit around and waste time with some charade where we all pretend we had no idea it could have been him until his name shows up on the list? Why? So Vic doesn't get mad?"

"Why would I get mad? I'm extremely pleasant," Victor replied.

"Fine, I'll say it," Jack said. "It was Henry."

"It wasn't Henry," said Victor.

"Henry Hilbert?" I asked. "I just met him, on Stage 13."

"How did he seem?" asked Jack. "Like a murderer?"

I didn't know what a murderer would seem like, but that felt like not the best thing to admit as I tried to convince this group to help me catch one. "He seemed normal. Sad," I said. "Can you all believe he's married now? Back in New York everyone thought he was queer."

That got no response other than silence. I'd stepped in something, but I had no idea what. "He is," said Victor finally.

"How do you know, Vic?" asked June right away.

"Oh, I ran into him at a pansy bar once," Victor replied. "Then I lived with him for fifteen years."

"So Henry used to be a part of the Ambassador's Club, from back before we even called ourselves that," Terry explained to me. "Then, '41 happens, and Devlin starts panicking about his leading men getting drafted, so he offers Henry an acting contract and says he'll turn him into a star."

"On the condition, of course, that he moves out of Vic's house and marries some boring blond idiot who happens to be woman-shaped," June added. "Which Henry did gladly. So after that we dropped him."

"Although some of us dropped him more than others," said Jack, looking at Victor pointedly.

"I *can't* drop him. My entire career is playing Henry's music; it's the only thing I'm known for," Victor protested.

"Now Henry hates us because he thinks we were unfair to him, so he's gone and taken his revenge by killing Fiona," Jack continued. "It makes sense to me."

"Look, is Henry bitter, arrogant, self-centered? Sure. But he was conducting the concerto," said Victor. "He was onstage with me the whole time. Granted, I wasn't looking at him, because he times the second movement all wrong, but I'm sure someone there saw him."

Jack leaned back, pursing his lips. "Oh. Right. I must've forgot he was conducting. If I was ever sober enough to know that in the first place. Hey, what do you call being soused at a concerto?"

"A requirement," said June.

Jack looked disappointed. "That's much better than what I was going to say. Three sheets to the woodwinds—don't look at me like that. Hey, what about Don?"

"Her husband?" I asked.

"You're mad," June said. "That's impossible."

"I could see Don," said Victor. "Terry?"

"I honestly don't know who did it," Terry said diplomatically. "But I do think it was probably Don."

"What's the motive?" I asked. "Get rid of Fiona? Move in another girl?"

"Revenge," said Victor. "Fiona was cheating on him. With half a dozen guys, if not more. She found them at nightclubs or at the Canteen, brought them around to the Ambassador's Club just like she brought you around. She was incredibly open about it; it's no wonder Don found out eventually."

"Bullshit," said June. "You all don't know Don as well as I do. I've done a dozen movies with the man. He's not a murderer. He's almost sixty, for god's sake."

"What does that have to do with anything?" asked Jack.

"Sixty-year-olds don't murder people," June explained, as if this were the most obvious fact in the world. "How can a man's blood run hot enough for murder if he can't get an erection?"

"Sixty-year-old men can get erections," said Victor.

"Read that somewhere, Vic?" asked Jack.

"Well, we all know Don and Fiona divorcing would have been out of the question," Terry said. "Don's at Pacific, and Devlin would have thrown a fit. Don Farris is one of the few male stars we have left. Devlin would never let him burn his career by admitting to being a cuckold. You couldn't cast Don as a romantic lead again after that story breaks."

"Don was at the Canteen that night," said Victor. "At least for a little bit. Jack and I saw him. He dropped Fiona off right as we got there."

Wheels were turning in my head. "Can we get into their house?" I asked. "There has to be something there, some proof we can take to the police or the press—"

"We can get in Don's house," Terry said. "This Sunday. He's hosting the memorial service."

Motive. Means. Opportunity.

I repeated the words to myself over and over as I walked back to my office, afraid I might forget them. When I was finally behind the shut door, I grabbed the nearest piece of paper and wrote them down. Perhaps they could help me solve not only Fiona's death but also the mystery of how the hell I was supposed to write anything.

So *Don't Count Your Coconuts* could have a murder in it—it was embarrassing it had taken me that long to get there, but I hadn't exactly been my best self lately. Yet I was quickly stymied again. Motive, means, opportunity all called for characters, and without Adam and Bev, where was I supposed to find those?

The prescription Irma had written for me was sitting on my desk, slightly crumpled from being shoved into my purse. *Why not?* I thought. I picked it up and headed for the pharmacy.

The line, as Irma had promised, was long, but it moved quickly. I assumed I would have to wait a bit after dropping off my prescription, but only a minute or two after handing the pharmacist the piece of paper, I was presented with a dark-brown bottle filled with oblong white capsules, free of charge.

I took one. Then, after considering that I'd been in the New York theater scene and knew my way around pills, took two more to ensure they would have an effect on me. I wandered across the walkway to the lot cafeteria for lunch as I waited for them to kick in. When I arrived in the big dining hall, however, I realized I wasn't hungry anymore, even though my stomach had been rumbling only fifteen minutes earlier. I bought a coffee from a coffee cart, parked on the corner of the New York Street and the Cowboy Street. I sipped my black, acidic lunch as I made my way back to the writers' offices, to June Lee's smiling face on the poster of the building next door. *Pacific Stars Are Heating Up Hollywood!*

Then the answer struck me, so clear and simple my heart began to pound. Why, Irma had practically suggested it to me. Adam and Beverly Cook weren't the only talented people in the world. I'd already met an entire social club full of some of the greatest wits of our generation. What if *Don't Count Your Coconuts* was a vehicle for June Lee? Something sexy, since Devlin would probably require it, but also a part that would really let her act? And a supporting role for Jack Kott, something physically comedic that would show off the lanky frame and elastic features his radio audience never got to see. And a side character for Victor Durand, a wisecracking piano player, who could provide a minute or two of Tchaikovsky to class the whole act up a bit. Terry could produce the whole thing, and we could make it together—well, now I was getting ahead of myself. But I could see it. I could see it all.

Christ, why had I not been drugging myself to write this whole time?

I was so inspired I clacked on the Remington until sunset. I finally went home, purely out of a sense of obligation and not because I wanted to, and spent the evening planning out scenes that I could write tomorrow as I forced myself to eat half a sandwich. I still wasn't hungry. I was so engrossed in the world I was inventing in my head it was like my physical body had ceased to exist.

Eventually, as the clock turned its way over to single digits again,

I forced myself to go to bed, even though I wasn't tired either. But as soon as my head hit the pillow—bang!

The sound startled me into sitting upright. Just when I'd convinced myself it had been the wind, I heard it again, this time clearer and louder and directly above me. My upstairs neighbors, who I'd never heard a peep from before, had decided to choose the one evening I was already looking at a restless night of sleep to start stomping around like elephants trying to imitate Fred Astaire. Just as I was wishing I had a broom with which to pound on the ceiling, the music started. Classical and Russian-sounding, I might have liked it if it weren't the middle of the night and accompanied by a symphony of stomps. Deliriously, I wished for a moment that I had a phone so I could call Victor and have him tell me what it was.

Pleasant melody or not, this was ridiculous. I put on a coat to cover my pajamas and headed for the second floor.

I gave the door to apartment 21 a much more polite knock than they deserved. There was no response, which infuriated me. It's not like they could pretend no one was home. I knocked on the door again and again, my polite raps turning into irate pounding. "I know you're in there!" I shouted, and this finally got a door to open—only not the one I was currently assaulting. An old woman peered out of the door to apartment 22.

"Will you keep it down?" she scolded.

"Me, keep it down!" I scoffed, offended. "They're the ones making all the noise!"

"No one lives there, you crazy lady," the old woman snapped back at me.

"You're the crazy one if you can't hear that music!" I said, even humming a bit of the Russian melody to prove my point. She slammed her door shut.

Once again, I banged on the door to 21, and once again, I got no response. As I stomped back down the steps, I half considered putting on some real shoes and finding a pay phone to call the police and make a noise complaint.

But when I returned to my apartment, it was dead silent.

By Friday morning, it had become my habit to arrive at the studio, grab a cup of coffee from the cart by the Cowboy Street, and use it to wash down two (or three, or four) of the pills. Soon enough, I would disappear into the warm haze of *Don't Count Your Coconuts*, hearing the voices of all my new friends as I typed lines for them to say. I didn't know if what I was writing was any good. That's not to say that I thought it was bad, but more to say that I wasn't considering its quality whatsoever. At least, I wasn't until Irma called me.

"Miss Laurence," she began, jumping right to the chase: "How's your script assignment going?"

I looked at the stack of pages to my right. "I think I might be… done," I said.

"That's wonderful," gushed Irma. "Bring it to me. I'll get it copied and distributed to the producers here."

After making a few minor tweaks to my final scene and straightening out the pages, I did as I was instructed and headed across the lot to Irma's office.

She smiled as I handed her my work. "Excellent. Well done! Did the pills help?"

The question put me off. I didn't want to admit that I needed to be medicated to do my job. But on the other hand, they had. "Yes," I said.

"I knew they would," she said. "They can have some side effects, though. Are you having trouble sleeping?"

Every night this week, the neighbors that I'd been told didn't exist had thrown a raucous party, complete with the same Russian music and what I could only assume was a bowling ball–dropping competition. "I have been having trouble sleeping," I said. "But it's not the pills. I have these horrible neighbors."

"Whatever the reason," replied Irma. "I'll prescribe you something for that too."

She opened her blazer and reached for the inside pocket, just like last time. Only now, a strange look came over her face as she found no special prescription pad there. "Huh," she said. "I must have used the last one up and forgot to replace it. I'll call the pharmacy myself, right now. They'll have it by the time you walk over there."

The prescription was ready, as promised, although this time I was left to wonder not only what kind of movie-studio secretary has her own prescription pad—but what kind of movie-studio secretary was writing so many prescriptions she needed more than one.

EIGHT

<del>《《◆》》</del>

"If I were to hum a piece of music, do you think you could tell me what it is?"

I felt a bit silly asking the question, but Victor answered immediately that he could. We were in his car, on the way to Fiona's memorial service. He'd offered to drive me once we realized we lived within a mile of one another, and I'd accepted after realizing Fiona's house in the Hollywood Hills was a half hour's walk uphill from the closest streetcar stop. "That's what Jack does to me on his radio show all the time," he said. "He has the band play something and then stop, and I have to finish the song. Hum away."

I started humming the music I'd been hearing—every night now—from my upstairs neighbors. It had lodged itself so firmly in my brain sometimes I swore I heard it sitting in my office or walking down the street. Victor recognized it almost immediately.

"Tchaikovsky concerto," he said. "In B-flat minor."

"My neighbors have been playing it every night," I said. "Loud enough to wake a graveyard. Now when I'm lying awake at two in the morning, I can curse Tchaikovsky along with them."

"Careful, you might be cursing me too. I recorded it once. Are they playing mine?"

"Not to shock your ego, but I wouldn't have the faintest idea how to tell the difference between you or any other piano soloist."

"Stab me in the carotid next time, I'll bleed out faster."

"Sorry."

"I'll tell you how. It's simple," he went on. "If the pianist is playing fast, it's me. If he's playing well, it's Vladimir Horowitz."

"You'll have to come over some night and tell me which it is," I said, adding, "Or tell me if you can hear it at all. It might be ghosts."

"Oh yeah?"

"I went up there one night to yell at them to turn it down, and no one was home."

He raised an eyebrow at me. "What are you on, and can you spare some for me?"

"Just something Irma prescribed for me." Before I could add that surely whatever the studio secretary had written for me couldn't possibly be *that* strong, Victor let out a loud clap of laughter.

"Oh, Annie, Irma and Devlin would shoot you up with horse tranquilizers if they thought it would make you churn out movies faster," he said. "Be careful with those. In fact, you should give them all to me. For safekeeping."

"Nice try."

"Worth a shot. He was queer too, you know. Tchaikovsky."

Something about the way he said *too* struck me as including me as well as himself. I wondered if I were so transparently "not the marrying type" that the whole world could read it on my face. "I didn't know that," I said.

"Well, you wouldn't, would you? The Russian government suppressed nearly all evidence of it."

"Then how do you know? Run into him at a pansy bar too?"

Victor only grinned. "Can't suppress everything, if someone wants to be found."

We pulled up in front of Don and Fiona's house, 2670 Beachwood Drive. Or at least, I assumed it was 2670. I couldn't tell for sure. The entire property was surrounded by a privacy shade of cherry laurel bushes twice as tall as I was.

I got out of the car and peered up at them, squinting into the sun. "Unbelievable," I whispered.

June had parked just behind us along the street, and Jack was slinking out of the passenger seat. "What is?" he asked.

I pointed toward the bushes.

"Aren't they tacky?" June said, joining us. Whereas I had put on a plain navy shirtdress and Jack had opted for a simple black—if a bit wrinkled—suit, June was wearing a low-cut, skintight black dress, with her hair curled and sprayed within an inch of its life. "Don had them put in a few years ago for privacy."

Victor scoffed. "He's so full of it. He hasn't been famous since the twenties. Why would—"

"The bushes are cherry laurels," I interrupted. "They're extremely poisonous."

"How do you know that?" asked June.

"It's the murder weapon in my play," I said.

Everyone went quiet for a minute. "That's our means," said Jack finally. "How absurd. Out in the open, staring us right in the face, and none of us would have even noticed it without you, Annie."

"Do you think when he put them in, he was already planning...?" asked June, unable to finish the question. "They've been there for years."

"It's possible," I answered.

"It doesn't seem like Don," June said.

"Just goes to show, you never know what another person is capable of," said Jack. Then he raised a camera I hadn't noticed he'd been holding and snapped a picture.

"What are you doing?" June asked him.

"Documenting," he replied. "It's evidence."

"You brought a camera to a funeral?"

"We're going to search the house, aren't we?" Jack said. "I thought it might be useful. In case we find something we can't pinch."

"Looks a bit suspicious to be carrying it," I said.

"Exactly," said June. "Give it to Annie. It'll fit in her enormous purse. Seriously, what are you carrying that thing for? Are you planning to hop in a boxcar and start a new life?"

"Maybe," I said as Jack handed the camera to me and I tucked it away. All four of us stood in silence a little longer, looking at the bushes.

"So Don did it, then," breathed Jack. "Wow."

The remark seemed to snap June out of some sort of daydream. "We're late," she said. "Let's go in."

A little ways down the driveway was a wooden gate, which we pushed open to reveal a large white mansion and a perfectly manicured lawn. I took a second to swivel my head around as we walked a brick pathway toward the front door. The lawn had a fountain, with two stone cherubs shooting crossing streams of water from their circular mouths. Fiona Farris had a cherub fountain in her front yard. Forget whatever dalliance she'd had with some sailor at the Canteen— that was the real career-ending information.

A butler let us inside before we even knocked. The house was airy and light and buzzing with sound as if this were any old cocktail party. We went to the spacious living room off to the right, where a waiter approached us with a tray of champagne. I thought this was a tad inappropriate but not inappropriate enough to not take one. We passed through a dining room so elegant it seemed impossible to imagine anyone eating in it, and then out a back door to a lawn even larger than the one in the front.

Nearly a hundred white folding chairs were set up, and even more waiters milled around with champagne and hors d'oeuvres. It could have been a delightful garden wedding if not for the dozens of photos of Fiona on easels around the lawn, each surrounded by an ominous wreath of black roses.

Terry had spotted us arrive and now quickly rushed to our side. We closed ranks in a tight circle. "You four are unbelievably late. Why am I only friends with actors, the least reliable people in the world?"

"I'm not an actor," said Victor.

"I know. I've seen the reels," Terry shot back. "June, what are you wearing? Do you have a hot date after this?"

"At least I cared enough to wear black," replied June, shooting a look at Victor, who was standing out like a sore thumb in a light-gray suit.

Victor waved off the insult. "Black is only for concertizing and funerals."

"It *is* a funeral, pal," said Jack.

"It's a memorial service," corrected Victor. "No body, no funeral."

"Why isn't there a body?" I asked. I realized too late how morbid of a question it was.

"Don wanted the body cremated right away," answered Terry.

The sentence hung in the air among the five of us. We were all so certain the rest were thinking it that no one had to say it out loud.

Was there some reason Don wanted to get rid of Fiona's body?

We were soon prompted by yet another butler to take seats out on the lawn. As the five of us settled in the back, a string quartet began to play a lovely, if perhaps too pleasant for the occasion, number. Even with Jack and June seated between us, I could see Victor huff. Terry put a hand on his knee to calm him down. "It would have been nice to have been asked," he muttered. "And *Haydn*?"

The quartet went on longer than anyone wanted them to, especially as the Los Angeles sun beat down on our necks. Starting to sweat, I took a big gulp of champagne. Finally, the strings wrapped it up, and Don Farris himself, in a crisp black suit, stood to address the crowd.

"I want to start by thanking you all for being here today," said Don, his voice projecting clearly across the large lawn. He was shorter than he looked in his pictures but just as charismatic: salt-and-pepper hair slicked back appealingly, soft blue eyes, a striking jawline. "It means a lot for me to know that Fiona was as adored by the world as she was by me."

"I've never seen half these people in my life," muttered Jack. Terry shot him a look. Next to me, June started to bounce her right knee.

"I wanted to tell the story of how Fiona and I first met over a decade ago," began Don. "I was taking a bit of time away from Hollywood and doing *Richard III* at the Longacre in New York. The regular critic for the *New Yorker* was out with food poisoning after eating some warm shrimp salad at Lindy's, so the magazine sent a fresh face just out of university to review me. That impertinent critic was a young woman by the name of Miss Fiona Ackerman. I would say, 'Thank god Hal Benson ate those off shrimp,' but I wouldn't want to sound...shellfish."

"Christ," said Jack, loudly enough that a few people turned around to shush him.

"The show—and my performance, in particular—were well received by everyone," Don continued, speaking with the relaxed cadence of someone who had told this story many times before. "Well, *almost* everyone." A few people in the crowd chuckled. "Miss Ackerman, however, had called my Dickie 'sporadic.' Not good, not bad—*sporadic.* I'd never had a performance characterized in such a way, and I didn't know what the hell it meant. So, naturally, I telephoned Miss Ackerman's office and asked her to meet me for a drink and a bite to eat. 'You can take me anywhere but Lindy's,' was her reply.

"You can imagine my surprise when I arrived at Sardi's that night to find that the cheeky critic who had humiliated me was also one of the most beautiful women I had ever seen! As we talked, I found she was smart, witty, perceptive, engaging. I asked her what she'd meant by calling my performance 'sporadic,' and she said that sometimes, I was brilliant, but sometimes, I was only eager to show off to the audience how brilliant I was being. She was entirely correct, and not one of the other critics—who had been in the game much longer than she—had seen it. By the end of the show's run, she asked me to marry her. You heard that right: she asked me. 'I think having the last name Farris would do wonders for me,' she said. 'Not because you're famous, but because Fiona Farris has a much nicer ring to it than Fiona Ackerman.'"

I chuckled a bit at that. She hadn't been wrong.

"Fiona and I…" Don trailed off, bringing his hand to his mouth and turning away from the crowd slightly. We had come to the part of the story he was not accustomed to telling at cocktail parties. "We always wanted to have a child," he finally choked out, suddenly on the verge of tears. "Both of us weren't raised in the best homes, and we always thought that perhaps we could heal that pain by starting a family of our own. Be the parents we had always wanted. But that dream wasn't in the cards for us, obviously. And I do wonder, if things would have turned out differently, if… Well, that's the tragedy of life, I suppose. You could get lost in the wondering."

"There's no way Don was still firing bullets, right?" muttered Jack.

I glanced over at him and noticed that tears were streaming down June's cheeks. Everyone else clocked this at the same time I did. "Aw, Junie," said Victor, leaning over Jack to place a hand on her knee. "Don't you know you're too pretty to be sad?"

"Wow, that sentimental crap really works on you, huh?" said Jack.

As I had in Victor's trailer the other day, I thought about what Fiona would say. "If only Don showed this much emotion in his pictures," I said. Even Terry stifled a giggle.

June smiled through a sob. "I know. I'm being ridiculous," she whispered. "The two of them would have been horrible parents, wouldn't they? They'd have to put the baby under a heat lamp to show it warmth. Still…poor Don."

Don was inviting anyone present who would like to offer a remembrance of Fiona to speak, and Henry Hilbert was making his way to the front. June's tears were immediately forgotten as all eyes snapped to him. "You have to be kidding me," said Victor. "Is it in bad taste to off yourself at a funeral?"

"Fiona Farris inspired me—inspired many of us—to be the best version of ourselves that we could be," Henry said, a wry smile on his face. "Because we knew if we didn't, we'd be done for."

The eulogizing lasted nearly ninety minutes. At first, it surprised me that none of the members of the Ambassador's Club seemed inclined to say anything; as the memorial wore on, it began to make sense. In the garish afternoon sun, the gushing, the weeping, took on an obscene edge. The colors were too bright, the emotions too performed, the lush backdrop of the Hollywood Hills too picturesque. Fiona had been a woman of smoky nightclubs and dim lighting. This sun-drenched monstrosity was for Don, not his late wife.

After the speeches, we were encouraged to stick around for drinks and light refreshments. ("What's a funeral without hors d'oeuvres?" Jack had remarked.) Sweating from baking in the sun, we migrated quickly back into the living room, where the Ambassadors once again formed a circle.

"All right, what's the plan?" asked June.

Everyone looked toward me.

"We split up," I began. "Between the five of us, we can cover the whole house quickly. Jack and I can take the areas that would be the most off-limits—upstairs, the basement, anywhere closed off to the party. I've never been here before, so I can pretend I'm lost if I'm caught, and Jack—apologies for being frank, but it seems like you're the most likely in this group to wander around somewhere and not know where you are."

"Two more glasses of this champagne, and I won't have to pretend to be drunkenly stumbling around," said Jack.

"And what are we looking for, exactly?" asked Terry.

"We already found the means, so focus on the motive," I said. "Diaries, stashed-away love letters, bank statements, bills. Anything that might have been a source of conflict between the two of them."

Victor nodded. "One more question: Ordinarily, I wouldn't complain about snooping around a dead woman's personal effects, but are we sure this is a good thing to be doing?"

"She's not just a dead woman," began June. "She's our friend—"

A voice from outside the circle cut her off, and we all clamped our mouths shut. "Lovely ceremony, wasn't it?"

Henry was forcing himself in between Victor and Jack. "Why don't you join our circle, Henry?" said Jack sarcastically as Henry practically shoved him aside. "I don't know if *lovely* is the right word to use to describe a memorial."

"Don't be silly," said Henry. "Things can be lovely even if they are unpleasant. Ever heard Sergei Prokofiev's *Piano Concerto in C Major*?"

"No," replied Jack.

"Well, maybe someday they'll put it in an Abbott and Costello movie and you can hear it then," replied Henry.

"We're in the middle of a conversation. Could you come back and insult our intelligence later?" asked June.

Henry laughed. He seemed so different from the sad, small man I'd run into on set the other day. Now he was smug and self-assured. "Oh, come on. You know I don't mean it."

"What do you want?" asked Victor.

"You're still going to be hostile to me at the funeral of our friend?" asked Henry. "Grow up."

"She wasn't your friend," said Jack. "Not anymore."

"Thanks for the reminder," replied Henry. "Anyway, I only came over to say goodbye, I've got to get home. The landscaper's coming by to talk plants for my new retaining wall."

"Wouldn't want to miss that," said Jack.

"Vic, can I give you a ride?" continued Henry. "I have something I want to talk to you about."

"You can do that here," said Victor.

"All right, fine. You know that concerto I've been working on?"

Terry pressed her eyes closed. "No. No concertos. We're months behind on your movie, Henry; we need you writing songs. You remember songs—they're three minutes long and you can tap dance to them?"

Henry waved this off. "I'm working on both. I'm a genius, remember? Anyway, my manager rang me the other night. Turns out Iturbi is stuck in Rochester for another month, so there's a free evening at the Bowl very soon if I decide I'm ready to debut it."

Victor's eyebrows shot up, and he turned to Henry with his whole body. "The Hollywood Bowl? Really?"

"So I thought perhaps I could give you a ride home, and we could discuss that."

"Unbelievable," June muttered.

Victor shot her a look. "Henry, I'd love a ride."

"Yeah, and maybe after that, you can take him home," said Jack.

"Hold on—you drove me!" I protested. "You're going to strand me here?"

"Yes," replied Victor. "Goodbye."

Henry waved at us all and led Victor away. "Thanks for all your help," Jack shouted at their backs.

"He's never going to get over the man if he keeps going home with him," said June.

"He doesn't want to get over him," Terry said. "He knows he *should* want that, so he acts like he *does* want that, but what he really wants is for Henry to leave his wife and come back to him and they'll be just like it was."

"That's pathetic," I said, perhaps to cover the part of me that wanted the exact same thing from my exes. "Henry's never going to do that. Why would he? He's getting everything he wants right now: the respectable married life and Victor at his beck and call."

Terry and June nodded emphatically. Jack only sighed. "Christ, this group gets catty fast when only one of the men is here. Forget him. Who among us hasn't been the one too caught up on a terrible ex?"

"Jack's right," I said. "We have work to do."

We split up: Jack heading for the basement, June for the kitchen, Terry for the front foyer to snoop through the mail table, and me for the second floor. Feeling a little sluggish from all the champagne and sunshine, I popped one of my pills—funny, as I'd packed them in my purse that morning, I was sure I wasn't going to need them. I waited for a moment when no one was looking and then tiptoed as fast as I could up the grandiose white staircase.

Upstairs was a long hallway, pristine and distressingly white. The floors were painted wood, the walls were smooth plaster, the doors— three on the left, two on the right—matched so well they were hard to spot. Fiona and Don must have employed a team of maids devoted only to scrubbing the baseboards.

Something drew me not to any of the rooms but down the hall, which bended out of my sight. Sure enough, it led to what was certainly the master bedroom, behind two open French doors. This room was bright and airy, with a large oak four-poster bed and more bright white, this time in the form of the plush bedding. Despite its loveliness, the room felt off to me, and it took me a minute to realize why: it was fake. There was not a single personal effect in sight—not a hairbrush, not a photograph. There was only one painting on the wall, a bland reproduction of a generic vase of flowers in the Impressionist style. There were no perfumes or lotions on top of the oak dresser, no half-finished books left open on the bedside tables. There wasn't a stray nickel or hairpin or even a dent in the bedspread from where a person sat to lace up their shoes. It looked like a sample room on the furniture floor of Macy's, for display purposes only.

What exactly was Don trying to display?

I tiptoed toward the bedside table on the right side of the bed and opened its one drawer. The items inside indicated this was Don's half: a prescription bottle of sleeping pills, an eye mask in a masculine stripe, a pair of men's slippers. Even these seemingly personal items felt unreal, as if the whole setup was a trap.

I shut the drawer and moved on to Fiona's side, only to find it completely empty.

My first reaction was to shut the drawer and open it again, as if my eyes were simply deceiving me. They weren't; the drawer was empty. A chill went up my spine. What kind of grieving widower, only a week out from his wife's tragic death, completely cleaned out her things from their bedroom as if she never existed? Someone who wasn't all too sad about her being gone, that was who. Someone who already had a woman in mind ready to take her place, perhaps.

I reached into my purse and found Jack's camera, snapping a picture of the empty drawer.

I went for the closet next, hoping to find an article of clothing that clearly had not been Fiona's, something to prove that Don had a mistress he was starting to move in. But like the nightstand, the half of the closet that had been Fiona's was completely empty. There were suits, dress shirts, ties, and dinner jackets, but not a dress or a blouse in sight. Desperate to prove now that Fiona had existed at all, had lived in this house, I opened each drawer in the oak dresser and found nothing but men's undershirts, men's socks, men's underwear.

It wasn't the realization that Don and Fiona's house was surrounded by poisonous shrubbery that made my heart begin to pound, or even finding out that Fiona's body had been quickly cremated so no further autopsy could ever be conducted. It was this. That while choking up on the lawn downstairs, upstairs Don Farris had been systematically erasing any trace of his late wife's existence.

Then, out of the corner of my eye, I saw movement.

"You know, I actually wasn't intending for guests at the memorial to be snooping around my bedroom," said Don Farris.

NINE

❮❮❮◆❯❯❯

I whipped around—my mouth hanging open like a trout, camera still in my hands—and tried to remember what I'd planned to say should this exact situation arise. "Someone told me—I... I had to go to the bathroom, but the bathroom downstairs was occupied, and someone told me there was a bathroom up here." Why was I saying the word *bathroom* so much? This explanation had sounded so perfect in my head as I'd tiptoed up the stairs and so idiotic now.

"Do you normally bring a camera into the bathroom?" Don asked me.

I looked at the camera. "It's not mine," I said, aware this explained nothing.

To my surprise, Don didn't seem upset. "I saw you sitting with June and Terry and them. Are you one of the Ambassador's Club? What's your name?"

"I haven't been officially inducted," I replied. "Annie. Annie Laurence."

He smiled at me, and in spite of everything, I felt myself relax a bit. He really did have a fantastic smile. "You know, Miss Laurence, I'm getting a little tired of making the rounds downstairs. Care to join me for a drink in my office?"

"That's all right," I said. "I should get back to my friends."

"Really," he replied. "I must insist."

Don Farris's office down the hall looked like the Broadway set of the study of a serious man, all mahogany bookshelves and red leather-bound tomes. This was at least a step up from the furniture store show-room that had been the bedroom, so I only somewhat warily slid into one of the brown leather armchairs by the unlit fireplace. Don poured an amber liquid into two cut-crystal glasses, his hand remarkably steady. Overall, he seemed surprisingly composed for a widower at a funeral. Was he putting on a brave face or merely forgetting to act the grieving husband?

I smiled and thanked him as he handed me a glass, then tried to examine it in a way that didn't look suspicious. It had come from the same bottle as the one he had poured for himself, but it would be dangerous to trust a move this man made. I took a sniff of the liquid, not sure exactly what I was looking for. It smelled like a normal brandy to me.

Don watched me with some amusement from the other armchair. He conspicuously took a very large sip from his own glass, so I figured it was safe for me to do the same. "Are you an actress, Miss Laurence?" he asked.

"A writer," I said. "At Pacific."

"Ah, how delightful," he replied. "Perhaps you'll write a picture for me someday."

"Perhaps," I said.

He smiled as he leaned back and crossed his legs. "You know, June begged me to take a part in the movie she's working on now, the Hilbert biography? There's a manager character—rather thankless part but would have been easy work. I refused. I can work with June; we've done a few pictures together, and we're on decent terms. But the rest of that little club, they think I'm the devil. Some old villain who managed to ensnare their friend for the nefarious purpose of building a life of love and hap-piness. They're all above that sort of thing, I suppose. Are you married?"

"No," I said.

"Then you'll fit right in," he replied. "Listen, I know what's going on here. The four of them suspect me of something. At least, Jack and Terry do. June's less sure, I'd bet, since she's actually had a pleasant conversation with me, and Durand can't be bothered to form an opinion that isn't about himself. But on the whole, they don't think the police are telling the truth. They sent you up here with that camera to snoop around on me, didn't they?"

"I was looking for the bathroom," I said.

"All right, sure," he said. "In that case, you can happen to mention to them that while you were looking for the bathroom, you ran into me, and I told you without a shadow of a doubt that I was nowhere near the Canteen the night Fiona died, so they can leave me alone. I dropped her off and then went to the Brown Derby on Wilshire. And if you don't believe me, you can ask the police, who reached me there by telephone that night." He finished his brandy in one large gulp and stood up. "Does that settle everything?"

I could have said, "Yes, thanks," and scurried out of there; I could have continued to pretend I had no idea what he was talking about. But half because I was imagining how impressed the club would be with my boldness and half because the pill I'd taken on top of the champagne and brandy had me feeling invincible, I said, "What happened to Fiona's things?"

The question instantly put him on the defensive, his shoulders huffing upward, his brow furrowing. "Oh, come on," he said. "I'm not sure why I need to indulge the petulant whims of a group of talentless, conceited hacks who think it's appropriate to giggle through a eulogy."

"You did serve champagne," I pointed out.

"It was Fiona's favorite," he shot back. "I know that because I loved her, very much."

"Then where's her clothes? Her books? Her makeup, shoes,

perfume?" I asked again. My heart was pounding, and I could see the whole situation with a sort of chaotic clarity. "For that matter, Mr. Farris, the Brown Derby is only a few miles from the Canteen. There were at least twenty minutes between when the concert started and when Fiona's body was found—even longer before the police would be trying to reach you. You could easily have been at the Canteen and made it back to the Brown Derby in that time to take that phone call."

"There's witnesses," said Don. "I was with a companion all night."

The word *companion* perked up my ears. "This 'companion' wouldn't have happened to be a woman, would it?"

He shrugged. "What if it were?"

"Surely you can see how a woman you were dining with while your wife was busy volunteering to serve her country might also have a reason to lie for you."

He traced the rim of his empty glass with his finger. "Don't just *imply* I was sleeping with her. Say it, if that's what you mean."

"You were sleeping with her."

"Yes, I was," Don answered simply. "And Fiona was sleeping with other men. She knew about my dalliances, and I knew about hers."

It only sounded like more motive to me. Kill your cheating wife and move in your mistress. A divorce would cause a hit to his career, but with this plan he could even gain some popularity if he played the sympathetic grieving husband just right. "And you were all right with that?" I asked. "Most men don't like it when their wives are out sleeping with other people."

"Did Mr. Cook mind when you were sleeping with his wife?" he replied calmly.

I leaned back in shock; I hadn't expected that one. "I'm not sleeping with Beverly Cook," I muttered, glaring at him. "Did Fiona tell you that?"

"I told Fiona that," he corrected. "I do theater, too, remember? Saw the two of you at one of Tallulah's parties, acting...rather appropriately for such a venue."

I winced, remembering the night. A punch had been served containing five different types of alcohol, resulting in extremely lowered inhibitions. "That wasn't what it looked like," I half-heartedly argued.

He held up a hand. "I'm not trying to be threatening," he said. "I'm only pointing out that since we're both people who have been involved in untraditional situations, perhaps you might be in a unique position to understand me. Sometimes one must put on a face for polite society that doesn't match one's private life. My marriage to Fiona was that face."

"Forgive me, Mr. Farris," I said. "But if all that is true, what about the cherry laurels?"

"What about the cherry laurels?" he repeated. His voice was calm, but the blood draining from his face betrayed him.

"The club told me you had them put in," I said. "They're highly toxic. I'm sure the landscaper would have warned you at the time. The leaves can kill a dog and, if you distilled them into a poisonous vapor, a person as well. Is that what you used to kill her?"

Don was quiet, as if in disbelief I had dared to even ask. I could hardly believe it myself, to be honest. "You're a horrible person," he whispered finally. "All of you. An entire club full of miserable, snide, pathetic human beings, devoid of empathy."

The string quartet had started up again downstairs, playing something jazzy and upbeat this time. "Your own wife's memorial has the air of a party scene in a picture that ends with Joan Crawford throwing a martini in someone's face, and I'm the one without empathy?"

"Yes, I put in the cherry laurels," he sneered at me, pounding his fingers into his chest. "Yes, the detectives determined that's what she used to commit suicide. Yes, I'll lie awake the rest of my nights, wondering if only I'd had a fondness for the way a different style of hedge looked, would she still be here? I'll be haunted by that choice the rest of my life. Does that satisfy you?"

His eyes were so wide they could have popped out of their sockets, the vein in his forehead so purple it could burst. Even though he'd gotten in my face in his rage, little bits of his spit dotting my cheeks, I felt eerily calm. "If she died by cherry laurel leaves, she didn't kill herself," I said evenly. "If that's how she died, she was murdered."

"I know they don't want to believe it, Jack and all them, but it's true. You can go back downstairs and tell them all to go to hell."

Don had become so worked up he had turned away from me, looking out the window as he took a few steadying breaths.

"She didn't think cherry laurel leaves could kill a person," I said. "She wrote that, in her review of my play."

He seemed to stop breathing for a moment. "What?"

"If you have a copy of it, I can show you—"

He turned away from the window, wheeling around to face me. "There wouldn't be one here; she kept her work stuff at the office— what do you mean? Are you serious?"

"I remember almost every word of that review. We all about had heart attacks as we were reading it for the first time," I said. "She wrote, 'That the murder weapon would be unsuccessful in real life detracts from the play's cleverness but not its impact.'"

Don sank back into the armchair across from me, running a hand over his chin as he stared into some middle distance. It was not the reaction of a murderer trapped by a clever line of interrogation that I'd expected. "How could the police have missed that?" he said, more to himself than me.

I was now in the awkward position of feeling I ought to comfort the man whom, moments earlier, I had attempted to force a confession of murder from. "Because they didn't investigate," I said. "Either through malice or incompetence, they had their answer before they even started. They only did enough investigating to back up a foregone conclusion."

Don's eyes snapped to mine, so hopeless. "What do we do?" he asked sincerely. "Go back and tell the detectives?"

"No," I answered. "There's a chance whoever the real killer is paid them off. If they know someone's onto them, it could tip the murderer off, put us all in danger."

He nodded solemnly, taking it all in. "Do you want to see Fiona's room?" he asked finally.

Don led me out of the office and one door to the right, which he pushed open to reveal another bedroom. The oak four-poster in this one was as nice as the one in the master bedroom, even if the room itself was much smaller. But what caught my eye right away was all the things. This bedroom was the opposite of bare: The nightstand had a pile of books on it; the dresser was topped with a jewelry box and an ashtray. A desk in the corner had a typewriter and a few papers stacked on it.

"We've slept in separate rooms for three years," said Don. "That's why none of her things were in the other room. After we tried and failed to conceive, our marriage became more of a friendship. We still loved each other, and separating would have been terrible for my career, so we stayed married and agreed that each of us could have our dalliances and the other wouldn't care at all."

I stepped inside, turning around slowly, not sure what to make of it all. Don followed me, closing the door gently behind us. "None of Fiona's friends knew about this," I said quietly. "They knew almost everything about her but not this."

"Fiona didn't talk to them about me much," he answered. "Being in love of any kind is a weakness, and that's not a group that's compassionate toward the weak. If they had learned we were practically living separate lives, not even sleeping together, she never would have heard the end of it. Please don't tell them."

It never occurred to me, when she was needling me about my greatest secret, that Fiona could have secrets she was hiding from me. "I won't," I promised.

"Look around as long as you want," said Don. "If there's anything that could help."

"I don't know exactly what I'm looking for," I admitted. "I came here looking for evidence that would convict you."

"There's none of that, unfortunately," he replied. "But come to think of it—she did get a telegram the night she died."

He went over to Fiona's desk, then opened and closed the drawers until he found it. "Here, this is it. July 25, 1943." He held it up to the light. "'NO RUSH BUT PLEASE SEND DRAFT WHEN YOU CAN. ACTUALLY YES RUSH.—M. J.'"

"Who's M. J.?"

"Marla Johnson. She's the interim editor of the *Dispatch*. Fiona had been working on a big column for weeks, and Marla had been hounding her to get it finished. It was going to run soon."

"And she killed herself right before the column she'd been working on for weeks was going to run?" I asked, raising an eyebrow. As a fellow writer, it both seemed highly unlikely and made perfect sense. "What was the article about?"

Don shrugged. "I don't know. We didn't talk about work. Her job was to ruin the lives of everyone in this town who might someday employ me, so it was easier to never bring it up. This one was massive, though. Normally, she wrote reviews, gossip. It took her an hour to write a column, max, but not this one. She must have had a story she wanted to take seriously."

"I have to find out what that column was about," I said.

"As I said, she kept all her work at the office," replied Don. "But the police told me I had to wait for them to go through it all before I could have any of it."

"If they ruled it a suicide, what does it matter?"

"I didn't ask questions."

"So it was about the column," I said. "Someone paid the police off to rule it a suicide, and now they're hiding the evidence from you to cover their tracks."

"Isn't this all a little…?" Don trailed off. "I think I might have indulged in a hope that I shouldn't have, coming in here with you. You didn't know my wife, Miss Laurence. She was ill—she had been ill for years, fighting this thing—and it finally got her in the end. You know, she probably only wrote that thing about your play to make a better column. I think it would be the best for all of us if you went back to the Ambassador's Club and told them you found nothing and you learned nothing. Let Fiona rest in peace."

"Perhaps you're right," I said. "We were all grasping at straws."

"Grief," he said. I waited for him to elaborate, but that was the beginning and end of the thought. "Shall we rejoin the living?"

I smiled and nodded, and as he held the door open for me to head back downstairs, I stuffed Fiona's telegram in my pocket.

I didn't see the rest of the club until first thing in the morning. Terry was inside when I pushed open my office door, her imposing frame in my leather chair startling me so much I almost spilled Cowboy Street coffee all over my white blouse. "Sorry. Did I frighten you?" she asked innocently, smiling a sadistic grin as I carefully placed the nearly overflowing cup of boiling-hot liquid down on the desk. "I wanted to make sure I was the first Pacific producer you saw this morning. Irma sent this around Friday afternoon."

She tossed me a bound set of pages, which I somehow managed

to catch through my flinch. *Don't Count Your Coconuts by Annie Laurence.*

With the memorial service on the forefront of my mind, I had completely forgotten I'd finished it. I'd been so drugged up when I wrote it that I had also completely forgotten at least two-thirds of the plot. "I read it on Saturday," Terry said.

"Did you like it?" I asked.

"No," she said. "It's terrible."

Even though I had wanted nothing to do with this script and could barely remember it anyway, I was still offended by her assessment. "It's not the sort of thing I normally write," I replied. "Mr. Murray assigned me a title, and that's what I had to go from. Horrible title too. *Don't Count Your Coconuts*? What, before they hatch?"

Terry put up a hand to stop me. "Enough. Maybe this will soothe your ego: I want to offer you a job," she said. "I want to bring you on to the Hilbert biography."

I was torn between excitement over being offered a job on a movie being made and utter dread due to everything I had heard about that picture. "I suppose that makes sense," I said. "Sounds like a not-very-good writer would be a step up on that one."

"There's two reasons I want to bring you on," Terry continued. "One: we've had five writers already, and I've had to fire all of them. Now every time I even make eye contact with a writer on this lot, they go running in the other direction. But you're brand new; you don't have any leverage. You literally can't say no to me, which makes you ideal for this project."

"How flattering," I said.

"The second reason is there was one thing in *Don't Count Your Coconuts* I liked," she went on. "Don't get me wrong. It's still very, very bad. But the characters... Freddy—that's a role for Jack, isn't it?"

Of course I had written it explicitly for Jack—for the way he spoke, the way he could control his features like elastic—but it suddenly felt mortifying to say so. When I'd been inspired by Beverly and Adam, they were with me, excited to see what I would come up with, always flattered by the thought I'd created a character only for them. I had no idea if Jack would respond the same way. "It could be," I said.

"Don't be coy," Terry replied. "Freddy's Jack; Lana is June; and the piano player character, you even named him Victor."

"I meant to change that," I said.

"Why bother?" said Terry. "Audiences love that stuff, an actor playing their real selves—or at least playing the version of themselves that we tell the audience is real. It's what we're trying to do in the Hilbert movie, having Jack and June and Vic play themselves, all coming up with Henry in New York together. And you've done that part wonderfully. Every line those three characters spoke, I could hear my friends saying. The story was a mess, the rest of the characters were flat, but those three worked. It was rather eerie. I found myself wondering if you've been eavesdropping on us."

"I suppose I find being in the Ambassador's Club inspiring," I said. Terry raised an eyebrow, and I quickly corrected my mistake. "Being *with* the club, rather. I know I'm not really *in* the club—"

"Whatever it is, it's exactly what I need for the Hilbert movie," Terry interrupted. "No one else knows how to write for them. I tried hiring Fiona to do it, but Devlin refused, which I suppose is fair after everything negative she's written about his studio. I tried letting everyone come up with their own lines, but June tries too hard, Jack doesn't try hard enough, and Vic can't think and act at the same time. So what do you say? Want to come aboard a sinking ship for no credit, no extra money, and no perks?"

"I'd love nothing more," I said.

TEN

—«‹◆›»—

Terry let me hitch a ride in her cart to Stage 13. It wasn't a far walk, but she explained that people respected her more if she arrived by cart. "Only the most important people at Pacific have access to them," she said. It hadn't occurred to me until then that she was that important, but I felt foolish after I realized it. Devlin had put her in charge of the picture that would launch his brightest new star—of course she was important. I glanced her way and gulped as it occurred to me that I would probably have to take this job seriously.

We once again entered Victor's trailer without knocking. June and Jack were already inside, and all three were doubled over with laughter about something. "Read that one again for Terry and Annie," cried June at the sight of us.

Jack cleared his throat, holding up a letter. "My dearest Don, I'm writing to request a new chaise from you, as the one I have is now permanently rank with our passion."

Terry and I groaned in disgust at the same time. From the couch, June screeched with laughter, doubling over into Victor's lap.

"Jesus," said Terry, snatching the letter from Jack's hands. Her eyes grew wide as she scanned the rest of it. I leaned over her shoulder to read for a sentence or two, but on a stomach empty with nothing but black coffee, it made me a bit queasy. I grimaced and turned away.

"I found Don's love letters in the basement," Jack said, his smiling eyes meeting mine.

"I surmised that," I said.

"There's a million of them here," he said, producing a small box filled with papers. "To Don from…everyone. Mary Martin. Lena Horne. Half a dozen women I've never even heard of. Some that aren't even signed. Safe to say Fiona wasn't the only one in the Farris house getting around."

"This one's just signed 'J,'" said Terry, tossing the letter back to Jack. "Is that you, Jackie?"

"Don's not my type," said Jack.

"Maybe you should reconsider," said Victor, handing Jack another letter. "It seems he has both remarkable technique and impressive stamina."

"No, no," said June, reaching over to snatch the letter away. "We shouldn't be reading these. It's not any of our business." The fact that she was nearly crying with laughter undercut her message somewhat.

"Just as well," said Jack. "Reading them was turning me celibate."

"You're already celibate," Victor said.

"Don't start with me, pal," joked Jack. "I might be going through a dry spell, but at least I have my dignity."

"Says the man having a drink at eight a.m.—"

"'Oh, Henry, I'd just love to hear your new concerto; sure, who cares if I leave my friend's funeral early?'"

"It was a memorial service, and it was over—"

"Drop it, boys. You're both at Pacific Pictures—neither one of you has any dignity," I said.

"Speaking of which," said Terry, "I've asked Annie to come on as our new writer for the Hilbert picture."

Jack, June, and Victor all looked at me as if I'd announced my grandmother had died. "Oh, darling, I'm so sorry," said Victor.

"You said no, right?" Jack asked me.

"I wasn't given a choice," I said. Terry shot me a look. "I'm delighted to come on."

"Can I have a monologue?" asked June. "I can cry on cue."

Jack had grabbed another letter from the box and was waving it around. "'My dearest Don: Memories of our night together still bring me to the very brink of ecstasy—'"

All four of us cut him off with a cacophony of groans and giggles. "Did anyone find anything else in the house?" asked Terry. "Maybe something less repulsive?"

"I found nothing," said June. "Other than some of Fiona's pills— which I took, if anyone wants any."

"That's inappropriate," said Jack. "But yes, I do."

"We were going after the wrong angle," I told the group. "Don caught me snooping around upstairs, and he convinced me. I don't think it was him."

"Thank you," said June. "That's what I've been trying to say—you all saw his eulogy! The man was genuinely grieving."

"Sweetheart, he's an actor," said Victor. "They can make you believe things that aren't real."

"But I did find something," I said, fishing around in my bag for the telegram. "Don told me that Fiona was working on a big article, some bombshell that required a lot more research than usual. It was almost ready to go. This telegram is from the *Dispatch* editor telling her to hurry up and finish it. This could be our motive. What if whoever killed her didn't want that article seeing the light of day?"

"Fiona wasn't working on an article," said Jack.

"How do you know?" asked Terry.

"Well, because we would know about it, wouldn't we?" he replied with a shrug. "We tell each other everything."

Victor scoffed at that. "Speak for yourself. I've got secrets."

"No, you don't," said Jack, rolling his eyes. "You are the one thing you can never stop talking about."

"Don thought her work stuff would still be at the *Dispatch* offices," I went on. "The police wouldn't let him have it, but I thought I'd go down there today and see if I could talk my way in."

Terry shut this down immediately. "No, no, no," she said. "You need to write. Send one of the actors. It's much easier to make a movie without actors. Jack, how about a field trip?"

"I'll do it," said Victor immediately. "Jack smells like booze—they'll never let him in."

"I've read the *Dispatch*. If he smells like booze, they'll assume he's an editor," Terry said. "But fine. Vic, go downtown. Annie, go write. I'm going to go find Henry and do my best not to dismember him. We'll meet tonight at the Ambassador's Club."

I was banished back to my office with a current copy of the script for the still-untitled Henry Hilbert project: a mess of differently colored pages, patchwork dialogue, and gaping holes that seemed as complicated as differential calculus. The yellow pages, I'd been informed, were scenes that had already been shot, and while I couldn't do much with those, I could rearrange them or trim them down or add in voice-over. The rest was mine to do with what I wished, and if I happened to come up with something that could be the title of a new Henry Hilbert song, for the love of god, would I call him up in the rehearsal studio and tell him? When I inquired how I was supposed to write Henry's life story if I didn't know it, Terry only laughed. "We're way past that," she said. "Make it up! I don't care if he saves the *Lusitania* from going down if it works in the script."

I took two pills and then, when that did nothing to make the pile of pages in front of me less intimidating, two more. The brown jar was nearly half-empty, even though I'd only had the thing a week. I made a mental note to call Irma soon and ask for a refill.

I worked in fits and starts for a few hours, only sporadically achieving the quiet, focused intensity I'd become so accustomed to when working on *Don't Count Your Coconuts*. It was a lot harder to write when you were actually trying to care. After a few hours, there was a knock on my door, and Jack poked his head in. "Can I take you for lunch?" he asked.

"I'm not hungry," I replied. I never seemed to be hungry anymore, which I chalked up to the heat. It was hard to muster up an appetite when you were sweating through your blouse.

"Good," he said. "Because when I said lunch just now, what I meant was a drink."

I looked at the mess of pages in front of me. Coffee wasn't helping, pills weren't helping... Might as well try alcohol. "Sure," I said.

Jack took me to a bar just off Hollywood and Vine, a narrow place that was nearly pitch-black inside despite it being just after noon and not a cloud in the sky. He ordered a scotch and soda, and I ordered a vodka martini. I liked the way the two drinks looked next to each other as the bartender slid them in our direction—one short and squat and warm, one tall and icy and glamorous.

"Look, I don't know if I mentioned this before," he began, "but I saw your play. I happened to be in New York doing a war bond thing, and Fiona took me as her plus-one. I loved it."

"Oh, thank you," I said.

"Seriously. As someone who wants to write and never managed to figure it out, my hat is off to you."

"You write one of the most popular radio shows in the country," I pointed out.

"Me and a dozen writers," he replied. "They do the work. I just show up and do silly voices. But you wrote something that's real, that was clever, and that moved people, and so I have to ask—what are you doing here? What are you doing taking a job on the Henry Hilbert movie?"

"I suppose someone forgot to tell Devlin Murray I'm a genius," I replied.

"I'm serious," said Jack. "Look, nothing's beneath me except politics, and even I'm too good for the Hilbert movie. Now, I'm doing it because I was told either I could play myself or John Garfield would, and that's the last thing I need—to find out John Garfield's a better me than I am. So why are you doing it?"

"Terry made it pretty clear that I didn't have a choice."

"She was trying to intimidate you. You have a choice," said Jack. "And even if you don't, even if she gets Devlin involved and he makes you, at the end of the day, you can always pay the fine and back away from your contract. That's an option left for you."

"I don't know how to explain this to a man with a studio contract and a weekly radio show sponsored by Lucky Strike, but I need the money," I said.

"Lucky Strike ended my contract after that thing I said about Judy Garland's marriage. I'm sponsored by Grape-Nuts now," replied Jack. "And don't give me that 'out of touch rich guy' thing. When my mother and I fled Warsaw, we had about thirty-five cents to our name. No, I don't mean quit and do some starving-artist bullshit. You had a play on Broadway. There's more studios than Pacific in this town. Go to RKO. Go to MGM. Find out if Grape-Nuts wants to get into the motion picture business. If Devlin doesn't think your play is good enough to make, if Terry's insisting you have to waste your time with this crap, call their bluff."

How funny, I thought, that he could only see me as a moderately successful Broadway playwright who had moved to Los Angeles to write movies. He couldn't see the unlovable, pathetic, desperate loser I was underneath. I almost didn't want to tell him. Maybe I needed someone who saw me that way.

I said nothing, and eventually Jack continued. "Maybe there's some other reason you feel you have to stay. I don't know. But take it from me—a man who wanted to be Upton Sinclair and ended up, well… making lazy cracks about Judy Garland's marriage on the radio: it eats at you like acid. The disappointment, the anger, the resentment. It festers and rots you from the inside out. I get so jealous. Of Vic, for doing what he loves every time he sits at a piano. Of Terry. She wanted to be an actress and it didn't work out, but she doesn't care. She found a way to be successful anyway. Sometimes I hate her for that. Fiona… Don't get me started. She had everything I wanted: the career, the respect—everything. My dearest friends in the entire world, people I've known for nearly twenty years, and sometimes I hate them with such a passion it scares me."

"You do?" I asked.

He nodded as he tilted his glass, nearly empty by now. "Sure. Booze helps. Money helps. Sometimes I forget, temporarily, that I'm miserable. But it always comes back. You just got to town… I don't know. I feel like I should warn you. You think, *Oh it's just one job, one thing to pay the bills, then I'll do what I really want.* And one job turns into two; two turn into half a dozen. The studios don't care about your passion; they're trying to make you into a perfect machine for printing them money. You can't trust your agents, managers; they only eat if you do. You're the only one who's going to look out for you out here. That's all."

I wasn't sure what to say to all that, which seemed at least as much about him as it was about me. Jack seemed to grow embarrassed every second the silence lasted. "Which isn't to say," he said finally, "that I

don't enjoy your company or don't appreciate what you're doing, helping us figure out what happened to Fiona—all the progress we've made,
it never would have happened without you. I don't want you to stop
coming around to our club. But maybe you should want more for yourself than writing a picture for a bunch of miserable old cranks like us."

"I like you all," I replied. "I liked Fiona a lot, and I like you all. So if
you do want rid of me, you'll have to try harder than that."

He smiled at me. "Careful," he said. "You start spending too much
time with us, I'll start hating you too."

If Jack was right about any of the things he was warning me about, I
didn't know. But he was proved to be wrong about one thing almost
right away: we were not making a lot of progress with Fiona.

The first setback of the evening was that the Cocoanut Grove was
closed when we arrived for our customary meeting of the Ambassador's
Club. Jack and I split a taxi from the studio, only to arrive at seven on
the nose and find June and Terry waiting on the sidewalk. Terry had
perched herself on the base of the tall white statue welcoming people
to the hotel, while June had her bare arms wrapped around herself and
was shivering dramatically.

"It's closed," Terry said to us before we'd even asked why they
weren't inside. "Private event."

"Oh, fantastic," muttered Jack. "Don't they know it's Monday night?
Who doesn't want a drink on a Monday night?"

"I'm calling a taxi and going home," said June. "It's cold."

"No, you can't leave," I said. "At least not until Vic gets here and tells
us what he found in Fiona's office." It was the first time I'd called him
Vic like the rest of them did, and I felt a sudden rush of remorse after
it slipped out. I half expected to be told off for being inappropriately
familiar, but the slip seemed to glide past everyone unnoticed.

"He never came back to set," said Terry. "He must have been at the *Dispatch* office all day."

"That, or the bastard finally offed himself," Jack blurted out, and even though it was the sort of dark joke they made about one another all the time, it hit everyone strangely now. Silence settled over us; I suddenly became very interested in staring at a wad of tobacco on the pavement. No one said a word until a few minutes later, when a car pulled up to the sidewalk and Victor got out of the passenger's seat, still fully alive.

"Of course that's where he was," Jack muttered, shaking his head. "Now I don't feel bad." It took me a moment to catch up, but then I saw it: Henry Hilbert was driving the car.

Henry waved at us sarcastically from the curb. "Don't worry. I have a dinner to go to. I won't ruin your night by sticking around," he shouted through the open window before pulling away.

"In my defense, I thought you all wouldn't see that," said Victor. "Why aren't you inside?"

"It's closed," Terry said.

"We could go somewhere else," I said. "The Brown Derby is right across the street."

"Don goes there," said Terry, Jack, and Victor, all at the same time.

I put my hands up. "All right, never mind. But we have to go somewhere, unless we want to discuss what Vic found at the *Dispatch* in the middle of the sidewalk."

He shrugged. "There's not much to discuss. They wouldn't let me in. I tried explaining she was my friend; I tried pretending she had something of mine I needed to get back—I even let out a 'Don't you know who I am?' or two. No dice. That's why I was with Henry, before you get all high and mighty about that. I thought someone more famous than me could pull some strings, but no. They're still waiting for the police to come pick up her stuff and not letting anyone in until they do."

"You didn't tell Henry what we're investigating, did you?" asked Jack.

"What possible difference could it make?"

"It's none of Henry's business. He might be a suspect—"

"He's not a—I'm not having this conversation again. I either need a drink, a sleeping pill, or for someone to knock me unconscious with a baseball bat; so if this place is closed, I'm going home."

"We might as well call it a night," June said.

"No!" I said, suddenly afraid if I let these people out of my sight, our entire investigation would fizzle out. Talks to regroup in a few days and come up with a new plan would get pushed back again and again until no one could be bothered anymore, and I couldn't let that happen to something this important. "We can go to my place. It's only a few blocks. I have wine and vodka. It's not very fancy but "

"You had me at wine and vodka," said Jack.

We traipsed the ten minutes or so north to my place, then shooed away the black cat hanging out on the stoop as Terry cracked some joke about what his presence meant for our fates. I unlocked my apartment door and led the group inside to stunned silence.

June spoke first. "Annie, you don't have any furniture."

I busied myself in the kitchenette, fussing with wine bottles and openers and glasses. "I know," I said as nonchalantly as I could. I hadn't wanted to bring it up beforehand in case it discouraged the group from coming over, but my apartment still consisted of a bed, a record player, and not much else. "I asked for furnished lodgings, and this is what Pacific came up with."

"Sounds about right," said Terry.

"Come on, when did you all become too good to sit on the floor?" asked Jack, collapsing to his knees.

"When I turned thirty," Victor answered, but he, Terry, and June reluctantly followed suit anyway.

I brought over the wine and the vodka quickly, hoping to distract everyone from their discomfort. "Some of us will have to drink from the bottle because I only have two glasses. I also don't have any ice for the vodka, so you'll have to think of Russia as you sip it."

"It's like we're playing that we're poor," said June, sniffing the merlot.

"A thing that famously never got anyone in trouble," said Jack, evidently volunteering to be one of the ones to forgo using glassware as he took a long swig from the vodka bottle. "Ask Marie Antoinette."

"Hey, I'm a single gal," I said playfully. "No use investing in furniture until I have a husband whose money I can spend." My back-to-back conversations with Terry and Jack earlier that day had left me with the nagging sensation I wasn't their friend, wasn't really one of them, didn't know anything about them at all. I saw a chance to try to change that. "Have any of you been married?" I asked.

"I'm divorced," said Jack. Once he said it, I vaguely remembered: some chorus girl back in New York; it hadn't lasted long.

"God bless him—he tried to make it work by marrying a woman too dumb to read," said June.

"I knew it was doomed when on my wedding night—Vic, you and Henry and Fiona were heading down to Henry's old place in Pennsylvania, remember?"

"That's right," said Victor. "You ditched her to come with us."

Jack started laughing so hard he choked on a sip of vodka. "I couldn't stand the thought of having to make conversation with her!"

"That's the level of devotion to one's spouse required for membership in our club," said Terry. "When an Ambassador gets married, we say, 'Til death or a better offer do us part.'"

"And you took them both, Ter," June said.

"My husband passed away in an accident a few years ago," Terry explained to me.

"Oh, I'm so sorry," I said. "I didn't mean to pry."

Terry shrugged. "I've learned not to have any sensitivities around this group."

"Terry, please. We would never make fun of the fact that you're a widow," said Jack. "We have boundaries. Unlike the boat your husband fell off."

"Hey, what does Annie's apartment have in common with Terry's husband?" asked Victor. "They both only have a sink."

Terry smiled and looked at me. "I married young, and he turned out to be a creep. Not that it would stop this gang from ragging on him if he were an angel."

"He is an angel, Ter," said June. "Because he's dead."

"What about you, Annie?" asked Jack.

For all the self-pity I'd wallowed in over Beverly and Adam, I had never thought through what I would say when asked outright about my romantic past. "I was in a relationship back in New York, but it didn't work out," I said blandly.

"With who?" Victor asked innocently.

"Don't tell them," warned Terry. "Unless you never want to hear the end of it."

"Let's discuss what we ought to be discussing," I said instead, neatly ignoring that I had been the one to bring up this tangent in the first place. "If her office is off-limits, how are we going to find out what Fiona was working on?"

The question threw us all into silence, each staring into our drinks and trying to come up with something—anything—to say. "Think, everyone," said Jack finally, as if that wasn't what we were already doing. "She must have said something about it, if it was so important. Some offhand remark, maybe?"

"I don't think she did," said June.

"Are we sure?" asked Terry. She was looking right at Victor. "No one can think of anything?"

"You know what I think?" Victor said. "I think we should get Annie some furniture."

"What do you mean?" asked Jack, figuring out the answer in the middle of the question. "Wait, do you want to—"

"Yes," said Victor, pressing a finger to his lips and tilting his head toward me. "But don't tell her what the plan is. Let's surprise her. Terry, you can get us a van from the studio, right?"

"You mean now?" she asked.

"Yes, I mean now!" He was already on his feet, urging the rest of us to follow suit. "Why not? Henry's on his way down to Newport to have dinner with Eliza's family. They won't be home for hours. He's a perfect target."

"Why is he having dinner in Newport? He needs to be working on songs," said Terry.

"And what better way to get back at him for slacking off?" said Victor.

Terry grinned. "All right, I'm in," she said. "I'm parked nearby. I'll drive us to the studio."

"I really think we ought to stay here and keep brainstorming," I tried to argue, but no one listened. "Instead of doing—what are we doing?"

"You'll see," said Jack.

ELEVEN

———⟨⟨⟨◆⟩⟩⟩———

After the five-minute drive to the studio, we parked in Terry's extremely close parking spot and were instructed to meet her at the wardrobe-stock building. While June and I waited outside— smoking and sharing swigs of warm, cheap vodka from a flask—Jack and Victor talked their way into the wardrobe building and emerged a few minutes later, wearing white work pants and white collared shirts. "I think they're technically housepainter uniforms," said Jack.

"They're perfect," said June.

Terry found us shortly thereafter and led us to a large white van in a back parking lot. "Three of you will have to ride in the back," she said, unlocking the rear door. Jack was already halfway in the passenger's seat, so Victor, June, and I clambered inside. Terry slammed the door shut behind us and then turned the key in the lock.

"Worried we might try to escape?" Victor asked her as she settled in the driver's seat.

"No, I'm planning to trap you and drive us all off the Santa Monica Pier," answered Terry. "Revenge for making fun of Bill drowning."

We drove far out of Los Angeles, the buildings that I could see out of the front windshield becoming more and more spaced out as we left

Hollywood and wound through the mountains. The sun had nearly set by the time we arrived at our destination, but there was light enough to see the gaudy white mansion on a street full of other gaudy white mansions, spaced generously far apart with large green lawns. Terry parked in the driveway.

"I'd forgotten how tacky this house is," clucked June, leaning over me to gaze out the windshield. "Such excellent taste in music and such horrible taste in everything else."

"That's Henry's house?" I asked as Terry came around to free us from the back.

"Why is his lawn in such a state?" asked Terry.

The sloping lawn in front of Henry's house was all torn up, with stacks of gray bricks piled everywhere. Victor rolled his eyes. "He's putting in a retaining wall. And the worst part is, he's excited about it. He talks about it constantly. It's disgusting. It's genuinely more upsetting to me than when he said he was going to marry a woman."

"That's how it goes," said Terry. "Marry a woman, move to the suburbs, get excited about landscaping."

"There but for the grace of God go any of us," Victor said. "All right, let's get to it. Come on, Jack. Hope you're limber."

"Me too," sighed Jack, melting out of the passenger door like a drip of ice cream down a cone. "Wait a sec—how is this going to work? Won't the maid recognize you?"

"She's never seen me. He sends her away when I'm coming over," said Victor. "That's the hallmark of a healthy relationship: no witnesses."

June and I leaned forward to watch out the windshield as Jack and Victor made their way to the front door and knocked forcefully. After a moment, a white-haired woman answered. Jack said something, pointing inside, and though she started to shake her head, the two went in anyway, full of confidence. A minute passed, then another. I had no idea how long whatever caper was going on in there would take, but June and Terry had their eyes glued to the door as if Victor and Jack would emerge any second.

It was only a few more minutes before they did, carrying a canary-yellow couch between them.

June and Terry indulged in a tiny screech of delight before Terry leapt into action, hopping out of the van to open the back door as Victor and Jack lumbered down the sidewalk toward the driveway. Both men were trying to appear as if this were easy, but Victor was already sweating and Jack's legs were trembling. They reached the open back door, and June and I jumped out of the way as the thing barreled toward us.

Victor hopped in the back as Jack ran around to the passenger door. "Hurry up, she's suspicious," he told Terry, who flung the key in the ignition and reversed out of the driveway like the cops were already on their way. In the back, June flopped on the middle seat of the couch, Victor and I on either side of her, Victor resting his head on her shoulder. We were all silent until we turned the corner at the end of the block.

"Well, Annie, you've got yourself a couch," said Terry.

All five of us erupted in full-body laughter, Victor's face buried in June's dress, Jack clutching his stomach, me wiping tears from my eyes.

"I forgot how fun that was," cried Jack, twisting his body to look at the three of us on the couch. "How come we don't pull pranks anymore?"

"You started getting paid to do it on the radio, and it lost interest for you," said June.

"Fair enough. Hey, Junie, next time we get in a cab together, start screaming that I'm kidnapping you. That one's a classic."

Both Terry and Victor started talking in unison about the last time they pulled this prank, on some pompous writer from the *New York Post* who had written something vile about June. I wanted to hear the story, wanted to steep myself more in the histories of this club, but I was having trouble focusing, with the way the words jumped quickly around the van. It was pitch-black outside, and yet somehow everything in here was a honey-colored buzz, warm and comforting, and my cheeks ached from smiling. I was happy, I realized, for the first time since I'd moved to this sun-drenched nightmare town, where studio execs decided what movies would be made based on titles scribbled in the margins of the morning crossword they did on the john. I had found people—*my* people.

The drive back to my place flew by, and we took our time unloading the couch from the van and bringing it into my apartment, not caring how many neighbors we disturbed with our carrying on and laughter. We arranged it by the window overlooking the street that I still hadn't managed to buy any curtains for. The yellow fabric wasn't my taste, the carved wooden legs and back too ornate for me, but I loved it far more than anything I'd picked out with Beverly and Adam. It was only a three-seater, but we all five managed to squeeze on it, with Jack perched up on the armrest, his hand on Victor's shoulders.

"You're officially a member of the Ambassador's Club now," said June, squeezing my hand.

Some inexplicable force drew all five of us to Vic's trailer Tuesday morning, some strange magnetic thing whispering in all our ears that as long as we stayed together, the glow of the night before would never have to fade. I brought the portable typewriter and balanced it on my knees on the gray couch in the corner. Terry hovered over my shoulder, glancing at the edits I was making and mumbling a suggestion or two. June was fighting Jack and Vic for space at the mirror in which to do her makeup, eventually perching herself on Vic's lap to paint on her eyeliner.

The scene they were to shoot that day took place in 1926, and lots of fun was being had at everyone's failed attempts to make themselves look twenty-one again: Jack caking on powder to hide the wrinkles on the sides of his eyes, Victor letting his hair fall loose in his eyes instead of gelling it back. "You should wear it like this more often," June was telling him, still on his lap, springing one curl. "You look like a sexy homeless person."

"Oh, just kiss already," heckled Jack.

"Who's kissing?" interrupted a voice. Henry appeared in the trailer's doorway, and I felt everyone tense up with anticipation. Was he going to say anything about the couch? Had he noticed? What witticisms were we each going to say as we denied it?

"June and Vic are getting married," said Jack. "He's just proposed."

Henry made a face. "That's illegal. She's Chinese."

"My God," said Jack. "Sometimes it hits me how we used to put up with you *every night.*"

"Now we only put up with him every day," said June.

"We need to talk about something," Henry said, and we all glanced at one another, our eyes dancing. "I need my couch back."

Incredibly, none of us broke, or even as much as lifted an eyebrow. "What couch?" said Vic after a moment, with pitch-perfect innocence.

Henry laughed in a way that sounded perfectly rehearsed to be as casual as possible. "We got home from dinner with Eliza's parents last night, and our couch was gone. The maid said two movers came and took it. She thought I'd arranged for it and forgotten to tell her."

"Maybe you did," offered June.

"Come on. I used to run that prank with you. We had Don Farris's armoire in our bedroom for years, remember? Tell me where my couch is so I can take it back, please."

We were all silent again, this time throwing in a few confused glances for good measure. "I didn't know it was possible to misplace a whole couch," said Jack.

"They do have feet," I said. "Maybe it walked away."

Henry slapped his thighs, his laugh becoming more aggressive. "All right, ha ha, you got me. You got me good. Henry the idiot, humiliated by the righteous Ambassadors. Congratulations. But I need that couch back."

"We didn't steal your couch," Vic said. "Terry runs a wing of a studio, June's a movie star—no one needs to drive to the suburbs for your secondhand furniture."

"I need my goddamn couch!" shouted Henry, all pretense of being in on the joke dropped. "It's Eliza's—it's a family heirloom. She knows I had something to do with this, and she's furious at me."

"No one cares about your sham marriage," yawned June.

"It's not a—is that what this is about? Eliza?" Henry threw his hands in the air. "I didn't have a choice! Why must you insist on punishing me for something I had no control over? Vic's made his peace with my marriage; why the hell can't the rest of you?"

"Maybe cause we're not getting from you what he is," Jack said. "You know. Concertos."

Henry shook his head. "I'm not sure what you want from me. You want me to marry him? I can't marry him. That's not my fault. This is how it's done out here. This is how it goes. Maybe if you cared about anything besides amusing each other with insults and drinking yourselves to death, you'd understand."

"I'd rather drink myself to death than sell my soul to the Devlin," said Jack.

"Oh, please," retorted Henry. "Any one of you would make exactly the bargain I made, except no one's asking it of you. You're stuck pretending you don't want fame only because no one's offering it, telling yourselves there's something smart and noble about jeering from the sidelines, when really no one wants you on the field. Wretched existence. No wonder Fiona killed herself."

Everyone erupted at that, except for Vic, who only sighed and shook his head. Jack leapt to his feet, clenching his fist like he might punch the guy. June and I both started shouting as Terry put her hands on Henry's shoulders to try to wheel him out of the trailer. Henry decided he had had enough of this and stormed out on his own. "Bring my couch back," he shouted as the door slammed behind him.

He wasn't gone for five seconds before Jack rounded on Vic. "What was that?"

"I don't know. He's a jerk."

"Not him—you! We're trying to defend you, and you just sit there—"

"I can defend myself."

"Maybe everyone should take a breath," Terry began, but everyone ignored her.

"Can you? Because he walks all over you, and you still play his work. It's seedier than if you two were only fucking," shot Jack.

"That's right," said June. "If you ever want to be more than the concert pianist who plays Hilbert—"

"Maybe I don't," said Vic. "Henry's a genius. He's a bastard but he's a genius, and the fact that he sees anything in me is the only reason I have a career. Does that make me the happiest man alive? No, but it makes me a regularly employed concert pianist. You only want me to let go of him so I'll have nothing else, so I'll be a miserable alcoholic like the rest of you."

"Spare us the moralizing. You're getting consistently laid, and you don't want to stop. It's neither special nor all that interesting," I said.

Everyone went quiet except for June, who began laughing through a hand pressed quickly to her mouth. I realized what I had done. I had been Fiona—but this time without trying. I'd slipped into my role unconsciously, shutting everyone up before things got said that couldn't be taken back. June had been right the night before: I was officially in the club now.

"Hear, hear," said Terry. "Besides, if we all start fighting now, it means Henry wins. And none of us want that."

"Did you see his face?" said Jack. "I thought he might punch someone."

"I wish he would have," June said. "I'd have liked to see Henry in a fistfight."

"We did him a favor," Vic said. "It's one of the ugliest couches I've ever seen. He ought to send us a fruit basket for getting rid of it for him."

"Especially since his maid couldn't be bothered to tip the movers," said Jack.

"Hold on a second—that's it," I said. "This is how we get into Fiona's office. They're waiting for the police to release her things? We'll be the movers. Say the police sent us to pack up her stuff and take it to Don's."

"That could work," said Jack excitedly, wagging his finger at me. "That could actually work."

"No way," Vic said. "They would never buy it."

"I could ask Don to help us," said June. "Have him call the *Dispatch*, tell them the police said to expect couriers to come today."

"No need," said Jack. "I can do a perfect impression of that fake British-intellectual thing he does. 'Oh, dahling, it's like I always say: George Bernard Shaw is dead.'"

"Shaw's not dead," said Vic.

"Then I won't say that. Good note."

"I could run over to props and have them make something official-looking," said Terry. "Some sort of letter—a work order from LAPD—"

"The housepainter costume's still at my house," said Vic. "I'll have to stop home and get it."

"No, no, you can't go. They'll recognize you," Terry said immediately. At Vic's proud puffing of the chest, she leaned over to smack him. "Because you were there yesterday, not because you once smoked a cigarette onstage at Carnegie Hall."

"I had an eighteen-measure rest. What else was I supposed to do?"

"Yeah, but you didn't need to start conducting with it," said Jack.

"Annie and I will go," Terry said. "This afternoon."

A few hours later, Terry and I headed downtown in a work van in what were technically welding coveralls but served the purpose of making us look like a legitimate-enough operation to have uniforms. The *Dispatch* offices were in downtown Los Angeles, a part of the city I hadn't ventured to since I'd arrived on the train. The sight of streetcars running past buildings taller than three stories made my heart ache suddenly for New York.

"Here's a little trick," Terry said as she parked the van just outside of the twelve-story redbrick building. I was busy folding and unfolding the prop sheet she had printed that morning to make it look like it had passed through more than one set of hands. "We need to act like what we're doing is perfectly reasonable and they're not going to have a problem with it. I guarantee you that's what Vic messed up. He's always assuming a fight, usually because wherever he goes, someone wants to fight him. But when you ask for a favor expecting the other person will say no, they start to suspect there's a reason they ought to say no. Always start on the same page. 'Of course you'll let us in. Why wouldn't you?'"

"Interesting," I said. "Yesterday morning, when you were trying to convince me to write a movie for you, you went with the tactic of telling me I had to do it or I'd be fired."

"Well, sure," said Terry. "If you have the ability to fire people, that's much more effective."

I handed her the sheet of paper, and we went into the front lobby and toward the elevators. My brain was spinning, coming up with a backstory for why two women would be working as movers—it was a family business, maybe, and all the men were overseas? Or maybe there'd been another job scheduled for today, and all the men were working that one?

Terry sensed I was already overthinking things. "You know, why don't you let me do the talking?" she said as the elevator dinged and the doors opened to the *Dispatch* front desk.

A receptionist greeted us, and Terry strode toward her confidently. "Hi. We're here for Mrs. Farris's things."

"Oh!" said the woman. "You're the movers? Mr. Farris did call to say you'd be coming."

Hopefully, Jack had kept it simple and not had too much fun with the improvising. "Couriers," said Terry. "We were told it was just a few boxes. Is there more?"

"No, no, a few boxes is right," the receptionist answered. "Only we haven't heard from the police yet that it's all right to release them."

"We have the order here," said Terry, producing the prop sheet. She handed it to the receptionist and strode confidently down the hall. "We're going to get started, if you don't mind? We have five more jobs today."

The receptionist didn't have the guts to stop us. "Five doors down on the left," she said.

I skittered behind Terry like a nervous cat. "That was something," I whispered as we passed door after door of clacking keys and ringing phones. "You could be an actress."

"Yes, I know," she replied. We'd reached the door emblazoned with "Fiona Farris." Terry took a moment to study it quietly before pushing it open.

Someone—the police or some *Dispatch* assistant—had already begun to box up Fiona's things. A few banker's boxes stood packed in the corner; a half-full one sat on the desk. Some of the larger items—a radio, a couple of plants, a cardigan draped over the back of the chair, never to be worn again—still remained scattered about. Terry got right to work, opening the desk drawers, so I headed for the filing cabinet. An album rested on top.

"Oh, it's one of Vic's," I said, picking it up. It was heavy—four records, at least. On the cover were illustrations of two men, back-to-back at two respective pianos; one working diligently in a cluttered apartment as an elevated train rolled past the open window, the other in full dress in a fabulous concert hall. Henry and Victor, back-to-back: the genius who wrote the songs and the disposable man who played them. *Henry Hilbert, Piano Concerto in C Minor*, it read; *Victor Durand, piano, with the Philadelphia Orchestra under the baton of Henry Hilbert*.

I snorted. Terry looked up. "What's funny?"

I showed her the cover. "'Under the baton,'" I said. "Sounds a little suggestive, no?"

Terry rolled her eyes.

"What?" I continued. "It's an accurate description, you must admit. Vic Durand is under the baton of Henry Hilbert."

"Sounds like the sort of triple entendre Fiona would publish," said Terry. "It's true, it's dirty, and then it's true again. Come on, put it in a box and let's get moving, before that receptionist catches on."

We loaded the first round of boxes into the van and were on our way down with the second when the receptionist did indeed stop us. "Ma'am, there must have been some mistake," she said. "I spoke with the Hollywood precinct, and the detective said the boxes are supposed to go to a house in Sherman Oaks, not to Mr. Farris's."

Terry didn't miss a beat. "Does the work order not say that? We must have brought the old one."

The receptionist forced a smile. "I apologize, but I can't let you leave until you bring me the correct one."

"Perfectly understandable," said Terry, setting down the banker's box in her hands on the receptionist's desk. "We'll bring back up the things we loaded already."

I put my box down as well, and the two of us headed for the elevator, managing to stay silent until the doors closed.

"We're booking it, right?" I asked Terry as soon as they did. She nodded. When the doors opened on the first floor, we ran for the van and didn't look back.

Once we were safely a few blocks away, heading down Wilshire, and confident we'd be out of the way before the receptionist realized we weren't coming back, I looked toward Terry. "Don told me the cops had to go through Fiona's things, and then he could have them," I said.

"Uh-huh," she grunted.

"If that's true, who the hell is in Sherman Oaks?"

Terry shook her head. "I have no idea."

In our one trip down to the van, we'd managed to bring four full boxes of the contents of Fiona's desk, Vic's record, and the cardigan—camel colored and a bit frumpy for Fiona, though I supposed that was why she kept it at the office. For some reason, when we brought all we'd found into my apartment, I slipped it on. It fit me like a glove, which meant it must have been large on Fiona, and was quite soft. If it hadn't been the middle of an August day, I might have kept it on.

"We don't have time to go through all this now," Terry said, but she was peeking into one of the banker's boxes as she said it. "They'll need us back on set."

"A quick look," I said, taking the lid off the box closest to me. "The club will want to know a bit of what we found."

This box had been surprisingly light, and I quickly assessed why. The inside was full of tubes of paper, rolled up and secured with rubber bands, some quite thick but others only a few pages. Sheet music.

"These belong to Vic?" I asked, tossing one to Terry, who slid off the rubber band.

"Looks like," she said, flipping through it.

I rooted around the rest of the box to see if there was anything else in there and found a small reporter's notebook at the bottom, no bigger than the size of my palm. I dug it out and opened it, flipping through the pages.

"Handwritten sheet music, so nothing that was published," Terry went on.

"'Handwritten'?" I repeated offhandedly. I was stuck on one page of Fiona's notebook, where her messy handwriting tried to work out a joke about Gene Kelly's nose. She'd gone from "can't see the dancing behind the nose" to "could sniff up Judy Garland" and then added "She's mostly cocaine these days." She'd refined the cadence in the final review that ran, as I recalled. Made it a little snappier.

"Maybe Fiona's piece was about how terrible he is at songwriting. You know, one time he wrote a funeral dirge, and Fiona said he should take a hint from the body and decompose it."

I snorted at the joke and flipped a page in the notebook, where I was met with a note that made my heart drop.

Annie Laurence—playwright—involved with the Cooks?

It was all I could do not to hurl the cursed thing across the room. I managed to keep it cool, knowing Terry was watching, and closed the notebook calmly. Terry had dropped the sheet music next to her and was back to rooting around in her open box. I was contemplating the least-obtrusive way to carry this notebook over to the trash can and toss it when I realized I had to stop her. Who knew what other incriminating details about me were in there? What else did Fiona have on Adam, Beverly, and me?

And then it hit me, the horrible thought: Was *this* the article Fiona was writing?

I took a deep breath and wetted my suddenly parched lips. "We should head back to the lot," I said, my voice only cracking a little.

"You're right," said Terry with a sigh, her knees cracking as she stood. With her back toward me as she headed for the door, I managed to drop the tiny notebook into my enormous purse, where it joined Jack's camera, which I'd been lugging around for two days.

We drove the few minutes to the lot in silence, me aware that I ought to be making conversation but too preoccupied to bother. Adam and Beverly had been at the Canteen the night of Fiona's death, but they'd left hours before. I'd watched them get into a cab. Unless they deliberately wanted me to think they'd left and then snuck back in later to—

What was I even thinking? Adam had been a philosophy major, a man obsessed with questions of morality and humanity. And Beverly was warm, kind—a friend to everyone she met. She knew the birthday of our milkman, for goodness' sake. They couldn't be capable of murder.

Then again, I never thought they would be capable of ripping my heart out of my chest, and they'd done that. And they certainly knew how to make the murder weapon.

The worst question of all was starting to sink in. If it had been Beverly and Adam—if, when I finally got to go through Fiona's things, I found it full of incontrovertible evidence that she was working on an article about us and that the two of them knew—what was I going to do? Turn them in to police? Not only would that tank my own reputation but I also didn't know that I could. I hated them, true, but I also still loved them. *Annie Laurence is under the baton of Adam and Beverly Cook.*

What was I going to do? I had no idea.

TWELVE

‑‑⟨⟨⟨◆⟩⟩⟩‑

I wanted to escape to my office, find a phone, and call Adam and Beverly. It seemed as if—if I could only hear their voices—I would know, somehow. But I had to follow Terry over to the soundstage, trying not to clutch my bag suspiciously close to me. They were shooting another '20s scene today, an utterly ridiculous one I'd written where Henry and Victor go to a producer's office to try to convince him to put one of Henry's songs in his revue. Even though I'd only drafted it yesterday, the lines all sounded foreign to me as I watched Henry and Vic say them. "In five years, everyone will know the name Henry Hilbert. You can either be the man who discovered a genius, or the fool who let him walk away." Had I really written that?

When the director finally yelled "Cut!" Vic made a beeline for us, leaving Henry looking confused and a little hurt, alone on set. "Did it work? Did you find anything?" Vic asked us.

"Kind of," said Terry. "Let's go to your trailer."

Vic lit a cigarette as soon as we'd cleared the soundstage. Once we'd gathered Jack and June in his trailer and all five of us assumed our usual seats, Terry spoke. "We got about half of it before they got wise and kicked us out," she said. Then she tossed the rubber-banded bit of sheet music over to Victor. She must have been carrying it this whole time, but I'd been so preoccupied with my own concerns I hadn't noticed. "Recognize that?" she asked.

Vic let his cigarette dangle from his mouth as he rolled the rubber band off the pages and studied them. "I thought this went missing," he said. "Fiona had this in her office?"

"What is it?" asked Jack.

"A song I wrote a few years ago," he replied. "I forgot about it, to be honest. I wanted it to be a love ballad, but it wanted to be an amorphous blob of displeasing sound. It won."

"Why was it in Fiona's office?" June asked.

"How should I know?" Vic shot back. "The last I saw it, it was in a box in my house with all my other old music. Henry accidentally took it when he moved out, and then the movers lost it."

"Fiona must have taken it so you'd never ruin a party by attempting to play it," said Jack.

"Please, I can ruin a party with my very presence," replied Vic.

"Maybe it's not just sheet music," June suggested. "Maybe she was using it as a code. The letters of the notes spell out a message."

"You've been in too many of Devlin's spy movies," said Vic. "It's old sheet music, that's all."

"You could at least check."

"It opens with eight nine-note chords," said Vic, already rolling the music back up and rubber-banding it again. "That's going to garble the message."

"Your love ballad opens with eight nine-note chords?" I asked. "I don't know a lot about music, but I think that's your first problem."

"Like I said, it wasn't very good."

"There was more of it," said Terry. "Almost an entire box."

"Are you accusing me of something, Terry?" he asked, putting out the cigarette and leaning forward.

"No one's accusing you of anything," said Jack with a little laugh. "Calm down. It's weird, is all."

"Because her article couldn't be about me. What would it say? Vic Durand is a homosexual? The *Dispatch* would never let her print it. Besides, Don said it was something she was researching, right? I'd love to know what her research process would be for that one."

"Yeah, to prove that, someone would have to talk to you for one minute," said Jack.

"I'm telling you, it's a code," said June again.

"You have to admit, it's strange," Terry said.

"Of course I'll admit that," said Vic. "Maybe I can figure out where her head was at if I see what all she had. Where did you two take it?"

"Annie's apartment," said Terry.

"I'll come over tonight."

"Not tonight," I said quickly. I needed time to go through the things on my own first and dispose of every reference to me and the Cooks.

"Why? Do you have a date or something?" asked June.

"Yes," I said, grateful for the lie. It wasn't until I noticed all four of them staring at me with disgust that I remembered that members of the Ambassador's Club hated each other's significant others with a fury. "It's a friend of my ex's," I added. "I'm only doing it for revenge."

Everyone seemed to take that as a valid reason for going on a date, and we moved on. "Well, we can't tomorrow; it's Canteen night," said Terry. "Thursday?"

"Thursday," I agreed.

I ditched the group for my office as quickly as I could. I didn't remember the phone number on the generic "We've moved!" letter the Cooks had sent me, but I remembered the street name, and "Cooks on Roxbury Drive" was enough for the operator to put me through. The line rang and rang. No answer.

Finally, I hung up. It was the middle of the day—they were probably both at work. Just for kicks, I asked the operator to connect me to MGM, where a sweet-voiced girl who sounded no older than eighteen told me I should write a letter if I wanted to reach my favorite MGM stars for a photo or an autograph. I thanked her and hung up.

With the help of a few pills, I managed to focus on work for a little bit, writing some awful scene for the whole group where Henry tells them he's moving to Hollywood to be a movie star. ("But you're the greatest composer the world has ever heard!" says Victor. "Now it's time for me to be heard *and* seen," replies Henry. I couldn't wait to forget I wrote that one.)

Finally, around seven o'clock, I'd finished a scene that was horrible, but no worse than the rest of the script, so I called it a night. I had a page boy send the scene to Terry for approval so she could make any edits and get it copied and ready to shoot for tomorrow. Then I started the long walk home.

I'd just reached my stoop when it occurred to me I should find a pay phone and try for Beverly and Adam again. But I wasn't going to have a chance. Victor Durand was sitting on my front steps, smoking.

"I knew you didn't have a date," he greeted me.

"I do have a date. I came home to change first," I said, stepping past him to open the gate. We rounded the corner and I unlocked my apartment door. "What are you doing here?"

"What, I can't drop in on an old stranger?" He didn't wait for an invitation to follow me in, peering around the nearly bare living room as if there might be someone waiting inside to attack us. "Honestly? I've been thinking about that music you said you found all day. It was gnawing at me, and I hate being gnawed at. It wasn't a sensation I wanted to experience every minute until Thursday. So I figured I'd wait until you got home and see if I could have a look at it sooner. I was going to call first, but apparently you don't have a phone."

"I've found if I don't have a phone, I can't call anyone it would be a mistake to speak to without a nickel and a sobering walk," I said. "Plus, it forces men who want to talk to me to come to my apartment, and then I can develop an interesting reputation."

Vic raised an eyebrow. "Huh. Men, you say? Is it these boxes here?"

"This one," I said, pushing the box of sheet music toward him. At least I was reasonably sure that one contained nothing but music, and unless there was a song in there titled "Annie Loves Adam, and Bev Loves Annie, and Annie Loves Bev, and Bev Loves Adam," I would be in the clear.

He took the box to the couch and began to rifle through it. Seeing no way out of this other than to try to go through the rest of the stuff ahead of Vic and hide anything I didn't want him to see, I sat down on the floor and started to rifle through the rest of the papers as quickly as I could, scanning each one only for my name or the Cooks and not paying any attention to anything else. "What about your date?" Vic murmured sarcastically.

"I'll leave him hanging," I said. "It was a revenge date anyway, remember?"

"Sure. Should we have a drink, then?"

Anything to calm my nerves would be welcome. I hoisted myself from the floor and tried to keep an eye on him as I went to the kitchen. We'd killed the wine the night before, so I went with the vodka, pouring us each a glass.

"You got a record, I see," he said as I handed him his, nodding toward the album I'd taken.

"That was in her office, too," I said. "She must have liked the soloist on it."

"Oh, the soloist is flawless," he said. "But the Philadelphia Orchestra's too romantic on the strings for Henry's music. I wanted to record it with the New York Phil, but Henry won. Put it on, you'll see. It makes the whole piece sound dated even though it's only four years old. Makes me feel halfway in the grave."

I found Side 1 among the five records in the book and blew the dust off both it and the record player, which hadn't been touched for months. Static played from the album and then the opening chords, the ones I remembered nearly shaking the floor beneath me when I'd heard it at the Canteen.

Vic had finished rifling through the sheet music. "Anything interesting in there?" I asked him.

He shrugged. "Some of Henry's songs, some of my songs. I can't fathom why she had it, unless it was part of some prank we never got to see pan out." To my relief, he settled back on the couch, listening to the record instead of investigating the rest of the boxes. Perhaps I could take it easy for now, go through the rest of it once he left.

"You have this piece of music to thank for your current employment, you know. This changed everything for Henry. People were starting to wonder if he wasn't a relic of the Jazz Age. This made him relevant again." The strings came in, lush and full, and he shook his head. "See what I mean? Too sweeping. We're not in Moscow."

"Sounds fine to me," I said.

"Insightful commentary. You should be a music critic. Annie Laurence says, 'I'm impressed they managed to play all those notes.' Let's change the subject. Are you sleeping with Jack?"

I almost spit out my vodka. "No. What? No."

Vic shrugged. "He's the famous, charming, single man and you're the new-in-town single woman. It felt like a not-irrelevant question. I'd warn you not to, though. The only thing Jack Kott knows how to do is self-destruct. You can either steer clear or be hit by the shrapnel. Unless there's some reason you're not sleeping with him." He tapped his glass. "Are you a lesbian?"

"I'm not answering that," I said with a scoff.

"I only ask because you carry around that enormous purse."

I forced my lips into a smile. "I'm not married. Let's leave it at that."

"Why? You know all about us, and we don't know anything about you, other than the fact that you live like a convict on the run." He paused. "Are you a convict on the run?"

"I wish," I said. "I had my heart broken, that's all. Lay on the floor practically comatose for a while and then decided to ditch town. Not that interesting of a story."

"Don't I know it," said Vic. "It was actually the morning we recorded this that Henry told me he needed to live 'respectably' now."

"No wonder you don't like this recording," I said.

"And I didn't even bring it up until I had mentioned the strings twice, so you know I'm not kidding about them. Wasn't that nice of Henry? People are only going to listen to this forever, long after you're dead, which you might as well be because you just lost out to a movie contract and a dumb blond. Now go play! But you know they say it's good for a pianist to be unhappy. Misery loves accompaniment."

"You had that one ready," I said.

"Do me a favor and act like it's new when I repeat it in front of the club," he replied.

"You know, our situations are similar," I said. Strange, it had never occurred to me before. The thought was oddly comforting, that perhaps it wasn't something wrong with me that had left me alone and floundering. "I was left because of a contract, because the relationship wasn't proper, because of... Well..." I gestured out the window, at the yellow Los Angeles sky that was quickly turning dark blue. "Because of this town, because of the studios, because of who people we'll never meet expect us to be. Because people who already make more money than us need to make even more money. Because out here, everyone's a product."

"Just wait until the day you're playing yourself in a biopic about your ex-boyfriend that never once mentions the fifteen years you spent devoting your youth to him," was the response.

I could see it happening, too: the film about Bev and Adam's rise to fame in New York, moving to Hollywood. I could see myself relegated to the supporting cast, the grateful playwright tossing flowers from the front row opening night, an extra cast to sit next to me as my fake husband. The thought made me sick. "I don't know how you do it," I said.

"You don't exactly have a choice," said Vic. "You can't go public without ruining your own career, and even if you decide you don't care about that, the studios will smear you. They'll say you're hysterical or lying, or if that fails—"

I never got to find out what the studios would do, because at that exact moment, a brick soared in through the window we were sitting under.

The window shattered above us, sending shards of glass raining down. I dove onto the floor, covering my head, purely on instinct. I thought at first we must have been bombed, that this was how the whole of Hollywood would meet its end. After a few seconds of relative silence, the only noise the record still turning unawares, I dared to sit up a bit and saw that was not the case—the world was still here. Something fell from my hair. I reached up to brush it away and only realized upon slicing my palm the thing that had fallen was glass, which I was now covered in. Vic was prone on the couch, hands underneath him. The window was totally smashed, the few shards that somehow remained upright still noisily cracking, threatening to topple any moment.

"You all right?" Vic asked.

"I think so," I said. "Get away from the window; the rest of the glass is going to fall."

"I'm scared to move," he replied. "I can't cut my hands. I'm playing the Hollywood Bowl in two weeks."

"Forget the Hollywood Bowl," I said. Reality was starting to set in, and my whole body began to tremble. "We could have *died*."

"Yeah, and even if we had, the union would still require my corpse to show up at the Hollywood Bowl in two weeks," Vic snapped, slowly inching his way up. "Brush the glass off me. No one cares if you cut your hands."

"God willing, I'll cut my whole arm off, and then I won't have to write any more of that movie," I muttered, helping him ease his glass-covered jacket off and using the sleeve to brush some of the shards sticking to the pomade in his hair.

"What the hell was that?" he asked.

Our eyes fell to the brick on the floor, gray and worn and eerily still for all the chaos it had just caused.

He shot to his feet. The movement forced the last remaining shards of glass to tumble in, and we both flinched at the sound. "Someone threw that at us? I thought it was Japan!"

"Thank God it wasn't," I said, but he wasn't listening, heading instead for my door. "What are you doing? Don't go out there! They could still be there!"

"I hope they are!"

"You're gonna fight an intruder? Without using your hands? What are you gonna do, kick him in the shins?"

"I'm not gonna fight him. I'm gonna give him a firm handshake and some tips to improve his aim."

I let him go, too afraid to follow, trembling as the clarinet wailed in the background and a heartbroken Vic from several years ago picked up the melody. After a moment, the present-day Vic returned, shaking his head. "Whoever it was, they're gone now. Not a soul out there except for that mangy black cat." He offered me a hand. "Come on. I'll drive you to my place. We can snort something and call the police."

"Maybe in the other order," I suggested, taking his hand. It wasn't until I grasped it, so steady, that I realized how dreadfully I was shaking.

He led me into the courtyard and out onto the street, where I stopped to gaze into the gaping hole that used to be my front window, now wide open for anyone to waltz right in. "What if someone robs me?" I asked.

"Robs you of what?" Vic immediately replied. He had a fair point. "I only live a minute or two away. The police will be here before that happens."

Vic lived only about a mile west from me geographically, but with its detached, elegant homes instead of squat cement apartment buildings, the neighborhood felt like a different world. His house was modern looking, two stories and all white, with a large patio on the second level—and the whole front lawn was swarming with cops.

He was out of the car practically before it had come to a stop, arms waving madly at the half a dozen or so police standing around. "What's going on? What's the meaning of this?"

Then we saw the gaping hole in his window too. Only his had smoke pouring out of it.

A next-door neighbor, apparently the one to hear the crash and phone the police, managed to coax us inside her place as Vic muttered obscenities at the cops, who wouldn't let him inside his house. I asked the neighbor if I could use the telephone, and I rang Terry.

"Call Jack and June too," Vic shouted when he heard who I was speaking to. "This is an emergency. I need every reassurance."

There was no answer at Jack or June's place, but Terry, who had still been at the studio, pulled up in record time. I could have kissed her I was so grateful for her presence, as Vic's muttering was turning into a full-blown tantrum. "My fucking piano!" he shouted at her as she walked in.

"Did something happen to your piano?"

"I don't know! They won't let me in there to see!" Terry went to give him a hug, which he swatted away. "Don't hug me. It's not so dire I need affection."

"It didn't look like that much smoke. Are you sure you didn't leave the oven on?"

"I've never used my oven, I'm keeping it pristine for my suicide," replied Vic. "You can hug the redhead instead. She got got too."

Terry looked at me, an eyebrow raised. "There was a fire at your place, too?"

"No, but someone threw bricks through both our windows," I told her.

"I bet it was Arthur Rubinstein," muttered Vic.

"You're in fine form tonight. Why would Arthur Rubinstein throw a brick through your window?" asked Terry patiently.

"Jealousy," Vic answered. "And I insulted his wife on Jack's show last week."

"Well, we can't narrow it down to just people you've insulted in public. There would be more people wanting to kill you than Fiona," said Terry. Her eyes suddenly flickered over to me. "Do you think this was related to...?"

"Two of us attacked? In one night? It sure seems like we're someone's target," I said. "Maybe someone who wants us to stop investigating."

"That's impossible," said Terry. "No one knows we're investigating anything besides the five of us. I haven't told anyone. Have you?"

"Don suspects," I said. "And Vic told Henry, when you were trying to get into the *Dispatch* offices."

"I didn't tell Henry anything," he retorted. "Not like he listens to me if I had. What a dreadful night. Did you get through to Jack and June?"

"I rang them both. Neither answered," I said. "Should we try to go find them? Make sure they're all right?"

"I'm sure they're fine," said Terry at the same time the police officer in the door said, "I can't let you leave."

All three of us rounded on him. "What do you mean, I can't leave?" said Vic. "I'm a prisoner?"

"The detectives have some questions for you," he explained.

"He's the victim," I snapped, "and our friends might be in trouble."

"We're sending a black-and-white for your friends right now," said a familiar voice. Detective Kiblowski appeared behind the officer, smiling like we were all old friends. "We figured we needed to talk to them too, after we saw the note."

"What note?" said all three of us at the same time.

Kiblowski held it in the air for us to read. "Found it tied around a brick inside, probably what broke the window."

In large block print letters, the note read: I'LL KILL YOU ALL IF I HAVE TO.

THIRTEEN

────※────

Kiblowski escorted us all to the police station, following in the squad car as Terry drove Vic and me in silence. Soon enough, Jack—followed a few minutes later by June—joined us in the blank off-white room, empty except for half a dozen uncomfortable blue padded chairs. "So," said Kiblowski, still smiling, "I have some news for you all. Given the break-ins at both Miss Laurence's and Mr. Durand's, and the particularly threatening nature of that note, we're reopening the investigation into Mrs. Farris's death."

"Why is that good news?" I asked.

"I didn't say it was," said Kiblowski. "I only said it was news. Although, wasn't it you that spent the night of Mrs. Farris's death trying to convince us someone at the Canteen had it out for her?"

"So you don't think it was a suicide anymore?" Vic said.

"We think there's enough reason to reexamine our initial findings, that's all. Especially now that it's going to be all over the papers that two of Mrs. Farris's friends were attacked. We may come to the same conclusion; we may not."

"If you'd listened to me that night, maybe Vic and I would still have windows," I said.

"I can't change the past, unfortunately, but I can try moving forward," began Kiblowski. "It's like Victor Hugo wrote: 'To rise from error to truth is rare and beautiful.'"

"I prefer that other Victor Hugo quote," said Jack. "'All cops should jump off a bridge.'"

Kiblowski shot him a sour smile. "Detective Cooper and I have just a few questions for each of you. Wait here. We'll be with you in a bit."

With that, he left the room, the door clicking shut behind him.

"Jesus," sighed Jack before turning to me and Vic. "Are you two okay?"

"I'm fine," I said.

"Physically, sure. Mentally, strap me down, sedate me, and lock the door," answered Vic. "Why didn't you answer the phone?"

"What?"

"Annie called you," said Vic. "Both of you. You didn't answer."

"I didn't hear the phone ring," said June.

Jack said nothing.

I closed my eyes. If whoever had thrown that brick through the window knew what we were doing and wanted to threaten us, get us to stop looking into Fiona's death, then it couldn't have been Beverly and Adam. I hadn't seen them since the Canteen, hadn't managed to get them on the phone today, hadn't even spoken to someone who could have passed on a message that I was investigating anything. The Cooks couldn't have thrown a brick through my window; therefore, they probably had nothing to do with Fiona's death either. I was surprised to find myself relieved by this conclusion.

The next conclusion was not so welcome. Terry had said it herself, back at Vic's place: only the five of us knew we were doing this. I wracked my brain for other potential culprits. Don knew we suspected foul play. But even if I'd been wrong to discard him as a suspect in Fiona's murder, he couldn't have been responsible for this threat. Don didn't know where I lived.

In fact, no one outside the four people in this room—and the Pacific Pictures driver who had picked me up from Union Station—had ever been to my apartment.

I opened my eyes. The room had been quiet for the several minutes I mused on this. I looked from each member of the club to the other: June, inspecting her cuticles; Vic, tapping his fingers on his thigh; Terry, staring at the ceiling. Jack and I locked eyes, each of us quickly looking away. Were all five of us slowly, silently coming to the same conclusion?

June sighed and shifted in her seat, opened her mouth like she was going to say something, and then shut it again. It had been too long with no one talking to start with small talk now.

"Are they watching us?" asked Victor suddenly.

"All right, I'll just say what everyone's thinking," said Jack, almost simultaneously. "You all think I did it. I found the body; no one saw me during the concert; I didn't answer the phone tonight—I can practically hear you all accusing me in your minds."

"That's not what we were thinking," I assured him, perhaps too quickly.

"Don't be ridiculous," June added.

"Certainly not," said Terry.

Everyone looked expectantly at Victor. He shrugged and kept tapping on his leg.

Jack went berserk. "Seriously?" he cried, shooting out of his chair. "You think I killed her? You think I threw a brick through your window?"

"I don't have an opinion," said Victor.

"You don't have an opinion about whether or not I'm a murderer?" said Jack, raising his eyebrows in shock. "Come on! You've known me for twenty years! How many times have I been there for your concerts, put you on the radio—you lived in my house for a week after Henry—"

"I'm not accusing you. I'm choosing not to have an opinion," Victor interrupted. "I'm done with all of this. Speculating about who killed Fiona, snooping around her effects. I'm not participating anymore. It's leading down a road I don't want to be on."

"So you don't think it was one of us?" said Jack.

June laughed at that. "'One of us'? What are you talking about? No one thinks it was one of us."

"The cops do," Jack pointed out. "Why do you think they've rounded us all up like this?"

"Because Annie and Vic are victims, and the rest of us are in danger," said June.

"Or we're both," I said. "We're the victims *and* the suspects. One of the five of us is targeting the rest."

June laughed again but a little less confidently this time. "We're not trying to kill each other. That's ridiculous. Why would we do that?"

The room once again went silent, probably as everyone counted up their own personal reasons for wanting to kill every other person in the group.

"At least you all know for sure it's not me," said Victor finally. Jack scoffed, and Victor shot him a look. "Pardon you, what was that noise? You think it *was* me?"

"I *don't* think it was you. I'm scoffing at the principle. You're allowed to suspect me, but I can't suspect you?"

"I don't suspect you. I'm a conscientious objector to the whole ordeal. And besides, the reason why we're here is that *my house* was just burned down."

"It was *burned*, not *burned down*," said Terry, hastening to add, "Not that I think you did it."

"Terry's right, though. You had a house fire," said Jack. "You weren't stabbed or shot at. You could have easily set it yourself. You're not even hurt!"

"Why would I set fire to my own house?"

Jack shrugged. "Maybe you did kill Fiona, and now you're trying to look innocent by making it seem like the murderer also came after you."

"First of all, I was with Annie all night," Victor shot back. "Second of all, I would never set fire to a room with my piano in it. That would be like you setting fire to that manuscript of yours—except *that* wouldn't be a tragedy. And I don't need to make myself look innocent. I *am* innocent. I was onstage when Fiona died, which you would know if you hadn't been soused to the eyeballs."

"Relax," said Jack. "I'm not accusing you. I trust you. All of you."

"I trust you all, too," I said.

"Me too," said June.

"It goes without saying," said Terry.

"Then why are we all saying it?" Victor snapped.

We fell silent again. The very idea of someone in the Ambassador's Club targeting its other members was absurd. These people had been there for each other, through thick and thin, for nearly twenty years. Fiona had introduced them to men with whom she was having affairs; Jack had ditched his newlywed bride to travel with them. And yet. And yet. Something Jack had said to me at the bar was stuck in the back of my mind, playing on repeat like a skipping record: *My dearest friends in the entire world, and sometimes I hate them with such a passion it scares me.*

Who was crueler to anyone in this room more than, well, anyone in this room? I'd be willing to bet none of Jack's radio colleagues made incessant cracks about his inability to write a novel. I thought of the one-liners about June having "used to be" an actress, the remarks about Terry's dead husband, the jokes about Victor's inability to write a song. The insults, the hostility always seemed not good-natured but certainly not *bad*-natured. Maybe it looked cruel to an outsider, but the Ambassadors had thicker-than-average skin. They'd known each other well enough and long enough to know each other's boundaries, and while they tested them frequently, they never pushed too hard.

At least, that's what I had thought. What if I had been wrong?

"You know, we never talked about that night," said Terry. "Maybe we should all go around, say what we were doing and what we remember."

"That's not a bad idea," I said. "It could help us figure out if there's something suspicious we missed."

"I'm not playing," said Victor. "We should be done with this. We're artists, not detectives, and some of us aren't even all that good at the former. Let's leave it to the police."

"I'm only pointing out, maybe it would help reassure everyone in this room that none of us had anything to do with it," said Terry. "After all, you did happen to have a big fight with Fiona ten minutes before she died."

"It wasn't a big fight," Victor replied.

"Then tell us your side of it," said Jack.

"All right, fine. Here's what I did that night: I arrived at the Canteen an hour or so before the concert. I was with Jack in the booth, drinking, but then we ran out of booze, and Jack left to go get some more. Henry showed up and we got into a horrible row. I'll even detail that for you. Henry told me not to get so indulgent with the rubatos in the second movement this time; I told him if he didn't like how I played it, he could play it himself, which got him all ruffled because of course he can't play it himself—not as good as I can, anyway—"

"No one cares," said Jack. "Skip to the relevant stuff."

"You wanted to know!" said Victor. "Henry stormed off. I was furious at him and went to take it out on Fiona. Got a bit dramatic with her—which I *never do*, you know—and then Terry broke it up and I went onstage, where several hundred people all had eyes on me for the next twenty-five minutes. Does that answer your questions?"

"Not at all," said Jack. "What were you and Fiona fighting over?"

Victor shrugged. "Don't remember."

"Bullshit. You don't remember the *last conversation* you had with one of your best friends?"

"When you put it like that, it makes me sound insensitive," said Victor. "Like I said, it wasn't really about her. I was mad at Henry, but he'd rudely declined to have me yell at him. Look, if I remembered every time I became hostile at someone, I'd never have space in my brain for the Tchaikovsky concerto. Terry was there—ask *her* what it was about."

"I didn't hear anything," said Terry. "Only got the general theme that you were upset and Fiona was defensive."

"Why is everyone ganging up on me? June also had words with Fiona earlier in the night, I heard," Victor said.

"No one ganging's up on you," said Jack. "We're having a conversation."

"I'll tell you my side," said June. "I have nothing to hide. I'd been on the dance floor since the start of my shift. A sailor I was jitterbugging with felt me up. I couldn't cause a scene on the floor, so I went to the kitchen and took it out on Fiona. I suppose that was the theme of the evening."

"Why did you take it out on her?" asked Terry.

June rolled her eyes. "Come on, you know why. It's always sort of seemed to me that if Fiona hadn't reviewed my first movie the way she had, I'd be a more serious actress. I wouldn't have to be a sexy spy, and people would know me for my talents, and men would respect me enough not to grope me in public."

"June, I mean this with the utmost sincerity," began Jack. Both him and Victor were already laughing. "You were never going to be a serious actress."

"Fuck you. Both of you."

"What happened after you left the kitchen?" I asked.

"Nothing, really," answered June. "By the time I returned to the dance floor, they were setting up for the concert. I took a seat and watched."

"And where were you tonight?" Victor asked.

"Hmm?"

"Annie called you, and you didn't answer."

June shrugged. "I didn't hear the phone. You must have called when I was in the shower."

"Bullshit again," said Jack. "You weren't at home. The cops sent a black-and-white out to Santa Monica to pick me up. You live seven houses down from me, but they didn't pick you up at the same time?"

"I suppose not."

"You're telling me they sent two cars from Hollywood all the way out to Santa Monica to haul us both in separately?"

June threw up her hands. "I don't know what to say! I was home all night. I ate some soup. I took a shower. I can't prove any of that, so if you want to think I threw a rock at Vic, go ahead. He did call us all miserable alcoholics the other day—maybe that was my motivation."

"Oh, please," muttered Victor. "We all know I was mostly talking about Jack."

"What kind of soup?" asked Jack.

"Let's move on," said Terry. "I'll go. I was working the volunteer entrance the night Fiona died, signing people in. About fifteen minutes before the show, I was hungry, so I went to the kitchen to get a sandwich. I should have locked the door behind me if I was leaving my post, but I forgot. I hope that wasn't how whoever did it—*if* someone did it… Well, regardless. I went in the kitchen, saw Vic and Fiona having words, and went over to break it up. I watched the concert a bit but then I got warm, so I stepped outside during the second part."

"Movement," corrected Victor.

"Second movement. That's when I ran into Annie and Jack. Jack had just wandered up to the second floor, drunk—"

Jack's eyes shot over to me. "I did?"

"You don't remember?" I remarked.

"No. What did I say? Did I say anything?"

Terry didn't wait for me to answer. "I told Annie I'd take Jack to the kitchen. It took us awhile. You were moving pretty slow, pal. But eventually, we made it in through the volunteer entrance and into the kitchen through the back way, and that's when we saw... Well, you know. Her."

We all fell into silence, the weight of what we were talking about striking us. "I miss her," said June.

Jack ran his fingers through his hair as he leaned his head in his hands. "Me too, kid."

"She would have solved it by now," said June. "If it had been one of us? She would have figured it out."

"Yeah, this redhead's a real poor substitution," muttered Victor.

"I suppose I'll go next," I said. "I saw June storm off the dance floor, and I followed her into the kitchen, where I got roped into making sandwiches until the concert started. Bette Davis told me I needed to fill out some paperwork, so I went up to that little unfinished room on the second floor, above the sound booth. During the second movement, Jack came up, and he was rather drunk, so I sent him off to the kitchen with Terry for coffee and food. I finished my paperwork and decided I'd take it down and watch the rest from inside—"

"Do you people always wander around so much during my concerts?" interrupted Victor. "It's only been my life's work for thirty-eight years. You could sit still for half an hour."

"—but the volunteer entrance was locked, so I had to go around," I continued.

"I locked it when I went in with Jack," interjected Terry.

"I was in the side alley and saw Terry and Jack and Fiona through the kitchen window," I said. "I ran around to the front to get help, but Terry was already getting security by then."

"So you were alone most of the night," said June, leaning forward to rest her chin on one perfectly manicured hand. Her dark-red nails once again perfectly matched the dark-red shade of her lipstick, and I wondered for one brief, cruel moment what kind of woman took the time to freshen up her lipstick before heading to the police station after her friends had been attacked in their homes.

"What are you implying?" asked Jack.

"Nothing," said June. "Only asking."

"Annie barely even knew us at the time," said Jack. "She didn't kill Fiona."

"I didn't say she did!"

"It was a probing question," said Jack.

"It's okay," I said to Jack. "That's the point of this—everyone asks all the questions they want. Everyone's cards on the table."

"Besides, Annie knew *of* Fiona before she met her," June said. "Fiona reviewed her play! And Annie's the only one here who got some benefit out of Fiona dying."

"What's that?" I asked.

"You got the job on the Hilbert movie. Terry wanted to give that to Fiona."

"Yes, that was my plan," I replied sarcastically. "Murder a woman I barely knew so I could infiltrate her drinking club under the guise of solving that murder and then secure myself what I've always wanted: a job on a sinking-ship movie at the last-place studio in Hollywood."

"I don't think you did it," June clarified. "I'm only asking questions."

"Jack, it's your turn," Terry said, clearly only butting in before things between me and June got any testier.

"I don't really have much to say," said Jack. "I don't remember much. Drinking in the booth with Vic. I remember running out of booze. That's when it gets fuzzy. I went to a liquor store, I think the one up on Hollywood. I came back to the Canteen and saw someone with horns coming out of the volunteer entrance, but I told you all about that already. I don't remember talking to Annie upstairs. I don't remember going to the kitchen. Seeing Fiona must have snapped me sober, because the first thing I remember is throwing up."

"Perhaps you killed Fiona but you were so drunk you don't remember," said June.

"Yeah, perhaps, but I'm not wild about you throwing that out there," replied Jack.

"I don't mean anything by it. I'm just pointing it out," she said.

"And where were you tonight?" I asked.

"I was working on my novel," said Jack. "I didn't want to tell you all, but I met a literary agent the other night, and he sounded interested. I wanted to polish it up before sending it to him. I didn't answer the phone 'cause I didn't want to be disturbed."

"The Great American Novel, brought to you by Grape-Nuts," said Victor offhandedly, as if being cruel about Jack's novel were a reflex rather than a genuine insult. June, too, impulsively giggled.

Jack did not take it impersonally. "Listen, I'm about sick of you tonight," he snapped, standing and crossing the room to where Victor sat. "Of the two of us, I'm not the one who had a fight with our friend an hour before she turned up dead. And I don't believe for one second you don't remember what that fight was about."

"I don't know how many times I need to explain to you people that while I'm an extremely talented pianist, I do need to physically be seated at the piano to play it," said Victor.

"What if you drugged her before you went onstage?" Jack was hovering inches from Victor's chair now. Victor studied his fingers, attempting to look bored. "What if you were working with someone else? What if you convinced her to commit suicide? That's just off the top of my head!"

Victor pointed at June. "What about her?"

June wrinkled her forehead indignantly. "What *about* me?"

"She also fought with Fiona, and her alibi's worse than mine. She could have easily pretended she was going to the bathroom and snuck into the kitchen through the back way. Or done any of those other things you're accusing me of."

"I suppose, yes, I could have done that," June said. "But so could Annie or Terry."

"Any one of us *could* have done it," said Terry. "That's why we're trusting each other to tell the truth. And since no one here said, 'And in these five minutes, I poisoned Fiona's coffee,' none of us did it."

"Sure," said Victor. "Now we all know, without a shadow of a doubt, that every single person in this room is innocent. So can we drop this? I don't want anything to do with this anymore."

Everyone fell quiet, and Jack settled back in his chair.

"I didn't like that," said June eventually. "That felt like we—like we *broke* something. Maybe we ought to—"

She didn't get to finish her thought. Kiblowski opened the door. "Let's start with Mr. Kott," he said.

FOURTEEN

—‹‹‹•›››—

After about fifteen minutes—during which time, not a single word was spoken among the four of us who remained—Kiblowski came back and pointed at me.

Cooper was waiting for us in an interrogation room, chewing on a toothpick. "Ah, if it isn't Detective Laurence," he said.

Before I had a chance to respond, Kiblowski jumped in. "Hey, Coop, give it a rest. The lady turned out to be right, didn't she? We have plenty of reason to suspect someone at the Canteen had it out for Mrs. Farris after all." He flashed me a smile and pulled out a chair for me. "Have a seat, Miss Laurence."

I did not care for whatever good cop, bad cop routine they were playing with me, so I took my seat without returning his smile. "Tell us what happened at your apartment tonight," he began.

"Vic was over. We were having a drink and listening to a record, and then someone threw a brick at us," I said.

"And then you left to go to Mr. Durand's?"

"To call the police. I don't have a phone."

"No neighbors in the building would let you use theirs? No pay phone nearby?"

I shrugged. "Vic suggested it. He lives close. Maybe another option would have been faster, but we weren't thinking clearly."

"I'll bet. That must have been quite the scare. Did you get a glimpse of who it could have been? See a car driving away, anything like that?"

I shook my head.

"I'd like to ask something, if you don't mind," Cooper interjected. Kiblowski gave him a go-ahead gesture. "Miss Laurence, you neglected to tell us during our first meeting that you wrote murder mysteries."

"You neglected to ask," I said.

"I managed to find a copy of your latest play," he went on. "I'll admit, it was a little shocking for us to realize the murder weapon was the exact same poison that killed Mrs. Farris."

I shifted in my seat. "I wasn't trying to hide anything from you," I said. "I didn't know that's how she died the last time we spoke."

"But you know now? It's not news to you?"

"Her husband told me at the funeral. You can ask him, if you don't believe me."

Kiblowski chuckled. "Don't worry, we believe you. It's a dark coincidence—we see them all the time. We actually think that maybe you can help us. Clearly, we didn't realize your potential value to our investigation the first time we spoke. You're a part of this Ambassador's Club now, aren't you?"

"Yes," I answered.

Kiblowski leaned in. "What do you make of it? Of them? Those friendships?"

I shrugged.

Kiblowski waited a moment for me to answer, then shrugged as well. "Well, I'll tell you what I see, then: they seem rather nasty, to me at least. Like the sort of people who think they can be as rude as they want if they wrap it in enough cleverness. I don't like people like that."

"Maybe that's because you don't have enough cleverness to keep up," I said.

"Must be it," said Kiblowski. "You seem to like them, so tell me what you see in them."

"They're intelligent, witty, interesting," I said. "They like a good drink at a bad club. They're fun."

Kiblowski nodded. "Sure, I can see that. But again—and let me know if I'm missing something here—none of them seem to like each other very much."

"People have different ways of showing how they like each other."

"True enough," said Kiblowski. "My father used to scream at me when I'd come home with a bad grade. Eventually, I figured out that was 'cause he loved me and he wanted me to have the best chance to succeed. He didn't know how to express it other than that."

I said nothing, not seeing what Kiblowski's undoubtedly made-up sob story had to do with me. He leaned forward, his elbows on the table. "All right, I'll just ask what's on my mind, then," he said. "I think you can be helpful to us. You're friends with the Ambassador's Club, but you're relatively new to the group, which means you know them but you're not biased. Your judgment isn't clouded. You can see these people for who they really are. Do you think any of them could be capable of murder?"

I hesitated. It had seemed to me in that waiting room that it had to be one of them. No one else made sense. But only twenty-four hours earlier, I'd been snug on a couch with those four, feeling a level of bliss I hadn't felt since, well, the morning of March 20, four and a half months ago, before Beverly and Adam extinguished the entire future I had planned for myself. How could any of the people who had made me feel so wonderful be capable of anything so awful?

"No, I don't think any of them are capable," I said finally. I was a member of this club now, 'til death or a better offer do us part. Two cops who had done nothing but disbelieve me and talk down to me weren't going to be the better offer that would get my loyalties to break.

"Fair enough," said Kiblowski. "How about this? If you're willing to keep an open mind about that, you could work with us from the inside. Report back to us if any of them start acting suspicious."

"I'm not going to spy on my friends," I said.

"They're not your friends," Cooper muttered. Kiblowski shot him a look, and Cooper shrugged. "You've known them for, what? A week?"

"Two weeks," I said, not realizing until it was too late how pathetic of a retort it was.

"I think my partner is only trying to point out," began Kiblowski, "that sure, you may be friends. But you can't learn everything there is to know about a person—about a group of people—in two weeks."

"They're not the kind of people who hide things," I said. "They tend to state exactly what's on their minds, for better or worse."

"Everyone is the kind of person who hides things, Miss Laurence," replied Kiblowski.

"That club has secrets," added Cooper. "Secrets they aren't going to tell a person who's only been hanging around a little bit. Secrets that could put you in danger. Secrets that maybe already have. A brick came through your window tonight, Miss Laurence. What will it be tomorrow?"

"They don't keep secrets," I said. "Not from each other."

"So you're not keeping any secrets from them?" asked Kiblowski.

I didn't answer that. The silence hung in the air for a moment before Kiblowski sighed and rose to his feet.

"If you change your mind, give us a ring," he said. "Detective Cooper will escort you out."

I wished I felt as confident on the inside as I'd managed to sound on the outside. Instead, I felt all shaken up. I bounced back and forth between wondering if one of the club could have done it, then feeling guilty for wondering. I worried they were having the same doubts about me, that whoever was left in that room was currently whispering to one another that it *was* strange I'd taken Fiona's job, wasn't it? I kept replaying sentences from that horrible hour in the waiting room. How much of that insisting we trusted one another had been honest?

The Ambassador's Club said terrible things to one another. How terrible were the things that weren't being said?

If only we could have a normal night together again, I felt, this would all be resolved. If we could go back to the Ambassador Hotel, to the giggling and the drinking and the insults, if we could be engulfed by it all again—my doubts would melt away. We'd remember some obvious thing we must have been missing, some person outside of us who could potentially want us dead. We'd go back to the police united and be done with this, once and for all, and then later look back and feel foolish over that night we spent thinking anyone in this club could ever harm one another.

But Cooper led me out of the station alone, not allowing me to return to the waiting room. I was thrown out into the now pitch-black night with only my anxious thoughts on a loop to keep me company.

I started walking, not even sure if I was headed in the direction of my apartment. I just needed to move forward. The police station was off on a side street, but I soon reached Hollywood Boulevard, where people spilled out of the restaurants and nightclubs around me, laughing and celebrating. The faint sounds of seven different jazz songs trumpeted out of every open door. I ignored it all.

Busted window or not, I had to get back to my apartment. If one of the four of them really had killed Fiona over the article she was about to publish, the evidence was currently sitting in my living room. Which meant I had to get to it before the guilty person did.

It wasn't Victor—I could be reasonably certain of that. He'd been onstage during the murder and with me during the attack. Besides, his big secret was unpublishable. Fiona could allude to him being a homosexual, but she'd already done that. Why would Victor care now?

That left Jack, June, or Terry. I considered what secret any of them might be hiding. Terry's husband: Had he perhaps died in more mysterious circumstances than she had led us to believe? It was an interesting theory, but with this group, it would be more likely if they had all helped Terry push the man overboard together. So what about June? I knew nothing about the romantic entanglements of June, despite having heard about Terry's husband, Jack's divorce, and of course Victor's ongoing Henry melodrama. Could there be a reason she played those cards close to her chest? A secret lover that Fiona had discovered?

Neither felt quite right to me, but my heart sank when I got to Jack. The man was an alcoholic. If anyone was likely to have secrets he was ashamed of, secrets that could jeopardize his whole career if published, it was the fellow who didn't remember what he did half the time. He'd even admitted to me, plain as day, that he sometimes hated Fiona. If she had planned to publish something devastating about him, it wouldn't be merely a nasty secret coming to light. It would be emblematic of their whole relationship: she the successful, respected writer, penning important columns for a reputable paper; he the deadbeat alcoholic who failed at everything.

Jack, June, Terry, or maybe Victor, if he'd been working with one of the other three. The answer, or something that could point to it, was in my living room.

I should have expected what happened next, should have known. Nothing had gone my way in months; why would the universe start cooperating now?

Someone—the police or my landlord, I couldn't be sure—had cleaned away the shards of glass and nailed a tarp to my empty window frame. It had already been too late. When I reached my apartment and unlocked the door, I saw that, of course, the only thing that remained from Fiona's office was Side 1 of the Hilbert concerto, still spinning silently on the record player.

Any chance the murderer wasn't among the five of us had gone out the window along with the contents of my apartment. Someone else who had it out for me might have been able to figure out where I lived, but no one else knew that stuff was there. One of my new friends, someone I'd laughed with on a stolen couch less than twenty-four hours ago, had murdered Fiona Farris.

An unexpected knock on the door made me jump. What did this night have in store for me now? "Hey, kid," Jack said with a smile as I opened the door. "Hell of a night, huh? Can I come in?"

"Sure," I said, wary of him but not sure what else I could say.

"I was halfway to Santa Monica when I realized both you and Vic would be needing somewhere to stay tonight," he went on. "And I was halfway to Vic's when I remembered I'm mad at him, so he can sleep in a ditch for all I care. So I came here." His gaze swept across the living room. "I thought you brought Fiona's work things here. Where are they?"

"Gone," I said. Not sure how much of my suspicions I should give away, I added, "The police must have taken them."

"Yeah," said Jack warily. "Maybe. Well. We can't do anything about that now, can we? Let's get out of here. Come on, I told the cab to wait. You're staying with me tonight."

"I was going to find a hotel," I said.

"No need for that. I have plenty of space," he replied. "Harpo Marx once snuck in and lived with me for a week, I had no idea."

"I wouldn't want to take Harpo's room," I said.

"I've got rooms for all the Marx brothers, including Karl," he said. "Annie, look, jokes aside, I really must insist. You were attacked tonight. I can't let you go stay in a hotel surrounded by God knows who."

I would have felt infinitely safer around a bunch of strangers than him, but it seemed he wasn't going to let it go. "All right, fine," I said, my mind racing. "But do you think we could stop somewhere for a drink first? My nerves are shot from all this excitement, and I don't know how I'll sleep otherwise."

He grinned. "You read my mind."

If I could get Jack half as drunk as he'd been the night Fiona died, I could ditch him and he might not even remember it. We ended up at Musso & Frank, where the bartender greeted Jack warmly and poured him a whiskey neat without him having to order. As I ordered the same, I wondered how many hours he'd spent nursing one of these—and then, when Jack downed it, I remembered that Jack Kott didn't nurse anything. Maybe it would be easier than I expected to get out of this.

He motioned for another round, which the bartender already had ready to go. "I must confess, there was another reason I wanted to see you alone tonight," he said. I was bracing myself to have to offer a romantic rejection—"It's not you, it's that there's a one-in-three chance you're a murderer"—when he added, "We ought to team up, the two of us."

"Team up against what?" I asked.

"Oh, come on, don't play dumb," he replied. "You heard the way things were going in there. It was one of us that did it. At least, that's looking extremely likely. I wish that weren't true—I wish that with all my heart—but I think we've all learned these last few years that wishing doesn't mean squat. If it was one of the five of us that killed Fiona, the rest of us are in danger. And not just physical danger. The cops have clearly narrowed it down to the five of us too. That means the killer's next move has to be pinning Fiona's death on someone else in the group. That's what we need to team up against. Because you and I? We're by far the most likely targets for a framing."

"I'm not a likely target," I said. "First of all, I didn't kill her—which I have to think would make it harder to pin on me."

"You'd think that, but this is Hollywood, kid. It's all about appearances," said Jack.

"Whoever killed her also threw a brick at me. I couldn't throw a brick at myself."

"The attack makes you less likely of a suspect, sure. You're probably in a better position than me, given that. But the attack matters less than the murder. And fact of the matter is, the night of the murder—from the start of the concert up until Terry and I found the body—I'm the only person who saw you, and you're the only person who saw me. Vic was onstage. June and Terry were in the audience. Say hypothetically, June's the one behind all this. Who is she gonna deflect blame onto? Terry, who could maybe scrounge up a witness; or you, who was alone? If one of them points at us—or worse, if the killer convinces the other two they should all three point at one of us—we're screwed. So you and I need to figure out which one of them is guilty before that happens and have each other's backs in the meantime."

He was acting as if it hadn't occurred to him that I might suspect *him*, that in fact I suspected him more than any of the other three. I wasn't sure how exactly yet, but I could use that to my advantage. I could pretend to go along with this and see where it leads. "All right," I said. "We'll be a team."

He let out an exaggerated exhale of relief. "I'm glad someone's on my side," he said. "Let's get out of here."

"We need to drink on our alliance first," I said, holding up my glass.

Jack held up his as well. "Mine is empty."

"Order another, then."

I didn't need to suggest it twice. Jack waved at the bartender, who nodded, not bothering with a fresh glass this time and refilling instead straight from the bottle. He raised his newly filled glass to mine. "To the two writers left," he said.

We clinked.

"Why don't you tell me where your head is at: Terry, Victor, June? You know them better than I do."

Jack rolled his glass between his palms and sighed. "That's the thing," he said. "I don't know. My brain's all jumbled up about it."

That answered surprised me. If he were the killer, I would have expected him to have a name ready to go, the person he had already decided would be the best to pin it on. "Talking it through might help," I suggested.

He nodded. "Here's what's sticking to me now: Vic could tell you the name of a waiter who messed up his drink order in '34, so he's lying about not remembering his fight with Fiona. Why would he lie about that? He's either embarrassed about what the fight was about— possible—or it's incriminating. But then again, he was onstage that night. He's the only one with a solid alibi."

"He could have been working with someone," I pointed out.

"Sure, thought that too. But if Vic needed help killing someone, he'd go to me. We just—that's the bond we have. You know, I met him my first night in New York City. I was doing vaudeville, far too young to be there on my own, and he was only two years older than me, playing piano in the band of the first theater I happened to book. He realized I was broke and hungry, so he took me out to eat after the show and then insulted my act the entire time. We started doing acts together, which were bad enough to ruin his chances of ever being a serious musician and good enough to ruin my chances of ever being a serious writer. We're bonded in that way only two people who have ruined each other's lives can be. So if he said to me, 'I need to kill Fiona, and I need help,' I probably would have done it. I probably would have helped him. I know that sounds terrible to say, but that's the truth." He shrugged and looked sadly down into his drink. "And now that I say that, I'm thinking...I would have helped any of them. I would have helped Terry, June, Fiona. You think I'm a monster for saying that, probably."

"No," I assured him. If anything, the admission was making me think he was less of a monster. I would expect Fiona's killer to deny up and down that he would ever harm a strand of hair on her head.

"Yeah, you do," he said. "Haven't you ever been that kind of close to someone before, though? You said you had a fella. Would you have killed for him?"

Would I have killed for Adam and Beverly, back in the good times? If they were in imminent danger—if they were being attacked on the street and I happened to have a knife on me—of course I wouldn't have hesitated. But something premeditated, something calculated, the way Fiona's death had been? It was harder to say. I pictured the three of us in the apartment: Adam in the chair by the radio, me and Bev lying on the floor. What if instead of leaving me, they'd asked me to help them kill Fiona Farris? "They wouldn't have asked me to kill for them," I said finally. "Not in a good way, not because they loved me so much they wouldn't want me involved—no. They didn't think enough of me to ask for my help with something like that."

Jack looked at me and raised an eyebrow. "'They'?" he said. "There was more than one?"

It was through sheer force of will alone that I stopped my hand flying to my mouth. I'd been so caught up conjuring images of them in our old living room, bathed in warm candlelight, that I'd completely forgotten to think before I spoke. "Turns out, I'm not the Virgin Mary," I said. And then, because I was already using the first distraction tactic I could think of for Jack Kott—alcohol—I went for the second: "Did you say earlier that a literary agent was interested in your book?"

This worked like gangbusters. Jack's eyes lit up. "Yeah, one of my writers on the radio show wrote a novel, and he invited his agent to the studio audience last week. He offered to read my manuscript, although he's not sure he can sell it, not with my name on it. That's the problem, you know. It's like Fiona said: people want a certain thing from Jack Kott. And it has nothing to do with me."

"But you *are* Jack Kott," I said.

He shook his head. "Not anymore," he said. "There's Jack Kott who entertains people on the radio, and there's Jack Kott who is me, here in front of you. And the longer I'm the former, the less I feel like the latter. I can feel myself flattening."

"What's the book about?" I asked.

He laughed at the question. "What do you mean, what's it about?"

I hadn't expected to have to explain that one. "You know, what's the plot? Who's the main character?"

"There is no plot," he said. "Do you want to know why? Because stories—stories where things make sense—don't happen."

"Ah. So it's modern, then."

"It's—are you making fun of me?" He grinned. "I take it as a compliment. The modernists got it right, I think. There's no reason behind anything. There's a whole war going on, you should understand that."

"There's reason behind the war," I replied. "To stop the Nazis."

"Then why are we also fighting Japan? Fighting Italy? Why are the Nazis killing people in the first place? There's no motive to any of it."

I was certain there was, but it had been a few months since I'd picked up a newspaper or read anything that wasn't a line of dialogue for a movie about the imagined life of Henry Hilbert. "Japan and

Italy are on the side of Germany because they all want to expand and be world powers," I said. I wasn't at all sure this was correct, and it sounded rather stupid. "And the Nazis are killing people because… because they're evil. They're Nazis!"

"My mom and I left Warsaw when I was four years old," Jack said. "We didn't have the money to all travel at once, and my mother already had a cousin over here, so my father and my older brother stayed behind. It was only supposed to be for a year or so. I got to go because I was the youngest, and at that time, women coming from Eastern Europe alone were all thought to be white slaves. My mom thought the younger the child traveling with her, the more she'd look like a mother than a prostitute. Maybe a stupid plan, but it worked. And then, three months after we got here, the U.S. started restricting the number of immigrants from Poland. My father and my brother couldn't get here. My mom tried to explain the law to me, and I didn't understand it. She said she didn't understand it, either, which is why she was sure it would go away. The law would be repealed soon enough; we only had to wait. We waited so long the first war started, and Germany invaded, and…" He shrugged.

"I'm sorry," I said.

"Don't pity me; that's not why I said all that… Or maybe it is, I don't know. No one gets into the radio business 'cause they lack an insatiable need for attention. I said that because I spent years trying to figure out the why, the *because* of my life. I wrote two hundred thousand words to try to solve it. You want to know why my novel is unreadable? 'Cause I realized there is no solving it, there is no meaning. Every part of it is vast and unreachable. Even beyond the war, the obvious tragedies. Why couldn't we all travel together, why did I get to go when my brother didn't, why were quota laws passed—there's no answer to any of those things. It's all absurd, it's all just…"

He stopped mid-sentence, then stood up from his barstool. Taking a few steps away from the bar, he began unbuckling his belt.

"What are you doing!" I cried. For a moment I thought he might be so drunk that he was about to take a leak right there on the carpet, but after unzipping his fly, he kept going, pulling one pale, hairy leg up and out of his pants. His shoe got trapped in the fabric, and he began to hop. I clasped my hands over my mouth as I laughed.

"I'm showing you—I'm—" Other patrons were starting to turn and watch now, which affected Jack not at all and only made me laugh harder. "Look at how meaningless everything is. I'm taking my pants off inside Musso & Frank's, and there's no reason for it, and it won't even matter in the end. It's all just"—with a final effort, he managed to kick his trousers up in the air, catching them gracefully—"absurd. Completely, totally—"

The restaurant's manager arrived. "Sir—"

"Yeah, I know," said Jack. "We were on the way out, anyway." He fished his wallet out of his pocket and tossed the bartender a stack of bills, then flung his pants over his shoulder like a scarf and offered me his arm. "Madame."

I took it.

I was still giggling as we rushed outside and around the corner into an alley. "Wow, it's easy to make you laugh, huh?" he said, doing a little shimmy as he tried to get his left leg back into his pants. "You ever want to be in the studio audience for *Grape-Nuts Presents: The Jack Kott Show*? I can pay you, but only in Grape-Nuts."

"Sorry, I only eat Wheaties," I said. "And I'm beginning to think I've struck an alliance with a madman."

"Now it's your turn," he said, refastening his belt. "To do something ridiculous. I know you have it in you. It's okay if it's not as good as mine, I'm a seasoned professional—"

I leaned in and kissed him.

If I surprised him, he didn't show it, kissing me back almost instantly, the slight five-o'clock shadow on his chin rubbing against me. After a few moments, when it became clear neither one of us was backing away from this, he put his hands around my waist, letting them rest on my hips. He kept them there when we finally did break apart, what seemed like an eternity later but was probably only a minute or two. "Now why," he breathed, his face so close to mine, "would you do a thing like that?"

Why had I done that? The only reason we had gone out for a drink was so I could get rid of him. This was the polar opposite of that, and I didn't care at all. Maybe it was the alcohol, but it felt both deeper and simpler than that. I wanted to kiss him, so I did. "I had no motive," I replied.

"Because now"—he stopped to kiss me in between words—"I have a motive, a very strong one." The way he pressed his lips to mine was so soft that it made me want to cry out to be kissed harder, to feel his stubble again. "To take you back to my place."

"They say you should buy a lady dinner first," I said. "But no one's ever accused me of being a lady."

Jack grinned.

FIFTEEN

-‹‹‹‹•›››-

I woke up the next morning in a daze, my mind warm and fuzzy. For a moment I didn't realize where I was, feeling nothing except comfortable silken sheets caressing my bare body as I lay in what felt like a cocoon of plush warmness. I had thought, for the last few months, that a cheap mattress on scratchy sheets with one pillow was comparable to most sleeping experiences. I'd been dead wrong about that.

Morning light streamed in through the French doors that lined one wall of Jack's bedroom, casting everything in a honey glow. I rolled over, opened my eyes, and nearly gasped. What had been nothing but darkness the night before had given way to a view of the ocean and the bluest of blue skies, like a set decorator had requested every California cliché. I settled back into the three plush pillows I'd arranged around my head. I should have started going home with rich men ages ago.

Jack stirred next to me, opening his eyes slowly to gaze into mine. "Morning, kid," he whispered with a smile, albeit one that disappeared quickly once the light hit him. He winced and pressed a hand to his temple. "Christ. How much did we drink last night?"

"I don't remember," I said. "I'm all right, though."

"To be honest, I had a few before the cops came," said Jack. "I can't write without being a bit plastered. With a man of my ability, it helps to not be able to see the words."

The mention of the others, of the police, of that awkward and awful night at the station, reminded me that a world existed outside of this bed. I pressed myself closer to Jack to try to stop reality from coming for us, but I could tell from the limp way he wrapped his arms around me that it was too late. The edges of the furniture had hardened; the light had turned cold and blue for the both of us.

"So what are we going to do now?"

Jack sighed. I felt his breath hit my forehead, warm and stale. "I ought to tell you—and this has nothing to do with you—I'm not really a, uh, traditional-relationship kind of person."

I couldn't help but laugh. If only Jack could see my relationship history. It would probably have sent him swan-diving off the palisades. How close I had come to spilling the beans last night! I would have to be more careful. "I actually meant—about our alliance. What are we going to do now?"

"Oh," he said, smiling in embarrassment. He had the cutest dimples when he smiled. "I suppose that is more important."

"Fiona's things were stolen from my apartment, so whoever threw the brick, we can assume that's what they were after," I said. "I suppose where we start is to look for that stuff. We can search Vic and June's trailers today. I can try to get into Terry's office—"

"No, no," said Jack. "This is like your play."

"What do you mean?"

"The scene in your play, when your leading man suspected that pretty blond had stolen the money—he didn't go looking for the cash."

"He told her there was more money somewhere else," I said. "And waited for her to try to steal that too."

Jack leaned back, smiling smugly. "You and Terry didn't get

everything from Fiona's office, right? So we pretend we got the rest. Say it's locked up in your office and then wait for someone to try to steal it."

"One problem," I said. "I would like—preferably—to not have another brick thrown at my head."

Jack frowned. "Hmm, so you're saying you still value your own human life? Interesting. Give it a few more weeks with us. We'll knock that out of you. All right. What if we make it easier to steal? Not your office but your purse, perhaps. No one needs to break a window to dig through an unattended purse."

"If it's too easy, they won't go for it," I said. "It'll look like a trap."

"You're right," he said. "So much for that plan."

"We'll keep thinking on it," I said. "There has to be some way to make it work."

"And the other thing?" he said. "You're all right with that? 'Cause I tried being the guy that marries the girl, and it didn't exactly work out."

"Is this your way of asking me to leave?" I said with a smile.

"I don't want you leave," he replied. "But I also don't want you to stay. And whichever you pick, I'm going to resent you for it. Aren't I charming? Now you see why I can't keep the women off me."

Downstairs, the phone rang. "Oh, thank God," said Jack. "If I kept talking, who knows what I'd say next?"

He disappeared down the stairs, not bothering to even put a robe on first, which made me giggle. When he returned a few moments later, he was holding a throw pillow in front of himself, which he tossed at me. "You'd better get up," he said. "Something's happened that hasn't happened in a month of Sundays: Henry's written a song. Terry wants us both on set."

"I can't go in like this!" I cried.

"I suppose you could put your clothes back on, but it's Pacific Pictures—no one will bat an eye either way."

"It's the same outfit as yesterday. Everyone will know." It was a distinctive outfit, too: slacks—of which I only had the one pair—and a white blouse with an elaborate design cut into the collar.

"What, that after we left the police station, you came right back to my place and stayed in one of my eleven guest rooms because your apartment is inhabitable? Yeah, I already told Terry that on the phone. Your pristine reputation is intact."

I was certain that it was not, that at least Vic, if not all three of them, would deduce the truth immediately, but we had bigger problems to manage. "All right," I said. "Do you remember where I put my purse?" I at least had a little makeup in there. I could attempt to look somewhat professional.

"It's over here," said Jack, picking it up from a chair by the window and carrying it over to me in the bed. "Christ, what do you have in here, anvils?"

"*Cosmopolitan* magazine says a cultured lady never leaves home without her anvils," I replied, accepting the bag and peering inside. "It's your camera, actually. I still have it, remember? What's it like to be rich enough to not notice—"

I stopped short as I saw something in my bag: Fiona's notebook.

Jack had gone into his closet and wasn't looking at me. I opened the notebook and flipped through, trying to find the note I'd seen scribbled about me and the Cooks. "Rich enough to not notice a camera missing?" Jack called, his voice muffled, likely from pulling an undershirt over his head. "It's fantastic. I highly recommend it."

I found the page and yanked it out, crumbling it up and stuffing it back at the bottom of my bag. I did a quick flip through to see if there were any other references—nothing.

"In fact," Jack continued, "Keep the camera. I'll buy another. How do you like them apples?"

He emerged from the closet, buttoning up a light-blue shirt and smirking as he waited for my response. I brandished the notebook. "Look what I found," I said.

Jack and I spent the cab ride to the studio poring over Fiona's notebook for any clues. It became obvious rather quickly that most of it—aside from the errant scribbled idea or random joke—had been filled one day when Fiona had gained access to a series of memos sent on the Pacific lot. She'd copied down dozens of them into her notebook, her handwriting growing messier and messier, presumably as she ran short on time in whatever office or storage room she'd snuck into. They spanned several years, the earliest being from '41.

> *MEMO: DM to IF*
> *12/7/41*
> *War inevitable now. We need to move on vetting my list of new*
>   *male stars. Who have you talked to?*

"Devlin Murray to Irma Feinstein," murmured Jack, running his fingers over the note. "Christ, look at the date. He didn't even take a day before thinking how it would impact the movie business."

The next page was obviously Irma's reply, dated the next day and providing a long list of initials and an update on each of them.

> *JG—Has heart trouble, unfit to serve. Excellent actor, strong*
>   *moral character. Move forward.*
> *VD—Failed screen test.*
> *PB—Married with children so will not be drafted yet, but*
>   *feeling pressured to enlist. Solid screen test but not worth the*
>   *resources as long as he's on the fence.*

HH—Excellent screen test, too old for draft, but has past issues.
   Will discuss in person.
JK—Unfit to serve but not star material. Too disagreeable.
   Would not recommend.

"Hey, JK, that's me," said Jack. "I'd forgotten about that. Yeah, around that time, I had a meeting with Irma, and she asked me all these questions about my past. I told her to go fuck herself. If only I'd known that was the first screening to turn me into Pacific's latest star, I'd have told her to go fuck herself and her whole family."

"HH must be Henry," I said. "And HH's past issues, we know who that is."

"This is a gold mine," said Jack. "This is the origin story of Eliza Hilbert, right here. Oh, and look: VD, that's Vic. Vic failed his screen test! Ha! Even I passed the screen test. I'm just an asshole!"

Jack was right: most of the memos were the origin story of Eliza Hilbert, back-and-forths between Irma and Devlin. They were always careful not to put anything damning in writing, but anyone who knew the subtext could tell what was happening. In February '42, Irma sent Devlin a list of names of women, mostly chorus girls on Pacific contracts. By March, the two had selected Eliza Sherman, and Irma had arranged for a dinner between the two of them to be crashed by paparazzi. By May, the two were married at the courthouse, and a column about their whirlwind romance had been planted in *Screenland* magazine. Immediately after the wedding, preproduction began on the Henry Hilbert biographical motion picture.

"But Fiona's article couldn't have been about Henry," I said. "No one would have published it."

"Maybe she wasn't taking the angle of Henry's…" Jack trailed off, mindful of the cab driver, although there was a partition between us. "If it was just about his marriage to Eliza, with the rest implied?"

"It's hardly worth killing over," I replied. "All Henry would have to do to disprove the article is stay married to her. Why go through the trouble? Especially when nothing here proves anything."

I flipped the page.

MEMO: IF to DF

6/7/42

Looking forward to lunch with you and June tomorrow. I know you have concerns about working with Kott and the rest, but we can minimize your interactions with them. June would really like you to come on board and so would Devlin, but we'll respect your wishes. Keep an open mind and let's all three discuss tomorrow.

"Who's DF?" I murmured. It was an initial we hadn't seen yet.

"Don Farris," said Jack immediately. "They wanted to cast Don Farris in the movie."

I remembered Don mentioning that to me: they'd wanted him for Henry's manager; he'd refused. It hadn't seemed like that big a deal—at least, not big enough for Fiona to be scribbling memos about it in her notebook.

Jack stared at it in silence for a long while, running his fingers over the words. "June," he said finally. "Why was Don getting lunch with June?"

"They've made a dozen pictures together," I said. "It makes sense they'd be friendly."

"Friendly, fine. I'm friendly with lots of people, but I'm not having lunches with them and my boss," Jack replied. "Just the three of us, tossing back cocktails and discussing my career? That's more than friendly. That's positively cozy."

"What are you implying?" I asked.

"It feels awful to even say it," said Jack. "But what if she was with

Don when she didn't answer the phone last night? There was that love note I found in Don's stuff, remember? It was signed J."

I let his accusation hang there. It made sense. Trying to stop an article from running didn't seem like enough of a reason to kill a friend. Getting rid of the woman who was married to the man you loved was far more plausible.

"But even if Fiona was out of the way, it's not like Don and June could get married," I mused. "It's against the law."

"Marriage. Who cares about marriage?" said Jack. "It's not 1915. They could still live together, have a life together."

It wasn't adding up to me. Fiona and Don weren't even sleeping in the same bedroom anymore. The only claim Fiona had on Don was the title of *wife*, and if that title wasn't available to June, what was the point of killing Fiona?

But on the other hand, who ever claimed that love made a person act rationally?

I flipped through the pages to see if there was more about Don and June that might persuade me one way or the other, but the rest of the memos returned to chronicling the disastrous production of the Hilbert movie. Henry was originally contracted to write ten new songs for the movie. That quickly got whittled down to six when it became apparent Henry was suffering from extreme writer's block. In March 1943, a ghostwriter was hired to write a few "Henry Hilbert" songs, but he failed to produce anything even close to satisfactory. You can't ghostwrite genius, I supposed. Shortly thereafter, Devlin attempted to buy the rights to Henry's older songs from MGM, but no dice. It was cheaper to keep the production stalled in limbo and pray Henry remembered how to put together a chord progression than fork over what MGM wanted for Henry's hits from the twenties. In April of 1943, Irma reported to Devlin that she'd put the fear of God into Henry, who insisted he would get Vic to help him. That was the end of the notes.

"There's not much here we didn't know already," I said. "The Hilbert movie is a disaster. Henry's marriage is a sham. Why did she bother to write all this down?"

"A total dead end for us," agreed Jack. "Other than the Don and June stuff."

"We can't let the other three know that this was a bust," I said. "As far as they're concerned, we haven't gotten a good look at the notebook yet, all right? It's filled with secret memos Fiona copied down, and they could say anything."

Jack nodded. We were close to the studio now, just a few blocks away. "I can't believe *two* of my friends have slept with Don Farris," he muttered.

"We don't know that yet," I said. "Don't jump to conclusions."

"I don't jump to anything," said Jack. "I get blackout drunk and then stumble backward into conclusions, knocking them over so they shatter into a million pieces."

"I'm not sure that's better," I said.

When we reached Stage 13, things were moving with an urgency I didn't know the crew of the Henry Hilbert movie were capable of. Apparently, the night before, while the rest of us had been sitting around the Hollywood police station or taking off our pants inside Musso & Frank's, Henry had sat down at his piano and plucked out a song called "For Sale by Owner." The lyrics weren't great ("if you can excuse / a heart that's gently used / you'll find mine's for sale by owner"), but the tune was all right, and everyone seemed so relieved to have something important to shoot, no one was being too critical. The song was for Elaine Larson, the blond tap-dancing star playing Eliza—who, of course, in this version of the story, had known Henry since '25 and was just as much in the group as June or Jack, even though the real Eliza would have been four years old at the time. If Henry had noticed any irony in writing a song about how love could be bought for the studio-mandated woman paid to play his studio-mandated wife, he didn't seem to care.

I was immediately banished to my office to write some kind of scene to lead into the number, my only directives being that it had to take place in the cabaret because there was no time to build a new set, and it had to have Henry at the piano because there was no time to record the song with a full orchestra. Terry told me, "I don't care what the characters say, as long as it technically qualifies as words." Who said making movies couldn't be creatively fulfilling?

I downed five or six pills (the tolerance had built up quickly, and I now needed nearly a palmful to achieve the same focused intensity that had spat out *Don't Count Your Coconuts*) and typed up something where Henry's friends think he's mad for falling for this silly chorus girl. But after Eliza sings his genius new song, the brilliance of the music convinces them otherwise, or something. The ending was a little unclear, but I figured Jack would at least get a kick out of saying, "Henry, you fall for a different chorus girl every week, and it never works out. Maybe you should try something different." I sent the pages off with a boy to get copied and distributed and headed back to set.

As soon I entered the soundstage, Terry yanked my arm, and I was dragged into a huddle with the rest of the Ambassador's Club. June, Jack, and Vic were all standing in a semicircle silently—June preening at her hair, Jack picking at the lint on his pants, and Vic with his arms folded. They were all in costume as their younger selves again, only this time it had the effect of making them all seem not quite real, like a painting that failed to capture its subject.

"All right, we're all here now," began Terry. "I think we can all agree that last night at the police station, things got out of hand. Tensions were high, and a lot of things were said. I don't want to litigate whether any of it was justified. I just hope we can all put it aside for today and focus on the work we finally have to do. Is that fair?"

"Yes," said June immediately. "Let's all move on and forget about everything."

"Hold on," said Vic. "We all but accused one another of the murder of our good friend last night. I don't know that Henry's movie is worth clearing that slate."

"We don't have to clear it," said Terry, at the same time June remarked, "No one really believes one of us killed her."

"I'm not sure that's true," countered Vic.

"You know, for what it's worth, the questions the cops were asking me? I don't think they think it was one of us," said Jack suddenly. "They were asking me all about Don."

Our eyes locked. I tried to suss out what he was doing, but he gave me a look that only said to go with it. "They asked me a few questions about Don, too," I offered.

"Don? They didn't ask me anything about Don," said Terry. "They only wanted to know about how much we despise each other."

"Same here," said Vic. "I told them I'd strangle each one of you if I could. What did they ask you, June?"

June looked as if she weren't sure how to answer. "I'm sure they asked me the same stuff as everyone else," she sputtered out finally. "I don't remember exactly what."

"It does make some sense," I said, not sure how much I believed what I was saying. "The things we got from Fiona's office were stolen from my apartment. They could have called Don; he could have guessed—he could have found my address from the studio files since they're the ones who put me up—"

"Fiona's things were stolen?" said Terry. "Well, shit."

"In fairness, the robbers might have wanted to take anything else, only Annie doesn't own anything else," said Vic.

"They didn't get all of it," said Jack. "One of Fiona's notebooks was in Annie's purse."

"Where is it? Does it say anything?" asked June.

"We don't have time right now," snapped Terry before softening a little. "Sorry. We'll look at it tomorrow night at the Club."

"Why not tonight?" asked June.

"It's Canteen night," Terry said.

"And I'm performing tonight," said Jack.

We all looked at him. "You are?" asked Vic. "I didn't know that."

"Sure am," said Jack. "And Annie is too. One of the sketches needs a girl, so she's going to do it with me."

This sounded like the last thing in the world I wanted to do, but Jack gave me a sly little wink, so I forced myself to nod.

"Unbelievable," said Vic, turning to me. "I asked you point-blank if you were sleeping with him, and you lied to my face! I'm furious. Being a degenerate liar is my thing."

June had a sudden case of the giggles and was shaking her head. "Oh, Annie. Tell me you just slept with him and didn't promise to read his book."

"We don't have time for this," said Terry, although she was grinning too.

"One more?" asked Vic. "It's good."

"Sure," relented Terry.

"Tell me, Annie," said Vic. "Does Jack need a whole team of writers to help him do a half hour of stand-up in bed, too?"

"Jesus, all right," said Terry. "I hope this means we have successfully put last night behind us. Remember that vow to move forward with a positive attitude when I deliver this next bit of news: Vic, we need you to sub for Henry's hands in the close-ups on the piano today."

Any lightness dropped immediately from Vic's demeanor. "No," he said emphatically. "Absolutely not. He's not taking credit for my hands."

"He's got a cut on his right palm," Terry explained.

"That's not my problem."

As if he sensed we were talking about him, Henry appeared, brandishing a bandaged hand. "I was putting in some bushes by my retaining wall," he explained. "Turns out, roses have thorns. Who knew?"

"Gee, someone oughta write something pointing out that dichotomy," said Jack.

"It's not serious," said Henry.

"Darn," said June.

"But it's unsightly, and we can't wait for it to heal before getting the shot," said Terry. "Be a team player, Vic."

"I'm a soloist. It's not my job to be a team player."

I slipped away as they continued to fight it out, heading for the coffee cart on the Cowboy Street. To my relief, I was only a few steps out of the soundstage when Jack caught up to me. "We're performing a sketch tonight at the Hollywood Canteen?" I asked.

"It's perfect," he explained. "You can see everyone from there. We can have eyes on all three of them at once. We'll make sure everyone knows you're leaving your purse in the booth instead of at coat check, and if any of them make a move while we're onstage, we'll see it." He grinned, obviously pleased with himself. "Pretty clever, huh?"

"Are you even on the schedule?" I asked.

"No, but Irma's been on me to perform since the place opened. She'll call the Canteen managers and tell them to give me fifteen minutes. I'll do some jokes, bring you out to do a sketch, we banter with the boys a bit, and we're done."

I considered this. It would be risky for whoever wanted the notebook to make a go for it while we might be able to see them, but it would be even riskier to leave possibly incriminating evidence in my hands. As long as they thought we were completely engrossed in the performance and didn't suspect a trap, it could work. And if it failed—well, the stakes were low. The only real risk to giving it a shot would be the public humiliation of my attempting to act. "All right," I said. "We'll try it. But we have to be careful. June's spying for the police."

He stopped in his tracks. "What? How do you know?"

"Because they asked me to spy on all of you. It didn't occur to me until just now, but of course after I said no, they asked someone else. June must have said yes. Did you hear how cagey she got when we asked what she talked about with Kiblowski and Cooper? That's because they spent their whole interrogation telling her how to spy on us."

"That means she's guilty," said Jack. I opened my mouth to protest, but he interrupted. "I know, I know. Jumping to conclusions. But—"

"We'll know soon enough," I said.

We walked for a moment in silence. "The cops didn't ask me to spy for them," he said finally.

"How would you have reacted, to being asked to collaborate with the Los Angeles police?"

He grinned. "Good point. Anyway, can you do me a favor real quick?"

"What?"

"Let me kiss you."

I expected him to be real showy about it, to lean me over his arm dramatically and give me an exaggerated smooch, as much for the amusement of the extras waiting to be called to set as it was for me. That wasn't what he did. He took both my hands in his and leaned in to give me a soft, sweet kiss that made my whole body buzz. I thought only one thing: *Oh no.*

His lips pulled away, but he let his forehead rest on mine for a moment, our hands still intertwined. "Actually, there is one more favor you could do for me," he murmured.

"Name it," I said.

"Can you write a sketch for us to perform tonight at the Hollywood Canteen?"

SIXTEEN

❖

The Canteen managers told Jack he could close out the evening, telling us we could go on at eleven thirty as long as we wrapped it up within twenty minutes, to give the band time to play a final couple of songs and spit everyone back out on Cahuenga by midnight.

At first I was relieved to have such a late spot. Jack had been on set all day shooting the "For Sale by Owner" number, so we hadn't had a moment to rehearse the terrible sketch I'd banged out in my office. The Canteen opened at seven, so we'd have plenty of time before we went on. When Jack didn't even wait until we'd reached the Canteen, however, to crack a flask in the back seat of the cab we were sharing from the studio—I started to worry. We had four and a half hours to rehearse, but it was also four and a half hours for Jack to drink.

"Hey, maybe we should both lay off," I said when he offered the flask to me. "We want to stay sharp."

"This is how I stay sharp" was his only answer. Then something out the window caught his eye. "Holy sh—look."

I followed his gaze to see June and Don, walking north together on Vine Street. The two were deep in conversation—June talking animatedly, Don with his brow furrowed in thought and his hands buried in his pockets. "They're walking to the Canteen together!" said Jack, whispering as if they might be able to hear us. "Everyone from Pacific is going to the Canteen tonight, and she chose to walk with Don?"

I had to admit, it was unusual. "Maybe they happened to be leaving at the same time and ran into each other on the street."

"I know what we'll do," Jack said, after taking another slug from the flask. "Let's wait for them outside the Canteen and confront them."

"*Confront* them?"

"I mean—talk to them. You know. Ask some questions."

We didn't have to wait long. Traffic snaked so slowly up Vine Street that by car, we only arrived at the Canteen a few minutes before June and Don did on foot. I watched June carefully as they rounded the corner, looking for any sign that she felt guilty for being caught. Nothing.

"Look who it is," Jack said as the two approached us. I tried to shoot him a look to keep it down. With the Canteen about to open, there were more than a few onlookers milling about, hoping to catch a glimpse of their favorite stars. The last thing we needed was an item in the gossip columns that Jack Kott had accosted a grieving widower in an alley. "Don, you don't normally show up to Pacific nights. What gives?"

"Normally, I didn't like putting my wife in the position of having to choose between spending time with me or her friends, who hate me," answered Don.

"I don't hate you," said Jack. "I don't think about you at all, most of the time. I merely dislike you when I'm reminded of your existence, like when a beet turns up in a sandwich."

"Don't be an asshole," June said.

Don only smiled. "How's the radio treating you these days, Jack?"

"See, this is why we don't like you. I tell you to your face, openly, that I dislike you, and all I get back is polite conversation. Be a man, Don. Fight back."

"You don't want that," Don replied. "Unlike you, I actually served in the military."

"There you go!" said Jack. "You could have worded it a little better. 'I was actually fit to serve'—that's nice 'cause then you also get a little jab in there about how I'm crazy."

"Ignore him. He's drunk," said June.

"Not yet," Jack replied.

"I'm going in to start my shift," said Don. "Thanks for the comedy advice, Jack. Always a pleasure."

"Hold on," said Jack. "It was nice of you to walk June over from the studio. Did you two have a nice talk?"

Don only tipped his cap and headed inside. Jack made a sour face, and June punched him in the arm. "What is wrong with you? The man's wife just died." Before either of us could respond, she had turned on her heel to follow Don through the volunteer door.

Jack sucked on his teeth as he watched her go. "I need a drink," he declared. "There's a bar two blocks north. Let's go."

"We have to rehearse," I said.

"One drink. We'll rehearse after. We have four hours."

I didn't know what to say. He'd been performing his entire life; surely he knew how much he could drink before a show and still go on. Who was I to stop him? "I'll stay here," I said. "I'm not thirsty."

"I'll be back soon," he said. "I won't be long."

He pulled me into one more kiss, and then he was gone.

I spent an hour reading over my lines in the unfinished room upstairs, and when I couldn't take it anymore I went down to the kitchen to make sandwiches. I couldn't go out on the floor without leaving my bag unattended somewhere, so kitchen duty seemed like the next-best option to occupy my hands and keep me from losing my mind with nerves. I was starting to get the feeling that Jack's and my performance would end the evening on an incredibly sour note.

Around ten o'clock, with Jack nowhere in sight, Bette approached me.

"Jack said you were part of his act tonight," she said. "Do you know where he is?"

"He had to run an errand," I replied.

I could tell from her raised eyebrow she knew exactly what kind of errand I was talking about, but she said nothing.

He'll be here, I told myself. Jack was known for the drinking, for the Communism, for the scandalous things he said on the radio every now and then, but he'd never had a reputation for being irresponsible. He'd never been a no-show on set or missed a broadcast, as far as I could recall. He was a loose cannon, but he could still reliably fire cannonballs.

At eleven, I headed for the sound booth, which was also the de facto green room, given the Canteen's limited space. Soon Terry, June, and Vic joined me, there for some strange preshow bonding that no one was quite sure we were friendly enough at the moment to be doing but all felt compelled to do nonetheless. I kept glancing at the clock on the wall, and Vic seemed to read my mind. "He'll be here," he said.

Sure enough, with fifteen minutes to spare, Jack waltzed through the stage door. I was relieved to see he didn't seem too drunk—he could walk, at least, which was a start. His hair was a bit disheveled, and his tie had become loose around the neck, but he was in one piece and knew where he was, so I breathed a sigh of relief. He winked at me as I handed him his copy of the script. "Told you I'd be back," he said.

"You also said you'd be gone an hour and have one drink," I replied. "We haven't rehearsed."

"I did have one drink. I didn't specify the size. And I never rehearse. Keeps the material fresh." He looked around at June, Terry, and Vic. "You should go get seats. You're going to want the best view in the house for the acting debut of Miss Annie Laurence."

"Opens her legs one time, and next she's debuting as an actress," muttered Vic.

"If that's a lead-in to a comment about me, you can shove it," June said.

"It wasn't going to be, but give me a minute. I can get there."

"Do you think my purse will be safe in the booth?" I asked Jack, maybe a little too loud. My debut as an actress was already off to an auspicious start. "The coat check girl was on a break."

"I can hold on to it, if you want," said June.

"June, you don't want to be responsible for her enormous purse," said Jack instantly, ushering the three of them out. "It'll be fine in the booth."

"Her purse really is enormous," I heard June mutter as they walked out to the street. "It's why I assumed she was a lesbian."

"Me too!" cried Vic.

Jack shut the door behind them and grinned at me. "Ready?" he asked.

The bandleader introduced Jack, and I had about five minutes alone in the sound booth to get my bearings. I cracked the door an inch to get a peek at the crowd. Vic and Terry were along the wall, all the way over by the snack bar. If either one of them were after my purse, they would have to go through the kitchen and out the volunteer entrance into the alley to get it. If they made a move, we'd be able to see it. I assumed June would be near the two of them and spent a moment scanning the crowd but didn't see her.

Jack had moved from his jokes into the setup of the sketch. "You know, I've always considered myself a serious writer," he began. That alone got enough of a laugh that I momentarily felt bad for making him say it. "This weekend, I'm actually going to dinner with some of my fellow serious writers. Sinclair Lewis, John Steinbeck, even Willa Cather's riding in. So to help me prepare, I've asked my dear friend Miss Annie Laurence to give me some notes. Annie?"

I took one last deep gulp of air and walked onstage.

The lights were surprisingly bright out there—nowhere near as blinding as a Broadway stage, but it still took my eyes a minute to adjust. There was only one mic, in the middle of the stage, so I made my way next to Jack. The seconds it took me to cross felt like days with all those eyes on me. The front row, sitting on the floor, were so close any one of the servicemen could have reached out and grabbed my ankles if he wanted to. Even this late in the evening, they were packed in like sardines and stretching back all the way to the door.

"Hi, Jack," I said, trying to keep the paper script I held in my hand still.

"Annie, you're a writer," said Jack. "What have you written?"

"I've had two plays on Broadway, and I'm working on a movie," I answered.

"A movie—that's swell," Jack said. "I like movies. They're like plays with no ambition."

Even though he'd spent the last four hours drinking, he wasn't reading from his script at all, just casually talking with his hands in his pockets as if this were the most average day in the world. As the boys laughed at the joke, Jack's eyes flickered toward the front entrance of the Canteen. I followed his gaze and saw what he saw: June was right by the door, and next to her? Don Farris.

"What have you written, Jack?" I asked, my voice cracking slightly.

"Thanks for asking," he improvised, and the genuine gratitude with which he said it—clearly making fun of how I was glued to a piece of paper to even recite my own résumé—got another laugh. "You know how everyone answers the telephone a little bit differently?

For example, I say, 'Kott residence'; my sister says, 'You've reached the Kotts'; and my mother says, 'Jack, stop calling. I'm not sending more money.'"

With my body angled toward the mic, Terry and Vic were right in my line of sight, but I had to look out a bit to see June. I adjusted my position to keep her in my sight line. "What about it?"

"Well, I write those."

"You write telephone greetings?"

"It's a very exciting market," said Jack. "Think about it. Books have been around for hundreds of years. If you want to write a book, there's a good chance some other fellow's written it already. But the telephone's only been around a few decades, which means there's lots more room for innovation. You ever hear someone answer the phone and say, 'Broom closet, this is the sweeper speaking'?"

"I haven't," I said.

"There you go. That'll be fifty dollars."

"Fifty dollars!" I exclaimed. Out of the corner of my eye, I saw Don lean in and whisper something to June. She nodded.

"Originality ain't cheap," Jack said. Our eyes locked—he had seen it too. "That's what I tell NBC. They have to pay me double or else I just repeat Fred Allen's show."

June and Don were on the move, heading for the front door of the Canteen. My heart started to pound. This was it—this was really it. They could be going for my purse.

To be honest, I was disappointed. To have it all—the murder, the threats—come down to a fit of jealousy over a man? I thought June had been better than that.

I tried to keep my cool, remind myself it wasn't over just yet. We had to act normally until we could get offstage and check my bag. Not until then would we know for sure what June and Don had done. "But, Jack," I began, hoping neither of them would notice that the hand holding my script had begun shaking like a leaf. "This is a dinner full of serious writers. You can't show up with—"

"Hold on, I have to stop you," said Jack. I looked up from the script, but he wasn't looking at me, instead gazing out into the crowd. At first I thought he was improvising, riffing on the sketch. Then he leaned into the mic. "June Lee, where are you going?"

"Jack," I hissed.

He ignored me. Out in the crowd, June turned around, confused. She and Don had nearly reached the door. "Yeah, I'm talking to you," Jack went on. "Why are you leaving early, in the middle of my show? With your dead friend's husband?"

The eyes of the several hundred servicemen immediately snapped to the back of the Canteen. A few of the others who had been standing along the front wall ducked away from Don and June, as if to say they weren't part of this. June's cheeks flushed. "What is your problem, Kott?" shouted Don.

"What's my problem?" Jack shot back. I grabbed his arm, and he immediately shook me away, so violently I stumbled back a few steps. "You killed her. The two of you did. That's my problem!"

Pandemonium is the only word I can find to describe what happened next. Half the crowd started running for June and Don, egged on by Jack shouting into the microphone not to let them leave. The rest of the crowd could only fall over themselves as they tried to get out of the way. A dozen or so volunteers swarmed the stage, trying to pull the microphone away from Jack. Out of nowhere, Terry grabbed Jack and yanked him back into the sound booth; I tried to follow through the swarm of band members who were coming back onstage to see what all the fuss was.

When I finally made it out the back entrance and onto the street, Jack was hysterical, hardly caring that dozens of strangers had assembled to watch him ranting in the street. Terry was doing her best to calm him down, but it was in vain. "They killed her, Ter, I know they

did. They're having an affair, and she got in the way. I know they did,
I know it. I know what I saw—"

A moment later, Don Farris rounded the corner with murder in his
eyes and knocked Jack square in the jaw.

Jack stumbled backward, hitting the ground as the crowd gasped. A
moment later he was back on his feet, lunging for Don, who grabbed
him by the lapel and sent him flying back once again. Terry leapt
between them, urging Don to stop in a calm but commanding voice,
and though his hands were still clenched in tight angry fists, he seemed
to listen. June arrived next, grabbing Jack as he attempted unsteadily to
rise to his feet a second time. "I'm not sleeping with him!" she shouted
in Jack's face, mascara pouring down her cheeks. "I just wanted a friend
who doesn't call me a slut all the time!"

I watched it all unfold in horror. How had this happened? In forty-
eight hours, the club had gone from laughing on Henry's stolen couch
to literally brawling in the street.

Vic appeared at my side and wordlessly handed me a cigarette. "I
tried to warn you," he said after I took it and lit it off the one in his
hands. "The only thing Jack Kott knows how to do is self-destruct."

"What do we do?" I said.

"Join the fray, if you want, or go home," he said with a shrug. "Not
my problem to care what any of you do anymore. Shame, really. If a
man says something clever but he doesn't have a club to repeat it to
later, did he even say it all?"

With that, he stalked off into the night. I was about to follow him
when I remembered something.

I knew as soon as I ran back to the booth what I'd find. The purse
was still there, at least. I'd have money to take a cab home or somewhere—on top of all this, my apartment still had a hole instead of a
front window. But I was right. When I reached my hand into the bag,
the camera was there, my keys were there, the crumpled-up piece of

paper that said I was in love with the Cooks was there…but Fiona's notebook was gone.

It was nearly one in the morning by the time I made my way back home. My plan had been, once again, to grab a few of my things and head for the closest hotel. But by the time I reached my apartment, I was too exhausted to do anything but collapse on the couch.

I was done with Los Angeles. I'd tried to start my life over with a move, tried to give it some meaning by solving Fiona's death, even tried to have an affair again, and look where it all had landed me. The message was clear: I was a failure in New York and a failure out here. It was time to pack in my dreams and give up. I'd finish out my contract with Pacific and be on the next train out. I'd go back to Westchester and be a shop girl, and once I was old and had inherited the house and lived there alone, the neighbors would develop all sorts of interesting gossip about me. "You know Miss Laurence, up on Church Street? She once had an affair with Adam and Beverly Cook." "The movie stars? With crazy old Annie Laurence? I doubt it."

I poured the last of the vodka into a mug and put on Side 1 of the Hilbert concerto again. I was asleep before either was finished.

The next thing I knew, someone was pounding at my front door.

I'd been having an uneasy dream I'd had a few times before, about showing up to the first day of rehearsals for a play only to find that I'd forgotten to write it. The knocking grew louder and louder, until I shouted, "Could somebody get that?" and woke myself up.

The tarp was making all the morning light that streamed into the apartment a moody shade of blue. I hoisted myself off the couch and made my way to the door.

Terry was there, dressed for work in a smart black suit and looking anxious. At first I thought she was here to round me up for not showing up to work on time, but surely after the events of last night, I would get a pass. "Jack's not here, is he?" she asked.

"Of course not," I said. "Why? Is he missing?"

"The cops took both him and Don to the station last night, but I don't know what they did with him after that. I just wanted to make sure you were alone. Can I come in?"

I stood aside, and she walked in, immediately settling on my couch. I lingered there in the middle of the room, not sure how to take this or even a hundred percent certain I wasn't still dreaming. "I don't see any way the club comes back after last night," she said.

"I'm sorry," I replied.

"What are you apologizing for? Not your fault," she said.

It was, in a way. I could have stopped Jack from going off to drink. I could have done more to discourage his paranoia over June and Don. Hell, the only reason we were on that stage was because of a plan he saw in a play I wrote. I sank into the couch next to Terry. It was only just now occurring to me that when Adam catches Bev going for the money in the play, it's merely a distraction that allows the real murderer to escape. How come both of us had forgotten that? "It feels as if everything is my fault," I said. "Fiona…everything. You were all so happy before I showed up."

Terry guffawed. "Don't think so highly of yourself. We were plenty unhappy. Maybe you were the catalyst for some things, but that club has been long overdue for someone to get punched in the kisser. I'm glad it's dissolving, quite frankly. I'm done keeping secrets for those louses. I came here to tell you something. Something I've wanted to say since the night Fiona died. I felt as if I had to keep quiet because we were all protecting each other. I told myself it wasn't my secret to tell, that he must have reasons for not sharing it with the group. But after last night? What's left to protect anymore?"

"'He'?" I said. "You mean Jack? What else did he do?"

She shook her head. "Not Jack. Victor."

SEVENTEEN

‒‹‹‹◆›››‒

I was going to need a cigarette for this. I went to my purse and fished one out, offering one to Terry, who declined.

"I heard what Fiona and Vic were arguing about the night Fiona died," Terry continued. "I pretended I hadn't because I didn't want to get Vic in trouble. I thought perhaps there was some context I was missing or that he was waiting for the right time to bring it up. But I'm done giving any of them the benefit of the doubt. The two of them were arguing about a column Fiona was working on."

My heart sank into my stomach. "Oh no."

Terry nodded. "I didn't catch all the details. I wasn't thinking too much of it in the moment. We all fight all the time, about all sorts of things. I assumed Fiona had made another quip about him and Henry in her latest column. But afterward, after Fiona was dead, I thought about it some more, and I'm certain it was more than that. Vic was telling her not to publish something, and Fiona was insisting that she had to. And he was upset. Furious. Normally, he's loud, you know—dramatic. But that night, he was very quiet. All that energy, boiled down—it was frightening. Fiona was frightened. I was frightened too."

"That's why he came to my apartment," I said. "After we stole Fiona's things. The article was about him. He had to get that stuff before we could see. He had someone throw that brick so they could get in— Henry, no doubt—"

"Maybe," said Terry. "Maybe not."

"Who else could it have been?" I said. The brick was still in the middle of my floor. I thought the police might have taken it for evidence, but apparently my case was not one they were too eager to solve.

"Henry has Vic wrapped around his finger," said Terry. "I'm not sure it goes the other way around. Besides, it wasn't the two of them alone. They were both onstage when Fiona died. Look, I don't know anything for sure. All I'm saying is there was a reason why I asked if Jack was here before I came in."

Suddenly, I felt like the world's biggest fool. Jack had told me himself he'd have helped Victor kill someone. Jack had been so insistent to team up with me, so eager to get us all looking toward June and Don. Had Jack even wanted to sleep with me, or was that part of the trick too?

"But what secret would Vic want to keep that Fiona would want to publish?" I asked.

"I don't know," said Terry. "And I don't want to know. Vic might be a murderer, but he's also working on a Henry Hilbert picture that Pacific has already sank three mil into. If he gets arrested, we'll have to reshoot all his scenes. And to be clear, I don't think you should be doing anything with this either. I'm only telling you because if you're going to get more involved with Jack, you deserve to know."

"Last night talked me out of getting more involved with Jack— believe me," I said.

"Good," said Terry. "Because Jack looks up to Vic like a dog to its owner. He follows him around, tells him everything. When push comes to shove, Jack's not choosing you."

"That's how the club works, isn't it?" I said. "'Til death or a better offer comes along? It's funny, I was starting to think I was part of the better offer, but turns out I'm…death."

"You do write about murder," said Terry. "Oh, speaking of, Henry's so behind on songs I got permission from Devlin to shoot the new concerto he's debuting at the Hollywood Bowl and put in a trimmed-down version of that. So I need some scenes from you that work that into the picture."

"I don't think I should work on this picture anymore," I said. "Two of the stars may have tried to kill me."

Terry shrugged. "Welcome to Hollywood."

Around here is where the story gets hazy. When I think back on the days after the dissolution of the Ambassador's Club, they have a dreamy quality. A softness, a one-dimensionality, like I was watching a film happening around me instead of experiencing it for myself. Several times those weeks, I reached out to touch something just because I was certain I wouldn't be able to, that nothing around me was real. The solidity of objects surprised me each time.

What I did with Terry's information, just as she'd suggested, was nothing. Saturday morning, the first thing I did when I arrived on the lot was not hatch some scheme to steal Victor's keys and break into his house and search it for Fiona's missing office stuff. I thought about it and then called Irma instead and asked for a refill of both the uppers and the downers. I started quadrupling both the recommended doses, which became quite effective for making myself a script-writing machine when the sun was up and practically comatose when it was down. If that's what this town wanted from me—to be a product— maybe it was easier to just lean in until I could escape. Products didn't have feelings, after all.

There was no better time for me to turn into a scene-generating robot, too, because Henry started writing songs at a pace that was reminiscent of…well, of Henry but fifteen years earlier. Within a few days, we had four new Hilbert tunes that, along with the excerpt of the concerto, would provide enough songs to string together something resembling a musical motion picture. All the new songs were sad, which ticked off Elaine Larson ("If you can't tap dance to any of them, what am I doing here?"), but each one was hauntingly beautiful— forlorn songs about love slipping through your fingertips. One song, "The Coldest Day in Spring," I loved so much I made a plea to Terry that it should be the title of the movie. She refused to even entertain the argument. "No," she said plainly, cutting off my speech with a confused expression. I couldn't tell if she was confused as to why I thought it should be the title or confused as to why I cared so much. "We're not calling it something that makes people think of pneumonia. It's called *Hat Full of Genius*."

I tried not to make a face. "Really? Because as the writer—"

"You're not the writer," she snapped. "You're the sixth person to write for this movie and the fifth not to get credit for it. Stop trying to make this art. It's not art anymore. It's now a Hail Mary to try and recoup some of the money we lost back when it *was* art."

If that disappointed me at all, it only lasted until I returned to my office and scarfed down three more pills. Suddenly, I could write any movie with any title.

In a way, the relentless pace of production was good for the five of us. It gave us all enough to do that it was less noticeable that no one was speaking to each other. From what I could surmise, June was still understandably furious at Jack, Jack thought June was wildly over-reacting, Victor seemed put out that the central drama of the group was no longer about his doomed affair with Henry, and Terry wanted nothing to do with any one of them. Days, maybe weeks went by with-out a word from anyone that wasn't related to where the best place for them to stand in a shot would be. I wish I thought about trying to make it better, trying to apologize to June for letting Jack get so drunk or something, but I didn't. I was in a haze, the days melting into one another, the nights wiped completely from my memory.

So when I say it was next Friday morning that Terry sent me to Calabasas, I'm only about fifty percent certain of that. It could have been Thursday, or Saturday. For all I remember, it could have been a Monday in December, but I have enough evidence of other events to conclude it was most likely Friday, August 13.

It began with the scene I'd written to lead into the Hollywood Bowl performance. I'd written the scene about a dozen times, actually, and Terry didn't like any version of it. According to her, my scenes didn't match the mood of the concerto they would be debuting. This proved difficult for me to fix, because I had never heard the concerto. Almost no one had heard it. Terry had listened to snippets before she pitched the idea to Devlin, but she was horrible at trying to describe it to me, using phrases like "tonally distressing" and "as if Stalin fucked Cole Porter," which I didn't find particularly useful. Finally, on probably Friday morning, exasperated with my latest unsatisfying take, she told me I should have one of Pacific's drivers take me up to Calabasas, where Victor and Henry were currently working on scoring the thing.

So that's exactly what I did.

The lawn was still in a state when I arrived, only this time half a dozen men were working on it, stacking bricks and hauling away dirt. I could hear a cacophony of piano music coming from inside the house as I approached the front door and knocked. There was no response, only more music, a flurry of sound that was, now that I was hearing it, accurately described by the phrase "tonally distressing." I knocked again, as loudly as I could this time, but received no response.

One of the landscapers took pity on me. "Mrs. Hilbert's out," he said. "If you need Mr. Hilbert, just go in, or you'll be standing out here forever."

I thanked him and opened the door.

The house inside was bland and unadorned, like they were still in the process of moving in. The foyer was so empty that my heels echoed on the tile floor. I followed the sound of the music down a hallway to my left. Two pianos, I could hear more clearly now, trading some discordant melody back and forth. Even from these tiny snippets of song, I could tell it was so much sharper, so much edgier than anything of Henry's I'd ever heard before, which excited me. I hadn't felt excited in days and found it to be a pleasant experience. The Hollywood Bowl was to be the final scene in the movie, and I already had a much clearer sense of what Terry was talking about. She didn't need a scene about how Henry Hilbert was still writing music; she needed a scene about how Henry was still a genius, still on the cutting edge of what music could be—still reinventing everything in '43 just as his *Sonata for the Millworker* had done in '24. Two decades of genius. A real hat full.

The music stopped abruptly just as I was about to round the corner, and for some reason I stopped, too, like a kid playing musical chairs. "That's lovely, that bit," I heard Henry murmur.

I decided not to make myself known yet, to eavesdrop on their conversation for a little longer and see if they might say something I could put in the scene. "It's all right," countered Victor. "Play me the strings again."

Henry started up on the piano, playing a melody that instantly displeased Victor. "Too fussy!" he shouted. "It's too la-di-da. You and the Philadelphia Orchestra, always out to make me sound like *Swan Lake*."

"You need some brass; that'll harden it," Henry said, offering some variation on the melody, which Victor rejected.

"No brass yet," replied Victor.

"You're not using enough brass. You're going to upset the whole section. Make them sit there all night to play a few notes at the begin-ning? They'll never work with us again."

"I didn't write the thing to woo trumpet players," muttered Victor. "You have any more coffee?"

He was already walking out of the room when he said it, which meant he was suddenly face-to-face with me. "Hi," I said.

"When did you get here?" he asked, an unlit cigarette dangling out of his mouth, the lighter practically forgotten in his hand.

"Just now," I replied.

"Eliza?" Henry called from inside the room, panic in his voice.

"Calm down, it's just Annie," said Victor. "What are you doing creeping around Calabasas?"

"I—Terry sent me up here to listen to the concerto," I replied. "Did you…? Did you write that?"

"No," said Victor.

"It was really good."

He took the cigarette out of his mouth and stuck it behind his ear. "Henry, she says it's good."

"But you didn't write it?" I asked. "Because I thought I heard you say—"

"I didn't say I wrote it," he replied, so confidently that for a moment I was convinced I must have heard wrong. "Henry wrote it."

Maybe sensing trouble, Henry had joined us in the hallway. "Vic's helping with the orchestrations," he said. "Which is normal. A lot of composers lack the ability to orchestrate. Different skill set."

"Oh," I said.

"Can I get you some coffee?" Henry asked with a smile.

I accepted and was ushered into the music room. The room was large—you could have fit a third piano in there—with floor-to-ceiling windows looking out on the backyard and miles of undeveloped farm-land beyond. Adorning the walls were framed posters from Henry's various shows, almost all of which I had seen in my New York days: *Strictly Confidential, The Ingenue, The Guest of Honor.* I walked the perimeter of the room, gazing up to admire each one as Henry went to retrieve the coffees ("Both the wife and the maid are out at the moment; I hope I can find it!"). Victor settled uneasily at the piano and began playing that same tonally distressing melody.

I could practically smell the awkwardness in the air, like I'd caught them in the act instead of orchestrating a concerto. I decided to cover this uncomfortable sensation with talking. "Terry thought the scene I wrote leading into the concerto wasn't working, so she sent me up here to listen to it for inspiration. And now that I've heard a little bit of it, I can see what she means. It's not really like anything I've heard. Very modern."

"Henry's a very modern composer," said Victor.

He was playing without any sheet music in front of him, I noticed. "How do you memorize all those notes?" I asked. It was such an obnoxious question that I was annoyed at myself for even asking it.

"I memorize them," he replied.

Henry returned with a tray of three coffees, placing it down on the piano. He handed me one, and I noticed the cut on his hand. "That still hasn't healed?" I asked.

He laughed and shook his wrist. "Not quite, no. It was deep."

"You said you got it from a rosebush?"

"Yes, that's right." He smiled and sipped his coffee.

"I didn't see any rosebushes out front, though," I said.

Henry tilted his head. "We decided they were too busy out front and moved them round to the side," he said.

"Annie, if you don't mind, we have to work," Victor interjected. "And if you get Henry started on his landscaping, we'll never get through it all."

"Sure, I'll get out of your way," I said, putting the coffee back on the tray. I was suddenly extremely hesitant to drink any liquids served to me by the two of them. "Thanks for all your help."

I practically bolted from the house and back to the car, where the driver seemed surprised to see me so quickly. "Back to Pacific?" he asked.

"Yes, thanks," I replied.

As we were driving away, I took one more glance back at the workers on the front lawn. The gray bricks they were laying for Henry Hilbert's suburban-fantasy retaining wall were the exact same shade as the one that had sailed through my living room window.

My mind was twisting as much as the car was on windy Mulholland as we made our way back to Hollywood. The memo in Fiona's notebook—what had it said? Henry was getting desperate with the songwriting, but Victor would help? What exactly did *help* mean? What if it was far more than providing the odd second opinion or musical variation?

What if the reason Henry Hilbert had been having trouble writing songs lately was because Henry Hilbert didn't write his own songs?

Now that was a secret someone might kill for.

I remembered Jack, stumbling backward into conclusions, and tried to slow down. What exactly had I heard? *I didn't write the thing to woo trumpet players.* It had been said so casually, and had gone unchallenged by Henry, that it sounded true. Henry said Victor was helping with the orchestrations. But *the thing* wasn't orchestrations. *The thing* wasn't a bar, a measure, or even a movement. *The thing* was the concerto that would debut at the Bowl in a week, under the name of Henry Hilbert.

But the deception had to go back further than that. The two of them hadn't even planned to debut this piece of music until Fiona's memorial service, so the concerto alone couldn't have been the reason

Fiona was dead. It had to have been going on longer, and—if I was right and this was the secret Fiona was planning to reveal—it had to be extensive.

I thought about Side 1 of the first Hilbert concerto, still resting on my record player. What had Victor said? It had solidified Henry's reputation, not just as a popular songwriter but as a serious composer. What if it was all a fraud? What if the Henry Hilbert the world thought it knew had never existed—he was just a handsome man in a nice suit?

Terry seemed surprised to see me back on the soundstage so quickly. "Did you hear everything you needed?"

I told her that I had indeed heard quite enough.

I was only on the stage for a minute, just passing through. Jack and Elaine were rehearsing "The Coldest Day in Spring." Jack tried to give me a little wave as I blew by, but I ignored him. I crossed the sound-stage through the back exit and went out to Victor's trailer.

It was still there, the tight coil of music, shoved in the same drawer. Pulling off the rubber band, I watched the pages unfurl and expand. I hadn't had the chance to look at them closely before, so I did so now. It was all handwritten, notes filled in with pencil, erased and written over again and crossed out and notated nearly to death. On the top, in neat careful lettering, it read "V. Durand. 1938."

I could hear our voices from that morning, all of us in this trailer together, whirling around me like ghosts. "*I wanted it to be a love ballad. It wanted to be an amorphous blob of displeasing sound.*" We had all bought it because it made sense. Jack had tried and failed to be a nov-elist, and June had tried and failed to be taken seriously, and Terry had tried and failed to be an actress, and I had tried and failed to be a mys-tery writer. Of course we would accept that Victor had tried and failed to be a composer. Of course we would *demand* that, even; members of the Ambassador's Club weren't allowed to be happy. Contentment undermined our aesthetic of not caring about contentment.

I was getting ahead of myself again. This pile of sheet music in my hands could still be just that. I needed to hear it. Unfortunately, there was only one other person I knew in Los Angeles who could play the piano.

I went back to the parking lot, where the kid who had driven me to Calabasas was still idling in his car. "Can you take me to Beverly Hills?" I asked.

I realized on the way they would probably both be at work, and prepared myself to perch on their front stoop until one or both returned. But the maid (unbelievable, they had a maid now) who answered the door told me that Mrs. Cook was not only in but that she would love to see me, and to wait in the parlor as she was still "putting on her face."

The "parlor" was a horrible white room with cavernous ceilings and gold curtains, hollow and two-dimensional and too well lit. I realized with a start that the green couch the maid pointed me toward was the one I had picked out with the Cooks a lifetime ago, back in New York. I almost didn't recognize it in this sterile place.

Beverly greeted me warmly, sweeping into the room in a light-blue dress with oversize buttons that looked far more expensive than anything I had seen her in before. She had lost weight when I saw her at the Canteen a few weeks ago and had lost even more since then, probably up to twenty pounds in total. It made her look fragile, sickly. I hadn't noticed it as much the last time we were face-to-face, but her hair—pulled up in some elegant knot—had changed from a warm dirty blond to an icier platinum shade. "Hi, darling," she said, pulling me into a friendly hug—obviously a performance for the sake of the maid. Can't have the help running to the *Dispatch* about the drugged-up, hysterical lesbian who got in a shouting match with Beverly Cook, MGM starlet.

"Your hair's gone Hollywood," I said.

She smiled, giving her head a little pat. "The girls at the studio lightened it for me. This shade is supposed to really pop in Technicolor. Do you like it?"

"I liked it fine before," I said.

She laughed. "It's nice to see you haven't lost your honesty."

The maid brought us coffee and a tray of little cookies. "Kate, how about you take the rest of the afternoon off?" Beverly smiled at her. "Let me and Miss Laurence catch up."

The maid agreed, and Beverly made nonsensical small talk about the weather—"It's hot but not too hot, wouldn't you say?"—until the back door had slammed shut. "What are you doing here, Annie?" she asked, her voice dropping practically a whole octave.

"Ah, there you are," I said. "For a second, I thought the bleach they put on your hair had soaked into your brain. Where's Adam? At work?"

"Sort of. He's…" She trailed off, as if debating how much she wanted to tell me. "He's at horseback riding lessons," she declared finally.

The thought of Adam on a horse made me giggle—him attempting to get the animal to gallop by a rational appeal to its sense of self-worth. I clamped my hand over my mouth, but Bev's eyes met mine, and they were dancing too. "I know," she said. "It's not even for a movie. MGM decided he needed a manlier hobby than translating old editions of Voltaire, so they decided he rides horses now. Once he's good enough that they can get a few pictures of him, they're going to do a whole *Screenland* story about how he rides every Sunday."

"I'll need a signed copy of that," I said.

"Done. It's better than my assigned hobby, at least. I've been tasked with losing twenty-three pounds. Not twenty-five; twenty-three on the dot. And I can't show my knees in public until I do. Apparently, I have fat knees."

"I didn't think slender knees were a thing anyone cared about."

"I didn't either, but it must be of the utmost importance," she replied with a laugh. "So that's our lives now. Adam rides horses, and I sit at home and wrap a tape measure around my knees."

We laughed for a moment, and then silence settled around us, me not wanting to ask if that made her happy and her not wanting to answer. What did it matter, if it made her happy? It was what she chose—what she continued to choose—every morning.

As the sun streamed down on her blue dress and her newly bleached hair, I was struck with the realization that I would never kiss her again. I would never wake up to the sight of her, never fetch her another roll of toilet paper while she was in the bathroom or start the coffee so it would be ready when she finally dragged herself out of bed. And with this realization, its corollary: that for the last few months, I *had* thought that one day we'd patch things up. That I had believed when they saw me in Los Angeles, they would realize how much they missed me, and everything would be perfect again. I had believed all that, not from any evidence but from the sheer grit of not wanting to let go, and what was worse—I hadn't even realized how completely I believed it until now.

We were trains on tracks speeding away from each other, and I no longer wanted to hold on for dear life.

"I came to ask a favor," I said after clearing my throat. "Could you play some sheet music for me?"

The piano was in another room, a bigger entertaining space with two separate white couches. Beverly made a face when she saw the sheet music. "Goodness, that looks confusing. What is it?"

"That's what I hope to find out," I said. "I was told it's a not-very-good love ballad."

"Doesn't look like any love ballad I've ever seen. And it's a lot of music for one song," she said, squinting at the top of the page. "Victor Durand wrote this? Isn't he a terrible songwriter?"

Even though I was certain he was a liar, and entertaining the possibility that he was also a murderer, part of me still felt a twinge of annoyance at Beverly with her stupid icy-blond hair insulting *my friend* Vic Durand. "Play it and let's find out," I said.

"I'm not the best sight reader, but I'll try," she murmured, beginning haltingly and unevenly to pluck out a melody. She didn't need to play more than a few notes before I knew. I knew exactly what it was, exactly what it meant.

It wasn't the same without the low notes. When I'd heard it at the Canteen, it was those opening deep chords, almost shaking the floor, that had reached right into my throat and seemed to grab it and clench it tight. The room began to spin around me. I pressed my eyes shut, and for a moment I felt transported in time: I was lying on the floor of the upstairs room at the Hollywood Canteen. Eight hundred soldiers and two hundred Hollywood volunteers were beneath me, and Fiona Farris, not one hundred yards away, was pouring her last cup of coffee.

My stomach clenched up into itself, as if I were going to throw up not just my lunch but maybe one or two of my organs. I grabbed at my abdomen, easing myself down onto the free corner of piano bench. Beverly either didn't notice my distress or didn't care, still plugging along at the keys. "Hey, I know this," she said, starting from the beginning, more confident on the chords this time. "This is the Hilbert concerto. We saw Iturbi play it once, at Lewisohn Stadium. Adam dragged us, remember? The second part's more famous. Let me find it."

She started to flip through the pages, then stopped. "No, this is just the first part, I think. Where'd you get this? It looks original."

"It *is* original," I said.

"In that case, it ought to be in a museum, not here on my out-of-tune piano," she replied, playing the opening bars one more time before putting a dramatic finish on the chords and smiling at me. "Well, solved that mystery! Shall I pour us something to celebrate?"

"I have to go," I said.

She pouted. "So soon? You only just got here."

"I know, I..." I trailed off. What did I do now? Where did I go; who did I tell? To the police? I had evidence Victor had written Henry's first concerto, evidence that Fiona knew that secret, but nothing that proved Henry and Victor had killed her. Motive, yes, but no opportunity—no explanation for how they could have pulled it off while both being onstage. I didn't like the unsettled feeling. When the mystery was solved in my play, the curtain came down, and if there were any holes in the story, I could only hope that the audience would have enough postshow cocktails to forget them by dawn.

Beverly took my uncertainty as being about her, and she reached over to gently brush my hand with hers. I looked up at her, startled, and before I could ask what on earth she was doing, her lips were on mine.

Apparently, I had spoken too soon about never kissing her again.

I knew I ought to pull away, but kissing her was something that required none of that horrible uncertainty, so I leaned in. As the embrace deepened, I braced myself against the piano, producing a dissonant set of notes, the awful love ballad of Annie and Bev. After a minute or two, she pulled away to focus on unbuttoning my dress, and I would have let her do it, only after the top two buttons, I saw her glance toward the windows.

"Unbelievable," I said. "You're in the middle of undressing me, and you're still concerned if the neighbors are watching." It was so ridiculous that all I could do was laugh. This was Beverly Cook now. She could kiss me on a piano, but she couldn't go back to being the woman I wanted to kiss. I slid away from her and stood up, producing another terrible chord.

"Oh, come off it," she said. "So I'm a monster because I don't want everyone and their mother watching?"

"You're not a monster," I said. "We're just two people who used to be in love but aren't anymore."

"But I am in love with you," she said. "You have to know that— when we made the choice to move—we didn't stop loving you."

There was so much I wanted to say to that. That leaving me like they had hadn't been a very loving way to treat me. That perhaps now she would know how it feels to have someone you love walk away from you. But I no longer wanted to hurt her the way she had hurt me; I only wanted to get out of the house. "I have to go," I said. "I'm sorry about your knees."

EIGHTEEN

-‹‹‹◆›››-

I could still taste the wax of Beverly's lipstick as I rode back to the Pacific lot. I dabbed it away with a hankie and focused once more on what I was going to do next.

Henry Hilbert was a fraud. Fiona had found out the truth and was going to publish it, which would ruin Henry's career. Henry had needed to stop her, and Victor would do anything for Henry. They'd killed Fiona, and when the Ambassador's Club got close to finding out the truth, Henry threw part of his retaining wall through my window (undoubtedly timed to occur while Victor was there, to keep him looking as innocent as possible) to try to scare us into stopping our investigation.

Those things, I was certain of. How you could kill someone while onstage—that, I had no idea.

It was a perfect alibi; I had to give them that. I admired it from a playwriting perspective. Hundreds of witnesses. The police would never have even considered them.

Maybe Terry had been right and Jack *was* involved. Victor would do anything for Henry, and Jack would do anything for Victor, allegedly. But I wasn't so sure. The club hated Henry, and if they knew he'd been riding Victor's coattails, they would only hate him more. None of them would kill Fiona to protect Henry.

Besides, with a secret this explosive, Henry and Victor would want to keep it between the two of them, not get more people involved. Which meant that somehow, with a thousand people watching, they'd killed Fiona Farris.

I went back to the lot, returned to my office, and took a few more pills. Then I returned to set, where I got chewed out by Terry for disappearing without warning before settling in to stare at Jack and Elaine as they serenaded each other for a few more hours. I wasn't watching, wasn't paying attention to any of it. My brain was busy churning away, not on the scenes I still had to write but on the beginning of a plan.

If Henry and Victor had killed Fiona because she'd intended to reveal their secret, the best way to figure out how they had done it—it seemed to me—was to let them think I was writing the same article. And see if they managed to kill me.

I spent a few days obsessively perfecting my plan, crafting it as if I were writing a play. I had to convince Henry and Victor that I knew their secret while somehow maintaining that I didn't suspect them of the murder. The more they thought I was an unsuspecting target, the more advantage I'd have in trying to catch them. It was a fine line to walk. I wrote out scripts, studied them like an actor, thought through every scenario until I landed on the best choice.

The whole club was back on set the next week to shoot the group scene that went around "The Coldest Day in Spring." (Had Victor written that one, too?) Everyone was still freezing each other out, but that was fine. I didn't need to talk to everyone—only one man.

I waited on set all morning for a chance to get Jack alone that would still look casual. I finally spotted him as he grazed at the snack table between takes, ripping open a box of raisins and forlornly looking around the room for someone to talk to. This was my chance.

"Hey, Jack," I said.

He swerved to face me, his eyes lighting up. "Annie, hi," he said, so happily it made me feel a little bad that I came with an ulterior motive. "You ever notice how you never see grapes anymore? It's only raisins. I know it's hard to move produce around in wartime, but I'd rather have a rotten grape than an excellent raisin."

"Sure," I said. "How have you been?"

He dumped a handful of raisins in his mouth and chewed. "Well, I lost Grape-Nuts as a sponsor after the news broke about how I punched Don in the face."

I remembered it as the other way around, but I nodded. "Sorry for that," I said.

He shrugged. "So I'm off the radio for now. Who cares? More time to focus on the book. Besides, it might have been a good thing. After the fight, there were all these stories about how I'd accused Don of Fiona's murder, which apparently brought a lot of attention to Fiona's case. Now there's pressure on the cops for them to actually do something. They were at my house the other night, Kiblowski and the short one, asking all kinds of bizarre questions. From the sound of things, they might arrest someone soon."

This was all news to me. "Do you know who?"

Jack shook his head. "No idea."

I wondered briefly if I should stop, wait for the cops to play out their investigation before I put myself in harm's way. But the police had made a lazy, incorrect conclusion before, and there was a distinct possibility they would do it again. I pressed on.

"Well, you'll never believe what happened to me this week," I said. "I found out what the big article Fiona was working on was about. I went back to the *Dispatch* offices and convinced them to let me see the rest of her things, and found her rough draft."

His eyes went wide. "You did? So was it connected? Is that why she died?"

I shook my head. "No, it couldn't be. The subjects of the article have a completely solid alibi. But it's still a huge story—one the world deserves to know. So I spoke to Fiona's old editor at the *Dispatch* and pitched that I use Fiona's research to finish her final article. Fiona would want that, I thought. The editor said yes immediately. It'll run in a few weeks."

"Incredible," said Jack. "You're really something, you know that?"

It felt strange to accept praise for a scenario I'd completely fabricated. "No, no."

"You are," he insisted. "I had given up, you know, after that night at the Canteen. I thought we all had. But here you are, still plugging away, and you didn't even know Fiona like we did."

"It's nothing," I said.

"It's something," he replied before going quiet. Then: "I really botched things that night, didn't I? We've all fought before but never like this. It's been two weeks. June's still not speaking to me. Terry only says one word to me at time. Vic talks to me but only 'cause he pities me. Can you believe that? A failed songwriter who couldn't pass a Pacific screen test feels sorry for me. And the worst part is, I don't even remember what I said, what I did to cause all this. I remember the outline of it, the general shape, but none of the details."

"You'd had a lot to drink," I said.

"I think I did that on purpose," he replied, reaching up to scratch under the collar of his shirt. "I knew I might have to say something awful to June that night, and I thought, *If I've had enough to drink, the awful things I say don't really count.* Because nothing counts when you're drinking—the things you do, the things you haven't done. And that's the thing about me: I'm always looking for a way to make the things I haven't done count less."

"I suppose I would only say to that, that you're Jack Kott," I replied. "And you've accomplished way more than most people will ever dream of. Your work has brought joy into the lives of millions of people."

"That's good," he replied. "No, that was a good start to an inspirational speech. I see where you were going with that, and I like it. I like it. But…" He shrugged and gave me a look. "What if I could have done more? And what if it's no one's fault but mine that I didn't?"

"I understand," I said.

"It all counts, Annie," he said. "Drunk, drugged, horny, sad, lonely—the mistakes all count."

"The good stuff counts too," I said.

"Sure," he replied. "But way less."

He was promptly called away by the director to get back to set, and he winked at me as he walked away. Jack would tell Victor about my forthcoming publication; I was sure of it. He was so lonesome, so desperate for conversation, there was a chance he'd stick his head out of the cab on the way home to Santa Monica that night and shout it to the whole town. The only thing to do now was wait for Victor and Henry to come up with a plan for my demise and hope I could stop them before they went through with it.

The volunteer entrance of the Hollywood Canteen was swarmed with more onlookers than usual when I arrived for my shift Wednesday night. Terry was stationed at the back door, and she handed me a clipboard to sign in. "What's with all the people?" I asked.

"Mickey Rooney" was the terse two-word answer I received as she snatched the clipboard from my hands.

Indeed, everyone inside was abuzz with the news that Mickey

Rooney would be performing tonight. I heard from five separate hostesses that when I saw him play the drums, I wouldn't believe my eyes. The men visiting the Canteen seemed a little more neutral about the evening's entertainment, although not unkindly so. I asked one man I danced with if he was excited for the show, and he answered, "Yes," with such a straight spine you would have thought I was his commanding officer, asking if he'd made his bed.

After a few hours of dancing, I was mostly excited for the chance to sit down. The first man I'd jitterbugged with had two left feet, and my right toes had spent the last few hours slowly turning a nasty shade of purple due to the multiple times they'd been stepped on. When the bandleader announced they'd be taking a quick break to set up for Mickey, I took the opportunity as everyone rushed to find a good seat on the Canteen floor to head into the kitchen in search of ice.

I struck out on ice, so—after a quick glance to ensure no one was around to witness this potentially disgusting solution—I popped myself up onto the counter to run my bare foot directly under the cold water. Disgusting or not, it felt amazing, and I had just closed my eyes and exhaled when I heard a voice.

"What are you doing?"

It was Victor. Of course it was. How could I not have been more on guard for this? The kitchen, during a Canteen show, the exact same as the time before. He was staring at me in a cross between contempt and confusion. How amusing, the idea that one could throw off a would-be murderer with absurdity alone. If I managed to make it out of this kitchen, I'd have to put that in a picture someday.

I still had to play dumb, had to pretend I knew his secret but not that he was Fiona's killer. "Hi," I said, swinging my legs out from the sink. It left a little arc of water droplets on the floor. "The Andrews Sisters weren't lying about getting corns for your country."

"Food is prepared in this room. Perhaps you could file off your corns elsewhere," he replied.

This was rather judgmental, coming from a murderer. "I wasn't filing them off," I muttered saltily. "Only trying to soothe the pain a bit."

He put up a hand. "Stop. I have already spoken more about your feet than I care to for the rest of my life. We need to talk about this article that you're writing."

"What article?" I asked innocently.

"There's no point in your denying it. Jack told me all about it," said Victor. "You're going to finish Fiona's article for the *Dispatch*. I'm here to warn you, you're not going to want to do that."

So this conversation was the warning, then—that made sense. Skipping right to murder would be extreme. "Why not?"

"Because Fiona had it wrong. It's not true."

"What's not true?"

He sighed. "I'm too exhausted to talk in circles with you. I recognize we're at cross-purposes here. I want to know how much you think you know. You don't want to tell me how much you think you know, in case I tell you something I assume you know but you don't actually know or think you know."

"I thought you were too exhausted to talk in circles."

"That was an ellipse. Look, we were friendly at one point. I stole Henry's couch for you. So can't we talk as friends? Because as your friend, I need to warn you, there's no merit to the story Fiona was writing, and it'll tank your career if you publish it."

"What career?" I asked with a snort.

"Fair enough. Then let's not talk as friends. Let's talk journalist to subject. You'll need to get a statement from me eventually, give me a chance to respond to your allegations. That's due diligence. So let's do that now." There was a loud cheer from the crowd in the main room, presumably as Mickey Rooney took the stage. "Go ahead. Ask me anything you like."

"All right," I said. "Did you write the Hilbert concerto?"

"No."

"You didn't let me specify which one."

"I didn't write either of them."

"Why did Fiona have a handwritten draft of the first concerto with your name on it?"

He shrugged. "I helped Henry orchestrate it. That's standard. It's like if Jack wrote a joke and you put it in a movie. You wouldn't say Jack wrote the movie, would you?"

"No," I said. "But if someone then handed me a piece of paper with Jack's joke on it and asked what it was, I wouldn't lie and say it was a love ballad. Why lie to us about that sheet music if it meant nothing?"

"Because no one in that room would have given it a rest if I'd told the truth," he replied. "'It's some orchestrating I did for Henry on his concerto'; do you think Jack or June would have let that fly? I'd get a lecture on how Henry takes advantage of me, and frankly, I've heard that tune enough."

"So Henry doesn't take advantage of you," I said.

"Of course he takes advantage of me. He just does it in ways I consent to."

"Interesting choice of words, because there's something else I noticed," I said. "Henry broke up with you and married Eliza, and suddenly he's unable to write the songs needed for the Pacific Pictures film that's going to anchor his new career as a movie star. Is that because you stopped writing songs for him once he left you?"

He didn't have an immediate answer for that, which told me that not only was it true, Fiona hadn't figured out that piece of it. I'd caught him off guard.

"And who could blame you for that?" I went on. "The man dumps you so he can star in a movie, then expects you to help him write it? Anyone would have told him to piss off."

"I did stop…helping him orchestrate, for a time," he said finally. "Yes, that's true."

"You were trying to shut down the picture," I realized. "MGM owns all the old Hilbert songs; if Pacific couldn't get any new ones, they'd cancel the movie, abandon their plan to make Henry a star. Then he could divorce Eliza, and everything could go back to the way it was."

"There's one flaw in your logic," he replied, taking a few steps toward me so he was only a few inches away. "If I wanted to shut down the picture, then I *would* want this article published, true or not. If what I wanted was to ruin Henry, why would I be standing here telling you not to run it?"

"Because you love him," I said. "You don't want to explode his whole career, just have it quietly fizzle out."

"I don't love anyone," he muttered. "Except myself and Chopin. And the fact remains, you don't have enough to take this to print. You have old sheet music, some memos copied down in a notebook, and a lot of conjecture. If you manage to finish an article that the *Dispatch* is willing to run—big *if*—Pacific will sue, Henry will sue, I'll sue. Your reputation is toast forever, and for what? So knock this off, if you know what's good for you."

His voice was low and remarkably calm. I could see what Terry had meant, about how frightening it was to see him so serious. Backed up against the kitchen counter, I couldn't help but notice how much taller he was than me, how one of his hands—big enough to stretch over an entire octave—seemed likely to also fit around my neck.

"I have three more things," I willed myself to say. "There was a cut on Henry's hand that I believe he got climbing through my window to steal Fiona's things from my apartment."

"Prove it," he said.

"I never told you what was in Fiona's notebook, so I have you admitting, just now, that you stole it from my purse."

"I stole your sleeping pills, too, while I was in there. Lock me up."

"And I have a brick from Henry Hilbert's retaining wall on the floor of my apartment. So would you like to amend any of your previous statements now? Because throwing a brick through my window and telling the Ambassador's Club you'd kill us all if you had to certainly seems like an overreaction to a story that isn't true and has no evidence."

"Let's go outside. I want a cigarette."

I ignored him. "That seems like an action you take to cover up a story that is true and has lots of evidence. That seems like an action you take when you don't want anyone finding out you killed Fiona over this."

"What? Christ! No, we didn't—what are you talking about? We would never have done that. Fine, yes—we broke your window. Yes, I stole that notebook. Yes, we threatened the club to try to get you all to stop looking into Fiona's death. But only because we knew Fiona was working on this story, that if you kept going, the whole club would find out. Henry and I didn't want our careers to be collateral damage of Annie Laurence's latest murder-mystery play."

"How am I supposed to believe that?" I asked. "You threw a brick at my head, but you're not capable of murder?"

"It was supposed to be a rock, not a brick—Henry's an idiot—"

"I'm supposed to believe that it's simply, what, a coincidence that Fiona was planning to write a column that would have been professionally devastating to the man you love, and then she died?"

"Yes," he replied. "Look, Henry and I only found out she was going to write that column a few hours before she died. She called Henry that morning for a statement. I didn't even know until Henry told me when he showed up for the performance. That fight we had in here was the first time I confronted her about it. You think I'd jump straight to murder? One fight that gets broken up and my next tactic is to try to kill her?"

Suddenly, I burst out laughing.

Again, Victor's eyes could have popped out of his head from sheer confusion. "What the hell is the matter with you?"

I was hardly sure myself. "Sorry, I…I just remembered. All this time, stealing documents from her office, poring over copied-down memos and—*she told me*. She told me your secret, that night. She told everyone in this room. You came in and she said—" Tears were coming out of my eyes now. It was all so absurd. All that intrigue for nothing! "'Here comes Henry Hilbert's right- and left-hand man.'"

In spite of everything, Victor laughed too. "Brutal, wasn't she? And smart. Boy, that got under my skin, as she knew it would. I spent the whole performance that night ruminating on it. As if I could play hard enough, I could prove it wasn't true, that it wasn't all I am. You know, I played it better than I ever played it that night. There was a decent chance if we had finished the show, I would have walked off the stage and told her to run it. Told her…"

"Told her you wrote the first concerto," I finished.

"I…," He trailed off before finally nodding. "Yes. I wrote it. The old concerto and the new one. I wrote them both."

"The songs for the movie?"

"Yes. Those too."

Frantically, not wanting to slow down in case he suddenly changed his mind about admitting to any of this, I started naming Hilbert shows. "*The Guest of Honor*?"

"Me."

"*6728 Hollywood*?"

"Me."

"*The Ingenue*?"

"Let me save you some time: Henry Hilbert hasn't written a song on his own since 1934. And only about half of the ones he said he wrote for two years before that."

I exhaled. My gut reaction was not that of the journalist I had been pretending to be; it was of the friend I knew I wasn't. "Why didn't you tell anyone? My God! Vic! Henry's won Oscars that should be yours! *Hat Full of Genius* should be about you!"

"Can we go out for a cigarette now?" He sighed. "I don't feel like revealing my deepest secrets while Mickey fucking Rooney plays the drums."

"Yeah," I murmured, in a daze. "This is the worst Andy Hardy movie yet."

"No, it's not," Vic replied immediately.

Cole Place was empty, all the lookie-loos who had shown up to see Mickey Rooney come in having left and the lookie-loos who would show up to see him leave having not yet arrived. Vic handed me a cigarette, and for one delirious moment, I wondered if I shouldn't take it, if it might be poison. This was absurd, I quickly realized, but nothing made sense anymore. It was strange—I'd thought for several days now that Henry was a fraud, but that hadn't prepared me to hear it directly from Vic's mouth. Any plan I had was out the window now. I took the cigarette.

"It started a long time ago," said Vic finally. "Back in '28. I'd been playing Henry's music for a few years with some success, but I wanted to compose. I wrote a sonata and debuted it in New York, and everyone said it was a knockoff of Henry's sonata. Even Henry said that. I wrote a few songs after that, and everyone said the same thing about those, too: *Imitations. Not artistically significant.* Were they right? I don't know. Maybe. But it always seemed to me that I wasn't getting a fair shot. People saw my name on a song and decided before they even heard it what kind of song it was, what they were going to think about it. So I stopped publishing the songs I wrote. Kept them all for myself.

Then a few years later, Henry was having trouble finishing the score for *Strictly Confidential*. And I had all these songs lying around, so I thought, why not? If all anyone's going to say is they sound like Hilbert songs, why not say they *are* Hilbert songs? So I let him have a few. And I'll tell you what: people liked them. When they thought Henry wrote them, they liked my songs just fine." He shrugged. "It wasn't that serious, at first. We'd joke about it. *À quatre mains*, we'd say. That's a type of composition; it means *four hands, one piano*."

"A French piano-composition joke," I remarked. "What's it like having such a relatable sense of humor?"

"You'll have to trust me that it's hilarious," he said. "Or it was, at first. But the lie kept getting bigger. Henry kept having writer's block; I kept giving him songs. I tried to break the cycle a few years ago and debut the first concerto under my own name. No one wanted it. Put Henry Hilbert's name on it, it debuts at Carnegie Hall." He looked at me. "What would you have done?"

"I wouldn't have killed Fiona over it," I said.

"We didn't," said Vic. "Don't say that. We broke a few windows, that was all."

"You also threatened to kill all of us."

"Only to try to scare you four into stopping this before we were caught! And we would have been, if any of you had looked at that box for five minutes—she had everything. She had all my old music; she had letters Henry and I wrote each other; she even had this drawing Henry did once, a little sketch of me at the piano, and underneath it he wrote, 'Afternoons at the Henry Hilbert Factory.' I don't know how she got it all—she must have been robbing me blind every time I threw a party in the last year. But hand to God, Annie, that was all." He pressed his right hand to his heart. "I would have told the world our secret if it would have saved her life, and I'd shout it from the Hollywoodland sign if I thought it would bring her back."

I dropped my cigarette to the ground and crushed it under my heel. I didn't know if I was drugged, naive, or insane—but I believed him. Maybe because I liked him, maybe because my head was still all messed up from seeing Beverly—no matter the *maybe*, I believed him. "But if you didn't do it," I said, not realizing until I started speaking that I was nearly on the verge of tears, "and Henry didn't do it, and June didn't do it, and Terry or Jack or Don or Bette Davis or—or—if none of them did it, then who did? Who killed Fiona Farris?"

I looked up in time to catch his expression softening into what seemed like pity. "Fiona Farris did," he said gently.

"But everyone agreed," I said. "Jack and June—they agreed with me. The suicide note was off, the police closed it too quickly—"

"June and Jack weren't there the first time she tried it," Vic said. "I was. I've known this all along, darling. I was trying to stay out of it, let you all go through whatever it was you needed to go through before you could admit it to yourselves. Fiona took her own life. She either had a bout of neuroses or her dosage was off or maybe she didn't want to face life if motherhood wasn't in the future. It was her reason to hold, and she decided not to share it with us. I'm sorry. I can understand you not wanting to face it. None of us want to. It makes us feel like we failed her, which maybe we did. Maybe instead of tearing the Ambassador's Club apart, all of this should have brought us closer together, made us vow to—I don't know. Be kinder to one another or something pathetic like that. Who knows. But we came out of this the way we were always going to come out of it: pointing fingers and shooting off our mouths and each one of us having to be the smartest one in the room. So Fiona's gone, and we've destroyed the club too."

"It's all my fault," I said suddenly. "I'm the one who pushed everyone into this. I'm the one who insisted—"

"Hey, relax. 'Everything's my fault' is just narcissism for pessimists; I should know. I screwed up too. Henry and I never thought that note would make the police reopen Fiona's case. All we wanted was for everyone to butt out, not turn on each other."

"You can consider me fully butted out," I said. "You and Henry? I'll never say a word."

"Thanks," he said. "I appreciate that. No one knows—no one but me and him. Can you believe that? I lied to my dearest friends for some man. If they ever found out, I dare say that would hurt their feelings quite a bit. Not that it matters anymore."

"It might again, one day," I said. "We should go back inside. I bet Andy Hardy is wrapping things up by now."

"I'm going home," he declared. "You've got me too chatty. Who knows what I might reveal to someone?"

"And normally, you're so restrained," I said.

The performance must have ended, as the door cracked open behind us, and a few Canteen hostesses came out to smoke. Vic nodded at me and disappeared down the street, leaving me to my whirlwind of thoughts.

NINETEEN

~~~≪≪◆≫≫~~~

Ibummed a cigarette off one of the other girls outside and wandered down to the corner to be alone. Why had I done this? Why had I done any of this? Why had I been so certain a woman I knew half a week couldn't have taken her own life? Vic was right—I wanted to be the smartest. Smart enough that the Ambassador's Club would like me, smart enough that Devlin wouldn't sideline me, smart enough that Beverly and Adam would regret leaving me behind. When you write a play that makes the audience gasp at the ending, you feel like a god. Had all this been me chasing that feeling again? Had I forgotten, like Jack said, that this was real? That this counted?

There was one thing I could do, at least. I put out my cigarette and went back inside, heading immediately for the coat check at the front of the building and asking for my purse. The bottles of pills, freshly refilled that day, jostled inside as I carried it to the bathroom, where I emptied both the uppers and the downers into the toilet quickly, before I could lose my nerve. From now on, any decision I was making, any ghosts I was hearing, I was going to be certain they were coming from my own brain. If that made me less than a perfect cog in the Pacific machine, so be it.

I had hardly rechecked my bag when I was pulled onto the dance floor. I almost declined, but it didn't feel right. I'd had an eventful day, month, year, but nowhere near as eventful as this sailor had had, would have. I looked at him and found my brain automatically blurring out his face, the way one did when caught up in the frenetic pace of the Canteen dance floor. This time, I actively worked to counteract the effect. I looked in his eyes (brown), studied the shape of his face (round, friendly, with a genuine smile and bushy eyebrows), noticed the way his arms felt around my waist.

"What's your name?" I asked.

"Les," he replied.

"I'm Annie," I said. "Where are you from?"

"Cincinnati."

"Neat. I'm from Pennsylvania. We're neighbors."

"I'll be sure to write home and tell the block we ran into one another."

I smiled. "Is this your first time at the Canteen?"

"It is," he said.

"What do you think of it?"

He looked as if he were about to stop himself from saying something. "It's fun," he said finally. "I liked Mickey Rooney. And it's always fun to dance. I love dancing."

"You can be honest," I said.

Les grinned. "Am I that transparent? It's grand that you all are doing this. But I do get this sense... I don't know. That we're supposed to be grateful for all of it? And it's not like I'm not. But I'd be more grateful to not be here at all."

"Of course," I said.

"One of the girls I danced with earlier... I said I was from Cincinnati, and she said, 'Bet you don't have many movie stars in Cincinnati!' As if the only thing I care about right now is movie stars."

"It's the only thing Hollywood cares about," I said. "So they assume it's the only thing everyone else cares about too."

"I can tell. But the sandwiches are good," he said with a shrug. "So there's that."

We laughed, and he spun me around as the song hit a crescendo, ending with a complicated dip that got a reaction from the other dancers nearby. I gave him a hug and we parted ways, each of us disappearing off into the crowd.

But our brief conversation lingered with me. This town was obsessed with stars. They were products, selected and crafted. I thought about Beverly, measuring her knees; Adam, taking horseback riding lessons. The memo Fiona had copied down, the long list of initials Irma and Devlin were considering for new male stars. Henry had been the chosen one, the new star to save the studio and get it through the war. How far would Pacific Pictures go to protect that investment?

The thing about endings, Adam had said, is they are intrinsically linked to beginnings. It had all begun here, at the Hollywood Canteen, one night in the kitchen as servicemen and MGM stars listened to a piano concerto. For all our following the trail of Fiona's article, we'd never done something so basic to any mystery. We'd never returned to the scene of the crime.

When the current song ended and I'd said farewell to the man I'd been dancing with, I made my way to the kitchen. With Mickey Rooney's performance over, it was back in full swing again. A couple of volunteers were making sandwiches at the island in the center; a woman was loading used cups into a dishwasher; a few of the Canteen managers were discussing the upcoming week's schedule over mugs of coffee. None of them paid any attention to me. I went over to the window through which I'd seen Fiona's body and looked out into the darkness. My reflection stared back at me, the kitchen behind me, reflected in the glass: the volunteers, the island, the sandwiches, the coffee…

"What's that?" I asked.

No one was listening to me, so no one answered the question. I squinted at the reflection. There was a piece of paper underneath the island.

I turned around, crouching down low and apologizing to George Burns as I reached in between his legs to grab it. The piece of paper had slid pretty far under the island. Finally, after a fair amount of groping around, my fingers curled around its edges, and I was able to slide it out.

It wasn't a piece of paper at all, I realized. It was a pad, a familiar one. I'd carried a piece of paper torn from it to the studio pharmacist my second week on the lot, exchanged it for a jar of white pills identical to the ones I'd flushed down the Canteen toilet.

Pacific Pictures Medical Offices, Office of Mrs. Irma Feinstein, Assistant to Mr. Devlin Murray.

How could this have gotten here? Irma told me she had lost it, but Irma didn't volunteer at the Canteen. All the Pacific nights I'd attended, I'd never seen her here, not once. It couldn't have been stolen by some pill-addicted Pacific actor either—Irma always carried it on her person; she told me that herself. Besides, who would need to steal it? The woman would have happily written you a morphine prescription if you told her it would somehow make Pacific Pictures money.

No. Irma Feldstein had been in this kitchen, and this pad had been deliberately placed to prove it. Whether it had originally fallen accidentally out of Irma's jacket during a struggle or Fiona had made a point to grab it, I'd never know, but Fiona had waited until Irma wasn't looking and flung it under that counter as far as she could. She knew enough to know if it were on her person, the police being paid off by Pacific could find it and dispose of it without telling anyone. Her only hope, her last resort, had been to stash it at the scene of the crime. One last chance for someone to put together another one of Fiona Farris's clever hints.

She had been smart.

I tucked the pad carefully into my pocket before claiming my things from coat check and leaping into the first taxi I saw. I went straight to Vic's house, where I banged on the door fruitlessly until the taxi driver, who was waiting, rolled down the window and asked if I'd like him to take me somewhere else. Not knowing what else to do, I gave him my address. I could find a neighbor with a phone and try to reach Vic at Henry's, assuming that's where he was.

I wouldn't get a chance. When I reached my apartment, I found not a stray black cat on my doorstep but Detectives Kiblowski and Cooper.

"Annie Laurence?" Kiblowski asked.

Why was he asking? He knew who I was by now. "Is something wrong?" I asked.

"You're under arrest," he replied.

I assumed I had heard him wrong and did that thing one does at loud parties when you haven't quite made out your conversation partner's words: smiled and nodded. It was only when he came toward me with a pair of handcuffs that the meaning of his words sank in.

"Wait, me?" I asked.

"For the murder of Fiona Farris," he went on.

"But I didn't murder her," I said, and as the words left my mouth, it clicked. I had started a rumor that morning that I was going to finish Fiona's article, hoping the news would reach the murderer's ears. It had; it just wasn't the murderer I'd expected it to be. Irma Feinstein, aware of everything that happened on the Pacific lot, had heard it too, and this was her way of ensuring I never ruined the studio's investment in Henry Hilbert.

I had to think fast. The only evidence I had against Irma was in my pocket. I had to get rid of it somehow before the police searched me. Kiblowski was narrowing in with the handcuffs. "Wait!" I cried. "Can I use the restroom?"

"You can use the restroom at the station."

"I'll cooperate with you, I promise, only it's my time of the month," I lied quickly. "I'm not sure it can wait—"

Kiblowski made a face. "Fine. But hurry up. Cooper, take her in."

Cooper watched me unlock my apartment door. "Leave the purse with me," he said.

Thank God I'd put the prescription pad in my pocket. I walked to the bathroom, as calmly as I could muster, and stashed the notepad in the tiny crack between the porcelain back and the wall, where I prayed no one would find it. I flushed the toilet, washed my hands, and went to meet my fate.

Kiblowski and Cooper took me to the same station in Hollywood we'd sat in the night Henry had thrown a brick in my window. Not that my treatment there the first time had been stellar, but this was far worse. I was fingerprinted, photographed, given a scratchy beige jumpsuit to put on, and shoved into an empty interrogation room. A glass of water had been kindly placed on the table for me. Unfortunately, my hands were handcuffed behind my back.

I waited for the detectives to arrive, which they did not. They must have been trying to psych me out, watching from somewhere, wanting to see me squirm. Well, I wasn't guilty. They could watch all night and would see nothing but a woman in handcuffs who would eventually need to go to the bathroom for real.

After maybe half an hour went by, it started getting hotter. I couldn't tell if this was deliberate—trying to sweat me out?—or if the air-conditioning had kicked off for the night. Ten minutes later, it became extremely cold. My body, which was now coated in sweat, became clammy and frigid. My teeth chattered. I had to hand this round to Kiblowski and Cooper: I would have put temperature-related mind games above their skill level.

I distracted myself by putting together the remaining pieces. Jack had said Irma had interviewed him about his past when considering him as a potential Pacific star. That must have been when Henry spilled the beans—the "past issues" that Irma had mentioned in her list for Devlin. Henry must have given Irma the sheet music, the letters, everything else from Fiona's office: the studio would want to hold on to that, make sure if Vic got any ideas about going public, he'd have no evidence to back himself up. Henry lied to Vic and said the movers had lost all the sheet music, and then Fiona stole it all from Irma's storage on whatever day she'd broken in and copied down all those memos. It was bold of her to take it. She must have thought no one would notice if it went missing. I wondered if that had been her mistake, the thing that had tipped off Irma and Devlin that a story was coming, the thing that had made Irma think about clever methods of poisoning she'd read about recently in scripts.

I sat there, shivering, for a long time, aching to wrap my arms around my torso. I was starting to lose track of how long I'd been sitting there. An hour? More? My head began to pound, the cold sweating got worse, my stomach began to rumble. Finally, I laid my head down on the cold metal table and tried to close my eyes, thinking I might as well get some rest if they were going to leave me here to rot.

And then it all started.

Thumping, footsteps, shouting, all coming from above me, out of nowhere and alarmingly loud. There were people on the roof of the police station! I bolted upright, my eyes wide in panic. If the station were under attack, would they leave me here, handcuffed and helpless? "What's going on?" I shouted, so loudly the sound bounced around the empty room. The noises were only growing louder and louder. Any minute now, I was certain someone would kick down the door to this room and take me as a hostage.

Then, the strangest thing—whoever was taking over this police station started to play music. Not a song I could recognize; something screechy and discordant, a hundred instruments being played by toddlers. As I was racking my brain for an explanation of why what had to be some kind of militia group was attempting to torture us with a terrible symphony, the truth dawned on me.

None of this was real. I was in a silent room. The only one who could hear these noises was me. I tried to take a deep breath but suddenly struggled to pull air into my lungs.

As if they had been waiting for panic to set in, Kiblowski and Cooper chose this moment to enter the room. "Sorry for the wait, Miss Laurence," said Kiblowski pleasantly, flipping through a folder as if the hours I had sat there were no more inconvenient than a delayed streetcar. "We had a lot of evidence to sift through before we got started."

I hadn't recovered from my first spiral, and this sent me only further down. I had thought this was a trumped-up arrest charge meant to smear my name to the public. I hadn't expected them to have evidence against me. How could they? I hadn't done it.

"Miss Laurence—may I call you Annie?—I'm wondering if we could go over again where you were on the night of Mrs. Farris's death," began Kiblowski.

"I was upstairs," I answered. "In the unfinished room on the second floor over the stage." Then, too eagerly and too suspiciously, I added, "Jack Kott saw me."

Kiblowski held up a hand, as if to say, *We'll get to that.* "Back all the way up," he said. "Where is this unfinished room?"

I wasn't sure what he was asking. "Upstairs?"

"Upstairs where?"

"At the Hollywood Canteen?"

"Ah," said Kiblowski. "So you were at the Hollywood Canteen. What were you doing there?"

"Volunteering," I said. "I volunteer as a hostess there."

"Interesting," said Kiblowski, nodding. "Why?"

"It's the Hollywood Canteen" was the only thing I could think to reply. "Everyone volunteers there. We have to."

"Sure," said Kiblowski. "Plus, I bet you meet a lot of successful people, volunteering at a place like that."

"I suppose," I said.

"That's where you first met Mrs. Farris, isn't it?" asked Kiblowski. "And the rest of that crew?"

I nodded.

"Do you happen to remember how?"

I tried to grasp for specifics. "I believe I saw them sitting together and went up and introduced myself," I said.

"Interesting," said Kiblowski. "And they invited you into their club, just like that?"

"Well, no," I said. "They invited me for a drink. I wasn't part of the club until—" I was halfway through the sentence when I realized perhaps I shouldn't confess to stealing Henry Hilbert's couch. "Until later," I finished.

Kiblowski smiled, and I felt a pang of dread, as if I'd said something wrong. "So volunteering at the Hollywood Canteen, meeting Mrs. Farris, being introduced to her friends—that was all rather good for you," he said.

"Yes, I suppose," I answered.

"Do you have other friends, Annie?" Cooper asked, a little pointedly.

"I just moved here," I said.

"So, no, then."

"Let's talk about that, actually," said Kiblowski. "Why did you move out here? I'm curious."

"I'd been offered a contract with Pacific Pictures," I answered.

"That's a long move, all the way from New York," Cooper said.

"Sure is," Kiblowski agreed. "I'm from Chicago, and the only reason I came all the way out here was—well, I'll just say it: my wife left me." I stared at him.

He let me stare for a beat, then shrugged. "You need a big kick in the pants to make a change like that, is all I'm saying. Anything like that happen to you, spurn you to move all the way out to California?"

"I'd been offered a contract with Pacific Pictures," I repeated, adding for effect, "I've always been a fan of money."

Kiblowski laughed. "Can't blame you there," he said.

"So," began Cooper, "you didn't move out here to follow Mr. and Mrs. Adam Cook?"

I probably would have handled a slap in the face better. My jaw went slack, my already uneasy stomach lurched. "I did *not*," I said, immediately regretting the forcefulness with which I spoke. It was too emotional. I'd exposed an open wound to a predator out for blood.

"Sounds like a touchy subject," said Kiblowski. "This Adam and Beverly Cook—do they think you moved out here to follow them?"

"I don't know what they think," I said.

"Well, you ran into them shortly after you arrived," Kiblowski said. "And they reacted poorly to that, didn't they?"

Something began burning at the back of my throat as I realized the only possible way he could know that. Was it before or after she'd tried to undress me against her piano that Beverly had spoken to the cops behind my back? "They did," I admitted. "But I didn't move out here to follow them. If they said that, they're wrong."

"Of course," said Kiblowski. "Still." He tapped his fingers on the table. "Pretty good timing on that Pacific contract. You know, maybe it was one of those situations where—you wouldn't have followed them on your own but that contract pushed you over the edge."

Saying anything felt like hurling myself in front of an oncoming train. "No," I said, tears starting to pool in my eyes. "I just needed to go somewhere. I needed a change. I needed—Pacific was the first offer I got. I would have gone anywhere. It just happened to be where they had gone."

"And why did you need a change?" asked Kiblowski, gentle all of a sudden, his voice a whisper. The tears had spilled over, and I was crying now, big fat embarrassing tears streaming down my cheeks that I couldn't wipe away. It was the first time, I realized, that I had cried for Beverly and Adam. I'd raged at them, cursed them, begged them to change their minds, wanted to kill them, wanted to kill myself, felt nothing inside, pounded my fists against the floor, pounded my head against the wall, smoked until my apartment was so full of haze I couldn't see a foot in front of me and drank until the room spun so much I couldn't hear my own thoughts. Not once had I cried for us, for the soft ring of blond curls around Bev's head as she slept that I'd never see again, for Adam's dimples and his big head and small smile that crossed his face just before he said something that would knock your socks off with its wit.

"You were involved with Mr. Cook, weren't you?" prompted Kiblowski after it became clear the lump in my throat was too big to allow me to speak. "His wife found out he was carrying on with the writer of the show they were starring in and dragged him out here to get him away from you. You saw the first opportunity to follow them and took it."

I wanted to kiss Beverly for this story, for this tiny lie that meant I didn't have to expose every single one of the raw edges of my heart to these men in this cold, dark room. I wanted to kiss her, and then I wanted to hit her. How easy had it been for her to lie like that? How easy had it been to deny me?

Kiblowski cleared his throat. "Annie," he prodded. "Is that what happened?"

None of this had anything to do with Fiona anyway. What difference did it make? "Yes," I said, sighing the word out. It felt like I had been trying to stay afloat but finally decided to sink down into the warm water. "Yes, I was involved with Mr. Cook."

"Did anyone else know you were fooling around with another woman's husband?" asked Cooper.

"The affair," Kiblowski corrected diplomatically. "Did anyone else know about the affair?"

I shook my head. "No, we kept it secret."

Kiblowski opened the folder in front of him and flipped through, producing a clipping from a newspaper, which he slid over to me.

Stars Shine, Ending Disappoints in Altogether Too Many Murders, the familiar headline read.

By Fiona Farris.

"Would you mind reading me that bit we have underlined?" asked Kiblowski.

I didn't have to look for the underline, and I didn't need to read it. That quote had been burned in my mind since that cold February opening night all those months ago. "Playwright Annie Laurence writes so lovingly for her two leads one wonders if the three don't spend their off-hours running lines among an extra-large bedroom set."

"Sort of sounds like one other person might have known," said Cooper.

So this was their angle, the story they'd concocted for me. I had killed Fiona because she knew about my affair.

"She was only making a joke," I said.

"To be honest with you, Annie, before this evening, I would have agreed with you on that," said Kiblowski. "Someone we interviewed brought up that article, and personally, I thought it was a reach. But then we brought you in here tonight and found something in your bag."

Kiblowski opened the folder one more time, and this time slid across to me the piece of paper I had torn from Fiona's notebook, all smoothed out for me to read.

Annie Laurence—playwright—involved with the Cooks?

"That's Mrs. Farris's handwriting," said Cooper.

I had nothing to say. I could only stare at Fiona's messy, slanted penmanship.

"Did you find this at the Canteen?" Kiblowski finally prompted. "Did it fall out of Fiona's pocket the night you met her?"

"I don't remember how I found that," I said finally.

"But you panicked when you read it, didn't you?" he went on. "Mrs. Farris knew, and she was going to reveal yours and Mr. Cook's secret to the world."

"You were only trying to protect the man you loved," said Cooper. They were really closing in on me, if Cooper was getting in on the nice cop game. "He'd only just moved out here. You didn't want Fiona Farris ruining his reputation before his film career could even get off the ground."

"How unfair would that be?" said Kiblowski.

"That's not what happened" was all I could say.

"So that's all that's going on here," said Kiblowski. "You happened to meet a woman who happened to make a joke about you that happened to be true and then she happened to be murdered by a poison you knew a great deal about," said Kiblowski.

"Yes," I said.

"I guess what I'm wondering is," began Cooper, "if this is all coincidence, why'd you spill your water on her?"

"What are you talking about?" I asked, and the second I said it, I remembered. I'd danced over to their table, then gotten a glass of water. I was standing nearby, eavesdropping—oh God, how embarrassing—then that couple had rammed into me, and I'd spilled the whole thing on Fiona. "That was an accident."

Cooper made a show of furrowing his brow. "You don't know what we're talking about, or it was an accident?"

"It was an accident," I repeated.

"So you do know what we're talking about," said Cooper. "Curious, then, that you didn't bring it up when telling us how you met Fiona."

"I'd forgotten," I said. "It wasn't that big a deal."

"Really?" asked Kiblowski, his eyebrows shooting up. "Because everyone else remembered. They all brought it up right away. Miss Lee, Mr. Durand, Mr. Kott. We asked them all, 'How did you meet Annie Laurence?' 'Oh, she spilled her water all over Fiona at the Hollywood Canteen.' So why were you the only person not to bring it up?"

"There's only one reason someone doesn't bring something up to the cops," said Cooper. "They don't want us to know."

"So it seems likely to me that you spilled that water on purpose," continued Kiblowski. "To have an excuse to talk to her. After you found that piece of paper there, you decided to worm your way into the group, get invited to drinks. Learn their patterns, gain Fiona's trust a bit. Am I wrong?"

He was, but on the other hand—was he? I had wanted to talk to Fiona, largely because of what she might have known about me and the Cooks. The night Fiona died, hadn't I been excited, daydreaming about the look on Adam's and Beverly's faces when they saw me talking to her? And if that were true, it was reasonable to conclude I had spilled my water on Fiona on purpose. And if that were true, it was reasonable to conclude...

"Let's get back to the night of Mrs. Farris's death," said Kiblowski, after it became clear I had no answer to why I'd spilled my water. "Where were you during the concert, again?"

I knew the answer to this one, but I was so turned around by now I hesitated before saying, "Upstairs, in the room above the sound booth."

"And you were in the kitchen before that, right? With Mrs. Farris?"

"Yes," I said.

"Annie." Kiblowski leaned forward, his elbows on the table. He lowered his voice. "Did you? Did you kill her?"

"No," I said.

"Are you sure?" he said, easy and unthreateningly, as if I were a child being asked if I needed to use the potty before leaving the house. "Maybe you asked Fiona if you two could talk during the concert. You didn't mean for it to happen, I bet. You only brought the poison to show her you were serious about never telling your secret. You didn't think she'd actually drink it. You didn't think she'd actually die."

The noise and music were hammering the inside of my skull now. I pressed my hands to my temple to drown it out. "Jack Kott saw me," I remembered suddenly. "Jack saw me, upstairs, during the concert."

"It's interesting, that," said Kiblowski. "When we questioned him the night of the murder, Mr. Kott had no recollection of where he was during the concert. We bring all of you back here a few days later, after you've become friends with him, and suddenly he does remember."

"He was in shock the night it happened," I said.

"I see," said Kiblowski. "So his story shifting there doesn't have anything to do with the two of you starting a sexual relationship?"

My mouth flew open, but the surprise passed quickly. Of course they knew that too. They knew almost everything else. I wondered who had ratted that one out. June, after she'd agreed to spy on us for them? "It doesn't," I said.

"I heard Jack Kott's a Communist," said Cooper. "Is that true?"

"I don't know," I said half-heartedly, already aware that it didn't matter. What was true or not true no longer mattered. It had been decided by Irma and Devlin and Kiblowski and Cooper before they had even put the handcuffs on me what I had done and why I had done it. It would be easier for them if I went along with it, but it wasn't necessary. They had proof Fiona knew a secret about me and proof the secret was true. They had my whereabouts during the concert completely unaccounted for, except for the changing testimony of the drunk Communist I was screwing, and the murder weapon in a script with my name on it. I'd written my own confession before I even walked in the room.

I was silent for a moment, and then I laughed. I had to. What other response could there have been? I was entirely screwed. I was definitely going to jail, and that was if I wasn't going to the electric chair. Boy, wouldn't Beverly and Adam feel sorry for me then? Execution—now that's how you stick it to your exes.

"I don't think I'd like to talk anymore without a lawyer," I said.

"As is your right," said Kiblowski, shutting the folder. "We're done, anyway. An officer will be in shortly to take you to a cell."

He pushed his chair back from the table, making an awful screeching sound, and headed for the door. Cooper started to follow him but then hung back at the last second. "Bet you won't be writing any articles for the *Dispatch* now, will you?"

His voice was so low and threatening I almost didn't hear him. I lifted my head, which I had hung toward the table. "What was that?" I asked.

"You heard me," he snapped, exiting the room and slamming the door shut behind him.

TWENTY

-<<<◆>>>-

I spent a sleepless night in a holding cell, alone except for the thumping and screaming and music and voices and chills and pains and thoughts flying through my head too fast for me to grasp and hold on to any one. After what felt like an eternity, I was shouted at to wake up—hilarious, since I hadn't even come close to falling asleep—and handed something sloshy and gray in a bowl that I believe was supposed to be oatmeal. Given the aggressive nature of my awakening, I expected something to happen after that, but nothing did. Hours passed. I was served a sandwich that I barely touched because nausea was flooding over me in waves so intense I couldn't see straight. When the guard came to retrieve my tray, I asked him if I wasn't supposed to have a phone call?

"You'll get a phone call after you're charged," he snapped, as if he were annoyed I hadn't read the jail handbook yet.

"And when will that be?" I replied.

"We have up to three days after your arrest to charge you" was the answer.

They were going to milk every one of those three days, I predicted. Every hour I was in here—not allowed a phone call, not allowed to share my side of the story with anyone—was an hour both the studio and the police could work on convincing everyone who might be inclined to believe me that I was a murderer. No doubt Kiblowski and Cooper were knocking on the doors of the rest of the Ambassador's Club right now, fake sympathy in their eyes. *We thought you deserved to hear the news directly from us...*

I lay down on the bed and closed my eyes, preparing myself to be there for a while.

Sure enough, nothing happened that day. Something did happen the next, but it wasn't related to my arrest: I started vomiting. It was a painful sort of vomit, too, the kind that seems less like a sickness and more like a cramp that sends your stomach contents upward like a geyser. The guard first accused me of faking it, which I would have laughed at if I hadn't been worried that laughing would start more half-digested porridge to erupt out of me. Once it became clear that I could barely even keep a sip or two of water down and therefore probably was not faking, a doctor was called, although he didn't arrive for several unbearable hours.

When the doctor did finally show up, an old man with graying hair and frigid hands, he wasn't exactly helpful. "Any chance you could be pregnant?" he asked.

"A small chance, maybe," I answered.

"Well, there's your answer, then," he said.

The fact that, even if I was pregnant, I was still unable to keep food or water down didn't seem to bother him. I asked for something to treat the nausea, and he said it should die down by the second trimester, an answer I didn't find helpful. Without even leaving me so much as a pack of ginger snaps, he was gone.

I didn't really believe that I was pregnant—Jack and I had used protection, and this felt more like the ceaseless vomiting that came with stomach flu or food poisoning than the waves of illness brought on by a strong smell or a moving train car I'd witnessed in actual pregnant women. But I had nothing to do but ruminate on the *what if.* Neither of us were exactly cut out for parenthood, but I did think (in a perfect world, one where I was not a murder suspect) Jack would try. He probably wouldn't be proposing to me, but he wouldn't run out on me either. He'd support me. He might even warm to fatherhood, eventually. I could see him giving the kid little bit parts on the radio, holding her up so she could reach the mic and grinning when the kid nailed it. It was one pleasant thought as the entire room spun around me.

Fortunately—or maybe unfortunately—by the end of the day, whatever bug I'd eaten had worked itself out of my system, and I was able to drink some ginger soda and eat a few crackers without incident. My pregnancy was apparently over. As the nausea lifted, I felt better than I had in days. I was exhausted, but my mind was clear, and the noises and thumping and ghosts even settled down too.

I had no idea what day it was, but I'd been in here two nights, which meant I'd be charged tomorrow or released that night.

Only I wasn't charged tomorrow. When I asked the guard about it—it had been seventy-two hours, hadn't it?—he told me that it was now Saturday, and weekends didn't count. I couldn't tell if he was lying to me or not. I'd been so preoccupied with vomiting, with the noises in the walls, that it hadn't sunk in yet that maybe I was in for more trouble than a ruined reputation and an expensive legal battle. As I lay there another entire day, a dark thought occurred to me: Maybe I'd never be charged. Maybe they'd let me die in here. If the police's case against me wasn't airtight—which I knew for a fact it wasn't, since I hadn't killed Fiona—maybe it would be easier to let me die in police custody. They could plant a suicide note on me too. *I'm sorry I murdered Fiona Farris; I can't live with the guilt anymore.* The thought of Jack reading that in the paper, thinking that of me when I was no longer around to set the record straight while a prescription pad that proved my innocence was left to rot behind the toilet in an apartment scrubbed clean and rented out to the next Pacific Pictures writer—it was nearly unbearable.

Not this, I told the universe, told myself. *Annie Laurence, you'll die someday in some stupid, senseless way—too many drugs or too much to drink or in some pointless frenzy of emotion, but not this, not this. Please. Not this.*

Finally, after two more horrible days, I was herded onto a bus with about a dozen other people, mostly men, all in the same beige jump-suits. No one bothered to explain where we were going, and I knew by this point that asking questions never produced satisfying answers. Maybe Jack had been right about the absurdity of the universe the night he'd taken off his pants in Musso & Frank's.

We arrived at a courthouse after a short trip, heading in not through the grand staircase at the front entrance but through a grimy metal door around the back, filing into the same room, where a judge called us one by one to the stand. I heard the charges of the other arrestees read out loud: Disorderly conduct. Aggravated assault. It dawned on me that I was the worst criminal in the room.

Sure enough, when it was my turn and the judge read out loud the charge of homicide, the men in the room gave a series of catcalls and wolf whistles, which were not at all silenced by the pounding of the gavel. Photographers started snapping pictures of me—none of the men had their picture taken. I was the star of today's proceedings, and I hadn't even had to lose twenty-three pounds of knee fat for the honor. The judge asked how I pleaded, and I said, "Not guilty." My bail was set at a couple thousand dollars, and I was returned to my row, cameras documenting my whole journey.

"Who'd you kill, baby?" the man next to me whispered in my ear.

"No one," I replied. "I'm being framed."

He grinned maniacally, giving me a wink. "Yeah. Me too."

I knew whatever I tried to do next to clear my name, Irma and

Devlin and the PR machine of Pacific Pictures would paint as the hysterical flailing of a guilty woman, making up nonsense because she was out of other options to save her own hide. They'd probably succeed at it too. But they were wrong if they thought I would let that stop me.

After returning to my holding cell for about an hour or so, I was marched to a room with a telephone. I wanted to call Jack, wanted him to tell me it would all be okay and bail me out and take me to his beautiful house in Santa Monica. I wanted to call Vic, tell him he'd been wrong, Fiona hadn't done this to herself. I knew neither of them would take my call after what was now four entire days of newspaper stories and police visits and gossip on the lot about what a crazy person I'd turned out to be.

I'd have to call the people who already thought I was crazy, before any of this mess. So I made my one phone call to Adam and Beverly Cook.

Beverly told me she and Adam couldn't risk being seen in public with me, let alone downtown picking me up from jail, but promised they'd find a way to help me nonetheless. It took all day, but finally— shortly after dinner—I was released into the custody of a grim-faced MGM employee with a severe hairline and hands so thick I wondered if he hadn't done a little murdering of meddling journalists himself. Without saying a word, he drove me not to the Cook house on Roxbury Drive but to a small bungalow in the Hollywood Hills.

"Where are we?" I asked when we arrived.

"It's an MGM safe house," he responded.

"You're kidding," I said.

"Sometimes in our industry, it's necessary to take meetings the press can't find out about," he said. "One example off the top of my head would be right now. So MGM has a few houses around town for that purpose. Your friends are inside; you can talk to them in private. I'll wait out here."

All this, I mused as I climbed the concrete steps toward the tiny house, for some lights and sound. Safe houses and jails and murder and sham marriages and knee weight loss and police bribes and horse-riding lessons—all for some pictures on a screen that weren't even real.

I didn't bother knocking, just pushed open the door to find Adam and Beverly seated on a brown leather couch. Beverly jumped up to hug me when I walked in. Adam didn't. "Oh my goodness, are you all right?" she squealed, pulling away to look at me and brush away a few strands of the tangled mess that was my hair. "We've been worried sick about you."

"I'm fine," I said, leaning past her to look at Adam, who was pretending to examine the freckles on his arms. "Hi, Adam."

"Annie," he replied, not looking up.

"We know you didn't do it, obviously," said Beverly. "They're printing all these awful lies about you—but we know you didn't do it."

"Did you do it?" asked Adam from the couch.

"No," I said. "I'm being set up. The head of Pacific Pictures and his weasel of a secretary killed her, and now they've arranged for me to take the fall."

"How dramatic," Adam said.

"How's the horseback riding going?" I asked him.

"What can we do to help?" Beverly interjected. "We'll do anything."

Adam grunted from the couch to indicate his objection to the word *anything*. He needn't have bothered. I knew Beverly was exaggerating since *picking me up themselves* and *letting me into their own home* were already off the table.

"A shower," I said. A few times over the last four days, I'd been permitted to stand under a pathetic stream of cold water for a few minutes, but it felt less like bathing and more like a fresh way to torture me. "I could use a shower. And something to eat."

"There's a bathroom upstairs," said Beverly. "One of my dresses is up there too—we thought you'd want something to change into. And we'll see what we can find in the kitchen."

The hot water felt so incredible cascading down my body, achy from the paper-thin cot and four days of inactivity, that I stood there for ages, only remembering that I needed to use shampoo and soap when it started to run cold. The dress Beverly had brought me was an old one of hers, red with white polka dots and a frilly detail around the bottom hem. It didn't fit me right—too big in the bust and too small in the waist—and the ill fit combined with my red hair gave the appearance of Little Orphan Annie Laurence. Still, it was hard not to be grateful. When I finally emerged downstairs, Beverly had made me a makeshift meal of a peanut butter sandwich, some applesauce, and a few shortbread cookies, which were stale but I ate anyway.

As they watched me eat, they made awful small talk about the pictures they'd worked on so far, either not noticing or not caring that I said nothing as I chewed on my sandwich. After I'd finished eating, Adam poured us all martinis, which I had to stop myself from downing in one sip.

Beverly was in the middle of describing her dance lessons when I interrupted. "Which one of you spoke to the police about me?" I asked.

There was a shared look between them. "We both did," said Beverly. "Together and separately."

"Because that's a large part of their story," I said. "They're saying I killed Fiona because she found out about an affair we had, that I followed you out here because I'm in love with Adam. If you really want to do something to help me, that's one thing: tell the police that isn't true."

They were quiet for a moment too long. "Sorry, Annie," said Adam finally. "But I mean…isn't it sort of true? You did move out here for us."

"Because you left me with nothing," I blurted out. None of us had expected me to agree with him, and we all took a second to blink at one another in shock. "You took my furniture, and you took my future. My play closed and I was too depressed to write another. I didn't have other friends. You two had been my only real friends. I couldn't tell my family what was going on, not all of it. I built a life with the two of you, and you took it away with no warning. Yes, I followed you out here, but not to win you back—not entirely. Without the two of you, I had nothing else. That's what I was following. That's why I came."

Neither of them knew how to respond to that. Adam folded his hands together and stared at them. Beverly's gaze wandered aimlessly around the living room. Finally, she cleared her throat. "You know, we're sorry if we hurt you—"

"You don't have to," I interrupted. "Let's all just move on."

Relief washed over their faces. "What's your plan now?" asked Beverly.

I exhaled. "Fiona was murdered because she found out a secret about Henry Hilbert," I said finally. "In my apartment, I have proof Devlin's secretary was at the Canteen when Fiona died. At Henry Hilbert's house in Calabasas is proof that Fiona was going to write an article about him. So I suppose I need to take my proof to Henry Hilbert and convince him to come clean on his own. Henry's evidence proves Devlin had motive, my evidence proves Irma had opportunity, and both of them found the means in the pages of our play."

"It's so grim," said Beverly with a shudder.

"But if Devlin and Irma are working with the police, how are you going to convince them?" asked Adam.

"If the police are in the pocket of the studio, it'll need to be undeniable," I said. "A public scandal. Something that makes arresting Devlin and Irma worth more than whatever sum of money they've been paid. If it's not that, they'll just poison my coffee, same as they did to her."

"I can drive you," said Adam immediately. "I don't want you getting in a car with anyone I don't trust."

This sudden flare of protectiveness made me soft. There was no future in which we were all back together again, but maybe there was one where we were something resembling friends. "Thank you," I said.

He glanced at his watch. "You'd better hurry, though. Hilbert's on at the Hollywood Bowl in an hour."

We stopped at my apartment, where, to my relief, the prescription pad was still hiding in its spot behind the toilet. The cops had clearly searched the place, but since there wasn't all that much to search, they'd mostly made a mess, probably out of a desire to appear intimidating. Was it really necessary to throw the ten dresses I owned onto the floor of my bedroom to conduct a thorough search of my enormous closet? I doubted it.

I thought about changing, but I didn't have time. Beverly's ill-fitting red dress would have to suit. I returned to the car, where Adam was waiting.

"Was it still there?" he asked.

"Thankfully, yes," I told him.

"Good," he said, starting the engine. We took off, Adam driving surprisingly fast, and ten minutes later we reached Highland Avenue. Traffic slowed as we joined the line of cars en route to the concert, snaking their way up a hill toward the parking lot. I glanced over and noticed Adam looked like he was on the verge of throwing up.

"What's wrong?" I asked.

"We need to talk" was his response, but he didn't elaborate further.

"All right," I said finally. "What about?"

"I think it would be best for everyone if we all pretended that story we told the police was true. You're a friend of Bev's I met in college once Bev and I were engaged. You and I had a brief affair, we all sorted it out, and now we're not in each other's lives much."

"Don't worry, I'm not going to go spilling our secrets to the press," I said. "If my case goes to trial, I'll stick to that story."

"Not just in the trial," he replied. "Between us. All of us. I think we should all forget anything more than that happened. Never mention it again, even when we're alone."

I looked at him, confused. He kept his eyes firmly on the road in front of him, his hands glued to the steering wheel. "Even when we're alone? Why?"

"Because—it's—" He sighed, exasperated. "With the police involved and the studio involved—"

"Are you worried they could be spying on you?"

"No, I'm not worried about that—Annie, I know you kissed her!" he exclaimed finally. "I know you came to the house the other day when I wasn't there and you kissed her!"

My jaw dropped, and I leaned back in my seat, stunned. "First of all, she kissed me—"

"That doesn't matter."

"It matters to me!"

"You got her alone and you—"

"I didn't know you weren't going to be there. It's not like I planned—"

"It's too much, on top of everything else. You've lost the privilege of talking frankly to us. You've lost your entitlement to our past," he said. "From now on, you're a friend of Bev's from college who I met once Bev and I—"

"Pull over," I said. "I'll walk from here."

He sighed again. "Don't be dramatic—"

"What do you care if I am? I'm only a friend of Bev's from college, who you met once you and Bev were engaged," I replied.

"It's all uphill from here. You don't want to walk it—"

"I don't mind a walk."

"You already look awful. Your hair isn't done; your dress doesn't fit. If you walk in this heat, it'll only be worse."

That was the final straw for me, the fact that he didn't want to spare me a walk not because he still liked me but because he was thinking of my appearance. I opened the door right there in the middle of Highland Avenue.

"If Devlin Murray murders me tonight," I told him as I got out of the car, "know that I died wishing I'd never met either one of you."

I slammed the door.

Despite Adam's concerns over my unset hair and my secondhand outfit, the guard at the stage door seemed completely unperturbed by my appearance. I explained I was a reporter, there to interview Mr. Durand for *Variety*. I didn't even get to the part of the fib where I'd forgotten my press badge before I was kindly given directions to the dressing rooms.

The stark white bowels of the Hollywood Bowl were poorly lit and eerily empty, silent except for the cacophony of thousands of concert-goers picnicking above us. Their muffled voices and piercing laughter gave me the feeling of walking through a crypt, hearing the faraway sounds of the living. I walked past a few closed doors until I reached the one labeled "Dressing Room B."

I stopped dead in my tracks. They were inside, all of them. I could hear their voices through the door: June screeching some one-liner, Victor responding, Jack laughing, Terry shushing. I hadn't expected them all to be there. The Ambassador's Club had been permanently dead only a few days earlier. How had so much changed?

I knocked on the door. After a few seconds, June answered, giving me a scoff, a very cold once-over, and an icy sneer. "I'll give you this," she began. "It takes guts to show your face here, that's for sure."

"Please tell me you don't believe it," I said. "I didn't kill her."

"Then now you know how it feels," she replied, "to be accused of something you didn't do."

"June, I'm so sorry," I said. "For everything."

"You've been arrested for my best friend's murder," she replied. "An apology isn't what I'm looking for."

"I'm being set up," I insisted. "I can prove it, but I need to talk to Vic."

June was about to slam the door in my face, but Vic spoke up from inside the room. "Let her in," he said.

Reluctantly, June stepped aside, holding the door open for me. The dressing room was much larger than the trailer in which the club usually gathered. It reminded me of the spacious room Beverly and Adam had shared backstage at *Altogether Too Many Murders*. A mirror stretched the length of one wall, a coffee table in the middle had been set up with meats and cheeses, and nearly every available surface was covered in bouquets of flowers. Vic was sitting at the makeup table in front of the long mirror, Jack leaning next to him, Terry perched on a couch in front of the finger foods. All three were glaring at me with looks that could kill.

I figured I ought to cut right to the chase. "I didn't kill her," I said, reaching into my bag to take out the prescription pad. "It was Devlin—Devlin and Irma. I found this at the Canteen kitchen, shoved under the island."

I could read it on Terry's face before I even produced the pad: it was plausible to her, and part of her was kicking herself for not thinking of it sooner. Whether Devlin was behind this particular murder, who could say, but there was no denying he could be behind some murder somewhere, that he had the resources and the influence to think he could get away with it.

Terry knew all that. The rest of the group was not so charitable. June came over to snatch the prescription pad from my hand and flip through it. "She could have dropped this anytime," she replied with a huff before letting it fall to the floor. I quickly bent down to pick it up. "It could have been under there for months."

"She had it when I first met with Devlin, a few days before Fiona died," I tried to argue. "Then, a few days later, she offered me sleeping pills and didn't have it. She had to call it in."

"That doesn't mean she's the one who dropped it," June argued back. "You could have stolen it from her. Planted the evidence."

"Sherman Oaks," said Terry suddenly. "The police told the *Dispatch* receptionist Fiona's things were supposed to go to a house in Sherman Oaks. Irma lives in Sherman Oaks."

"A lot of people live in Sherman Oaks," replied June.

"You have to trust me," I pleaded.

"Why would we do that?" Jack asked, his eyes piercing mine. "You've been lying to us from the beginning. Ever since you pretended to spill a glass of water on Fiona to get close to us."

So that had made it to the papers. "I only wanted to be your friend," I said. "And I was, I think. Wasn't I?"

"No," said June, almost laughing. "It's when you came along that everything went south. You had us all convinced our friendship was poison, when it was you all along."

I understood now. They were all back to wisecracking in a dressing room, not because they'd forgiven each other but because they'd bonded over not forgiving me. "Fine, you don't have to like me. But please." I looked at Vic. "She died over it."

He stared at me for a moment, then dropped his gaze. He reached over and grabbed a cigarette, lighting it with shaking hands.

"Died over what?" said Jack.

"The prescription pad proves they had opportunity," I said, still looking only at Vic. "If you and Henry come clean, that proves they had motive."

"Oh no," said Terry, turning to Vic. "What did you do?"

"Nothing!" scoffed Vic.

"Then what did Henry do?"

"Wait," said Jack. "Devlin killed Fiona over something Henry did?"

"No," said Victor, looking at me. "No, you're wrong. It wasn't that. It was a suicide or it was—it wasn't that." He lowered his voice, as if that would keep the other people in the room from hearing him. "Devlin and Irma didn't know."

"Henry told them," I said. "In the interview—Jack said Irma interviewed him, all about his past. They surely did the same for Henry. He told them, and then he gave them all the evidence, and he lied to you and said movers lost it."

"Henry wouldn't have done that. He wouldn't have told them," Victor responded, but he didn't sound certain of that. "It was our joke. À quatre mains. Our secret."

"Like Henry hadn't thrown you under the bus before," said Jack.

"You don't even know what the hell we're talking about," snapped Victor.

"Then enlighten us," June said.

"Nothing. We're talking about nothing," Victor declared. "I have to debut a concerto in front of seventeen thousand people in fifteen minutes. This is not the time for this. Annie's guilty. They arrested her. She's a stalker who followed some MGM actor out here, and when she couldn't weasel her way into his life, she weaseled her way into ours."

"I'm not a stalker!" I shouted. "We were in love! I'm done hiding it or denying it—we were in love! His name is Adam, and his wife's name is Beverly, and we were—all three of us—we were all together, I loved both of them, and they both loved me. And I know that might not make sense, or it might make me look worse in your eyes, but I don't care anymore. That's the truth. The three of us were together for seven years. Seven years! We had just bought new furniture. We were planning for the future. And they got MGM contracts and dumped me because the chance to be a Hollywood star was worth more than me. I did follow them out here, in a way, but can you blame me for that? They took everything I had, and I only wanted it back. Is that worse than what you did, for the man you love?"

Everyone only stared at me, and I found myself wishing one of them would crack a joke about me, anything to make the moment less mortifying. I felt as if I'd sliced open a vein and were bleeding out on the floor.

"What did you do?" Terry finally asked Victor again.

"It doesn't matter," I said. The initial terror was melting away, and with it came relief. If Irma and Devlin managed to lock me up for good—or worse—the truth was out there now. "Nothing matters. Only that they want me to pretend it never happened, and I don't want to do that. Their names are Adam and Beverly Cook, and I was in love with them, and they were in love with me, and it was real. It was. I don't want their lies to be the final say on my life. But don't worry about it. I'll leave now. Break a leg, or whatever it is you say to pianists. Break a finger."

"Well, you don't say *that*," cried Victor, but I was already halfway out the door.

"Annie, wait—" called Terry. I halted, turning back as Terry addressed the rest of the group. "Is this the justice we want for our friend? If Annie's right and we do nothing, Irma and Devlin walk free."

"I don't walk anywhere," said a voice behind me.

TWENTY-ONE

———⫷⫸———

Devlin Murray, with Irma right behind him, stark-brown victory curls high as always, sidestepped me and entered the dressing room. Terry leapt to her feet. "Mr. Murray! We weren't expecting you," she said cheerfully.

"I'm spending a lot of money to film this concert. I figured that earned me a ticket," Devlin replied. "What were you all saying about me?"

"Only that once we shoot this concert, the Hilbert picture's done and we can all walk away free," Terry improvised without missing a beat.

"Ain't that the truth." Devlin's eyes suddenly fell to me. "You're the writer of mine who got arrested for killing that reporter," he realized.

"Yes," I said.

"What the hell are you doing here?"

"Bail?" I answered meekly. I realized I still held Irma's prescription pad in my hand, and I quickly hid it behind my back, hoping neither of them had seen it.

He moved on, leaning over the coffee table to grab a few slices of prosciutto, wiping his greasy hands after on the inside of his jacket. I saw Jack narrow his eyes as he watched the two of them move about the room. "Hi, Irma," he said.

"Mr. Kott," she replied.

"I like your hair," Jack went on. "Have you always worn it like that?"

"I want to talk to you all about something," Devlin interrupted. "I was thinking: it doesn't make much sense for the Hilbert picture to end with someone else playing the Hollywood Bowl."

"Henry's conducting," said Terry.

"Can they switch?"

Victor snorted, which caused Devlin to glare at him. "No, you can't switch the soloist and the conductor minutes before the show starts. This isn't a movie set. What we do requires talent and rehearsal," said Victor.

"We just spoke to Henry," said Irma. "He said he would be willing."

"Oh, did he? How swell of him. I'm unwilling," said Victor. "Terry…"

"Like you said, Devlin, we're spending a lot of money to film this thing. Let's stick to the plan," said Terry smoothly.

"Fine," Devlin conceded. "Then after Durand finishes the ditty—"

"Concerto, for fuck's sake, it's an entire concerto—"

"Don't swear at me. After whatever it's called is done, we'll have them switch for the encore. As long as we have some shots of Henry, we can fake that he played the whole thing in editing."

"Aw, come on, Devlin," Jack interjected. "It works just fine for the picture to have Henry conducting and Vic playing. The conductor's more important than the soloist anyway, right, Vic?"

"Yes, that's what I always say," replied Victor. "A conductor is *not* merely a metronome with narcissism."

"Switch for the encore," Devlin declared with a tone of finality.

"I was trying to help you," Jack muttered to Vic.

"I said a conductor's *not* a metronome with narcissism. What if I refuse?"

Devlin, who had been heading for the door already, turned around to take in Victor again. "What do you mean, what if you refuse? I'll cut your Pacific contract, that's what."

"Can you cut it with cocaine?" replied Victor.

June laughed. Devlin shook his head. "Terrible people, all of you. You make the convicted murderer look good."

"I'm not convicted," I argued.

"Well, you are fired," he said.

"You can't fire someone for being arrested," I said. "I'm innocent until proven guilty."

"Not according to my morality clause," Devlin replied. "This whole room could study that morality clause! Who let me make a multi-million-dollar motion picture with a bunch of fairies, Commies, and Chinese?"

Laughing to himself, he started out the door, Irma following him.

"How is being Chinese against the morality clause?" June muttered.

"He can drag me off the stage if he wants. I'm not giving Henry the encore," said Victor.

"Everyone, shut up," said Jack, quietly but forcefully. He moved to the door, crossing the room in two giant strides, and peered out into the hallway after Irma and Devlin. "Oh no," he said. "Oh no."

"What's the matter?" June asked.

Jack darted back into the room, closing the door behind him. "Horns," he whispered. "Remember I said the figure I saw leaving the Canteen that night had horns? It was Irma's hair, her victory curls—I saw her!"

"No," said June.

"Holy shit," said Terry, turning to me. "You were right. You were actually right."

"I tried to tell you," I said.

"No, we can't do this now—we can't," pleaded Victor. "I have to perform. Can this wait until after the show?"

"No!" cried Jack. "Annie could be in danger—"

"Yes, yes, it can," countered Terry. She lowered her voice. "As far as Irma and Devlin know, Annie's going down for it and no one has any idea she's innocent. She's not in any danger—not yet, at least."

Jack had started pacing the room, his hands buried in his hair. "All right," he said finally, looking at Victor. "Let Henry play the encore, okay? I don't want you literally dying out there."

"That's funny," said Victor. "I was just thinking Henry will play that encore over my dead body."

The five of us made our way over to stage right, where Henry Hilbert was waiting in the wings. He perked up at the sight of us. "Look, Terry. There's a camera back here. One of the ones that records sound, too," he said excitedly, pointing to the stationary camera resting on a tripod, its unblinking lens staring at us. "Maybe we could stage some business for Vic and I to do when we come off."

"I could kiss you on the mouth," offered Victor.

Henry recoiled. "Shhh, it could be on."

Terry rolled her eyes. "We're not wasting film to shoot this. It's one of the spares for the boys onstage grabbing close-ups, since we can't stop the concert if a camera breaks. Although"—she turned to me—"it's not the worst idea. Want to write a scene real quick?"

I shot her a look that said she must be nuts. Terry quickly backed off, but it was enough to cause Henry to notice me. "What's she doing here? Isn't she…?"

"A murderer?" Jack finished. "Yes. We all are. We killed Fiona together, and now we're coming for you. Don't drink the water at the conductor's stand."

"You shouldn't joke about that," scolded Henry. "That isn't funny. Seriously, what's she doing here?"

Before he could get an answer, the stage manager came over to usher him onstage to lead the orchestra in "The Star-Spangled Banner." He gave Victor one last encouraging pat on the shoulder. "Give 'em hell," he said.

"Don't fuck it up," Victor replied.

Henry's hand lingered there. "See, this is a nice visual," he said. "The stage behind us like this? We should be filming this."

With that, he turned and headed onstage.

The crowd erupted into thunderous applause, and Henry took it in from the conductor's stand with an "aw, shucks" demeanor and a handsome smile. I did have to hand it to Devlin and Irma on that one: I personally wouldn't have gone shopping for replacement movie stars in the world of fortysomething composers, but Henry had a certain charisma, even beyond the goodwill around him from being one of the most popular songwriters of the last twenty years. The crowd refused to stop cheering, and eventually Henry just began the national anthem instead of waiting for the noise to die down.

After we'd finished standing for our country, Jack, June, Terry, and I settled into a handful of folding chairs that had been set up for those watching from backstage. It wasn't until I was collapsed in that chair in the dark of the wings that I realized how destroyed I felt. The sandwich hadn't stuck to my stomach at all, and I was already hungry again, and my dry throat ached for a glass of water. More than anything, though, my head felt like it was made of sandbags. I longed to lay it down on Jack's shoulder next to me, but I doubted it would be welcome. I snuck him a sideways glance to see if he would look at me, but his gaze remained fixed ahead, watching Victor methodically crack each one of his knuckles.

Onstage, Henry turned around to speak into the microphone that had been placed behind the conductor's stand. "I'm thrilled to be here to debut my latest work," he began, switching tones from celebratory to sober as smoothly as an actor reading lines. "As many of you know, while composing this concerto, I lost a dear friend of mine. So without further adieu, allow me to introduce Mr. Victor Durand to play the *Concerto for Fiona.*"

Victor came out to significantly less applause than Henry had, and even though I couldn't see his face, I could tell from the slump of his shoulders that this annoyed him. He settled in at the piano off to Henry's left and gave Henry a little nod.

The piece began with a literal bang, a large drum going off that caused me to jump in my seat. This was followed by a blast of trumpets, the strings following in a frantic piece of music that sounded like a train crashing forward. As quickly as it arrived, it all ceased, leaving the piano alone, a slow and sour, angry melody.

I couldn't help but remember the first time I saw Vic play at the Canteen, the night Fiona died. That night, the first movement seemed to fly by; tonight, every second seemed to take a lifetime. There were no languid, romantic melodies in this piece to carry one away in emotional reveries. Vic struck each note as if it were a drum, demanding that attention be paid. This close to the orchestra, the vibrations through the air sent me reeling. I gripped the seat of my chair and shut my eyes. The music began to pick up the pace, growing more and more frantic, making me dizzier with each forward dive in the tempo. The air around me felt anxious and electric, as if one spark could burn this place to the ground.

The first movement finally came to an end, and Jack leaned over to me. "Henry might be an ass, but boy, he really can write 'em, can't he?"

The second movement began, quieter and prettier than the first, a glockenspiel joining Vic's twinkling on the keys. I opened my eyes and could tell immediately from the look on Jack's face that something was wrong with me. "Christ, but you're pale," he said. "You okay?"

I tried to shake my head, but the action made the whole wings swim. It wasn't the energy of the music making me feel dizzy, I realized. I was dizzy. "I think I might throw up," I managed to say.

Jack jumped to his feet, taking my arms and lifting me out of the chair before reaching down to grab my purse. June looked at us, concerned. "Where are you going?"

"Annie needs water," explained Jack. "We'll be back."

His warm arm around my waist, Jack led me out of the wings and back into the labyrinth of white backstage hallways. We made our slow way to a women's restroom, where Jack kicked open the door and helped me sit against the wall. The cool tile felt good on the backs of my legs and my neck. He ran a handkerchief under the sink and then knelt in front of me, pressing it against my forehead. "Better?"

"Thanks," I mumbled.

"I'm going to get a cup for some water. Don't move, okay?"

"Really? I was thinking I might go out and play the encore."

Jack managed a small smile as he headed for the door. "Ah, she has jokes. That means either everything's fine or she's on the verge of death. Seriously, Annie, stay put."

He needn't have sounded so worried. I was perfectly happy to lean back and close my eyes. I could still hear the music in here, but it was softer, not grabbing me by the chest with its pulsating anxiety anymore. The room was no longer spinning so violently around me. Once Jack returned and I could have some water, I thought, I'd feel just fine.

I heard the door and opened my eyes. Only instead of Jack, I was face-to-face with Irma.

She must have followed us, as she didn't seem surprised to see me. I saw her take in my state on the floor for a heartbeat only. Then she dove for my purse.

I screamed, even knowing it would be useless with the roar of an eighty-piece symphony only a few yards away. The only thing I could think to do was to roll on top of my bag, pinning it between my body and the ground. She grabbed me by the hair and tried to pull me off it. "Give it to me!" she shouted.

"Give what to you?"

"Don't play dumb!" She smacked me across the back of the head, sending stars across my field of vision. "The prescription pad. You had it in your hand the whole time we were in that dressing room. Do you think I'm blind?"

She had dug her knees into my back by now, lifting me up by the hair again and then letting my head crash forward onto the tile. I cried out. "Jack—"

"Jack's not coming back," she said.

The words sent a chill down my spine, and she took advantage of my momentary weakness to once again bash my head into the floor. This time everything went black, but thankfully only for a moment. I came to with the taste of blood from my nose running down into my mouth. "Do you think I won't kill you, too?" she sneered. "It'll be worlds easier to kill you than it was to kill her. I'll be thrilled to not spend hours skulking around the Farris front lawn collecting poisonous leaves first. We won't have to make it look like a suicide with you, because no one cares enough about you to want to see your body after."

It wasn't the repeated blows to the head that got to me. It was this. That after twenty-eight years of life on earth I had nothing to show besides two exes who wanted to pretend we had never dated, four friends who wouldn't miss me if I were gone, and a handful of uncredited scenes in the motion picture telling of the made-up life of Henry Hilbert. I was just as much of a fraud as he was, only I hadn't even been successful at it.

I went limp, and Irma grabbed me by my shoulders and yanked me over, taking the purse into her arms. I didn't fight it. I only wanted it all to be over.

It wasn't. Irma dug through the purse, confirming the pad was indeed inside before looping it over her shoulder and barking at me to stand up.

"Stand up?" I repeated. "Why?"

"You think I'm going to leave you here on the floor for the whole woodwind section to find in five minutes? You're coming with me."

Irma marched me out of the bathroom, shooting furtive glances around us as she led me down the hallway. The concerto was in its bombastic third movement now, the music loud and unwieldy.

Devlin appeared from around a corner, jogging up to us. He grabbed my free arm and helped to muscle me down the hall. "Did you take care of Kott?" Irma asked him.

Devlin nodded. "Had him escorted out. Where are we taking this one?"

"Out back. Our guys are on the way," answered Irma. "We'll say she attacked me in the ladies' washroom. They can bring her in for that, keep her for violating the conditions of her bail."

The music reached a final crescendo and applause erupted from the audience. *Good for Vic*, I thought stupidly.

"We'd better hurry," said Devlin.

"We still have the encores," Irma reminded him. "I told Henry to play the whole sonata. That'll buy us ten minutes, at least. Fifteen if he milks it."

"I hate classical music," muttered Devlin. "How am I supposed to know what a tune's about if there aren't any words?"

The applause died down, presumably as Henry returned to the stage and sat at the piano. Except then a voice came booming out across the canyon that was not Henry's.

"I was told I'm supposed to let Henry play the encore," said Victor into the microphone. "But I feel like hearing Chopin, and Henry can't play Chopin. So let's have some Chopin."

Victor began to play some wild, frantic piece. Devlin stopped in his tracks, and Irma nearly stumbled as the action forced her to stop as well. "That motherfucker," cursed Devlin, his face suddenly beet red. He released his painful grasp on my bicep and stalked off toward the stage. "We told him—in no uncertain terms—he was not to play! I'm going to break every last one of that man's fingers! No one disrespects me like that in this town and gets away with it!"

Irma turned to look after him, seeming to be too afraid to tell him to stop, and I saw my chance. I gathered up any remaining strength I could find and elbowed Irma square in the chest. As she went down, arms flailing, eyes wide in shock, I grabbed my purse and ran.

I was hardly thinking. If I had any plan at all, it was only to get back to the wings, to where June and Terry could possibly help me. Irma screamed at Devlin to stop me, but I was past him before he realized what was happening. I reached a sign pointing toward the stage and followed it, only to discover once I was through the door that while stage right had been host to stage managers and friends watching in the wings, I was on stage left, utterly alone except for a second spare camera, again fixing me with an unblinking stare. I'd have to run out on the stage, I thought. They couldn't murder me in front of seventeen thousand witnesses, not if they still hoped to pretend I'd committed suicide. Although it'd be a shame to ruin the Chopin with my broken nose and hysterical ranting. I'd be playing right into the deranged stalker story Irma and Devlin wanted to tell about me, too. The crazy killer running onstage in the middle of a piano solo while bleeding profusely would be all over the papers, but there was nothing else for it.

Unless—was there?

I had only moments to set up my plan, and no certainty if I'd done it right or if it would work at all. Within seconds, Irma and Devlin had found me.

"You take one more step towards me, and I run out on the stage and tell the whole world what you did to Fiona," I told them breathlessly.

Devlin only laughed. "You think that will work? You're nobody. I own a movie studio. Between now and the day your trial starts, we'll have every paper in town printing stories about how crazy you are. I'll send my friends at the police station to harass any friend you might have until it's not worth it to believe you. Make no mistake: Pacific Pictures owns your story, and Pacific Pictures will decide how it ends."

"Then let's write an ending that works for all of us," I said. "I'll hand over Irma's prescription pad, the one you lost at the Canteen while you were killing Fiona. In exchange, you tell the cops to drop the charges against me. Everyone walks away."

Devlin scoffed. "You think we need some silly prescription pad?"

"No, Mr. Murray, I don't think *you* do," I said to him before turning to look at Irma. "It's your name that's on it. You that did the dirty work. Do you trust him not to let you take the fall for all of it? Killing Fiona was his idea too. I'm sure of it."

Irma hesitated, then held out her hand. I could have melted in relief. I reached into my bag and handed her the pad. She tucked it away inside her jacket. "Thanks," she said, then turned to Devlin. "Tell Kiblowski to shoot her."

Before I could process what was happening, Devlin was on me, pinning my arms behind my back with one hand and covering my mouth with the other. I tried to scream, but it was muffled enough that no one could hear me. Devlin started to drag me away just as whatever Victor was playing now came to a conclusion and the audience began to applaud.

"That was Chopin, *Étude Number Four, in C-Sharp Minor*," he said into the microphone. "Like I said, Henry can't play it. In fact, there's a lot of things Henry Hilbert can't do."

Devlin and Irma weren't listening to him anymore, but I was. I managed to wrestle free of Devlin's hand just long enough. "Vic—" I shouted, and his head snapped up. Our eyes locked. It was only for a moment as Devlin proceeded to muscle me out of sight, but I swear I saw him smile.

"Enough of this," Vic said, for all of the Hollywood Bowl, for the live radio audience, for the five cameras positioned around to canyon to hear. "Henry Hilbert didn't write that concerto. I did."

Devlin stopped in his tracks and shut his eyes, as if this were a dream he could wake up from. Onstage, Vic continued. "I'm serious. I wrote the concerto you just heard. I wrote Henry's last concerto. I wrote every song that's been published under his name for the last nine years. Understandably, a lot of people want me to keep quiet about this, but I'm done. I suppose you could say I don't want their lies to be the final say on my life."

Whatever plan they had to take me out back and shoot me like a dog was abandoned. Letting go of me, Devlin stalked onto the stage, Irma right behind, begging him not to do anything rash. "Ah—here's my boss," announced Vic at the sight of him. "Mr. Devlin Murray, ladies and gentlemen! I suppose that concludes the evening's performance. Thanks for coming to the world-famous Hollywood Bowl. Henry Hilbert is a fraud. Drive safely!"

Devlin tore the microphone off its stand and grabbed Vic by the lapels. I didn't wait around for them to shoot me amidst the pandemonium. I ran.

I made it to Vic's dressing room just after they did. June and Terry had managed to separate Vic from Devlin. As Henry wailed in the corner, Vic poured himself a drink.

"Here's what we're going to do," Devlin shouted. "I'll tell the papers that you're on drugs—"

"True," said Vic.

"That you're mentally insane—"

"Also true."

"And having delusions of grandeur."

"They're not *delusions*—"

"How could you do this to me?" shouted Henry. "I should have told you to go to hell. The first time you showed up at my apartment—'*Mr. Hilbert, I'm such a fan*'—I should have told you to go to hell."

"Let's get one thing straight: *You* invited *me* over."

"You could have written under your own name," continued Henry. "I never stopped you—I never asked for this! You've ruined me!"

"They killed her over it," said Vic. "You might not believe it—I didn't at first—but it's true. Annie figured it out. It's not worth it. It's not worth it anymore."

"This is all horseshit," roared Devlin. "You're going to publicly acknowledge you were lying, high, insane—I don't care which. I'm carting you off to an institution tonight, and after six months in an asylum, I might let you work again. If you refuse, I know a guy who will break every bone in your hands before you finish wiping your ass at the Trocadero bathroom—"

"You're the insane one if you think I'm working for you ever again. Besides, I prefer the Cocoanut Grove."

In the blink of an eye, Devlin had Vic by the throat, the glass in Vic's hands tumbling to the ground. June screamed. Terry grabbed Devlin, muscling her way in between the two.

"You have no idea," Devlin spat, "the amount of money I've spent to turn that marshmallow into a star. I'm not letting you ruin my picture over a murder allegation you'll never prove and some secret you've been perfectly content to keep for a decade." Devlin rounded on Henry. "I bet on you precisely because you told me he would never tell! You told me you were certain!"

Devlin finally released his grip on Vic's throat. Vic gasped for air, stumbling forward. He braced himself against the counter and looked to Henry. "Oh, Henry..." he said quietly. "Tell me you didn't. Tell me you weren't the one who told them."

Henry was a mess now, sobbing and shaking. "I had to," he managed to say. "Irma brought me in—she said that if Pacific was going to make me into a star, they had to know everything—they had to be prepared—"

"And when Fiona told you what she was writing—when she asked you for a statement—you told them that, too?"

"I'm so sorry," whispered Henry. "I had to. For the movie...I had to... I didn't know he was going to..."

"You knew all this time," said Vic. "You knew all this time the two of them killed her. You spoke at her goddamn funeral—you monster—"

"I didn't know," said Henry. "Not for sure—"

"You suspected! And you didn't tell me! Didn't tell anyone!"

"I couldn't!" cried Henry. "My movie—"

"You idiot!" Vic shouted. "That's not real! It's a movie! Fiona was real!"

"All right, folks, here's what we're going to do," said a voice. Detective Kiblowski had appeared in the doorway, Cooper to his right leading along a handcuffed Jack. Irma lingered behind them, a smug smile on her face. "Miss Laurence, Mr. Durand, you're coming with us and Mr. Kott."

"Like hell I am! What did I do?" snapped Vic.

The sides of the room, I observed, were starting to change color, from white to gray to black. After a moment, I realized this was not due to some magic hue-shifting paint but that my field of vision was starting to go dark. As the police attempted to restrain Vic, I waved Terry over to me.

"I'm about to faint," I whispered.

"No wonder—you're gushing blood—here," Terry tried to put a handkerchief against my nose. I swatted it away.

"No time," I said, keeping my voice low. "I got them, on camera.

Irma and Devlin confessing. One of the spare cameras, off on stage left… Don't let the cops get to it first."

Our eyes locked, and Terry nodded.

Some handcuffs were placed on me once again, and Vic, Jack, and I were led down the hall and out of the back entrance to a waiting police car.

"Is it true, what you said?" Jack said to Vic once they had piled all three of us in the back seat. "You wrote all that music?"

"Yes," said Vic.

"And that's why Fiona's dead."

"Yes."

Jack was quiet for a moment. "You could have told me," he said finally. "You could have at least told me."

"Jack—"

It would be the last thing I heard before everything went black.

TWENTY-TWO

If I had been in any state to appreciate irony, I probably would have found it amusing that it was an amateur movie that brought down the movie studio. Accounts of Devlin and Irma's taped confession were in the papers, snippets of it played on the radio, a handful of daring movie theaters even played the whole thing in their newsreels. I missed all of that. If you want to avoid having to spend a month in the mental hospital, I would recommend not telling the doctor who is resetting your broken nose that you have also been hallucinating noises from the vacant upstairs apartment for the last month and a half.

The time I spent in the hospital was mostly a blur, days that blended together with nothing to pass the hours besides sleep, which was nearly impossible to come by given the constant agitated noises of my fellow neurotics. The police came several times in the first few days to take statements from me, although none of them were Misters Kiblowski or Cooper. If that had anything to do with them losing their jobs for taking bribes from Pacific Pictures to cover up a murder, I could only speculate.

Sometime early on, I was told I had visitors, and my heart leapt at the thought of seeing June, Jack, Vic, and Terry again. Imagine my disappointment when my old acquaintances from college, Mr. and Mrs. Adam Cook, strolled in.

"You know, you're a hero," said Adam at one point, and Beverly nodded enthusiastically in agreement, too-blond curls bouncing. "You managed to stop Devlin Murray before he killed again."

"It wasn't even the first time, you know," added Beverly. "He had some actor's mistress killed back in '39 when she threatened to go public about their relationship. And he tampered with a crime scene to cover up for a star who had killed her lover."

"Everyone's talking about you," said Adam. "The whole world will want an interview once you're out of here."

He said it like it was exciting news, something I should look forward to. "That sounds exhausting," I said.

"No, you should be thrilled!" cried Beverly. "Every studio will want to turn this into a movie! You'd better start thinking about who you want to play you." She batted her eyelashes and giggled.

"This has been the worst year of my life. I'm not turning it into a movie," I snapped.

She forced a smile. "You're tired," she said. "We'll come back another time, how's that?"

They never came back.

It was June who came next, strolling into my room about two weeks later, two cigarettes dangling from her mouth. She lit them both and handed one to me as she perched on the edge of my bed. "Okay, so here's the latest," she began, like we were two friends catching up for drinks and not two neurotics who had both accused the other of murder. "After the public outcry and the arrest, Devlin appointed his kid to take over, but of course no one wants the kid of the murderer running the studio, so the board is trying to oust him. He's holding firm, but the studio's hemorrhaging money. Everyone's either leaving on principle or the kid's selling contracts to try to get enough money to fight the takeover."

"Hi, June," I said.

She wrinkled her nose at me, as if to ask why I would waste time on greeting her when there were more important things to discuss. "Hi, Annie? So the point is, Terry got a job at Paramount, I'm following her there, and she dispatched me to come see you because, apparently, you've got a script with a great part for me."

I had no idea what she was talking about. It felt like I hadn't ever written a word. Finally, it came back to me. "Oh, you mean *Don't Count Your Coconuts*? It's not great. Terry read it. She liked the dialogue I wrote for you but that was it."

"Not that," said June. "I'm not making another movie where I play a sexy Asian lady on a beach—fuck no. She meant *Altogether Too Many Murders*." She took a drag on her cigarette. "Good title. Has a ring of truth to it."

"Terry wants to make that?" I said. "And you want to be in it?"

"Terry said it was good. Is it not good?"

"No, it's good," I said. "I meant…after everything I did."

"Oh." She shrugged. "I did some stuff to you too. Jack told me you guessed it, actually. Remember?"

"Memory's not my strong suit these days," I remarked.

"The detectives asked me to spy on the club for them and report back," said June. "And I agreed. I told them all about you and Jack—I saw that made it to the papers, how you got your Commie boyfriend to cover for you. So you and Jack embarrassed me at the Canteen, and I got you arrested. Let's call it even. I'd rather hold grudges against people who are less fun."

"It's forgotten," I said. "Figuratively and literally."

"Terry wants me in the part your ex-girlfriend played," said June, her eyes twinkling. "Hope you're okay with that. You weren't planning to take it to MGM and try and win her back?"

"No," I said, so quickly that both of us laughed. "No, I… I wasn't planning on that."

"How did that even work?" she asked. "All three of you, together? Like, if you and Mrs. Cook wanted to have a round, did you have to wait for Mr. Cook to come home first…?"

I laughed, and blushed, and buried my head in my hands. "No!" I said.

"So you all must have been constantly going at it, like, all the time."

"A usual amount, it was a—"

"Just a den of sin over there, huh."

I hadn't laughed in a very long time, and my abdominals were hurting already. "It was mostly very dull," I said. "I would write, Adam would read Russian literature, Beverly would play the piano…"

"Oh, that does sound boring. At least Vic will be jealous. He's thought for years he's so interesting because he's queer, and now here you come along, liking them both."

"How is he?" I asked.

June pursed her lips, took another drag on her cigarette. "He's been holed up in his house for three weeks. We all have, I suppose. I went to see him a couple days ago, and he didn't say a word to me the whole time, just sat there and played Chopin. I'd ask him how he was feeling or if he's been sleeping all right, and be met with an unblinking stare and a nocturne. It was terrifying." She paused. "It's hitting Jack hard. He met Vic when he was like fourteen, you know? Fourteen and on his own in New York City, and Vic kind of took him in. I think he always looked up to him, like an older brother. You don't want to find out your older brother's been lying to you for a decade. Especially if the reason is because…because he thought you wouldn't be happy for him."

"Would you have been?" I asked. "If everyone knew, if he was beloved by the world…would you have been happy for him?"

She exhaled, picking a piece of lint off her black skirt. "I can't answer that," she said finally. "At least, not any answer that makes any sense. Yes, I would have been happy for him. I would have been thrilled for him. And no, I wouldn't have been happy for him; I would have been bitter and jealous and mean. I'd take every chance to stick it to him and pretend I was doing it for his own good. I did that already—why flatter myself and think I'd be any better if he were more famous? But on the other hand, maybe I would have... I don't know. Taken some comfort in it all. If he could do it, if he could break free of the nonsense, make things, be rewarded for it, be seen for it... Who knows? It might have given me some hope." She laughed a bit. "So, yes and no, and I don't know, and the question's a dumb one anyway. How's that?"

"Makes sense to me," I said.

"So, Paramount," she said. "You coming?"

"Are we going right now?" I asked.

"Nah, we can wait until you're busted out of the loony bin first."

"I suppose if that's happening, there's something else I'll have to do," I said.

"What's that?"

I laughed. "I'll have to buy some furniture."

June laughed too. "About time, Annie Laurence. About time."

Hollywood Memorial Park was only a few blocks away from the lot. I had to walk past it each Thursday night when heading from set to Paramount night at the Hollywood Canteen. Each week I thought perhaps I'd stop in; each week I found I wasn't ready. July 25, 1944—one year to the day since she died—I decided it was time.

I went in the morning. The air was already thick with July heat. The woman at the front had directed me straight ahead, and as I crossed the lawn, I recognized a familiar figure in a wrinkled white shirt, undoubtedly standing where I intended to go.

I almost turned back. He'd dodged seeing me face-to-face so many times over the last eleven months, I had assumed he never wanted to speak to me again.

So imagine my surprise when I tapped him on the shoulder and his eyes went joyfully wide, pulling me into a hug. He smelled the same, clean and oaky with an aftertaste of booze. I inhaled. "Annie Laurence," he whispered. "You have no idea how good it is to see you."

"Interesting to hear, Jack Kott," I replied. "You've been doing a pretty spectacular job of not taking my calls."

"Yeah, I… I'm sorry about that, kid. I'm sorry."

"It's all right. I understand."

I put a hand on his shoulder, and together we looked down at the simple flat stone marking Fiona's interred ashes.

FIONA ACKERMAN FARRIS
22 April 1908–25 July 1943
"The show was rubbish, but the ending was killer."

"Who wrote that?" I asked.

"She did," Jack replied. "It was in her will."

"She thought of everything," I said.

"Want to share a drink with her?" asked Jack, producing a flask from his pocket. "One last time?"

It was 8:30 in the morning, but I did. We settled on the grass, Jack pouring a little out before handing it to me. "I saw your movie, you know," he said as I took a sip. "*Altogether Too Many Murders*. It was really something. You can actually write; June can actually act—who knew?"

The movie had been doing surprisingly well, with June's performance in particular receiving raves. I was already hard at work on the next one, spending my days typing away in my office on the Paramount lot and my nights drinking with Terry, June, and a handful of others.

But I wasn't sure Jack—who, as far as I knew, hadn't worked or even left the house in a year—would want to hear about all that. "How's the book coming along?" I asked, returning the flask.

He rolled his eyes. "A stupid obsession. I don't want to talk about it."

I raised an eyebrow. "Last I remember, you might have found an agent interested in it."

He smiled, and his eyes dropped to the ground. "Didn't pan out."

"I'm sorry."

"It's fine. I'm over at Warners now. They're making a series of B pictures around me, where I go to different exotic places and have adventures. The first one's called *Kott Goes to Cairo*. I get cursed by a mummy. Not exactly high art, but something's gotta pay the bar tabs, right?"

I couldn't figure out a way to ask the next question on my mind. "I have to say something, Jack, and it's going to sound stupid at first, but you have to promise to push past that. I'm going somewhere with this."

"You can't say anything as stupid as *Kott Goes to Cairo*."

"When I was in jail those few days, I fell sick. I'd stopped taking all those pills Irma gave me, and I was vomiting constantly. They called a doctor in to see me, and he said I was pregnant." Jack's eyes widened, and I could see the math turning in his head. "No, no. I wasn't pregnant. He was just a shit doctor. But for a moment there, I thought— *Well, what if?* And the answer wasn't the worst thing in the world."

"You want to bear my fruit, Annie?" he deadpanned.

I laughed. "No. Not yet, at least. Only that there was a moment where I saw us together, and I didn't hate it. I thought maybe you might be up for…trying something like that."

For a writer who'd had an entire year to prepare this speech, I mangled it horribly, but I hoped I had gotten my point across.

Jack was silent for a moment, looking out across the lawn. "Annie, you don't want to do that. You're the new thing now. You're it. You don't want to tie yourself to a lead brick like me."

"We don't have to get tied," I said. "Let's start with dinner."

"There's no point," he said, chuckling. "I can see how it will all play out—can't you?"

"Enlighten me," I said.

"All right. Fine." He took a breath and another sip. "I take you to dinner, and then another dinner, and another, and unless you wise up and drop me before then, I marry you within a year. Why wouldn't I? Look at you; look at me. I'd be a fool not to.

"Meanwhile, my career keeps dwindling off because I'm a miserable drunk Commie who's only talented unintentionally. And your career takes off, you're the talented, fresh-faced writer of *Altogether Too Many Murders* starring June Lee, after all.

"I'll try to be happy for you, but I'm not. You understand that— I'm incapable of it. Vic lied to me for a decade 'cause he understood that. But you won't be able to lie to me, so instead you'll resent me, for being jealous and angry all the time. For spending my nights at the bar instead of home with you. I'll grow to resent you because when I look at you, I see you seeing my potential, and if I can't see my own potential, I don't have to feel bad for not living up to it. Failing is fine. I can numb the pain of failing, but I can't numb the pain of you watching me fail.

"I'll become bitter; so will you because you don't understand why I hate you so much when you did nothing wrong, and you'll be right. When you're at the peak of your success, you'll feel guilty instead of proud. You'll write a movie for me instead of the big stars you could be working with, but I won't be grateful for that—no, I'll grow even more bitter. I'll feel like less of a man, whose wife has to dim her light to help him shine. And you'll say it's not like that, that you genuinely want to work with me, but I'll know it's a lie, and the whole crew will know it's a lie, and I'll have to hear every time the director yells, 'Cut,' little whispers here and there about how, oh, a *serious* actor like John

Garfield would be so much better in this role, how it's a good story but Jack Kott is ruining it.

"And they'll be right too. The picture will be a dud, and you and I, we'll plod along for a few more years just to keep up appearances, not wanting to admit that it was the thing we tried to make together that ruined us, but it will already be over. I'll sleep with some chorus girl, and you'll be relieved to have a reason to divorce me. You'll have tanked your career with our movie and be stuck writing B pictures the rest of your life. If you're lucky, being married to me will only leave you with a drinking problem and not a pill problem too. We can't be together; we can't be an item. I can see how it all plays out, Annie. It's not good."

"None of that is real," I said. "The only thing that's real, the only thing that counts, is how we feel about each other right now."

Jack smiled, sadly and gently. "And you deserve to find someone else who thinks like that," he said. "'Cause it ain't me."

"Well, then," I said, feeling the warmth of the California sun on my face. "Maybe sometime you could meet me and some friends at the Ambassador Hotel for a drink."

"Sure," he said. "I'd like that."

AUTHOR'S NOTE

-◄◄◄◆►►►-

The Hollywood Canteen was a real place, spearheaded by Bette Davis and John Garfield. Located on Cahuenga Boulevard, just south of Sunset in Hollywood, it was a venue exclusively for servicemen—no officers and no civilians allowed. Inside, everything—food, beverages, entertainment—was free. The Canteen was staffed almost entirely by volunteers from the film industry, who worked as hostesses, busboys, kitchen staff, coatroom clerks, and more. Every night featured entertainment from big-name bands, floor shows, and of course jitterbugging with the Hollywood hostesses. Attendance was between fifteen- and twenty-five hundred servicemen a night, entering and leaving in shifts so everyone could spend an hour inside.

Stars who performed at the Canteen over its three years of operation included Lena Horne, the Andrews Sisters, Duke Ellington, Abbott and Costello, Mickey Rooney, Judy Garland, Marlene Dietrich, Bob Hope, Frank Sinatra, Burns and Allen, Jack Benny, Louis Armstrong, Orson Welles—the list goes on and on. Sundays at the Canteen were dedicated to classical concerts, and the Canteen had its own eighty-piece orchestra. World-renowned pianists Arthur Rubinstein and José

Iturbi both appeared in the classical Sunday concerts, as well as conductors Otto Klemperer and Leopold Stokowski.

What fascinated me about the Hollywood Canteen was the tension between the genuine tirelessness and selflessness of many of its volunteers, and, as historian Kevin Starr puts it, the "crass self-promotion" of it all. The Canteen was popular with servicemen and spoken of fondly by many who attended. It was also a way for Hollywood to applaud itself for its valuable contribution to the war effort, even as many of its stars managed to avoid active duty. This sour taste is perhaps best embodied in the pretty offensive 1944 Warner Brothers film *The Hollywood Canteen*. Shot on a replica set of the real Canteen, the film featured sixty-two stars playing themselves and centered around a loose plot of mostly small-town country-boy servicemen falling over themselves, unable to believe their luck as they encounter stars at the Canteen. As Starr writes in *Embattled Dreams: California in War and Peace, 1940–1950*:

> *"Not a single servicemen in* Hollywood Canteen *emerges with any discernible autonomy when fortunate enough to meet a real live Hollywood star from Warner Brothers… Hollywood Canteen was not a film…about how brave these young men were as they headed in harm's way…[but] rather a celebration of how good Hollywood was to be on hand personally to send them off."*

Hollywood in the studio system was constantly churning out stories, and not just for the screen: stories about itself and stories about the stars it created in what Karina Longworth describes as "the meat grinder of the star machine." What did it mean to turn your humanity over to this system? What did it mean to resist it?

In addition to Starr's book, the following sources were essential to researching both the Hollywood Canteen and Hollywood during

World War II: *The Hollywood Canteen: Where the Greatest Generation Danced with the Most Beautiful Girls in the World* by Lisa Mitchell and Bruce Torrence; *The Star Machine* by Jeanine Basinger; *Hollywood Victory: The Movies, Stars, and Stories of World War II* by Christian Blauvelt; *Hitler in Los Angeles: How Jews Foiled Nazi Plots against Hollywood and America* by Stephen J. Ross; and Karina Longworth's *You Must Remember This* podcast.

I first became obsessed with the idea of writing something about the lives of the early twentieth-century wits after reading *With Malice Towards All* by Dorothy Herrmann. Other books that helped round out the characters in this book include *She Damn Near Ran the Studio: The Extraordinary Lives of Ida R. Koverman* by Jacqueline R. Braitman; *A Wayward Quest: The Autobiography of Theresa Helburn*; *Hedda and Louella* by George Eells; *All the Sincerity in Hollywood: Selections from the Writings of Fred Allen*; and *Memoirs of an Amnesiac* and *A Smattering of Ignorance* by Oscar Levant. Caleb Boyd's meticulous documentation of Oscar Levant's film and radio appearances in his paper "Oscar Levant: Pianist, Gershwinite, Middlebrow Media Star" was another valuable resource.

Each member of the Ambassador's Club is inspired in some part by a real person, although I have taken many liberties as well as combined traits from many different people. Those people include Dorothy Parker, Robert Benchley, Anna May Wong, Theresa Helburn, Oscar Levant, George Gershwin, George S. Kaufman, Judy Garland, and Alexander Woollcott. Each one of these extraordinary individuals is worthy of an entire book on their own, and I can only hope I've done them some justice as I've inelegantly crammed them all into one.

It was a challenge to write jokes that sounded like they could have been written by the great wits of the early twentieth century but were not. Most of the jokes the members of the Ambassador's Club tell each other were written by me. A few I did not write: Jack's "*Beethoven's*

Fifth" joke is an old chestnut that's been used in many forms by many sources, although I first heard Al Jolson say it on a 1949 episode of *Kraft Music Hall*; Victor telling Annie he memorizes all those notes "by memorizing them" is paraphrased from Arturo Toscanini as recounted by Levant in *Memoirs of an Amnesiac*. It was also Levant's observation that "under the baton" sounds, as he put it, "sexually suggestive." Any other similarities between any other jokes in this book and quotes from Dorothy Parker, Clifton Fadiman, Oscar Levant, and Alexander Woollcott are a coincidence. I'm sure the similarities exist. They wrote a lot of jokes.

READING GROUP GUIDE

❦

1. How do the circumstances of Annie's arrival in Los Angeles point her toward Fiona Farris? What does she want to gain by making friends with Fiona and her contemporaries?

2. Describe the Hollywood Canteen. What was its intended purpose? How do Annie's feelings about that mission change throughout the book?

3. Fiona's reviews are known for their incisive wit and sly allusions. What makes her writing dangerous?

4. How would you describe Adam and Beverly Cook? Would you pursue fame if it cost you an important relationship? Do Adam and Beverly have the same level of resolve when it comes to their studio-mandated hobbies and appearances?

5. The Ambassador's Club is extremely hostile to outsiders, especially romantic prospects. Why do they see other people as threats? Why do they decide to allow Annie into the fold?

6. How does typecasting affect June and Jack? Why do we expect
    consistency from creators and celebrities?

7. Morality clauses allowed Golden Age Hollywood studios to care-
    fully control the images their stars projected on- *and* off-screen.
    Why was that control so important to them? Do you think celeb-
    rities in the modern era receive the same type of scrutiny?

8. Victor's announcement at the Hollywood Bowl concert saves
    Annie. Why did he choose that moment to speak up? Was the
    cost of his honesty what he expected it to be?

A CONVERSATION
WITH THE AUTHOR

—«‹◆›»—

The Ambassador's Club's repartee is so fast and dynamic. Are you the type to jump into a battle of wits or watch from the sidelines?

Who doesn't love kicking back with an ice-cold beer on a warm summer evening to watch a battle of wits from the sidelines? I'll never forget the time I was at a battle of the wits with my dad and I caught foul language.

Many of the characters' true relationships are hidden or sidelined in favor of their public images. How do you think that affects our understanding of history?

Whenever there's a new hate movement trying to disguise their hate as mere "concern" over the "rise" of [trans people/gay people/nonbinary people], I think we should all try to remember that there is no past where these people did not exist—only a past where they were not allowed to exist openly.

Jack, June, and Victor all struggle for one reason or another to make careers that are satisfying to them. How did their initial industry obstacles become more personal mental blocks?

All of these characters deal with industry obstacles in ways that are perhaps self-sabotaging, but I wouldn't say they are just mental blocks. June is a Chinese actress at a time in history when Asian women in Hollywood films are reduced to oversexualized stereotypes. The rare Hollywood movies that were about more complex Asian characters often cast white actresses in those parts. This is still a problem in Hollywood today! Jack and Victor's career struggles are less extreme and not rooted in racism but are similar in other ways. Jack is a radio comedian and people like him as a radio comedian. Whether his modernist war novel is good or not is irrelevant. When the world repeatedly tells you that your only value resides in one small aspect of your full humanity, that you should put away and shut up about the rest, is it a mental block or an understandable reaction to turn to drinking, drugs, cynicism to drown that pain?

The theft of Henry Hilbert's couch is hilarious. What's the best prank you've ever pulled or received?

The couch theft is based on what real prank members of the Algonquin Round Table would pull: dressing up as movers and stealing each other's furniture. Personally I hate pranks and have never pulled one in my life. I would never, for example, steal one sock from each pair from the laundry of a person in my building who took my wet clothes out of the dryer while the cycle was still going so they could put in their own. I'm above that sort of thing.

While things are looking up for most of the Ambassador's Club by the end of the book, Jack still isn't able to imagine anything but pain and self-sabotage in his own future. Why does he cling to his pessimism?

Jack is the sort of person—as many smart and anxious people are— who sees bad things happening as inevitable, that pessimism is how the world really is and optimism is just self-delusion.

As a comedy writer yourself, what was the most fun part of writing for the Ambassador's Club? Were you intimidated at all by the historical figures who inspired them?

The group scenes for the Ambassador's Club were the most fun and also the most challenging. When you have that many characters who all have opinions and all love the sound of their own voices, it's difficult to keep the scene moving in the direction it needs to move in. I was intimidated only by my wanting to do right by the people who inspired the Ambassadors. I wanted to write characters that were three-dimensional, funny, and full, not flattened or infantilized by their struggles.

ACKNOWLEDGMENTS

I want to first thank everyone who bought, read, reviewed, shared, reached out to me about, hosted an event for, came to a signing of, and otherwise supported my first book, *The Woman with Two Shadows*. It means the world to me.

Pretty much every time I have a conversation with another writer, I find myself saying, "Wow, my agent is nothing like that," in response to their complaining. Abby Saul is a dream to work with in every regard, and I feel so lucky to have her as well as all of #TeamLark on my side.

Thanks to my editor, Shana Drehs, for taking all the swearing in this book in stride, and for her thoughtful and meticulous edits. Findlay McCarthy at Sourcebooks also provided helpful notes and encouragement. Thanks to the rest of the Sourcebooks team: copy editor Rachel Norfleet, production editor Jessica Thelander, proofreader Aimee Alker, art director Heather VenHuizen, senior graphic designer Stephanie Rocha, production designer Laura Boren, and the marketing and publicity team, including Cristina Arreola and Molly Waxman.

I am eternally grateful for the feedback and support of Katie Avery,

Amanda Freechack, Tiffany Ho, Rebecca Rosenberg, and Audrey Wong Kennedy. This book, and possibly its author, would not exist without them.

Huge thanks to the USC Library Special Collections and the USC Cinematic Arts Library for letting me view their Oscar Levant collection, particularly Sandra M. Garcia-Myers and Billy Smith.

Additional thanks to Brittany Axworthy, Andie Bansil, Audrey Beauchamp, Laurie Bolewitz, Ross Brenneman, Kristen Damiani, Taylor Dariarow, Jake Farrington, Ibet Inyang, Matt Mahaffey, Brian and Christy McElhinny, Rebecca Munley, Jeremy and Lyndsay Palmer, Daphne Pollon, Mary Sette, Adrienne Teeley, and Taylor Wolfe.

Thanks to my favorite place in the world, the Los Angeles Public Library. Much of this book was written in the Art, Music, and Recreation Department. Thanks to those librarians for constantly fetching me out-of-print biographies of 1940s concert pianists.

Thanks to my parents.

Thanks to my cat, Lucille.

Finally, this book is for Hop On—now canonically immortal.

ABOUT THE AUTHOR

—⫷◆⫸—

Sarah James is the international bestselling author of *The Woman with Two Shadows*. Originally from Pittsburgh, Pennsylvania, Sarah received an MFA in writing for screen and television from the University of Southern California. She lives in Los Angeles, California, with her cat, Lucille.